A BICYCLE MADE
FOR TWO

A BICYCLE MADE FOR TWO

Mary Jayne Baker

An Aria Book

First published in UK in 2018 by Mirror Books

This paperback edition published in 2022 by Head of Zeus Ltd,
part of Bloomsbury Publishing Plc

9 7 5 3 1 2 4 6 8

A CIP catalogue record for this book is available from
the British Library.

ISBN (PB): 9781801108386
ISBN (EB): 9781801108362

Cover design © Head of Zeus
Typeset by Siliconchips Services Ltd UK

Printed and bound in Great Britain by
CPI Group (UK) Ltd, Croydon CR0 4YY

Head of Zeus
First Floor East
5–8 Hardwick Street
London EC1R 4RG

WWW.HEADOFZEUS.COM

Author's Note

Please be aware that although real events and bodies relating to the organisation of the 2014 Tour de France are referenced in the course of this story, many details, including the process by which the Tour route was decided, have been invented by the author.

To my lovely and supportive Firths: grandparents Eric and Maura, mum Sandra and naughty little sister Erica. Thanks for everything, family.

My Friday nights were not like other girls', I reflected as I laced up the black leather corset.

Tom poked his head around the bedroom door just as I'd finished tucking in my cleavage.

'You ready yet, wench? It's been your shift for five minutes.'

I jumped. 'God, learn to knock, can you? I could be starkers in here.'

'Excellent, I've always said we need to try something different on the weekends. Fun Bags Friday, we'll call it. Corner the lad market.'

'Yeah, and you can explain to Dad why you've reinvented the place as a family Hooters bar.'

'Look, hurry up. I need to take over in the kitchen so Deano can go for his break. He'll play pop if we keep him waiting.'

'OK, OK, keep your jerkin on,' I said, stuffing my dark brown curls inside the unattractive Mrs Tiggy-Winkle mob cap that went with my costume.

He wasn't wrong. Ever since Dad had become too ill to keep up with cooking duties, it felt like we'd been dancing round our diva-ish new chef Deano. Dad said a temperament like that was the sign of true talent. Tom said it was the sign of an arse.

I laced up the leather boots and stood to examine myself in the mirror.

Ugh.

'All right, I'm ready. Come zip me.'

'Hey, treat for you tonight,' Tom said, grinning at me in the mirror as he fastened my skirt. 'Mr Squeezy Sauce. Thought I'd save him for you; I knew you'd want to give him the star treatment.'

'Harper Brady? He's here?'

'Yep. Can't wait to tell Dad.'

I shook my head. 'Not tonight, Tom. He's not good at the moment.'

He frowned. 'Bad afternoon?'

'Yeah. Gerry's sitting with him now.'

'OK, if you close up I'll relieve Gerry after my shift.' He patted my arm. 'You take a night off Dad duty. You look jiggered.'

'I am a bit. Thanks, bruv.' I turned to face him. 'So what do you think Brady's doing here? I wouldn't have thought he'd be caught dead in a place like this.'

Tom shrugged. 'Maybe he fancied slumming it for a change. Hey, think we can get a signed photo to put behind the bar? It'd be great PR.'

I curled my lip. 'You can ask if you want. You know I don't groupie.'

'Come on, you nearly wet yourself when that boy band bloke came in last year.'

I tilted my nose, trying to look superior. 'That was

different. He was childhood nostalgia. That band were massive when we were kids.'

'Yeah, childhood nostalgia you wanted to hump.'

'I did not. Shut up.'

'Still. Harper Brady,' Tom said, a faraway look in his eyes. 'I bet he's the biggest name we've had in.'

'He certainly knocks that bloke from *Last of the Summer Wine* out of the water.' I groaned. 'God, I hope he doesn't expect special treatment. Celebrity diners give me a pain. If he tries to order off the menu he can explain it to Deano himself, see how he likes the heavy end of a skillet.'

Still, as celeb customers went I had to admit Tom was right: this one was a pretty big deal. Oh, we got the occasional soap actor or washed-up pop star coming along to check us out – the quirky medieval theme restaurant with the pulled hog platters and spiced mead on tap, tucked away in a forgotten corner of the Yorkshire Dales. Then when they'd had a good laugh, off they buggered back to their usual highbrow dining establishments to tell people how hilariously ironic they were. We didn't mind. A visit from a name was usually good for a few weeks' spike in business.

But we'd never had a name as big as Harper Brady.

The family were well-known locally. Harper's mum Sonia had made a mint back in the nineties when she'd patented a design for the upside-down squeezy ketchup bottle, and when she'd passed away, her only son had got it all. He'd lived it up as a jet-setting playboy for a while, then, not content with being a gentleman of leisure, he'd blown the lot on acting lessons in the hope he could make a name for himself in TV.

If there was any divine justice, that would've been the end of the story. A few acting tutors would be living the high life on the squeezy sauce millions and Harper Brady, spoilt trust fund kid extraordinaire, would be forced to get a proper nine-to-five like everyone else. But no. In the most irritating twist of fate ever, it turned out he was actually bloody good at acting. Now he was twice as rich and just as handsome, with a legion of adoring fans and a string of TV credits to his name.

I made a mental note to make him wait for his food.

Downstairs in the restaurant, I spotted Harper near the front of the queue. He was perfectly groomed as always, in a designer suit and tie – I mean, a waistcoat and everything; talk about overdressed – with his long flaxen hair stylishly gelled like he was the lost member of One Direction.

I couldn't tell if the good-looking, slightly scruffy man he was chatting to was with him or if they'd just struck up a conversation. However, there were certainly eyebrows raising among the other waiting diners. Harper preened slightly when he clocked the looks of recognition directed towards him, all the while talking to his friend as if he hadn't noticed a thing.

I screwed on my brightest customer smile for the middle-aged couple at the front of the queue.

'Welcome to Here Be Flagons. Can I take the name you booked under please?'

'It is, it's him!' the woman in the loud purple hat hissed to her husband. 'It is, I know it.'

I hemmed loudly to command their attention. No response.

'It's nice when stars patronise these little local places, isn't it?' her husband whispered back.

I tried again. 'It's just, there's rather a queue, so if you wouldn't mind—'

'Yes, yes, dear.' The woman lowered her voice and leaned forward confidentially, enveloping me in a cloud of evening primrose. 'I don't know if you've noticed, but that's Harper Brady behind us.'

'Lovely. So if you could just give me the name your reservation's under, I can get you to your table.'

The woman turned back to her husband. 'I'm going to ask for a photo with him,' she whispered.

'Go on, go on,' her husband said, nodding vigorously.

'I will. I'm going to do it.' The woman giggled. 'Will I do it?'

'Yes, do it!' Her husband smiled at me. 'I'm sure the young lady can wait.'

There were mutterings now as those waiting wondered what the hold-up was.

'Well no, actually—' I began, but the woman had already turned to face Harper.

'Oh, Mr Brady, is it really you?' she asked, her mouth forming an O of fake surprise. Harper looked round, annoyed at having his conversation interrupted.

'No, it's really Abe Froman, the sausage king of Chicago.'

The woman carried on beaming, failing to notice the sarcasm. 'Me and my husband are such huge fans,' she gushed. 'We've seen everything you've ever been in. Everything, even back when no one had heard of you.'

Harper scowled. It was clear the suggestion there was

ever a time he'd been less than megastar famous displeased him.

'I don't suppose you'd consider letting me take a photo of the two of us?' the woman blundered on. 'My friends will never believe me.'

'A selfie?' Harper curled his lip. 'I couldn't consent to anything so crass, I'm sorry.'

The woman's face fell. 'Perhaps... an autograph then?'

Harper lowered his voice. 'Look, lady, I'm here to enjoy a quiet night with a few close friends. I don't appreciate having my identity broadcast to all and sundry, and I appreciate still less having my conversation interrupted by fat menopausal hatstands. How about a little respect for my privacy?' He lifted his voice so I could hear. 'I don't know why the staff here allow their customers to be badgered this way. Disgraceful.'

The woman sagged. 'Sorry,' she mumbled. 'I didn't think you'd mind.'

'Well I do.' Harper looked as if he might be incubating a few more choice insults to go with his hatstand line, and I came out from behind the desk to rescue the situation.

'Follow me,' I said firmly to the woman and her husband. 'Never mind about the name.' Looking hurt and bewildered, the two shuffled along behind me to an empty table, where I left them gazing with unseeing eyes at the wine list.

I beckoned to Jasmine, our pretty teenage waitress, and she came shimmying over. Somehow on her tiny, swaying hips, 'medieval tavern wench' looked pure catwalk.

'Get them a free bottle of whatever they want, with our apologies,' I muttered. 'My dad'll go spare if he hears about this.'

'Right.' Jasmine went to take the couple's drink order, and I headed back behind my desk. The smile I summoned for Harper Brady was anything but warm, and possibly threateningly toothsome.

'Welcome to Here Be Flagons. Can I take the name you booked under please?'

Harper acted as though he hadn't heard, chatting away to the man with the rumpled sandy curls.

I leaned across the desk to give his shoulder an irritated tap. 'There are people waiting, so if you can make it quick, sir—'

Harper turned to me with surprise. 'I'm sorry, what?'

'The name you booked under. I'll need it to seat you.'

'Seriously? You're asking my name?' He let out a short laugh, rolling his eyes at his friend, and leaned forward to let me get a closer look at his face. 'How's this? Good enough?'

I stared impassively into his eyes. 'Look, if you haven't made a reservation I can't let you in. We're full tonight.'

'You must be joking! I've been queueing quarter of an hour.'

I was enjoying myself now, doing my best nightclub-bouncer-with-a-dictator-complex. I folded my arms across my chest.

'Sorry, mate. No reservation, no entry.' After a second's pause, I added, 'More than my job's worth.'

BAM. Have that, Harper Brady. I'd always wanted to say that.

'Look, I don't have time for this. I'm meeting my agent, I have to—' He drew a deep breath and lowered his voice. 'Come on, don't pretend you don't know who I am. You know my name.'

I kept my expression fixed. 'I can promise you I don't.'

He goggled. 'You're having me on. Haven't you seen *Stitch*? *The Chester Files*?' He reeled off a load more of his TV credits, but I remained inflexible.

'No. What're they, films?'

The way his mouth fell open was worth losing out on the PR value of a big-name diner. Next to him, the handsome friend's mouth twitched at the corners.

'Look, maybe I can sort this out before we both starve to death,' the other man said.

He pushed Harper behind him and leaned one arm against the desk, letting the twitch at the corner of his lips spread into a warm smile. After hesitating a second, I returned it. Next to him, Harper almost reeled to see his friend's charm working where his celebrity had failed.

'We booked online,' he said. 'It's under my friend here's name.'

'Which is?'

'Tell her,' he said to Harper.

'Fine. Harper Brady,' Harper said sulkily. He scrutinised my face for any sign the name meant something, but I let go of not a flicker.

'OK, yes, there's a booking here for Brady,' I said, scanning my reservation list. 'Can I see some ID please? Sorry, but we are very busy. When there's a lot of demand for tables I have to be extra cautious.'

Total bollocks, obviously, but I was having bags of fun.

'God! What is this, The Ivy?' Harper pulled out his wallet and shoved a driving licence in my direction. 'You know, I'll be making a complaint about this to your manager. Bloody ridiculous.'

'For what, doing my job?' For form's sake I checked his ID and ticked him off the list.

'For being deliberately rude and obstructive. Don't think I'm joking.'

I saw him scanning my cleavage, jutting out in the nothing-to-the-imagination leather corset, while he told me off. He wasn't above having a perve in his righteous anger then.

'Come on, what's his name, your manager? He'll be receiving an email about your conduct.' He sneered unpleasantly. 'Have fun on the dole queue, love.'

'It's a her actually. Lana Donati.'

'Right. And what's yours?'

'Lana Donati.'

His friend snorted, then quickly turned it into a cough. Harper grabbed his driving licence, shot me a last resentful glare and stormed off into the restaurant.

'Bit hard on him, weren't you?' his friend said. 'Not that it wasn't hilarious.'

'Couldn't help myself. I heard what he said to that fan before.'

The man smiled. 'So you do know who he is.'

'Yeah,' I said, smiling back. 'But don't let on, eh?'

He made a zipping motion across his lips. 'Not a word.'

'So what's your connection to him?' I scanned the athletic figure and broad chest. 'Not his minder, are you?'

He laughed. 'No, I'm his cousin, sadly.' He held out a hand. 'Stewart McLean.'

'Oh, right,' I said, shaking the hand absently. The name sounded vaguely familiar. 'Family meal?'

'Research date actually. Harper's got a part as a cyclist. He's been shadowing me the last few days.'

'You cycle?'

'Occasionally. Anyway, I get a consultant credit, so, you know, pretty cool.' He glanced over his shoulder at the queue. 'Oh. Sorry, everyone, I'm holding you up.'

He stood to one side to let me deal with the other customers, but he didn't go sit with his cousin. Actually, when I glanced over to Harper's table I saw he'd been joined by someone else – a busty blonde woman in an almost invisible black dress who'd been seated by herself at the bar for the last half-hour. Charmless git that he was, the man didn't seem to want for company.

When I'd dealt with the last pair's reservation and Jasmine had taken them to their table, I turned to Stewart.

'So. Sounds like you're going to be a star,' I said.

'No autographs, please.' He tossed his curls comically. 'You really manage this place, Lana?'

'Actually I own it – well, my family does. My dad bought it when he emigrated from Italy and turned it into this place.' I gestured round the candlelit room, plastered all over with mounted boars' heads, replica halberds and painted coats of arms while Dad's favourite CD, *Harpsichord Renaissance*, played on a loop in the background. It felt like a Chaucer lecturer's drug-fuelled nightmare.

'It's original, I'll give him that.' Stewart followed my gaze, taking it all in. 'Why the medieval theme though? I mean, not that the costume doesn't suit you, but it's a bit… well, Here Be Flagons? Yikes.'

'You don't need to tell me,' I said, smiling. 'Just his sense of humour, I suppose. Only my dad could build a business around a single pun.'

'Is he working tonight?' Stewart asked. 'A pun-obsessed

Italian with a medieval history fetish sounds like someone I need to meet.'

I flushed. 'No, not tonight. He's… not well.'

'Ah, right. Maybe another time.'

'No, I mean he's really not well.' I had no idea why I was telling him that, this stranger. The words just seemed to fall out of me. 'Cancer, you know? Bastard cancer.' I cast my eyes down. 'Terminal.'

'Oh God,' Stewart said, a look of concern spreading over his features. 'I'm so sorry, Lana.'

I shrugged. 'Not your fault, is it?'

He looked puzzled. 'Well, no. That's just what people say. You know, when they…'

'…when they don't know what to say,' I finished for him, smiling. 'Sorry, didn't mean to be rude. Years of inhaling soup fumes has sent my sense of humour careering into the surreal a bit. If I make you uncomfortable, feel free not to tip.'

His puzzled expression lifted into a smile. 'No, I like you. You're kind of weird and funny.'

'Gee, thanks.'

'Don't be offended: attractive qualities in a tavern wench. They lend her that air of sophisticated unpredictability that always leaves you checking for your wallet.'

I laughed. 'If that was a chat-up line, it needs work.'

'It wasn't.'

I blushed, wondering if I'd misjudged the flirting. 'I know. Just a joke.'

'This one's going to be though. Fancy grabbing a drink sometime?'

The blush deepened, with a more pleasant sensation this time. 'Er, yeah. That sounds nice.'

'When are you free? Next week?'

'Thursday's good. That's our quiet night so I can get off early.'

'Pick you up at eight then?'

'Yep, perfect.'

'You know, for the first time tonight I'm glad I let Harper talk me into coming out.' Stewart sighed theatrically. 'Suppose I'd better join him, before Legs Eleven over there smothers him to death. See you, Lana.'

2

'Ow,' I said when I felt a punch on my arm fifteen minutes later.

'So what happened while I was in the kitchen?' Tom asked.

I nodded at Stewart, who'd grabbed himself a seat at Harper's table. 'First I humiliated a famous actor-stroke-sauce playboy, then your man there was so impressed he asked me for a date. Stewart, his cousin.'

'Bloody hell, really?' Tom said. 'What for?'

'Maybe, just maybe – impossible as it is for my own dear brother to believe – he fancies me.'

'Nah. Must be on drugs.' He looked more closely at Stewart. 'Yep, deffo. Face of a twenty-a-day ketamine guzzler if I ever saw one.'

'You're just jealous. When does anyone ever ask you out?'

He drew himself up. 'I'll have you know I got chatted up just before you started your shift. Six-foot-five fireman with abs like a griddle pan and one of those weird bum chin things that make you look hot and chiselled.'

'Right. And where is he?'

'Oh, I turned him down. I can't be expected to throw

all this—' he gestured down his lanky frame '—away on just any old scrubber.' He nodded to Harper. 'So what's Mr Squeezy Sauce like then?'

'Humble. Modest. A pleasure to talk to.'

'Really?'

'Nope. He's an arse.'

'Who's the collagen job with him?'

'Dunno, she was at the bar when he came in,' I said. 'He mentioned something about his agent.'

Tom snorted. 'If she's his agent, I'm his bloody stunt double.'

'She is a bit heavy on the silicone for a theatrical agent, isn't she?' I watched the woman drape herself over Harper as she purred into his ear. 'And kind of… gropey.'

Tom's smartphone buzzed in his pocket. He yanked it out and swiped at the screen.

'I don't believe it!' he hissed, staring in disbelief at his phone. 'That… *bastard!*'

'Eh? Who?' I tried to get a peek at the screen over his shoulder.

'Harper Brady!' He thrust the phone at me. 'He's only gone and given us a one-star TripAdvisor review! I just got a Google alert.'

'Son of a bitch!' I glared at Harper. 'When did he do that? He hasn't had that woman's tongue out of his ear since he got here.'

'He must've done it on his phone while she was licking him.' Tom scanned the review. '"Long wait, rude staff, historically inaccurate decor. Food mediocre at best. Don't waste your time." He hasn't even had his bloody food yet! Ooooh. Right, I'm responding.'

I put a hand on his arm. 'Don't, Tommy. Wait till you've calmed down. It'll only make things worse if you do it while he's here.'

'Don't worry, I'll be firm but fair.' He started tapping at his phone. 'Wait – "running jump" isn't hyphenated, is it?'

'Seriously, Tom! Leave it.'

'OK, OK, I'm kidding,' he said, putting the phone down. 'I'll wait till tomorrow. See if I can fob him off with a voucher or something. He won't take it, but it'll show anyone who sees his review that we made the effort.'

'Yeah, that's better. That's what Dad would want us to do.'

Someone tapped my elbow and I turned to find a worried-looking Jasmine, shuffling nervously.

'What's up, love?' I said. 'Deano picking on you again?'

'Not yet.' She glanced over her shoulder at Harper's table. 'It's those people. The man says he's a vegan.'

Tom groaned. 'Why am I not surprised?'

'Well, did you read him the vegan options?' I asked. 'Not that he isn't perfectly capable of doing that himself, but he seems far too busy not getting a room.'

'Yes.' She shuffled again in embarrassment. 'I read them, but…'

'For God's sake, Jaz, stop fidgeting; you look like you need the loo. Get it out, can you?'

'He says he's a special kind of vegan. Something called a living foodist.'

Tom's eyes saucered. 'A *what?*'

'A living foodist. They only eat organic veg or something. And when I told him I didn't know if we had anything for that, he said he wanted to speak to the manager.'

'Oh Christ,' I muttered. 'Why tonight, Tom? Why did it have to be tonight? The first time I've pulled in over a year and he comes in with the fad dieter from hell.'

'You want me to go?'

'No, you'll only end up shouting at him over that review.' I looked at Harper, who was giving me smug side-eyes from his table. 'Anyway, I get the impression I'm the one he wants.'

I marched over to Harper's table.

'Is there a problem, sir?' I said from behind a fixed smile.

'I'll say there's a problem,' Harper snapped. 'Your menu's – Claudia, can you leave my ear alone a sec? – your menu's the bloody problem. Is this stuff really not organic?'

'Some of it might be. It's locally sourced, at least. We get it from farms in the area.'

'I didn't ask if it was local, I asked if it was organic.' He folded his arms. 'I can't eat anything non-organic. It raises my blood pressure.'

I shot a look at his almost-empty bottle of champagne. Apparently that didn't have any effect on his blood pressure.

'Look, we do our best to cater for special diets but for something that niche you really should've phoned ahead,' I said with forced patience.

'It never occurred to me I needed to phone ahead just for organic veg. I thought all restaurants were using it now by default.' He curled his lip. 'All *proper* restaurants.'

'This isn't the big city, Mr Brady. We provide wholesome food with a twist, which is what our customers want.'

'Well it's not what this customer wants, darling, so sort it.'

Stewart shook his head. 'For God's sake, Harper, just

have the soup. She said it's locally sourced. That's ethical, isn't it?'

'It might be ethical but it's not healthy,' said the ketchup millionaire. 'I don't want my veins poisoned with fertiliser, thanks very much.'

Stewart sent me an apologetic smile. 'Sorry about this, Lana. He'll have the soup.'

'I won't. I'll have something organic or I'll leave.'

'You'll have the soup,' Stewart said firmly. 'Or you can research your own bloody role.'

'No, it's fine.' I managed a bright smile. 'It's fine, I'm sure we can sort something. I'll speak to the chef.'

In the brushed aluminium of the kitchen, Deano was stirring a pot of rabbit stew, his spiky scarlet-dyed hair looking almost demonic in the glow of neon. He was giggling to himself and humming snatches of Christmas tunes – in May – just one of the odd habits that made us wonder if he wasn't faintly insane.

He looked round when he heard me come in. 'Hey, Lana-banana! Always a pleasure, never a chore.'

Then he lifted me up by the hips and planted a massive smacker on my lips.

'Bleurghh,' I gagged when he put me down. 'Don't *do* that, Deano! How many times: not appropriate to snog the boss. You remember that little chat we had?'

He shrugged, turning back to his stew. 'You're Italian, aren't you? I thought you were a passionate and demonstrative people.'

'I'm half Italian. The other half's English, which means

I'm a reserved and sexually repressed people who save the passion for a spot of missionary on a Saturday night.'

'You speak for yourself, love.'

I curled my toes inside my boots, preparing for what I knew was coming.

'Deano…' I said in my most wheedling, persuasive voice.

'Yeah?'

'Think you can manage a special request?'

He turned to face me, frowning. 'No I can't. I'm finishing in an hour.'

'Please. As a favour. You can have all my tips for the night if you do it.'

'Hmm. What is it?'

I scrunched my eyes closed so I didn't have to look at his face.

'Living foodist,' I mumbled.

'What the *what?*'

'Living foodist. Organic vegan. We've got one in.'

I risked opening one eye. As expected, Deano's face was the perfect storm of horror and disgust.

'But… but why?' he faltered. He gestured helplessly over his hand-selected ingredients and bubbling pots, as if the idea of someone rejecting all that lovely food was culinary blasphemy.

'I don't know, some bollocks about fertiliser and blood pressure.'

'But… the venison! I did it in red wine. *Red wine*, Lana!'

I put a soothing hand on his arm. 'I know you did,' I said in the special softly-softly tone I saved for when he was going off on one. 'But there'll always be those who don't appreciate great artists. You're like the Vincent van Gogh of the kitchen, that's all. I bet after you're dead, your rabbit stew recipe'll be worth buckets.'

'And there's honey-roasted oxen steaks, and the turnip and rosemary pottage – I spent hours on that,' he went on, ignoring me. 'What's wrong with the pottage? It's vegan and it's delicious and I spent hours on it.'

'Is it organic?'

'Well I don't bloody know, do I? It's delicious, that's all I know.'

'You said that already.' I sighed. 'Look, isn't there anything you can do? It's that sauce guy, Harper Brady. He's already given us a one-star review. One tweet could do for us.'

'I don't care if he's the bloody pope!' Deano said, his voice getting more high-pitched by the second. 'He can come in here and explain what the problem is with my delicious vegan pottage or he can bugger the buggery off.'

'Come on, Deano, you're not a comedy French chef in a Looney Tunes cartoon,' I snapped, abandoning the soothing tone. 'You haven't got the moustache for it. You've got one job: to keep those knobheads out there in pulled hog and pottage. So drop the attitude, OK?'

'This isn't attitude, it's commitment to a craft.'

'Two years of catering college and he's Marco Pierre White,' I muttered. 'Look, will you do it for me? I'm having a shit night. Brady's been nothing but ball-ache, and I was exhausted before I even started my shift.'

His expression softened. 'Phil worse, is he?'

'Yeah. I was up most of last night.'

Deano scrutinised my face. 'You do look tired.' He rolled up his sleeves. 'All right, Lana, because I love you. I'll send the kid to the farm shop for supplies. It'll only take her five minutes on the scooter. Sure I can whip up a quinoa surprise or something.'

I exhaled with relief. 'You're a star. I'll let Jasmine know she needs to pop out.'

'Am I allowed to snog you then?'

'No. But you can slap my backside every second Saturday for the next three months.'

He grinned and held out a hand for me to shake. 'Deal.'

Harper guzzled the bean casserole Deano made him with every sign of relish, although it must've been a little dry judging by the rate he knocked back the fizz. By eleven, every diner except the Brady party had paid up and gone.

The blonde woman was still draped over Harper, giggling, and – I strongly suspected from the look on his face – quite possibly copping a feel under the table. Stewart, giving up all pretence at being sociable, had taken out a book. Stifling a yawn, I came out from behind the bar and approached Harper's table.

'Can I get you the bill?'

'No. Just another bottle of champagne,' Harper said without looking up. His voice was thick and heavy. More champagne sounded like the last thing he needed.

'I'm afraid the bar's closed. I can bring you some coffees if you like.' I scanned his droopy expression. 'Some black coffees.'

Harper opened his mouth to object, but Stewart jumped in first.

'Thanks, Lana. Just the bill.' He looked at Harper. 'Don't forget you're filming tomorrow.'

I rang their orders through then brought the bill to them on a little tray. Customers usually got an After Eight as well, but I'd decided Harper didn't deserve an After Eight. I might not have the power or influence of a Harper Brady but in this restaurant I was queen of the bloody After Eights and damned if I'd let him forget it.

'Right, come on then,' Harper said when they'd paid, standing up.

'See you next week, Lana?' Stewart said as he tucked his book away.

I smiled. 'Looking forward to it.'

Harper stared at his cousin. 'You're not serious, Stew. You fixed up a date with the waitress?' He looked me up and down. 'You could at least have gone for the fit one.'

'The "fit one" is sixteen, Mr Brady.'

'Shit, she's not, is she?' he said. 'Dodged a bullet there. They should make these kids show ID before they let them buy make-up.'

Claudia laughed and nuzzled his neck. 'You're funny,' I heard her whisper.

'It's waitress-owner to you anyway.' I walked to the door and held it open. 'Goodnight, sir.' I shot him a sarcastic thumbs-up. 'Oh, and thanks *so much* for the review.'

When they'd gone, I locked up and dragged my exhausted frame upstairs. Harper's table was still a mess, strewn with empty wine bottles and dirty goblets, but that could wait until morning. Mentally I added it to my list of chores, right after waxing the ornamental lute and taking the Brasso to the suit of armour.

The first room on the left was Dad's. I knocked softly, and a second later Tom's head poked out.

'He awake?' I whispered.

'Barely. I just gave him the last of his drugs.'

I opened the door gently. Dad was propped against a stack of pillows, his eyes heavy. The book Tom had been reading to him was lying open on the end of the bed.

Dad smiled sleepily when he saw who it was and beckoned me to him. I sank into the chair by his bed, Tom sitting down at the other side, and took the hand he offered.

'Well, little girl, and are you looking after my business?' he asked, his speech slurred from the morphine.

'Always do, don't I?' I said. 'We're doing great, Dad. Every table full. We sold three bottles of champagne too.'

'Ah.' He breathed a sigh of satisfaction. 'And how is my Lana?'

I smiled. 'Should I be worried you don't ask that first?'

'No point. I know you're too clever not to tell me you're fine.' He yawned heavily. 'Like your mother was clever. Too clever.' He gave a little laugh.

'Have you had fun with Gerry today?' I asked softly.

'Not much fun for him, I think, but it was good to see him. He says I owe him a pint at the Fox when I'm well enough. I think he's trying to take advantage of my bad memory.'

Tom laughed. 'Sign of a true Yorkshireman. You'll never want for company while you still owe drinks, Dad.'

'So do you have any restaurant gossip for the old man? I miss watching the people.'

I shot a look at Tom. I didn't want to tell Dad about the whole Harper Brady TripAdvisor fiasco when he was this drugged up; it might upset him. In the morning, if he was better, he could laugh about it.

'Deano had a bit of a strop,' I said. 'Had to cook bean casserole for a fussy vegan. I thought he'd pop when he realised they didn't want his precious marinated venison.'

Dad smiled. 'Quite right too. A talented lad, that one. I was like him once.'

Tom winked at me. 'She's not telling you the real gossip, Dad. Ask her about Stewart.'

Dad's forehead knit into a groggy frown. 'Stewart? Who is Stewart?'

I flushed. 'Just someone I met tonight. We're going out next week.'

'On a date?'

'That was the general idea, yes.'

He laughed. 'Well, I hope you don't scare him away with your sarcasm.'

Tom shook his head. 'She's a terrible flirt now you're not around, Dad. Fluttering her eyelashes at the customers to get bigger tips than me.'

I saw Dad wince, pressing his eyes closed for a moment.

'Is it hurting?' I said quietly.

'A little, that's all. Just a little. So he likes my Lana, this Stewart?'

'Yeah. I think so. I mean, I hope so.'

'Then you must bring him to meet me.'

I smiled. 'A bit soon for that.'

'You think I'll frighten him off, hey?'

I patted his hand. 'I don't want you to tire yourself out grilling him on his intentions, that's all.'

'I'll be good.' His eyes were half closed now. 'Well, I'm glad you met a nice boy. I always hoped I'd see you find someone to take care of you.'

'No need for you to worry about that. I can take care of me.'

'I know you can. But the best thing is to have someone take care of you, and you do the same for them. The best thing.' He sighed, and I knew he was thinking about Mum. She'd been dead nearly twenty years – so long that to me she was just a shadow from my little-girl memories – but for Dad the pain was raw.

He looked over at Tom. 'You too, Tomasso. When will you find yourself a nice boy?'

Tom flinched. 'Do you have to call me that? Tomasso Donati sounds well pretentious.'

'Ha! Your mother wanted Thomas, but I overruled her. We have to have something of the homeland.'

'Then you could've opened a bloody Italian restaurant,' Tom muttered, glancing down at the medieval costume he hadn't had time to change out of. But he was smiling.

Dad pointed a shaking finger. 'Don't change the subject. You hope I'll fall asleep before you answer, don't you?'

Tom grinned. 'Maybe.'

'Well, I think it might work,' Dad said, yawning. 'Go to bed now, kids. You'll have a busy day tomorrow.' He blinked in confusion. 'Tomorrow's Friday, isn't it?'

'Saturday, Dad,' I said. 'Today's Friday.' One side effect of the medication and irregular bedtimes was that Dad tended to lose track of time.

I stood and leaned over him to plant a kiss on his cheek, blinking back a tear. His appearance had changed so much over the last few years, it was hard to believe the gaunt, pain-riven face belonged to the same man as my strong, energetic dad.

'You get some sleep, OK?' I whispered. 'Maybe we'll go out in the morning if you're up to it. Love you, Papa.'

He smiled. 'I like it when you call me that.'

'I know you do. Night night.'

I left the room, closing the door quietly so Tom could say his goodnight. He came out a second later, his usual grin vanished. When he wasn't smiling his face looked tired and careworn, the way I knew mine must too. Instinctively, I clung to him and burst into tears against his shoulder.

'Oh God, I wish we could make it stop,' I whispered. 'It's hurting him more than he tells us.'

'I know, sis, I know. Me too.'

3

'And you're absolutely certain I look OK?' I asked Tom, twisting my neck uncomfortably as I tried to get a look at my back in the mirror.

'For the two hundred and ninth time, Lana, you look fine.'

'Oh God, fine? Just fine? Fine doesn't mean fine, it means crap – everyone knows that. It's what you say when you think someone's got docker hips and an arse the size of Finland.'

'Look, I'm your brother. Don't you think if you had an arse the size of Finland, I'd be first in line to tell you?'

'Hmm. Suppose there is that.' I yanked up my strappy top a bit to hide some of my stare-inviting cleavage. 'Ugh, big boobs are a nightmare. They make perfectly respectable River Island tops look like fetish gear. Don't know what blokes see in them.'

'Me neither.'

'I don't look too desperate, do I?' I yanked it up a bit further. 'Or too frumpy? Like I'm trying too hard to hide it?'

'Fine. You look fine. Arse the size of a modest peninsula at most, just the right ratio of fabric to flesh and with hips

26

like the most feminine of maritime workers.' He stood up from the edge of his bed and gave me a little shove towards the door. 'Now bugger off. I need to change for my shift. Just relax and enjoy yourself, OK?'

'Yes. Relax. Right.' I took a deep breath. 'Sorry. Don't want to mess it up, that's all.'

'Never seen you this nervous before a date. You must be keen on him.'

My eyes widened. 'What – does it show? You swore I didn't look desperate!'

Tom groaned. 'Here we go again.'

I jumped when a buzz sounded on the intercom, letting us know there was someone waiting at the foot of the stairs to our flat.

'It's him!' I hissed. 'What do I do?'

'You answer it.'

'Answer it. OK, I can do that. I think.' I gave his arm a squeeze. 'See you in the next life, Tommy.'

'Just have fun!' he called after me as I headed down to the restaurant.

Stewart was waiting at the bottom of the stairs, smiling warmly.

'Um, hi,' I said, fighting back a blush. 'So… you're here.'

'Seem to be.' He leaned forward to kiss my cheek. 'Good to see you again, Lana. You look nice.'

'Oh. Thanks. You too.'

He was looking pretty sexy in his smart-casual ensemble, a well-tailored blazer slung carelessly over a tight grey T-shirt. I tried not to stare at the athletic lines of his body under the clinging cotton.

'So, um, you want to come upstairs for a minute?' I

asked, fighting back the fizzing sensation that had sprung up in my stomach when he'd kissed me.

'If you promise you'll still respect me afterwards.'

I smiled, relaxing a little. 'To meet my dad, you daft sod. He asked if we could stop in before we headed off.'

'Oh. OK.'

He followed me up the stairs.

'I'm sorry about this,' I said as we made our way to Dad's room. 'First date and you're already getting roped into meeting the parents.'

'No need to apologise, Lana. I'd love to meet your dad.'

'It'll be nice for him to see a new face. He can't get out and about much now; it gets him down.'

Dad was wide awake, sitting up in bed doing the *Guardian* crossword as the dying sun streamed through the windows. I was glad Stewart was meeting him on one of his better evenings.

It was in the early days following Dad's diagnosis, when he was still on cooking duty in the restaurant, that Tom and me had started noticing the flickers of pain. They were few and far between then: the occasional wince, leaning against a worktop to steady himself. Then they'd started to get more frequent. Now, nearly seven years later, they weren't flickers any more. The agony was ever-present, and the hardest thing was having to read it there in his face.

But he did his best to summon the old, jovial Dad as I bashfully guided Stewart by the elbow into his room.

'Um,' I said when I'd shuffled in.

'Lost for words? That makes a change.' Dad put his crossword to one side and nodded to Stewart. 'A shy little flower, my Lana. And if you believe that then trust me, you'll believe anything.'

I smiled. 'Don't you start embarrassing me, old man.'

'Who, me? Never.' Dad crossed himself solemnly.

Stewart laughed. 'Stewart McLean,' he said, holding out a hand. 'Good to meet you.' He flashed an anxious look at me. 'Er, sir.'

Dad smiled as he shook Stewart's hand. 'Phil will do fine. Sit down, lad. My daughter tells me I'm supposed to—' he shot a look at me '—grill you on your intentions. Lana, was that the phrase?'

'Dad's good at grilling,' I told Stewart. 'He's a chef, you know.'

Stewart smiled a little uncertainly as he took a seat in Tom's chair. I claimed my usual place on the other side of the bed.

'Stewart McLean.' Dad looked thoughtful. 'I know that name from somewhere. Are you from Egglethwaite?'

'No, I live about ten miles away. Out Halifax way.'

'And what is it that you do?'

'I'm a cyclist.'

'Cyclist...' Dad blinked as something clicked. 'Not the Stewart McLean who set a new record in the Etape du Dales last year, surely?'

'Er, yes, that was me,' Stewart said, flushing slightly.

Dad looked impressed. He was a big follower of cycling. Personally I wouldn't know a spoke from a sprocket, but if Dad thought Stewart was a big deal in the sport he must be someone to be reckoned with.

'Well, there's a coincidence. I've just been reading about you.' Dad thumbed through his newspaper with a trembling hand. 'Top ten athletes to watch, it says here. Stewart McLean, number six.' He gave Stewart an approving nod. 'Very good.'

Stewart smiled. 'Does that mean I've got your blessing to take out your daughter?'

'I'm afraid you have to get that from her. I'm not allowed a say now she's so very grown up, she tells me.' He turned to me. 'Where are you going, Lana?'

I shrugged. 'Was thinking the pub.'

Dad waved a dismissive hand. 'Pfft. The Fox is not a romantic place for a date. You want to go somewhere you can be alone.'

His lips were twitching at one side, the familiar teasing smile. I was hardened to it now, but when he'd embarrassed me like this in front of boyfriends as a teenager it'd been excruciating. Nice to see there was one old hobby he could still enjoy.

'Nothing wrong with the Fox,' I said. 'If we run out of things to talk about, we can play darts.'

'Worse and worse, little girl. Every Italian bone is crying.'

Dad beckoned me to him. I stood and leaned over the bed.

'Take him up to Pagans' Rock,' he whispered. 'You can see the stars there.'

'Pagans' Rock? It's a bit of a walk, Dad.'

'All the better. At this time of the night you can have it to yourselves. Take some champagne from behind the bar if you like.'

I smiled. 'Take it out of my wages, you mean?'

He shrugged. 'Of course. We're not made of money.'

'Do you mind?' I asked Stewart. 'It's about a mile uphill but it's well worth seeing.'

He looked bewildered. 'Er, no. Sorry, where are we going?'

'Local beauty spot, my dad's favourite. Shame to waste a lovely evening like this indoors really.'

'Have fun,' Dad called after us as we left. 'Be back by eleven, Lana.'

'I'm not sixteen any more, Dad!' I called back.

'OK, midnight then.'

Stewart smiled as he followed me downstairs.

'Takes good care of you, doesn't he?'

'Oh, he's just teasing. Anyway, he likes you; I can tell.'

'I like him. He's a brave man. I can see he's in pain.'

'All the time,' I said soberly. 'I'm glad you got to meet him like he was today.'

'What was different about today?'

'He's so out of it a lot of the time now, with the drugs. That was the old Dad. He... we don't see too much of that guy any more.'

I nipped behind the bar, nodding to our second waitress Debbie on barmaid duty, and passed Stewart a bottle of champagne from the fridge. He tucked it under one arm while I slipped a couple of flutes into my handbag.

We left and started walking up the cobbled main street towards open countryside.

'So. You're a proper cyclist,' I said to Stewart. 'My dad doesn't raise an eyebrow for just anyone, you know.'

He laughed. 'Not sure there's any such thing as a proper cyclist. But I do it for a living, if that's what you mean.'

'Another celebrity diner for our collection. I'll have to tell my brother – he'll be made up.'

'Well, I don't know about that. Harper's the celeb in the family.'

'Mmm. I bet he doesn't let you forget it either.'

Stewart grimaced. 'Yeah, sorry about him. He was on his absolute worst behaviour that night, for some reason. Hope he didn't give you too much of a headache with that living foodist bollocks.'

'That wasn't so bad, but the arsey review we could've done without. That's the last thing a small business needs.'

'He didn't leave you a review, did he?'

'Yeah. One star, and I know he posted it before he'd tried the food. Bastard.'

Stewart looked mortified. 'Oh God, I'm sorry, Lana. I'll get him to take it down.'

'Oh yeah, that reminds me.' I fished in my bag and handed him a little square packet. 'For you.'

He frowned at it. 'What's this?'

'After Eight. Don't tell your cousin.'

'Right,' he said, blinking. 'Er, cheers. I'll smoke it later.'

We passed Holyfield Farm, the last outpost of civilisation before nature took over, and made our way along the wooded footpath that led up to Pagans' Rock. The sun was just sinking into the horizon, splashing the sky auburn and gold.

Stewart was walking close by my side. My fingers accidentally brushed against his and he glanced down to see what was tickling.

I flushed, yanking my hand away. 'Sorry.'

He smiled. 'Here,' he said, taking my hand and twining

my fingers in his. My stomach fluttered at the exciting, unfamiliar press of skin on skin. The tip of Stewart's thumb made soft, lazy circles on the backs of my fingers as we continued our walk hand in hand.

'This is nice,' he whispered.

'Yeah.' The word came out like a sigh.

'Good to find out what you look like out of uniform, by the way.'

I smiled. 'Everything you expected and less, right?'

'Dunno, I think I could adjust to it.' He ran an approving gaze over the long chestnut waves cascading over my shoulders, for once free of the elasticated cloth cap that had been making my working life an ear-pinched hell since my teens. 'Not that the Mother Goose look wasn't rocking for you. Still, I like non-wenchy Lana best.'

He gave my fingers a squeeze.

'Bit of a scramble here,' I said as we approached the grassy verge leading up to Pagans' Rock. 'Think you can handle it?'

'Hey. I'm an athlete.' He glanced up the steep incline. 'What is this place anyway?'

'You'll see.'

By the time we'd put dignity aside and scrabbled hamster-like to the top, we were both out of breath, even the athlete. But it was worth it to see Stewart's face.

'I never knew this was here,' he said in a hushed voice.

'Not many people do. Us locals try to keep it quiet.'

'I can see why.'

A huge, flat rock jutted from the edge of the tree-circled heath we were standing on. Far beneath curved the serpent arches of Egglethwaite's old railway viaduct, reflected in the sunset-fired square of the reservoir behind. With the moors rising up behind, blushing with the embers of the day, I had to admit Dad was right: when it came to romantic settings, there was nowhere like Pagans' Rock.

He'd brought my mum here when they were courting and, scratched somewhere in the stone among hundreds of other lovers' marks, you could still find their initials. Soppy buggers.

'Beats the pub, right?' I said to Stewart after a moment's silence while we drank the view.

'It does,' he said quietly. He nodded to the viaduct. 'Does that thing still get used?'

'No, they shut it up back in the sixties. It just sits there now. Impressive old thing, isn't it?'

'It is pretty spectacular.' He smiled. 'Still, for me tonight's more about the company.' He nodded to the flat surface of the rock, carved all over with the messages and initials of more than two hundred years' worth of visitors. 'Shall we sit?'

'OK.'

I scrambled onto the rock and sat down, crossing my legs like a yogi – the flexible levitating type, not the picnic-basket-stealing type – and Stewart lowered himself down next to me. He uncorked the champagne I'd borrowed from the bar with a satisfying pop-fizz as I rummaged in my bag for the flutes. When he'd poured us both a glass he put one arm around my shoulders, his fingers curling lightly around my upper arm.

The height was quite dizzying, when you took the time to drink it in. As a kid it had always made me nervous being this close to the edge of the rock, even clinging tightly to my parents' hands. But with Stewart's reassuringly solid arm around me, I felt safe enough. I nestled into it, a thrill shooting through me as his fingers started trailing gently over the bare skin of my arm.

'Cold?' he whispered when he felt me shiver. 'You can have my jacket if you want.'

'I'm OK. Just ticklish.'

He grinned. 'One day, I promise you'll regret telling me that.'

'Feels nice,' I murmured, letting my head drop onto his shoulder. 'Don't stop.'

It'd been so long since I'd been out with a lad, I'd been worrying myself sick beforehand that I'd have forgotten how you were supposed to do it. Tom had been right when he'd said it was the most anxious he'd seen me. My dating nerves seemed to follow a formula that went something like 'length of time since last date multiplied by how much you like the guy equals how much of a tit you're terrified you'll make of yourself'.

But now I was actually there, Stewart's soft fingers brushing my skin as we inhaled the mingled scent of cherry blossom and champagne drifting to us on the breeze, it all seemed quite easy. The setting was right. The closeness was right. Stewart was right. Somehow, it was all… just right.

Although there was one thing missing. Wine, check. Sunset, check. Sexy man with magic fingers, check. All we needed now was…

'We could do with some music, couldn't we?' Stewart said.

'You read my mind,' I said, smiling. 'Just a sec.' I fumbled in my jeans for my smartphone and fired up a bit of Kirsty

MacColl. Instantly the dulcet sound of her familiar Brit-country stylings blared from the tinny speaker. Not the most romantic playlist, but it was all I had on there. Anyway, it helped me relax.

Stewart laughed. 'What, no Barry White?'

'I like Kirsty MacColl,' I said with a shrug.

'Bit before your time, isn't she?' He examined my features. 'Unless I've seriously misjudged your age. In which case, kudos to your Botox guy.'

'I'm twenty-five,' I said, smiling. 'S'pose it reminds me of my mum. She loved a bit of Kirsty. It's one of my earliest memories, her dancing me round the kitchen to "Don't Come the Cowboy" while Dad cooked.'

'Where is your mum?'

'Dead. When I was five.'

His eyes filled with sympathy. 'You've had some bad luck, kid,' he said gently.

'Yeah.' I summoned a smile. 'Come on, let's cheer up. Here. Lie back with me.'

He cocked an eyebrow. 'Hello.'

I nudged him. 'To look at the sky, I meant. Cheeky person.'

We lay back on the rock, side by side. The day had drifted into dusk now, the sun all disappeared, and the moon was just peeping through a wispy lavender cloud. Stewart shuffled closer so our sides were touching and reached for my hand.

'So how did you manage to get rid of Harper this evening?' I asked. 'I thought he was shadowing you.'

Stewart shrugged. 'Gave him a fiver, sent him to the pictures.'

36

'Didn't look like he was asking you much about cycling on your little dinner date last week.'

'Yeah, he managed to make it all about him as usual. He used to pull this sort of thing when we were kids too. Comes of being a spoilt only child.'

'And that girl Claudia's his agent, is she?' I said. 'They seemed... inappropriately close.'

'Mmm, he seems to have a few of them. And funny thing: he always wants to meet them at some isolated dive in the middle of nowhere. Er, no offence.'

'She's never from a theatrical agency though.'

'She's from some sort of agency. Not sure it's got the word "theatrical" in front of it.'

My eyes went wide. 'No way. She's an *escort*?'

'Yep,' Stewart said with a grin.

'God. That's probably the most exciting thing that's ever happened at Flagons.' I inclined my head to take a sip of wine. 'How come he brought you along?'

'Dunno, cover? Easier to explain if he gets papped.' Stewart rolled so he was leaning over me on one elbow. 'Not such a bad night from my point of view though. I got to meet some interesting people.'

I flushed. 'I'm not interesting.'

'I'm interested in you.'

'Why?'

'Not exactly sure.' He swept my breeze-tossed hair back from my forehead. 'Something here, I think,' he said, running one finger around my eye.

I felt my cheeks burning. With Stewart's face so close, my first-date nerves were back in force. It'd been a long time since I'd had a pair of lips that near mine.

My eye had started twitching, probably making me look at least a little deranged. Maybe that's why Stewart was smiling.

Shit, he was going to kiss me, wasn't he? Could I remember how to do it? What if my tongue did something weird, or I opened my mouth too quickly? Or too wide? Oh God, it was a minefield. Kissing was second-date territory, definitely.

Guiding him away, I sat up and grabbed the wine bottle.

'Top-up?' I asked brightly.

He sat up too, frowning. 'Something wrong, Lana?'

'Look, could we just talk for a while? I'm… I mean, don't want to inflate your ego too much, but I'm kind of out of practice at all this. I wouldn't mind taking it slow.'

'Of course, whatever you want. Here.' He took the wine and filled our glasses, then slipped his arm around me again. 'We've got all the time in the world.'

I sipped the wine gratefully. 'So tell me about you then. How did you get into cycling?'

He shrugged. 'They took the stabilisers off one day and that was it, never looked back.'

'Come on, tell it properly.'

'All right, if I must,' he said with a smile. 'I used to love biking when I was a kid, belting around on a BMX. Then when I was ten I joined my school cycling club and it all grew from there. We used to go on trips – Lakeland, the Peaks.' His eyes shone. 'The hills and the open road from the saddle of a bike, the wind in your face just like you're flying: I couldn't get enough of it. You ever cycle, Lana?'

I shook my head. 'Not like that. I can just about manage

to sit on the thing without falling off. When did you start competing?'

'In my teens. My mum pushed me into it at first. I loved the freedom of being on a bike but I never really had that drive to be the best. Once I'd started though, the rush of it: it was addictive.'

'Winning?'

'Partly, but the personal challenge too. That need to be better and better every time. I couldn't imagine not competing now. It's my life.'

He was gazing towards the viaduct, almost like he was talking to himself. Eventually he shook his head to bring himself back to where he was.

'Sorry,' he said with a guilty smile. 'We do tend to get a bit religious about it. Probably sounds weird when you're on the outside looking in.'

It did a bit, but it was still inspiring, seeing how committed he was. It wasn't something I could quite get my head round though, that compulsion to win. Maybe it was a testosterone thing.

'Anyway, enough about me,' Stewart said. 'I already know about that guy. Tell me about you. This is actually my first ever date with a medieval serving wench.'

'Really? You haven't lived, love.'

He laughed. 'So was that what you always wanted to do?'

'What, dress up like a pillock and shove my tits at people over a plate of hog flesh?' I shrugged. 'Not especially. It's a living.'

'Then what did little Lana dream?'

'Oh, I don't know,' I said with a sigh. 'My brother's a couple of years older, and it never occurred to him he'd do anything but go into the family business. He's more entrepreneurial. Takes after Dad.'

'But you're not.'

'Not like Tom. I used to waitress for a bit of pocket money when I was at school, but I never thought it was something I'd be doing forever. I used to imagine...' I smiled. 'It's stupid really. I had this thing about the stars, when I was a kid.'

'Right.' He frowned. 'You wanted to work for *Heat*?'

'No, the other kind,' I said, laughing. I lifted my eyes skywards, where a couple of glowing pinpricks were just becoming visible against smoky velvet. 'I was fascinated by them. Wanted to be an astronomer.'

'Horoscopes?'

I nudged him. 'Astronomer, not astrologer. Study the skies.'

'How old were you?'

'About four, when it started. We visited a planetarium on some family holiday and there was this amazing light show, every star in the heavens. We had to lie on our backs in a domed room while a voice-over told us about each galaxy and constellation.'

He was looking at me keenly.

'Here.' He took my hand and guided me down so we were lying on our backs again. 'Like this?'

My eyes darted over the stars, picking out the constellations like old friends.

'Yeah,' I said softly, squeezing his hand. 'Just like this.'

'Then what happened?'

'Oh, I was obsessed for a bit. Used to watch *The Sky at Night* religiously every week. You couldn't get into my room without stepping on a rocket or a Lego astronaut for a while.'

'So what, you grew out of it?'

'Not exactly. I mean, the rockets and astronauts disappeared, but it still interested me. I actually started looking into BSc courses at a few unis.' I sighed. 'But then Dad was diagnosed, and I knew I was needed here. He's only got me and Tom since Mum died: the rest of his family's in Italy. Three years is a long time to be away, especially when—' I swallowed '—when we didn't know how long we'd get to keep him, you know?'

'He wouldn't have wanted you to stop your education, would he?' Stewart said gently, rolling over to look into my face.

'No. That's why I never told him.' I gave a bleak laugh. 'He probably thinks working in the restaurant's my dream job.'

'You should tell him.'

'I can't do that. And I am happy, Stewart, honestly.'

He reached for my cheek, brushing the back of his fingernail over a wet patch that had appeared under one eye.

'Not sure I believe you.'

'Not sure I do either.'

He was scanning my face again. I wondered if my mascara was smudged.

'Think I still owe you a tip from the other week, don't I?' he said at last. 'You can have it in the form of a hug if you like.'

'Yes.' I smiled weakly. 'Yes, I think I'd like a hug.'

We both sat up. The arms went round me, hot and

strong, and I let myself relax. God, it felt safe in there. The combination of smells, of wine and aftershave and sweat, so human and so real, went with the sense of serenity that filled me. Stewart's fingers meshed behind my back, keeping me right up against him.

'Sorry,' I whispered.

'Why sorry?' His voice sounded different this close to my body. I could feel it, deep and soft, vibrating through the cheek that was laid against his neck.

'For crying at you. You can probably tell I don't date much.'

'Then it's time we changed that.' He held me back a little to smile at me. 'You know, if you'd told me this time last week I'd be on a night out with a sobbing medieval tavern wench…'

'And I'd be spilling my life story to a random customer…'

He laughed. 'It does feel slightly surreal. But I'd like a bit more of it, all the same.'

'I think I would too.'

'I'm back to intensive training on Monday but if you give me your mobile number I'll call you soon as I get a break, OK? My turn to pick the venue for the next date, I think.' He glanced at my phone, blaring out Kirsty as she unromantically griped about inappropriate footwear. 'And the music.'

'As long as it's not harpsichord.'

'Nothing medieval within spitting distance, I swear.' He drew a finger down my cheek. 'I was thinking a nice tapas restaurant I know. Big on the mood lighting and easy jazz.'

I smiled. 'Sounds perfect.'

'I really like you, Lana. I know we just met last week, but I think this could be... something, you know?'

'Yeah,' I whispered. 'Me too.'

'In that case, don't suppose you'd be interested in carrying this date on at my place?' he asked, smiling. 'I've got an impressive selection of euphemistic coffee you can sample.'

I shook my head. 'Don't spoil it, love.'

'Sorry,' he said gently. 'I like being with you, that's all.'

'Let's just enjoy right now. We don't need to rush, do we?'

'Like I said. All the time in the world.'

My eyes were locked into his. Suddenly I wasn't worried about uncontrollable tongues or lips, and kissing wasn't a minefield but a simple, natural thing that was just right for the moment. I tilted my lips up to Stewart's and relaxed in his arms as our mouths joined, feeling happier than I had in a long, long time.

4

'Here you go,' Gerry said, dumping my Guinness and Tom's Boltmaker down on the table. 'And make sure you tell your old man I bought you both one. He can scratch it off against that pint I owe him.'

'Why is it you two always seem to owe each other drinks?' Tom asked, claiming his beer.

'Because they're as tight as each other, that's why,' Sue said, nudging her husband in the ribs as he sank back into his seat.

He shrugged, wiping a fleck of foam off his moustache. 'You knew what I was like when you married me.'

Tom groaned. 'Can you cut out the bickering, guys, just for today? This is our first night out in months. We don't want to waste it giving you two marriage guidance.'

Gerry grinned. 'Just keeping the old lady on her toes.' He gave his wife's sizeable backside a hearty slap. 'If there's one thing your Uncle Gerry can teach you about women, son, it's you've got to treat 'em mean to keep 'em keen.'

'Still not getting the whole gay thing, is he?' Tom muttered to me.

'He'll get the hang of it when you meet someone.'

'Heh. At the rate I'm going he'll be waiting a while.'

'Any news then, kids?' Sue asked in a gentler voice.

'Nothing since we saw you last,' I said soberly. 'Could be days, could be weeks. Nothing to do now but keep him comfortable.'

'And how are you both feeling?'

'It's like... like we're in some sort of hellish limbo,' Tom said in a low voice. 'I mean, we're dreading it, obviously. But part of us just wants it to be over.'

He reached out to take my hand and I gave his fingers a firm squeeze.

'Is that bad? To feel that way about it?' I asked Sue, too aware of the pleading note underpinning my tone.

'It's not bad,' she said softly. 'You don't want to see him hurting. We've been just the same.'

'You look knackered, the pair of you,' Gerry said, radiating concern. 'You sure he wouldn't be better off in the hospice now he needs round-the-clock care?'

'No. He's not going there.' Tom looked almost fierce. 'He wanted to be at home when he – when it happened. That's what he said so that's what's going to happen.'

'He wouldn't want you making yourselves ill over it.'

'You think we'd be any different if he was in the hospice?' I grabbed my phone off the table and quickly scanned the screen, just to make sure Dahlia, Dad's nurse, hadn't texted. 'That'd be worse. Knowing we couldn't be with him straight away if he wanted us.'

'Fair enough, petal,' Gerry said gently. 'You know what's best. If we can do anything, just let us know.'

There was silence for a moment, everyone staring into their pints.

I'd been eighteen when Dad had been diagnosed and barely twenty when he'd found out the cancer was terminal: not much more than a kid, trying to prepare myself for the loss of the second parent in my young life. But nothing, nothing had prepared me for the daily agony that was the very end of the end. It was good of Gerry and Sue to drag us out and try to take our minds off it for an hour or two.

'Well, he wouldn't want us moping,' Gerry said at last. 'We brought you out to cheer you up, not make you cry.' He lifted his pint. 'Tell you what, here's to absent friends. My best mate Phil, as good a lad as ever drew breath, who never cheated at pool when he thought anyone was looking and never dodged his round when he thought you were too drunk to notice he'd only got you a half. Wish you were here, mate.'

'To Dad,' we echoed, clinking glasses.

We went quiet for a minute, each alone with their memories.

'So how's the maypole dancing, Gerry?' I asked after a while, summoning a bit of cheerfulness to lighten the mood. 'Will the farm be extra fertile this year or do we need to sacrifice Tom in a giant wicker man?'

Gerry shot me a look. 'It's morris dancing, young lady. The maypole hardly comes into it.'

'Yeah, pull the other one, it's got bells on.'

Sue groaned. 'Do you know how many times you've done that joke?'

'And still it never gets old.'

'It bloody does, you know.'

I shrugged. 'That's only your opinion.'

Tom glared at me. 'Oi. Did you just call me a virgin?'

'Probably the closest we'll get round here. You haven't been out with a lad in nearly three years.'

'Bloody hell.' He knocked back a morose gulp of his pint. 'The sad thing is, that's true.'

'It's no good picking on him, Lana,' Sue said. 'I don't see you going out with many boys. What about that young chef with the punk-rocker hair your dad likes?'

Tom snorted. 'Deano?'

'That's the one. Phil was always full of him.'

'I'm all right, thanks,' I said. 'Deano's lovely but he's about ninety-nine per cent whacko. Not for me.'

'What about the band then? You must meet some pretty trendy young men there.'

I laughed. 'Egglethwaite Silver's not Oasis, Sue. There's only three of us under fifty.'

'Seems to me you're past the point where you can afford to be picky. It's been over a year for you as well.' Sue paused to take a sip of her pint. 'What was his name, the bike man?'

'I don't know who you mean.'

'Come on, you remember. That cyclist you went out with who never called you.'

'No, I don't remember. I don't remember Stewart McLean at all actually.'

Tom drew a zip over his lips. 'Nix on the S-word, Susan. We don't mention that guy.'

'Well, it's time our Lana got back out there if you ask me.' She skimmed down my body. 'What size are you now, love?'

I winced. OK, so I'd gained a bit of weight in the last year. Caring for Dad, it'd been too easy to grab a ready meal or some restaurant leftovers before I took over from Tom for the evening watch. Still, I was far from an unhealthy size. Bloody Sue, she always had to ask.

'Mind your own business.'

'Mmm. You want to come to Slimming World with me?'

'I don't need Slimming World. I just need to look after myself a bit, that's all.'

Gerry shook his head. 'I don't know why you girls can't let yourselves be. Nothing wrong with a bit of jiggle. Gives us fellers something to hold on to.' He leaned back to cast an appreciative look at his wife's backside.

'I should've filed for divorce the day he grew that bloody moustache,' Sue muttered.

'So any news from the village society this month, Gerry?' Tom said, diplomatically changing the subject. 'Has the Egglethwaite knicker thief been caught yet?'

'Nope. The Knicker Nicker's still on the loose.' Gerry took a long draught of his pint. 'To be honest, I'm glad. That's the only excitement we get in those meetings. Otherwise it's just planning permission for sheds and what type of paper to use for this year's newsletter.'

'Why did you join then?' I asked.

'Oh, you know. Do my civic duty, look out for farmers' interests. Fill your dad's spot when he couldn't manage it any more,' he said. 'Boring as shite though. No word of a lie, we spent half an hour in the last meeting looking at yellow Dulux swatches. Talk about watching paint dry.'

'Why? Are they doing up the temperance hall?'

'No, they're after getting in on a bit of this Tour de France publicity. You know, the Grand Départ? It's in Yorkshire next year.'

'It's not coming near here though, is it?'

'Dunno, the route's not been announced yet. The society thought it'd be good to show support though. The least we can do is get one of those yellow bikes up outside the Temp.'

I fell silent, staring into my Guinness while the conversation moved on. As the alcohol hit my tired old brain, an idea started to form.

'Lana?' Gerry said. I looked up, realising he must've asked me a question.

'Hmm?'

'You all right, petal?'

'Yeah. And why shouldn't it anyway?' I murmured, half to myself.

'You what?'

'Why shouldn't it come here as well as anywhere?'

Sue frowned. 'What on earth are you dribbling about, girl?'

'The Grand Départ. Why shouldn't it come through Egglethwaite? We're as good as the next Dales village, aren't we?'

'We're no better than the next Dales village either,' Tom said. 'Three farms, a pub and a cobbled street is about what it boils down to for us. What's so hot about that?'

'Setts,' Gerry said.

'What?'

'They aren't cobbles, they're setts. Broader and flatter.' He shook his head. 'Everyone gets that wrong.'

Tom waved his hand dismissively. 'Cobbles, setts, badgers,

who cares? What I'm saying is there's a million villages like ours. What've we got to make them choose Egglethwaite?'

I looked around the Sooty Fox, filled with villagers laughing and chatting over their weekend pints.

'We've got us,' I said. 'The village might be two-a-penny but the people are pretty special. That's what Dad always says.'

Sue looked doubtful. 'You can't cycle on people, Lana. They'll want sweeping landscapes, gorgeous views. Stuff that makes good telly.'

'We've got that,' I said, warming to my subject now. 'The view from Pagans' Rock – the viaduct. The moors. We've got it all, guys! Why shouldn't it be here? It has to go somewhere.'

Gerry was frowning. 'No offence, but what's in it for us? I don't fancy my farmland overrun with tourists, ta very much. It'll upset my sheep.'

Sue tutted. 'Sod your sheep. There's more to life than bloody Swaledales, Gerry Lightowler.'

'Spoken like no true farmer's wife, lass. And I'll be telling them you said that too.'

'Why do they call them farmers' wives?' Tom asked.

'Because they're married to farmers.' Gerry rolled his eyes. 'Kids.'

'Yeah, but Sue's a farmer too, isn't she? Why aren't you a farmer's husband?'

'Well, because…' Gerry stopped, looking perplexed. 'Dunno.'

I shook my head at Tom. 'See, you've introduced him to feminism now. His poor Yorkshire head might explode.'

Sue glared at me. 'Oi. No one insults this old man but me.'

'Well you certainly do it plenty for the lot of us,' I said. 'Look, we're getting off the point. What about the Tour? Honestly, I really think it's worth looking into.'

'It's a nice idea, but really, Gerry's – well, something not approaching wrong,' Sue said. 'It'd be a lot of hassle for not much return.' She nudged her husband. 'Best you're getting, lad.'

'It'd be a massive boon for businesses though, all that tourism. Reckon you could pitch it to the society, Gerry?'

'Hmm. Not convinced, love, sorry.'

'But come on, guys. We could make history here!' I could see Gerry still hesitating and put on my best puppy-dog eyes. 'For me, eh? Dad'd want you to.'

Gerry took a meditative suck on his pint. 'Well, I'll bring it up,' he said at last. 'But don't get too carried away, Lana. For all we know the route's already decided. We'll see what happens.'

My phone buzzed on the table. I fumbled for it and hastily swiped at the screen.

'Oh God,' I whispered. 'Tommy, we need to get home. Right now.'

5

'For God's sake, Flash. Get on with it, can you?'

The fat Border collie puppy stared at me as he sat on his hind legs under a tree, for all the world like a furry black-and-white gnome.

I waved the plastic bag at him accusingly. He carried on staring.

'All right, I get it. You want some privacy. Just hurry up, that's all.'

I turned away to look across the daisy-foamed landscape. It was an overcast summer's morning, the sun just breaking through. Long beams of light – God's fingers, Dad called them – bounced off the viaduct and shattered on the reservoir behind. There was a bleak, empty beauty to those grey arches, which today I couldn't help hating.

I glared at the sunbeams. What did they have to be so bloody shiny about?

My phone buzzed and I yanked it out of my pocket.

T minus two hours. You going to be much longer?

'You done yet, pupster?' I called to Flash. 'Uncle Tommy says time to go home.'

I turned to discover Flash had finally done his business and was standing proudly next to it, tail wagging, like he expected to be awarded the Turner Prize any minute.

'Good boy,' I said, giving him a stroke. 'Come on then. It's time.'

Back at the restaurant, Tom was waiting downstairs for us in his suit and tie.

'Oh good, you're back,' he said with a sigh of relief. 'Was worried you'd forgotten the time. Are you going to change?'

'I'll just put Flash in his bed.'

But Flash was way ahead of me, tearing through the restaurant and up the stairs. I found him on the landing by Dad's room, scratching at the door.

'No, boy. You can't go in there.'

He whined, staring at me with big, pleading eyes.

'I said no, Flash! Go to your bed.'

But it was too late. Flash had managed to push his way in with his nose. Sighing, I followed.

The curtains were drawn, just enough light peeking through to bathe the room in a dismal gloom. Dad's book was lying face down on the bedside table next to his pain medication. I found Flash sitting in the Dad-shaped depression in the middle of the bed, whimpering.

'You're a naughty dog. He's not here, see? Come on.'

I turned as if to make for the door, but Flash didn't move. He just carried on whimpering.

'Come on, you daft pup! Don't you hear me? He's not here. He's gone.'

I glanced at Dad's book, still open at the last page Tom had read to him. *The Road to Wigan Pier*, George Orwell – he loved that one.

Had loved. He *had* loved that one.

Sinking into my chair by the bed, I burst into tears.

'It's no good, Flash,' I whispered to Dad's little puppy. 'He can't cuddle you any more.' I reached out to stroke him, a furry blob through the mist of tears. 'You'll miss him, won't you? Me too, my lamb.'

'But at least he's out of pain.'

I looked up to see a Tom-shaped cloud walking towards me. A heavy hand landed on my shoulder and I seized it gratefully.

'I know, I know. It was a prison to him. I'm a selfish cow to wish him back again.'

'No you're not. You're his little girl.' He gave my hand a slightly ferocious squeeze. 'He should never have gone like this. Fifty-two, what age is that? That *fucking* disease...'

'And so we're orphans. Twenty-six and I'm already a bloody orphan.' I stood to hug him. 'Oh God, Tommy, how're we going to get through today?'

'Together. No other way.' He patted the back of my head. 'You'd better get your suit on. The car'll be here in an hour.'

When the funeral car pulled up outside Cedarwood Crematorium, a gaggle of mourners were outside chatting to Sal, the kind-eyed humanist celebrant Dad had chosen to conduct the service.

'This isn't everyone, is it?' I murmured to Tom. There were only about ten people: Aunty Clem and her husband, who'd flown out from Italy specially, and a few folk from the village.

'I announced it on the Facebook residents' group,' Tom said. 'Maybe there's more on the way.' But he sounded concerned.

Sal came forward to greet us as we stepped out of the car. 'How're you both doing?' she asked when she'd given us a hug each.

Tom managed a smile for her. 'Been better, I think.'

'Of course you have,' she said. 'Well, I'm here to worry about the difficult stuff. You two just say if you need anything else from me today.'

That was one thing I really liked about Sal. Ever since Dad had asked us to send for someone to help him plan his funeral, she'd been the perfect combination of sympathy and efficiency, none of the faux-sentimental nonsense you got so often from strangers. It was exactly what we'd all needed. I think Dad might've been a bit in love with her by the end.

'Where's the coffin?' I asked. I was dreading seeing it.

'Inside.' She gave my arm a squeeze. 'Look, I know today's going to be tough. There's not really any such thing as a joyful funeral, is there? But remember your dad wanted this to be a celebration of his life. Think of the happy years you had together, and try to see it as... well, a closing.'

'All I can think of is that he isn't coming back.' I let a little sob escape. 'My dad's gone and he isn't coming back.'

'If he came back it'd be to pain.'

'We know,' Tom said. 'God, we saw enough of that. It should make it easier, but... well, it doesn't.'

'Just hold on to the fact he loved you, and he was proud of you,' Sal said gently.

I let out a damp laugh. 'I know he was, daft old bugger.

Imagine being proud of a pair of screw-ups like us, eh?' I gave Tom a nudge, and he shot me a fond smile back.

'Come on then, guys. Let's get this over with.'

Tom gave an involuntary laugh as we followed Sal into the crematorium.

'God, Lana, it's the whole village!'

It certainly looked like it. The place was packed to the rafters with Egglethwaite folk, standing room only apart from a couple of chairs at the front that had been saved for us. There was Deano and Jasmine and Debbie from work; there was the butcher, Jean from the flower shop, Billy the landlord of the Sooty Fox...

But before I could properly take it in, my eyes were drawn to the long wooden box up front by a pair of curtains I knew hid the furnace. An image of poor Flash, whimpering quietly in the depression that still held the shape of Dad's body, appeared uninvited in my mind.

'Oh God, he's in there,' I whispered to Tom, sudden panic sweeping through me. My head felt tight and uncomfortable, as if I had my restaurant cloth cap on and it was shrinking around my brain. 'Dad's in there, Tom!'

He shook his head. 'Dad's gone. What's in there... it's not him. It's empty.'

But I couldn't take my eyes off the coffin. I stared at it in horror, feeling like I might black out.

'I can't do this,' I muttered. 'Tommy, I'm so sorry, I... I can't watch.'

'Lana!' he called after me, but I was already running for the exit.

Outside I sagged against the wall, panting, trying desperately to calm the frenzied beating of my heart.

My dad… they were going to…

'So you're here, are you?'

Sue had followed me out and was holding me in a stern gaze, arms folded.

'Yes, I'm here,' I mumbled. 'Just about.'

'What're you doing outside? There's a lady vicar in there waiting for you so she can get started.'

'Celebrant.'

'What?'

'Celebrant. She's not a vicar.'

She shook her head. 'Your dad and his funny ideas. Are you coming in then?'

I swallowed a sob. 'I can't, Sue. The coffin… I can't watch it go in.'

'Don't make me Mum at you.'

'You wouldn't Mum at me.'

'I would. I'll Mum you up properly, girl, so just you get in there and give your brother some support.'

'But—'

'Don't "but" me, Lana Donati. I bought you your first bra.'

I frowned. 'What's that got to do with it?'

She ignored me. 'With her last breath, your mother said to me. "Sue," she said. "Watch that those kids of mine always look after each other. Especially Lana."'

'I thought her last words to you were "For God's sake, when I'm gone make sure Filippo gets rid of those curtains"?'

'Well, this she said with her eyes.' She rested a gentle hand on my arm. 'I know it's tough, but that's the way life is. You love someone, then the day comes when you lose them and there's just the memories left. It's a kick, but there it is. You and your brother need each other now. So pull up your knicker elastic, get back inside and look after him like your old mum said, eh?'

'Which mum?'

'Both of us.' She slipped an arm around me. 'He's not in there, chicken,' she said softly. 'He's somewhere else, somewhere it doesn't hurt any more. It's just a box, that's all: a big, empty box of nothing.'

'That's what Tom said.' I sighed. 'Poor little Tommy. We've just got each other now.'

'No you haven't.'

I smiled. 'No. Thanks, Sue.'

'Just you look after poor little Tommy and let me and Gerry look after poor little you.' She passed me a tissue and I blew my nose noisily. 'We're on Mum and Dad duty now.'

'Is that why you're so bossy?'

'No, that's because I enjoy it.' She guided me back towards the crematorium. 'Time to say goodbye now, my love. Time to live your life.'

Inside, everyone had taken their seats, music playing softly in the background.

Ugh. Harpsichord Renaissance. Still, it was what Dad wanted.

Sal was behind the lectern, waiting to start. I leaned heavily on Sue as she guided me down the aisle, trying not to focus on the coffin in case I freaked out again. All I could see from the corner of my eye as I passed were the blurred colours of Dad's football scarves, Bradford City and Napoli, crossed over the top.

'I'm sorry, Tommy,' I said when I was seated by him, giving his knee a pat. 'I'm here now. Won't leave you again.'

He smiled weakly, eyes soaked. I could tell he was past the point where speech came easily.

Sal cleared her throat, and the hum of conversation died down.

'I only knew Filippo Donati for a short time,' she said. 'And I could fill pages with the usual fluff: how he was larger than life – which he was, even when I knew him at the end; how much he loved his kids, his friends, his community; the energy he brought to everything he did. But I won't, because no one can tell you the kind of man Phil was better than him.' She scanned the sheet of paper in front of her. 'So I'm going to let him tell it, by reading the eulogy he wrote himself.'

I reached for Tom's hand and gripped it tight. Sal had asked if we wanted to hear what Dad had written before the service, but we'd foolishly decided to put it off for as long as we could.

'When I was a little boy in Naples, they made us study a poem by an Englishman called John Keats,' Sal began, reading Dad's words. 'I forget most of it now, but one line was "Now more than ever seems it rich to die". When I was a child I thought what a foolish thing that was to write, because nobody wants to die. These English must be a strange bunch, I thought.'

Muted laughter hummed around the room.

'And I laughed, because I was ten years old and I knew, as all ten-year-olds know, that I was going to live forever,' Sal went on. She took a deep breath, voice trembling. 'But writing this, I understand what Mr Keats meant. Because now I am dying, and yes, it is rich, filled with a wistfulness that's sweetness and pain in equal parts. I didn't live forever, but I lived well, and I lived happily. I fell in love with a beautiful woman – my Paula – who, for a reason I don't understand to this day, loved me too, and I brought up two wonderful children, Tom and Lana, to become two wonderful adults. I lived amongst the immortal beauty of the Yorkshire Dales, the hills and valleys that became my home and whose people took me into their hearts, and for every ounce of pain there was a ton of pleasure. No man should be mourned who has loved and been loved.' She looked at Tom and me, the tears rolling down our faces. 'Don't cry, kids. Don't regret a single day of your precious, precious lives. Love, and live, and when you reach the end you'll see that no amount of pain can rob of you of the sweetness that comes from knowing you leave the world a better place for having been in it. Remember I'll always love you, and live. That's all. Goodnight, my dears.'

Tom's hand was gripping mine so hard the knuckles were white, but I barely felt it.

Sal put the paper down. 'And now it's traditional to have a moment's silence to remember the person who's gone. But Phil didn't like silence. So instead we're going to take a minute to turn to our neighbours and give them a hug, as he wanted us to.'

There was a hum of conversation as people stood to follow Dad's last request, embracing, shaking hands, kissing cheeks: there was even some laughter. It was beautiful.

I turned to Tom and hugged him tightly.

'The last thing he thought of was us,' Tom said in a choked whisper.

'I know. Let's try to do what he wanted.'

6

Bereavement or not, we couldn't afford to close the restaurant, especially with custom as bad as it had been recently. Deano, Jasmine and Debbie were all brilliant, taking extra shifts so Tom and me could have some downtime in the weeks following Dad's funeral, but after a fortnight it was back to business as usual. To be honest, it was a relief to have something to take my mind off things.

My first evening back, I looked around the restaurant and sighed. It was a Saturday, which a year ago would've meant a full house. Tonight only about a third of the tables were occupied.

Dad had been the heart of Here Be Flagons, even after he'd got too ill to keep up with chef duties. Ever since we'd learned he was coming to the very end it felt like the whole place had been infected with a residual gloom that even the customers had picked up on.

I tapped Jasmine's shoulder as she passed by with a dish of wild boar casserole for Table 12.

'Jaz, I'm just going to check on Deano then I'm taking my break. Think you can manage?'

'Yeah, take as long as you need, Lana. Debbie and me should be able to cope.'

I cast a glum look around the thinly peopled restaurant. 'Yes. I think you should.'

She threw me that look before she went, the one that'd been in everyone's eyes recently: a blend of sympathy and gratitude, because it was us and not them. That's what it seemed like anyway. I was sick of it.

It was a relief to go see Deano in the kitchen. Deano didn't do the look. Deano was just Deano: touchy-feely, loud and friendly, like a giant, scary muppet. Over the last year, I'd come to realise he was actually the closest friend I had. Which was weird because he was still trying to snog me at every opportunity.

'Hey, Lana-nana! Come check this out,' he said, beckoning me to him with excitement glittering insanely in his insane brown eyes.

I blinked at the cooker top. 'It's a pan.'

'Not just any pan. This is top of the range, Mum got it for me. Brought it in because I couldn't wait to use it.'

'Why? Is it a magic pan?'

'It is when I'm cooking with it.' Deano gestured to the pan's surface. 'Look! Non-stick, titanium-coated, super-efficient heat distribution... I'm telling you, Lana, if Jesus Christ had been into cooking, this is the pan he would've used.'

'Nah, that's the old *Last Crusade* trap, isn't it? Jesus would've used a simple wooden skillet and your fancy pan'd make Nazis turn to dust.'

'All right, the Dalai Lama then. Or Gary Lineker. Anyone awesome with great taste in pans.' He caressed the handle reverently.

I squinted at him. 'Did you name the pan, Deano?'

He drew himself up. 'Certainly not. Don't be ridiculous.'

'Oh God. What's it called then?'

'*She* is called Katie, if you must know.' He turned away from Katie the pan to look at me. 'So how're you getting on then, boss?'

I sighed. 'As well as I can, I guess. Thanks for asking.'

'Well, there's asking and there's doing. Here.' He lifted a small casserole dish off the top of the oven. 'Nothing special, just chicken and veg. I thought you and Tom probably wouldn't feel like cooking.'

I took it from him gratefully. 'Ta, love. You know, you don't need to keep looking after us.'

He waved his finger at me. 'But ahaha. This is all part of my master plan.'

I rolled my eyes. 'Go on then, I'll bite. What's the master plan?'

'To make my fortune by marrying you and taking over your half of the business.' He shrugged. 'Or Tom, I'm not fussy. Whichever of you calls dibs, all this could be yours.' He gave his hips a little wiggle.

I couldn't help laughing, but there was a bit of sigh in there too. 'Think you might need a new plan, mate. The way things are, you'd make better money on the dole than marrying into the Donatis.'

'Oh, all businesses go through slumps. It'll pick up. I'm planning a whole new menu for the autumn.' He gave my bottom a comforting pat. 'Go on, Lanasaurus, take your break. We've got things covered down here.'

Upstairs, I dumped the chicken in the kitchenette and went

to chill on the sofa while I waited for Tom to get back from wherever he'd disappeared to.

Flash was curled up in his bed, watching me with one eye open. He was only a baby; he hadn't quite got the hang of playing asleep yet. As soon as my bum hit the leather, he abandoned the pretence and leapt into my lap to give my face an enthusiastic bath.

'Oof. Don't you be getting hair on the wench gear, pup,' I said, tickling him between the ears.

After a few minutes, a pungent smell of dripping and vinegar assaulted me and Tom came in with a greaseproof packet tucked under his arm.

'God, Tom, not chips again,' I groaned. 'You'll be a blimp in a few months. Then you'll have Sue nagging you about Slimming World.'

'Oh, shut up and take some calories for the team.' He collapsed next to me and shoved the packet my way.

'Why don't you just ask him out before your arteries seize up?' I asked, ripping along the paper and helping myself to a chip. 'The social embarrassment can't be worse than heart failure.'

'Don't be daft, I'm British. Course it bloody can.'

Flash looked up eagerly when he smelt the chips. I hesitated, then handed him one. He was getting spoilt rotten since Dad had gone, but we couldn't help babying him a bit. After so long caring round the clock for someone, it was easy to feel a bit bereft with only ourselves to look after. The little sheepdog Gerry had given us to comfort Dad in his last few months was all we had left.

'Come on, you've fancied that lad in the chippy for

months,' I said to Tom. 'Are you just going to guzzle chips twice a week until he notices you?'

'In the absence of a better plan.' He pinched a chip off me. 'Hey, I found out his name today.'

'Well, that's progress I suppose. What is it?'

'Cameron. You know, I've always thought he looked like a Cameron. His hair says Cameron.'

'You told me last month his eyes said Craig.'

He shrugged. 'Close enough.'

'You're liable to get a slap off Deano anyway,' I said, feeding Flash another chip. I nodded towards the kitchenette. 'He made us chicken for tea. If he finds out you ruined your appetite with chips, it'll be no pudding for you.'

'Where is he on the crazyometer today?' Tom asked. 'I'm on kitchen duty with him in half an hour.'

I made a swirly motion next to my ear. 'Oven's on but nothing's cooking.'

'Oh God, what this time?'

'He's developed an inappropriate relationship with a lady frying pan called Katie.'

'Right.' Tom blinked. 'Well that's certainly a new one.'

'Yeah, he's getting worse. But he's a good lad.' I sighed. 'Dad always liked him.'

'I know.' Tom snorted. 'So Deano's a pansexual now, is he?'

I groaned. 'God, that's terrible.'

'Better than your morris dancing gags.'

My phone buzzed from somewhere inside my corset, and I reached into my cleavage for it.

Tom curled his lip. 'Do you have to keep your phone in

your boobs, sis? It's disturbing watching you grope around in there.'

I shrugged. 'Sorry. Whoever the genius was behind these costumes obviously didn't think there was any need to include pockets for all our wench paraphernalia. Bet any money it was a bloke.'

'Well? Gerry or Sue?'

'Gerry.' I swiped at the bosom-warmed screen to answer the call.

'Hiya,' I said. 'You know, you don't need to check up on us every day. We're fine, honestly.'

'That's not why I'm ringing. It was the meeting last night.'

'I told you, Gerry: joining the Egglethwaite Morris Men is not a valid way for Tom to cope with grief.'

'Not that meeting, the village society,' Gerry said. 'I pitched your Grand Départ idea like you asked.'

'Oh God, did you?' I grimaced. 'Honestly, forget it. I don't know what I was thinking.'

'No, they loved it. Rodge wants you to come to a meeting with the other local business owners to discuss it. Only if you're feeling up to it, he said.'

'You're kidding!'

'Nope. It's Sunday. Think you can face it? They've asked for you and Tom to present your proposal.'

'Proposal?' My eyes widened. 'What proposal? I never made a proposal!'

'You proposed we woo the Tour de France people so we can get the route through Egglethwaite,' he said, sounding impatient. 'And then you asked me to sell it to the society and I did – against my better judgement. What's the problem, lass?'

'That's hardly a bloody proposal, Gerry. It's an idea, that's all. I never thought I'd have to be the brains of the operation.'

'You don't, you just have to make a case. Me and the missus'll be there to support the pair of you.'

The pair of us. I shot Tom a guilty look as he nibbled obliviously on a chip. I couldn't help feeling he'd been dragged into this somehow.

'They're not expecting a PowerPoint or anything,' Gerry went on. 'Just tell them why you think it'd be good for the village.'

'But it was just an off-the-cuff suggestion! God, if I'd followed up on every mad pub idea I've had in my life, I'd have arm-wrestled Bear Grylls and run a marathon dressed as a panto dame by now. Are you seriously telling me I've got five days to flesh this thing out into something solid?'

'Basically, yeah.'

I lowered my voice. 'How many of them are there?'

'Eight.'

'Shit!'

'Plus the business owners.'

'Bollocks!'

'And they're opening it up to interested villagers too.'

'Fuck!'

He laughed. 'On behalf of your old man, I should probably tell you to wash your mouth out.'

'You son of a bitch, Gerry,' I hissed. 'What've you got me into?'

'Me?' he said in a surprised tone. 'I just do as I'm told. When the womenfolk give me instructions, I follow them.

I'm no mug.' He sighed. 'Look, just come to the meeting and say what you said in the pub. If the society go for it, you don't have to take it any further.'

'Ugh. Fine. But next May Day I'm sabotaging your bells. When you lot find your dingers missing, remember who to thank.'

'If you really wanted revenge you'd sabotage the beer pumps,' he said. 'See you Sunday, pet.'

'Oh God, what's up?' Tom said when I'd ended the call.

'Who said there's anything up?' I dislodged Flash and walked to the window. The long-empty shop across the road was covered in scaffolding and I wondered fleetingly what they were doing to it.

'Your stupid wenchy face says there's something up. What've you got us into, Lana?'

'Nothing,' I said, throwing myself back on the sofa. 'Just the tiniest thing. It'll take half an hour, tops.'

'What'll take half an hour, tops?'

I screwed my eyes closed and peeked at him from under one lid. 'Wehavetogiveapresentationtothevillagesociety,' I mumbled in one breath.

'We have to what?'

'Village society. Presentation. Us.' I opened my eye a little wider, then closed it again when I saw the incredulous look on his face. 'Gerry's fault.'

'But what on?'

'BusinesscaseTourdeFrance.'

'Seriously. Stop doing that.'

I sighed. 'That idea I had at the pub, the night Dad... that night. The village society want us to go to a meeting and make our case. If we're feeling up to it, they said.'

'*Our* case?'

'Yeah. Not sure how you got press-ganged. Sorry, Tommy.'

He looked thoughtful. 'Well, that's not so bad,' he said at last. 'Much as it kills me to say it, it's actually a great idea. Plus it'll take our mind off, you know... stuff.'

'You what? You hate public speaking. You're, like, the shyest person ever.'

'Yeah, and you're the mouthiest person since Eve was a lass. Between us we should cope.' He squeezed my shoulders. 'You were right, this is Egglethwaite's chance to be part of history in the making. Let's make Dad proud and bloody well do it, eh?'

7

'Pheeeeewwww.' I exhaled slowly through my teeth.

'What're you doing that for?' Tom asked.

'Doing what?'

'Making that weird noise. Deano's cheese souffle's not repeating on you, is it?'

'It's a breathing exercise, dumbass. I'm psyching myself up.'

'Wish I'd psyched myself up with a stiff drink,' he said, huddling further back into his corner. 'Oh God, they'll start arriving any minute. Another fine mess you've got me into.'

'What? You were the one who said it was a good idea!'

'Suddenly it's not looking quite so hot. Why the hell did we come so early?'

OK, so perhaps it had been a mistake, arriving at Egglethwaite Temperance Hall – or the Temp, as locals tended to call it – a full half hour before the Tour de France meeting. We'd wanted to avoid entering to the stares of a packed room. But now we were here, cowering in the hideous tangerine meeting room as we waited for anyone else to arrive, I was desperately wishing we'd called at Holyfield Farm for Gerry and Sue on the way. Now we just had more time to worry about this bloody presentation that according to Gerry wasn't a presentation but clearly, clearly was.

'Oh. Evening, you two.'

I summoned a weary smile for the chairwoman of the WI as she flounced in. Or rather, no longer Egglethwaite Women's Institute but Egglethwaite Ladies Who Lunch, as they'd rebranded since Yolanda Sommerville – Sue's best friend and bitterest enemy – had been elected chair.

Yolanda had pink hair. She liked shawls, *Heat* magazine, men half her age and being the most shocking person in the room. She made me want to gnaw off my own earlobes and fry them in garlic.

'Hi,' I said.

'Hello, darling.' She shot a suggestive smile at Tom. 'Tall and dark, just how I like them. How are we then, Tomasso?'

'Still gay, love, sorry.'

She shrugged. 'Well, let me know if you change your mind. I do so relish a challenge.'

'Yeah. It doesn't actually work like that.'

'I've a bottle of elderflower gin in my larder says it can, handsome,' she said, grinning. 'Try everything once except incest and morris dancing, as the saying goes. Don't tell Gerry I said so, of course.'

I shook my head. 'For God's sake, Yo-yo, give the lad a break. You know, sexual orientation aside, you're old enough to be his mother.'

'They call us cougars these days, my lovely,' she said, tossing her shawls affectedly. 'We're very now, you know.'

'You're very deluded, you know,' I muttered. But our conversation was cut short by the arrival of Gerry and Sue with a handful of society members. Gradually the room filled, until there was a standing crowd of about thirty people.

I felt a hand grip my wrist.

'How the hell do I let you talk me into these things?' Tom muttered.

'How the hell do I talk myself into these things?' I scanned the expectant crowd in a panic. 'Oh bollocks. Look at them all. I bet they think we know what we're talking about and everything.'

'Oi. Language. No swearing allowed at meetings, Gerry said.'

'No fucking swearing, are you fucking kidding? There's a room full of assorted morris men and their mates staring at me. And I bet that joke about it having bells on isn't going to ice any turnips either.'

'It never did.' Tom patted my shoulder. 'Well, don't worry, sis, you can do it. I have every confidence in you.'

'Me? Us! Don't you dare pull out on me now.' I grabbed his arm as he tried to sidle off. 'Stay put or I throw you to Yo-yo.'

The chairman, Roger Collingwood, was clearing his throat for quiet. Tom and me put on our best calm-and-confident faces as we waited to be introduced.

'Hm-hmmm,' Roger began. 'Ladies and gents. Welcome to this extraordinary meeting of the Egglethwaite Village Society. There is no agenda tonight, or rather—' he laughed nasally '—or rather, the agenda is an agend*um*. Only one item is before us. As we all know, Le Tour leaves Yorkshire next year, and we wish to consider how it could in any way benefit our little village. We have gathered you together, residents and business owners, to give your views.'

There was a buzz of conversation among the assembled crowd.

'If we could get on the route it'd put a lot of custom my way,' Billy, landlord of the Sooty Fox, called out. 'Are there wheels in motion to get us under consideration or what, Rodge?'

'It might bring custom your way, son, but it'll do me no favours.' Kit, one of Gerry's farmer friends, leaned across the crowd to talk to Billy. 'You don't have land to worry about. I don't fancy my fields trodden into muck and my cows scared into miscarriage by a load of oblivious townies.'

'He's got a point,' Gerry said. He shrugged in our direction. 'Sorry, kids, but he has.' Sue glared at him.

'Gentlemen, gentlemen,' Roger said, holding up his hand. 'You'll have an opportunity to say your piece when we've heard – oh.' He broke off to acknowledge the man who'd just entered. I caught a brief flash of a too-familiar face, topped with sandy curls, before it blended into the crowd. 'The new cycle shop owner, I assume? We've just started; you haven't missed anything.'

I pressed my eyes closed.

'It's him, isn't it?' I muttered to Tom in Italian.

'Yes. It's him. Sorry, Lana.'

Stewart McLean. The man who never called. He was back.

8

I risked peeping out of one eye. Stewart was at the back of the crowd. He didn't seem to have noticed me.

He looked different than he had on our one and only date – God, it seemed a lifetime ago now. Still handsome, but there was something in his face, a certain... I don't know, a sadness? He was paler too.

Ah, he'd spotted me. He caught my eye and smiled – the smile hadn't changed, at least. It was still warm, sexy, enticing. Full of lies. Bloody well smiling at me! After a year!

I pretended I hadn't noticed and looked the other way.

'What's he doing here?' I muttered to Tom.

'I don't know, do I? Ignore him. And stop speaking Italian; everyone'll think we're talking about them.'

'We are talking about them.' I glared sideways at Stewart. 'One of them.'

Roger was blinking at us. I flung him an apologetic smile.

'Sorry. Just practising what we want to say. Er, in Italian, so... it'll be a surprise.'

'Ah. Very good.' He turned back to the crowd. 'So before we get into a debate, I'm going to hand over to a couple of our younger business owners. Of course we all knew Phil Donati, who ran the restaurant for many years until he sadly passed away last month. I'd like to thank his children Lana and Tom for coming at this difficult time, to make the case for the Grand Départ passing through Egglethwaite. This was their suggestion so I know they'll have some persuasive arguments.'

'Oh God. Class Four Nativity,' I heard Tom mutter.

We both remembered The Great Class Four Nativity Disaster. Tom had got the plum role of innkeeper – well, it was a plum role given most of his class were playing farm animals. He even had a line: 'No room at the inn'. Just five words; he'd spent weeks practising them in different voices in front of the mirror. But when little Joseph and Mary, a Tiny Tears doll stuffed up her frock, knocked at his door, Tom just gaped like a halibut for a full minute before waving a welcoming hand and saying, 'Yeah, come on in'. After that he was relegated to Junior Donkey for the rest of primary.

And it looked like the nerves that had ruined the Class Four Nativity were back tenfold tonight.

'Stay strong, Tommy,' I whispered. 'We can do this.'

'Speak for yourself.'

'Er, right. Hi,' I said to the crowd, trying not to look at Stewart. I fixed my gaze on Sue, who smiled encouragingly. If I just pretended I was talking to her, maybe I could get through it. 'Yeah, so, as you all know there's been a successful bid by Welcome to Yorkshire to bring the Grand Départ here next year. It's expected to lure big crowds from all over the country – the world even – so I thought, well, why shouldn't we get a wedge of the cheesecake? We're most of us business owners here and I'm sure we wouldn't sniff at the extra trade.'

There was a faint murmur of conversation. I couldn't tell

if people were interested and discussing what I'd said, or bored and talking amongst themselves.

Tom came to back me up. 'If the beauty of the Yorkshire Dales wooed the Tour organisers, then maybe the beauty of our little patch can bring them here. We've got as much scenery as anywhere.' His voice was shaking with nerves, poor little donkey, but he struggled manfully to the end. 'My dad always said he wouldn't swap this corner of the county for the whole world, and neither would I.'

'Why should they choose us though?' Billy said. 'I certainly wouldn't object to a full pub for a few days, but I don't see what we've got to offer over other villages. The scenery's bonny enough, Tommy lad, but nothing that can't be matched by our neighbours.'

'There's the view from Pagans' Rock,' I said, determinedly avoiding Stewart's gaze. 'That's impressive by any benchmark.'

'I'm not denying that,' Billy said. 'Still, can Pagans' Rock alone cut the Dijon? Oakworth's only a few miles away: they've got a hundred views, and a heritage railway. Hebden Bridge has got the canal; Haworth's got the literary thing going for it. What's Egglethwaite got? One good view and a cobbled street.'

'Setts,' I heard Gerry mutter. Sue nudged him in the ribs.

'He's not wrong, darling,' Yolanda said to me. 'The competition is rather stiff, isn't it? Yorkshire's got Herriot Country, Emmerdale Country, all sorts of countries. And here our little village is, in the middle of... well, Nowhere Country.'

'No. We're Brontë Country, aren't we?'

'Well, just, I suppose. But we're not close enough to Haworth for anyone to notice us.'

MARY JAYNE BAKER

'OK, maybe we're not in the tourist bit,' Tom admitted. 'But only because no one outside the area knows we're here. That could be part of our sales pitch, couldn't it? The hidden treasure angle? Nothing to lose by trying.'

'There's a lot to lose for us farmers,' Kit said. 'Suppose we're successful? Your restaurant and the pub might do all right off it, and Caroline's B&B. I don't see what's in it for the rest of us.'

'A lot of churned-up land and worried animals, that's what,' Gerry said. He shot me an apologetic grimace.

Kit nodded. 'Some of us are quite happy being a hidden treasure, ta all the same.'

'It's once-in-a-lifetime though, isn't it?' It was Mrs Wakefield, head teacher of our old primary school. 'I'm not a business owner, but I'd certainly welcome the chance to be part of something as historic as this. And the children would be so excited. We could plan a whole term's activities around it.'

'That is a point,' Roger said. 'My grandchildren would love it.'

'History's all well and good, but what about my walls then, eh?' Trevor, founder of the Egglethwaite Wallers, piped up. 'Our volunteers have spent the last six months getting all the drystone walling round here sorted out. I don't fancy a load of bloody tourists leaning on it, knocking the capstones off.'

'There wouldn't necessarily be any damage. Not if we put safeguards in place.'

I didn't need to look up to see who'd spoken. I still remembered that voice, vibrating through me the night he'd held me against his body up at Pagans' Rock.

'Ah. Mr McLean. Please do give us your view, as a newcomer to the area,' Roger said. He gestured to Stewart, who moved through the crowd to the front.

'I used to take part in things like this pretty frequently – nothing as big as a Grand Tour, but some fairly high-profile events. I'd be more than willing to contact the organisers on your behalf to find out what measures could be taken to protect land and livestock.' He nodded to Trevor. 'And walling, of course.'

Yolanda turned wide eyes on him. 'Oh my goodness! I've just realised who you are.'

He smiled. 'When the shop opens next month, I'll be just another business owner. But if I can help with cycling contacts, I will. I'm new here – I'd like to make a few friends.'

There was a hum of interest as everyone put a name and a face together and came up with four.

'I'm sure we'd be grateful for any help you can offer, Mr McLean,' Roger said. 'With you backing us, perhaps Egglethwaite wouldn't be such a lost cause after all. How many other villages have their own celebrity cyclist?'

'Just a local businessman, Mr Collingwood. I don't cycle any more.'

Didn't cycle any more? The man who'd told me competing was his life didn't cycle any more? Then again, he'd told me he was going to call me too and that had been a web of lies.

I tried to tone down my glare a bit. I didn't want to draw attention to myself.

'Well, perhaps I can move things forward with a suggestion,' Roger said. 'Let's say that Egglethwaite will put in a bid to be included on the Grand Départ route.' He held up a hand as Kit opened his mouth to object. '*If* the organisers are able to put safeguards in place to protect local farmland, and *if* the route hasn't been decided already. And may I further propose that we form a dedicated committee to pursue this?'

'Isn't that your job?' Sue demanded. 'I thought that's why we had a village society, to follow up on things like this.'

'As I'm sure your husband has told you, Susan, the society has many important issues to deal with,' Roger said stiffly. 'This would be far too time-consuming to add to our monthly agenda on top of everything else.'

'Ah, now, I'm glad you brought that up. Another pair of Marks and Spencer's finest went missing off my line the other day. Silk as well. Have you got any leads on that knicker thief yet or what, lad?'

'Maybe he's making himself a parachute,' Gerry muttered. 'Ow,' he said as his wife dug him in the ribs.

Roger drew himself up. 'We're pursuing a number of leads. Can we stay on topic, please?' He looked over at us. 'I really feel something like this should be business-led. What are your thoughts, Lana?'

'My knickers are fine, thanks, Roger. Still got a full set.'

It was worth it to see him blush.

'Your thoughts on the Tour, young lady,' he said sternly. 'Would you be willing to join a committee?'

I hesitated, glancing at Tom. How far did we really want to go with this?

'Oh. Right,' Gerry said as Sue elbowed him again. 'Look, Rodge, it was good of Lana and Tom to come tonight, but I'm not sure they're in a position to commit themselves to anything more right now. You know it's a tough time for the family.'

'Of course, thoughtless of me,' Roger said. 'There's no pressure, you two. Whatever you feel comfortable with.'

'I'd like to join the committee,' Tom said.

I blinked at him. 'Would you?'

'Yeah. We suggested it, the least we can do is follow it through.' He lowered his voice. 'And it'll be good for us, Lana. We should be doing something.'

I thought of Dad, and his last message to us. Making a difference...

'Well, perhaps you're right,' I said. 'OK, Rodge. Count yourself in two Donatis.'

'Thank you. I'm sure we all appreciate it.' He looked around the rest of the crowd. 'Any other volunteers?'

'Ow! God almighty, our lass, can you give it a rest?' Gerry muttered as Sue dug her elbow into his ribs again. He turned to Roger. 'All right, me and herself'll join. Anything for a quiet life.'

'You?' Roger said. 'I thought you said it was a terrible idea.'

'Not as terrible as upsetting the wife, believe me.'

Roger shot a look at Sue, who had her formidable face on, but he was a sensible man and managed to refrain from nodding.

'OK, that's four,' he said. 'Any more for any more?'

'Count me in too,' Stewart said. 'Seems like something useful I can get involved in, if I'm going to be part of the community.'

For God's sake! What the hell did that man think he was playing at? He was the last person I wanted to be on a committee with, as no doubt he well knew.

'And me,' Yolanda said. 'You know me, Roger

Collingwood: anything for the village.' She shot a flirtatious smile in Stewart's direction, making it pretty clear what the anything she'd do for the village was.

Roger beamed. 'Six, excellent. Well then, on that note I think we can end the meeting. Thank you for coming, everyone.'

9

Once the meeting was officially over, I barged through the crowd, determined to get out before I had to speak to Stewart.

'Wait up, sis! I want a word with Rodge before we go,' Tom called.

'I'll see you at home!' I shouted over my shoulder, steaming ahead to the exit.

But it was too late. I'd no sooner made it through the door when I felt a hand on my arm. Bloody long-legged cyclists, you just couldn't out-stride them.

'Lana. Wait a sec.'

I turned to face Stewart – slowly, to avoid any impression I was either angry with him or keen to see him. It was the nonchalant turn of a woman who didn't care. A woman who went on hundreds of dates with gorgeous eligible bachelors, of which he was the least gorgeous, the least eligible and by far the least memorable.

Well, that was the intention. It actually came out more drunken pirouette.

Stewart was smiling broadly, for all the world like the last year hadn't happened. Bastard. But the smile faltered a little when he clocked the black look on my face. No matter how hard I tried to be the woman who didn't care, my brow would seem to knit into the resentful frown of the woman who cared so much that at any moment she might either burst into tears or lamp him one.

'Hi,' I said. Carelessly.

'Er, hi. Good to see you again.'

He blinked a few times, as if lost for what to say next. His cheeks were pink with shame. Well, I hoped it was shame. If it wasn't it bloody well ought to be. The other meeting attendees were streaming past us on their way to the pub, and I made a valiant effort to stop various parts of my face twitching.

'So, um, how've you been?' Stewart fumbled at last.

Single. Lonely. Haunted by the face of a dying loved one.

'Fine,' I said.

'Good. That's good.'

'You?'

'OK. Well, up and down.'

'So you stopped cycling then, did you?' Tone-wise I was aiming for cool and casual, but it came out more accusing.

The blush deepened. 'Yeah. Invalided out. Knee injury.'

'Sorry to hear it.'

'You still wenching?'

'Only when I need to eat, pay bills, that sort of thing. So yes, most nights.'

Another silence. The broad smile was long gone now, and I let him sweat. Buggered if I was going to be the first to bring up our doomed first-and-last date.

'Lana, are we OK?' he blurted out at last.

'Why wouldn't we be?'

'Just, you know, last year and everything. Us. And now,

with this group and everything and me living here and… everything.'

'Last year?' My fake nonchalance was so palpably, pungently fake it probably triggered every polygraph within a ten-mile radius. 'Oh! Pagans' Rock,' I fake-remembered airily. 'Right, yeah. Long time ago.'

'Pagans' Rock.' He stretched out a hand, then pulled it back again, looking confused. 'You know, I meant to call you, after that night. Honestly I did. It was… something came up.'

Something came up. That was it, was it? The best I was getting? Something came up that'd lasted a whole fucking year, apparently. That was one impressive something.

I almost asked what, but bit my tongue. He was perfectly capable of telling me if he wanted. I wasn't going to let him think I cared a spit about him or his somethings.

'It's fine.' I summoned a forced smile of my own. 'Honestly, Stewart, I'd forgotten all about it.'

'Right. OK. Good. That's good.' Not a glimmer of disappointment. If anything, he sounded relieved. 'So are we OK to work together on this Tour de France thing?'

'Course,' I lied. 'Be useful to have your expertise on board.'

'And we're friends? I'd like us to be. Just friends, that's all.'

'We're… neighbours.'

'Lana, what're you – oh.' Tom pulled up short and cast a worried glance from me to Stewart, taking in the matching blushes we'd painted between us. I don't know what Stewart's was in aid of, but mine was a generous shot of humiliation with a solid rage mixer. On the rocks.

'Sorry, am I interrupting?' Tom asked.

'No, we're done. Come on, Tommy, let's go.' I gave Stewart a curt nod. 'See you around.'

'Yeah. Bye, Lana.' He put one hand briefly on my shoulder before I left, and I felt a very gentle pressure. 'Hey,' he said, his voice softer. 'Sorry to hear about your dad, kid. He was one of the good guys.'

'Oh. Thanks.'

'What was that all about?' Tom muttered as I took his arm to guide him away.

'Stewart McLean, that's what,' I said once we were out of earshot, finally giving vent to my pent-up rage. 'Can you Adam and fucking Eve it? Asking if we can be friends. Friends! After a year! What a first-class, prime-cut arse monkey.'

'Right. Arse monkey.' He frowned. 'What's an arse monkey, sis?'

'It's a monkey made of arses. Or an arse made of monkeys; either could apply.'

'You're being very unfair on monkeys, you know.'

'Stewart *bloody* McLean! God, I wish Dad were here to give him a slap.'

'You want me to give him a slap?'

'No. I think I'd have more fun doing it myself.' I squeezed his elbow. 'Thanks for offering though.'

'Well, I am the man of the house. It's my job to defend the wenchfolk now.'

'Stewart *bloody* McLean! Where the hell does that guy get off? Swanning into my village, name-dropping all his cycling contacts.' I waved my hands. '"Oh, hey, little people, it's me, yeah? Stewart McLean, king of the cycling arse monkeys.

Hey, I know everyone who's anyone in the biking world and my cousin invented fucking ketchup. Perhaps I can fix your tiny village problems with my humongous ego."'

'That's what he said, is it?'

'Pretty much.'

Tom sighed. 'Look, Lana, do we have to do this? We already did The Slating of Stewart McLean pretty thoroughly when he stood you up a year ago. Not sure I've got the energy to go through it again.'

'He didn't stand me up. He just never called me. Prick.'

He threw an arm around my shoulders. 'Ah, you're too good for him anyways.'

'Brotherly bias. But cheers.'

'I don't know why we bother with the dating lark, you know. It's more trouble than it's worth. I swear, I'm this close to resigning myself to a life of celibacy and death by chocolate.'

'Chocolate.' I stopped walking. 'God, I could murder some chocolate peanuts. And a Guinness.'

'Ugh, me too. Pub?'

I nodded. 'Pub.'

He followed us to the bloody pub too. Stewart, I mean. I spent the time it took to drink one Guinness stubbornly trying to avoid his eye, which would keep drifting my way, even though he was way across the room chatting to Roger and Yolanda.

'All right, that's all I can take,' I said to Tom once I'd downed the dregs of my pint. 'Even my own sodding local's been invaded. Come on, let's go.'

Tom finished the last mouthful of his beer and stood up. 'Yeah, we should get home. The dog'll be waiting for his walk.'

We went back to the restaurant to pick up Flash then headed to the viaduct. Our pup was still enough of a baby to enjoy his favourite game of darting in and out of the arches, playing hide-and-seek with us. As soon as we let him off his lead, he bounded off to do a preparatory weave-and-sniff of his territory.

'Echo!' I called under one of the arches, leaning back and feeling my spine mould to the brickwork. A shiver of satisfaction ran through me as a faint whisper drifted back on the wind, like the dream version of my own voice. *Echoooo...*

Tom smiled. 'You remember playing that with Dad?'

'Course,' I said, smiling back. 'Me and you at one end, Dad at the other, meeting in the middle so between us we'd echoed every arch. I used to think it was bad luck if we didn't do them all.'

I could almost see the old us in front of me, little ghosts: me a good few inches taller than Tom then, even though he was two years older. And Dad... Dad. Young, strong, full of dash and fun, like he could go on forever. I'd honestly believed he would, then. A kid's quiet faith in immortality.

Tom saw me blink back the rogue tear threatening to escape. He put his arm around my shoulders and we were silent a moment, gazing into the past.

'Impressive bugger, isn't it?' Tom said quietly, nodding up at the viaduct curving above us. 'You can see why Dad loved it.'

'Imagine how it must've felt when a train went over. Bet it was like being in a thunderstorm.'

'I was thinking, we should look into getting a memorial bench up at Pagans' Rock,' Tom said. 'Better than a plaque at the crematorium.'

'Yeah. He'd like that.'

We fell silent again. I scrunched my eyes closed, trying to imagine the rumble of a passenger train; how it would've felt against my spine.

'So. You and Stewart,' Tom said, breaking the silence.

I opened my eyes again. 'There's no me and Stewart.'

'There's a historical you and Stewart.'

I snorted. 'Barely.'

'Hmm. Thought I might have to do my best "leave it; he's not worth it", the way you were glowering at him in the pub.'

'Wouldn't give him the satisfaction,' I muttered darkly.

Flash came bounding up, yipping excitedly, which meant he'd checked his territory for threats, piddled everywhere he needed to piddle and now he wanted to play. We wandered after him, and I leaned down to claim a stick.

'Here, give it us,' Tom said. 'You throw like a girl.'

'Do not. Shut up. You do.'

He took the stick off me and chucked it as far as he could in the direction of the reservoir. Flash disappeared after it, only the lightning marking on his tail visible in the cloud-thinned moonlight.

'So what is our policy on Stewart McLean?' Tom asked. 'You sure you're OK to be on this committee with him?'

'Too right I am. I'm not letting him drive me off it. It was my bloody idea.'

'What'll you do then?'

I shrugged. 'Ignore him and get on with it, I guess. It'll get easier.'

'If you say so.'

Flash came galloping over with his stick and after a brief tussle I threw it back into the night. Then I turned to look at the viaduct.

'Shame really, isn't it?' I said.

'Hmm?' Tom said absently, his eyes still on Flash.

'The viaduct. The way it just sits there.'

'Well, what else is it going to do? They're not going to start running trains over it again, are they?'

'It's in great shape though, for its age. Shame it's nothing but furniture for a nice view.'

I was silent for a moment, running my gaze over the dramatic arches. Another brilliant Lana Donati idea was forming – two in as many months. I was on fire.

'I reckon it should be opened up,' I said. 'Other viaducts have been.'

'I know what you mean. It does seem a waste.'

I turned to him, eyes glittering. 'This is it, Tommy! This is what Egglethwaite's got to offer the Tour. Not just the view – the viaduct.'

He blinked. 'What, like, open it up to cyclists, you mean?'

'Open it up to everyone.'

'But… well, how?'

'Dunno. I could talk to Roger. Imagine it though.' My eyes hazed as I gave in to imagination. 'The viaduct open, lined with spectators and TV cameras, billions watching as the pelican speeds along—'

Tom shook his head. 'Peloton, dumbass, not pelican.'

'Whatever. Come on, where else has got that?'

'You're doing it again, Lana,' he said in his best superior big-brother voice. 'Running away with yourself. If it's been left all these decades, there must be some pretty strong reasons no one's done it already. Maybe it's beyond repair.'

'Then why not knock it down?'

He shrugged. 'Well, it's picturesque. That doesn't mean it could be got in a condition to support hundreds of cyclists and spectators in a year.' He nuggied my hair. 'Try not to get too excited about it, eh, sis? It's a nice idea but it might not be possible.'

'Still.' My mind was far away, imagining a horde of cyclists whizzing along the viaduct to thousands of cheering fans. 'History being made, right here in Egglethwaite. If we can do it, our kids' kids'll still be talking about it.' I glanced up at him. 'What Dad wrote to us in his eulogy: making things better. Don't you think this is what he meant?'

He looked sober. 'OK, when you put it like that…'

I beamed at him. 'So are you with me?'

Flash dropped his stick so he could let out a yip of support and I nodded to him. 'Thanks, boy. But I mainly meant your Uncle Tommy, no offence.'

Tom sighed. 'Always am with you, aren't I?'

I gave his back a pat. 'Knew I could count on you. Right. Let's crack on with it then, eh?'

10

Summer was always a busy season for Egglethwaite Silver Band, second only to Christmas. Six weeks after Dad's passing, I finally felt ready to relieve the pensioner who'd been drafted in to cover First Trombone and get back on the concert circuit.

At eleven and thirteen, me and Tom had both been sent for music lessons with Eric Spiggott, the kindly old gent who'd trained up junior band members back in the nineties. Tom had lasted about a month on the cornet before jacking it in, but I'd found the trombone strangely addictive. It'd seemed like an exciting secret code, learning how those black blobs could be combined with slide movements to make beautiful music – well, OK, tuneless raspberries in the early days, but I'd eventually developed a pretty pure sound. Fifteen years later I was still at it, the only female band member under fifty.

'You did very well today, Lana,' Roger said following an afternoon on the park bandstand, my first day back. 'I'm pleased to see you've been practising the "Pink Panther" solo.'

Wherever there was a village group that needed a leader – or a conductor – there was Roger Collingwood, who loved being in charge almost as much as he loved the sound of his own voice. Not the chairman Egglethwaite needed, but the chairman Egglethwaite deserved. Still, I liked him, pompous and blustering as he was. It was people like Roger who kept the village running.

'Thanks, Roger.' I glanced around at the old men who made up the band, decked out in their daft maroon blazers with the gold epaulets on the shoulders. 'It's good to be back.'

'And how is Egglethwaite's newest committee getting along? Anything to report?'

'We haven't had our first proper meeting yet, but possibly.' I lowered my voice. 'Look, that old railway viaduct in Thornton – they had it opened up as a right of way, didn't they?'

'That's right. Why do you ask?'

'I just wondered what was to stop us doing that. It could help woo the Tour people, and be a lasting legacy afterwards.'

'It's a nice idea, but… well, that type of thing can cost hundreds of thousands, Lana.'

'Still, it's worth looking into. Have you got anyone you can put me in touch with?'

'I know someone on the town council, but I wouldn't get your hopes up. It's highly unlikely we'd be able to get it opened in time for the Tour, even if the cash is there.' He gave my arm a pat. 'Still, it's nice to see the young people taking an interest. Us old folk were starting to worry the village would descend into anarchy once we weren't around.'

I laughed. 'Well, I'll try to see it doesn't go too "last days of Rome" when you retire.'

'Ah, yes. Yolanda.'

'Heh. Mentioning no names, eh? Thanks, Rodge.'

The gig had been fun but wearying and I was exhausted by the time I'd walked back up the steep cobbled street to Here Be Flagons in the hot July sun, dangling my trombone case.

Far too exhausted to deal with the good-looking blond pillock who was standing outside his new shop, giving directions to workmen putting up a huge sign – 'McLean's Machines: Cycle Repairs, Hire and Sale'.

'Afternoon, neighbour,' he said with a military salute. 'Who're you supposed to be, the chocolate soldier?'

Ugh. He would have to see me in my band uniform: the only outfit I owned more embarrassing than my medieval costume. Of all the humiliating…

'Funny.' I tried to pass him, but he fell into step beside me.

'You need a hand with that?' he said, nodding to the trombone. 'Looks heavy.'

'I can cope, thanks. I've been managing it fifteen years without a big, strong man to help me.'

'Bloody hell. You must have some right hook on you by now, love.'

'Keep following me and you'll find out.'

He frowned. 'Was that a joke?'

'Yes, Stewart. It was a joke.' Gallows humour, but still.

'Look, you did mean it when you said we were OK, didn't you?'

I stopped walking to look into those guileless grey eyes. God, blokes could be obtuse sometimes.

'I'm tired, that's all,' I said at last, giving one eye a rub as if to prove it. 'I'll see you next week for the cycling group meeting.'

'Right.' I was hoping he'd take that as a cue to sod off, but he was still following me, right to the door of the restaurant. 'Hey, I was thinking we could do with a funky new name. "Egglethwaite Cycling Group" doesn't pack much punch, does it? How about—' he waved his arm with a flourish '—"The Pedal Pushers"?'

I nodded to his shop. 'You got a drawing board in there?'

'Well, have you got anything better?'

'I've been thinking about the actual event, mate. The name of the group hardly seems the key issue.'

He looked a little crestfallen. 'I've been thinking about the event too. I contacted the organisers today.'

'What? But we haven't had our first meeting yet!'

'Exactly. I thought if I got in touch now, I'd have something to report back.'

'We need a plan first, you div! You can't just crash in, all guns blazing.' I thought about the viaduct. 'We don't even know what it is we want.'

'I didn't mention the village. Just asked what safeguards would be in place to protect local land when it all kicks off, that's all. And I put feelers out via a friend on Team Sky to find out whether the route's still being decided.'

'Hmm.'

'I haven't scuppered it, Lana, promise.' His eyes sought mine. 'No need to be angry. We're on the same side, aren't we?'

'You need to consult the whole group before you do stuff like that.'

'And you need to relax,' he said. 'You're pissed off at me, aren't you? Just these subtle signals I'm picking up on, like calling me a div and threatening to punch me in the face. I mean, call me Mr Oversensitive...'

'Let's just say you rub me up the wrong way.'

'Look, if this is about last year—'

I snorted. 'Don't flatter yourself.'

'What then?'

I pushed open the door to the restaurant. 'I don't like cocky bastards who show up in my village and try to take over, all right? Five minutes you've been part of this community. Your business isn't even open yet and somehow everywhere I go, all I hear about is Stewart bloody McLean. Don't think whatever celebrity status you've got'll carry any weight with me.'

'I'm not trying to take over. Or flaunt celebrity, if I've got any,' he said, putting a hand on my arm. 'Just to help. I want to make a difference, same as you.'

'Right. Well you go home and do that then. I'll see you next week.'

'No hard feelings though?'

'Oh, hardly any.'

I watched him saunter back to his shop. God, I hated that guy.

Inside, I changed out of the despised band uniform and went to veg in front of the telly with Tom and Flash.

'Good gig?' Tom asked when I chucked myself down next to him.

'Well the little old ladies watching the Bowls seemed to

appreciate some background music. And I managed to stay in tune for the whole of Dvořák's "New World Symphony", which might be a first.' I nodded at the TV, which was panning around a sweeping moorland landscape. 'What're you watching?'

'Oh God, it's hilarious. Profile on Mr Squeezy Sauce for *Look North*. They've got him poncing about on the moors.'

I watched as Harper Brady tramped into view, dressed in a fashionable jacket and trainers that'd fall apart in about five minutes if he was a real walker.

'As both an actor and a man, I was moulded by this landscape,' Harper's voice said over the visual. 'In many ways the moors were my mother, suckling and nurturing me from the cradle.'

'Grim,' I said, curling my lip. 'Now I can't even enjoy a walk on the moors without thinking about Harper Brady breastfeeding.'

'My latest role, as a war-scarred veteran who regenerates himself through the healing power of cycling, was directly inspired by my experience of growing up surrounded by the beauty of moorland like this,' Harper continued. 'I owe my home a great debt.'

Tom snorted. 'You what? His role as a battle-scarred soldier was inspired by growing up round here as a pampered little rich boy?'

'That must be the part he was shadowing Stewart for.' I nodded to the remote. 'Turn it off, Tom. I can't bear any more.'

Tom pressed the standby button and Harper's latest ego trip blinked out.

'He's not giving his cousin much credit for inspiring him, I notice,' I said.

'Did you see Stewart putting his sign up outside?'

'Yeah. We had some words actually,' I admitted. 'About the Tour plan.'

'Hmm.' Tom chucked a worried look in my direction. 'You're sure you'll be OK at the meeting next week?'

'I told you, Tommy, I'm fine. I'm past it. I mean, it was only that one night; it's not like he's my ex or anything.'

'That's the spirit.' He gave my knee a slap and stood up. 'Right. I'm off down the chip shop before we open.'

I shook my head. 'Honestly, bruv, this is getting daft. You can't just keep popping in until you're twenty stone and crying into a fishcake butty. Ask the lad out already.'

'Not today. Maybe next time.'

'Right.' I levered myself off the sofa. 'You're staying here. I'm going to the chippy.'

'Don't you dare!'

'You trust me, don't you?' I called as I grabbed my coat from the hall.

'Absolutely not.'

'Come on, what's the worst that can happen?' I came back in and started counting on my fingers. 'OK, possibilities. One: he's not gay.'

'And I'll be too humiliated to show my face in there ever again.'

'Won't do you any harm after months on the all-chip diet.' I put up another finger. 'Two: he is gay and doesn't fancy you. Short period of moping, knock to your self-confidence, then you move on.'

'And three?'

'He is gay, does fancy you, happily ever after ensues. So that's a one in three chance of happily ever after, right? Pretty good odds.'

Tom shook his head. 'You'd never make it as a bookie, sis.'

'Look, I won't tell him you like him or anything. Just a recce.'

He squinted suspiciously at me. 'What sort of recce?'

'I'll just, you know, engage him in conversation. Flirt a bit, see if he responds.'

'Right. And how will you know if he's gay or he just doesn't fancy you?'

'A girl can always tell.' I ruffled his hair. 'Leave it to little sister, OK?'

II

When I got to the chip shop, an attractive lad with dark, floppy hair and glasses was behind the counter.

Right. Flirting. Oh God, how did you flirt? Eyes were involved, weren't they? Eyes and hair. Girls in books were always tossing it about, like they were advertising L'Oréal or something.

Yolanda. That was it. I needed to channel Yolanda, the queen of flirting.

I tried giving the old eyelashes a flutter, chucking in a bonus hair-toss, but Cameron just blinked at me.

'Er, hi,' I said, narrowly biting my tongue before I added, 'What's a nice boy like you doing in a place like this?'

'Hi,' he said. 'What can I get you, love?'

'Fish and chips once with scraps, please.'

'Coming up.' He grabbed his fish slice and started piling chips into a sheet of greaseproof paper. 'Hey, do I know you?' he asked, squinting into my face.

Was that a chat-up line? Ugh, this was hard. Yolanda jumped up a notch in my estimation for making it look so easy.

'You might've seen me around. I run the restaurant at the top of the village with my brother.'

'Yeah, probably what I'm thinking of. The cute one – Tom, is it? You look a bit like him.'

Cute, what did that mean: cute? Cute like an adorable little kitten? Or did he mean it the way Americans said it, like, shaggable cute?

'Look, are you American?' I blurted out. 'I mean, are you gay?'

He blinked at me. 'Er, yeah. I mean, what?'

I blushed furiously. God, I was making a right mess. Tom was going to kill me.

'Actually, mate, can you hold the fish?'

'I'm sorry?'

'Me too. That's why I'm changing the subject before I die of shame. You give me chips, I'll give you money and we'll forget the whole thing, OK?'

He smiled. 'My mum is from Vermont, to answer your question. Vinegar on them?'

'Oh. Um, yes, please…'

'Look, you seem a lovely girl,' he said as he shook Sarson's generously over my chips. 'I'm very flattered and all that, but you're not really my type. Sorry.'

'Oh God, that's brilliant,' I said with a smile of relief. 'You are gay.'

'No. I'm bi, if you really want to know.' He shook his head. 'You know, it's not every day I get quizzed on my sexuality by customers. You were asking me out, right?'

'Not exactly. Er, hey, do you like cycling?'

When I got home, Tom was waiting expectantly by the living room door. While he wasn't quite hopping from foot to foot, it looked touch and go whether he wouldn't start any minute.

'Well?' he demanded.

I tossed him the packet of chips. 'There's a guy works down the chip shop swears he's on the non-dichotomous continuum of sexual orientation.'

'Right.' He frowned. 'And in English we say…?'

'In English we say you're in.'

His face brightened. 'He is gay?'

'Bi apparently, but I think he likes you. He said you were cute. And he's half American so that means fit in proper English.'

'Ha! Seriously? Oh my God!' He threw himself at me for a hug. 'Thanks, Lana.'

I patted his back. 'I made a bit of a hash of it actually, but we got there.'

He let me go, looking nervous again. 'So what do I do now?'

'Has it really been so long you can't remember? You're as bad as me.'

'The sad thing is it actually has. Not quite got the nerve to just stroll in and ask him out.'

I tapped my head. 'Don't worry, Tommy, it's all here in your sister's cunning brain. I invited him onto the cycling committee.'

'Did you? Why?'

'It'll give the two of you chance to get to know each other, won't it? In a social situation where you're not divided by a chippy counter. Cracking idea, though I say so myself. Plus, we need all the help we can get.'

I felt a buzz in my jeans pocket and yanked out my phone.

'Roger Collingwood,' I said, frowning. 'What does he want? I only saw him a few hours ago.'

'Hello, Lana,' Roger said when I answered. 'Listen, are you sitting down?'

'Not yet.' I struggled out of my coat and chucked it over the arm of the sofa, then plonked myself down. 'Now I am. What's up, Roger?'

'Were you really serious about that viaduct idea?'

'Course, why?'

'Good, because I popped into the village archives at the temperance hall to research it. I thought I could find out why it hadn't been tried before.'

'And?'

'As it turns out, it has. Someone in the village looked into getting it opened eight years ago.'

'Don't remember that. Who was it?'

'Are you sure you're sitting down?'

'I told you I am,' I said impatiently. 'Come on, who?'

'Filippo Donati.'

My eyebrows shot up. 'You're kidding!'

'I'm not. I'm holding a stack of his paperwork on making it a right of way here.'

'But why didn't he say anything to us?'

'It doesn't look like he got beyond initial research; 2005 – that's when he was diagnosed, isn't it?'

'Yes,' I said, blinking. 'God, yes, that's right.'

'Maybe that's why. Listen, I'll get it all copied and pop it through your letterbox.'

'Thanks, Rodge, you're a saint.'

'What was that all about?' Tom asked when I'd hung up.

'You'll never believe it. The viaduct – well, you know

how I said it was just the sort of thing Dad would want us to be doing?'

'Yeah?'

'Turns out he had the same idea. He was looking into getting it opened when he got his diagnosis.'

'Shit! Really?'

'Yep.' I shifted in my seat to look at him. 'Well, that decides it, doesn't it? Bugger the memorial bench. We're giving our old man a viaduct.'

Roger dropped a fat packet through our letterbox the same evening. I didn't have time to look at it until my shift finished, but by the time Tom was done with maître d' duties I was more than halfway through.

'Bloody hell, Tommy!' I said when he'd joined me at the coffee table.

'What's it say then?'

'The viaduct. It wasn't just an idea; Dad had a whole plan. Looked like he was well into it by the time he started the first round of chemo.'

Tom gave Flash, between us on the sofa, an absent stroke. 'Yeah. He got pretty tired after that.'

'He's left us all the blueprints,' I said, scanning the paperwork. 'Structural survey, financial viability, everything! Good old Dad.' I pointed to one item. 'Look at that.'

Tom glanced at the spreadsheet. 'Whoa. Is that true?'

'Figures add up. Forty grand a year it's costing to keep the viaduct in its current state.' I looked up. 'Dad estimated it'd only cost around fifty to get it done up.'

'Then why don't the council do it already?'

'Dunno, accountability? No one pays attention to money spent on maintenance. Knocking down or fixing up: that's when questions get asked.'

'What can we do then?'

'Fight, of course! Get the whole community behind us. Then the council would have to listen.' I tweaked a sheet of paper out of my pile. 'Look.'

There was a sketch among the paperwork, another of Dad's creative talents. It showed families, cyclists, horse riders, walkers, all making their way over the arches; our long-dead viaduct, alive and useful again.

'When did he find time to do all this?' Tom said.

'You know what he was like. Probably planning a big reveal, just to see the look on our faces.' I glanced up from the sketch, eyes shining. 'Know what this means?'

'Hard work?'

'Well, yes. But it means we can do something he really wanted. The viaduct open; the Tour making history on it!'

Tom looked doubtful. 'It is a good idea,' he said hesitantly. 'But I'm worried about you, sis. Why so feverish? You're grieving; you need to take things slowly.'

'But it's what Dad wanted. That means it's what we want too, isn't it?'

'I just can't help feeling you're setting yourself up for disappointment. Dad wouldn't have wanted that.'

I frowned. 'All right, genius, what would he have wanted?'

'It doesn't matter now, except to us.' He flung a comforting arm around me. 'Dad's gone, Lana. It's like the coffin. It might be the same size and shape and weight as Dad, but it isn't him. Dad's... not here. Not any more.'

'He's here in us. And damn it, I'm going to make sure

everyone knows it. They won't forget him; not while I've got breath.'

'Who said they'd forget him?' Tom said quietly. 'You're being defensive against an argument no one's made.'

I blinked back a tear, staring down at little fuzzy Flash on the sofa. 'Maybe I said it.'

'How do you mean?'

'Maybe I'm scared. Scared of forgetting him myself. It's only been a month, and already, when I try to picture his face…' I looked up at him through eyes claggy with tears. 'I need this, Tommy. Let me fight. It's all I've got.'

'Is it healthy though?'

'Healthier than your chip habit.'

'Ah, that's different,' he said with a smile. 'Puppy love.'

'You're twenty-eight. You're not a puppy any more.' I sighed. 'And it's the same really, isn't it? Fear of losing a dream. That's why you're too scared to ask Cameron out. A dream's better than nothing.'

'I'm not nothing, am I? Or Gerry or Sue. You're not alone, Lana.'

'No. But I miss my dad. And this feels like… like closure.'

12

'Now are you sure you and Deb can manage?' I said to Jasmine as Tom and I prepared to leave for the first cycling meeting. We'd planned it for a Thursday, always a quiet night in the restaurant – especially these days. 'There's another barrel of honey mead in the cellar if we run out, and, oh, tell Deano I got more cream; it's in the fridge—'

'We'll be fine, Lana,' she said, standing on tiptoes to kiss my cheek. 'You worry too much. I'll just let Deano know I'm here then I'll get my costume on.'

'What's with her fashion sense lately?' Tom asked as he watched the teenager's knee-high rainbow socks and hotpants disappear into the kitchen.

'Trying to impress Deano. She's got a crush on him.'

'Ha! Seriously?'

'Yeah. Stockholm's, I reckon. Come on, let's get this over with.'

When we got to the pub, Yolanda and Sue were already at a table, glaring at each other.

'Oh God, what now?' I muttered to Tom.

We got a drink each and headed over.

'Believe me, Susan, nothing can have been further from my mind than offending you,' Yolanda was saying. 'I made the merest suggestion of a tweak to your recipe.'

'You what?' Sue said. 'You didn't even use my recipe! That's a bloody Nigella recipe, that is. I know because she always calls for too much flour.'

'All right, what're you two arguing about today?' Tom asked as we took our seats.

Sue glared at Yolanda. 'Ask her ladyship.'

'Well, Yo-yo?'

Yolanda shrugged. 'She would insist on us using her supposedly fabulous recipe for lavender scones at the cake sale last week. I made one teensy change and now she's all huffy.'

'One teensy change my wobbly backside, love,' Sue said. 'You didn't even use it! Trust me, my mam invented that recipe. I can taste the difference.'

'Are there really that many recipes for scones though?' I said, taking a sip of my Guinness. 'Surely they're all the same: flour and butter or whatever.'

I could tell by the look of horror both women turned on me that it was the wrong thing to say.

'Sorry,' I mumbled.

Sue shook her head. 'And your old man a chef.'

Yolanda reached over to give my hand a pat when Sue mentioned Dad. 'How are you both doing, my loves?' she asked gently.

She was only being nice, of course. Still, I was getting heartily sick of that question. What did people expect the answer to be? 'Yeah, I'm crying inside, thanks, but I'll probably get over it in a year or so'?

'As well as we can,' I said.

'Where's Gerry?' Tom asked, picking up on my tone and deftly changing the subject.

Sue jerked her head towards the door. 'Having a fag.'

'So we're just waiting on Stewart,' Yolanda said brightly.

Sue shook her head. 'Don't you be flirting with him all night, Yolanda Sommerville. We're here to work, not set you up with a lad half your age.'

'Still. That could be a nice bonus for my community spiritedness, couldn't it?' Yolanda lowered her voice. 'Lovely pert bottoms, these cyclists.'

'Are you going to be OK, love?' Sue asked me quietly.

For a second I thought she was talking about Dad. Then I realised she meant Stewart.

'I'll manage.' I sighed. 'Much as I hate to admit it, he will be useful to have on board. Let's just all stay civil. Sure we can manage that.' I glanced from her to Yolanda. 'As long as we keep off the scones.'

I noticed Tom blush deeply and followed his gaze to Cameron, who was at the bar.

'Oh. Yeah. Actually, there is someone else coming tonight,' I said. 'I recruited us a new member. The lad from the chippy, Cameron. Big cycling fan. Er, his mum's from Vermont,' I added by way of an introduction. It was the only thing I knew about him.

Sue glanced over my shoulder to get a look at Cameron, then back to Tom's pinkened cheeks.

'I see.'

She didn't need to say any more. Sue was sharp as a needle when it came to our love lives.

'Hiya,' Stewart said, sinking into a free seat next to Yolanda.

'Oof! Bloody hell, lad! You gave me the fright of my life.' Sue patted her heart, her huge bosom jiggling alarmingly. 'Where did you creep from?'

He shrugged. 'I've been here the whole time you have, having a drink with Kit over there. Didn't you see me?'

'No.'

'They call me The Spectre,' he said, tossing his curls. 'I walk like the night. You look behind you, and fzzt! I'm gone.'

Yolanda giggled. 'You're funny, aren't you? I like that in a man.'

Sue snorted. 'What you like in a man is oxygen and a Y chromosome. Everything else is optional.'

I suppressed an eye-roll as Cameron came over to join us.

'Hi,' he said, hovering nervously with a carrier bag clutched in one hand and a pint in the other. 'Er, can I sit down?'

'Course you can,' Sue said, indicating a chair. She smiled a welcome. 'Thanks for joining us.'

Cameron took his seat. He seemed on edge, his eyes darting around as if he was wondering whether he'd made a big mistake in agreeing to come.

I gave Tom a nudge. He'd come over all Class Four Nativity, staring into his drink to avoid eye contact.

'Er, hi,' he said to Cameron, his cheeks a fetching shade of pink. 'Nice to see you. You look different without your... chips.'

'Thanks. Oh, that reminds me.' Cameron reached under the table for the bag he'd been carrying. 'My treat. Chips and scraps, right? You normally come in today, so when you didn't, I thought maybe you'd, um, run out of time. I put a buttered teacake in too – I know you like them.'

'Oh, right, yeah.' Tom took the bag, just brushing Cameron's fingers. 'My favourite,' said the man who'd told me earlier that if he ever saw another chip he'd vom.

'So, you know, if you wanted to come in next week as usual, er... I could have them ready.'

Tom beamed. 'Thanks, Cameron. I'll do that.'

Yolanda looked bored while this conversation she had no part in went on.

'Forgive me, but aren't we supposed to be discussing the Tour de France?' she said. 'Why is everyone talking about chips?'

'We need Gerry first,' I said.

Sue waved a dismissive hand. 'Oh, don't wait for him. He'll be hiding out there chain-smoking until he's sure what he's so hilariously dubbed Sconegate is done with. Let's make a start.'

'OK, who wants to go first?' Stewart asked.

Tom elbowed me. 'Our Lana does. She's had another brainwave.'

'Don't hurt yourself, will you, hun?' Yolanda said. I shot her a look.

'Well, Lana, what've you got?' Stewart said.

I reached into my handbag for the paperwork Roger had copied and tweaked out Dad's sketch.

'This,' I said, holding it up.

Yolanda frowned. 'Is that our viaduct?'

'A vision of it, courtesy of Phil Donati. This was Dad's brainwave. I'm just custodian.'

'When did your dad do that?' Sue asked.

'Eight years ago apparently,' Tom said. 'Never said a word, the sly old bugger.'

'Sorry, I'm confused,' Cameron said. 'I thought Lana said this committee was about trying to get us on the Tour route.'

'That's just the idea,' I said. 'I was thinking about what Egglethwaite had to offer over other places, and – well, we keep talking about the view from Pagans' Rock. What makes that so special? The viaduct. That's what our dad thought.'

'So Dad sketched his vision of what it could be,' Tom said.

'It's a nice drawing, darling, but how does it help us?' Yolanda asked.

'Because it wasn't just a drawing.' I shook the rest of the papers out of my document wallet and spread them over the table. 'There's a whole stack of research relating to getting the viaduct opened up that Dad was working on before he started chemo. But this is most important.' I pointed out the structural survey done a decade ago.

'Why?' Cameron asked.

'Because it says the viaduct's sound. All it really needs is tarmacking.' I swept my hand over an imaginary vista. 'Picture it, you lot! A train of cyclists darting over the arches, helicopters getting footage of the reservoir and moors. It'll look incredible on TV.'

'Will it bear the weight?' Sue asked.

I shrugged. 'It could take a train, I'm sure it can cope with a few bodies.'

'Even yours, Susan, I'm sure,' Yolanda said with a smirk.

'Those arches look well reinforced.' Sue shot her a filthy look.

Stewart remained silent while this conversation went on.

'It won't work,' he said at last.

I frowned. 'What do you mean, it won't work? Why shouldn't it work?'

'Come on, Lana, don't be naive. You really think it's possible to get a viaduct that's been neglected for fifty years opened in such a short time?'

'He's got a point, darling,' Yolanda said.

I glared at her. 'It's worth making enquiries, isn't it? I told you, the structure's sound.'

'Let's be logical.' Stewart started counting on his fingers. 'One. We don't even know if we're going to get a shot at the Tour route yet. It might already have been decided.'

'That is true,' Tom said.

'That doesn't matter though!' I looked from one to the other of them. 'It's worth doing regardless of the Tour.'

'Well, let's park that for now.' Stewart held up another finger. 'Two. There may not be funding. Grants are competitive, and local authorities are stretched these days.'

'We could always try community fundraising if they turn us down.'

Stewart pulled my dad's costing sheet towards him. 'Fifty grand though. You really think we could raise that in a tiny village like this?'

'If we think up good ideas.'

'In just a few months?'

I hesitated. 'Maybe.'

'OK, three. The time. It'd be nigh on impossible to get the money raised and work done in time for the Tour.' He put up one last finger. 'And four. After all that, we might not even get selected for the route and it'll have been a lot of hard work for nothing.'

'It wouldn't!' Angry tears stung my eyes. 'Even if we don't get the route, it'll be a lasting legacy. We just have to fight.'

'Um, why're you standing up, sis?'

I looked down at Tom. He was right: without realising it I'd jumped to my feet.

'Why is he being so obstructive?' I practically yelled, pointing to Stewart. 'Because it was me who suggested it? Is that it, Stewart?'

Stewart looked concerned now, and a little frightened. Through the cloud of rage I noticed the same look on every face around the table.

'I'm sorry, Lana,' he said quietly. 'I had no idea you were so invested or I wouldn't have – look, I was just trying to point out the flaws objectively, that's all. I don't think any of us want to give our time to a dead end, do we?'

'It's *not* a dead end!' To my disgust, I burst into tears. 'My dad didn't think so. Oh God… I have to get out of here. I can't do with you all staring like that.' Turning from the sea of worried eyes, I practically ran to the door.

In the Fox's little beer courtyard, Gerry was leaning against the wall, smoking a roll-up.

'What're you doing out here?' he asked.

'Same as you. Hiding.'

He stubbed his cigarette out against the wall. 'Something upset you, petal? You sound choked up.'

'Yeah.' I sniffed. 'Dad stuff.'

'Thought that must be it.' He beckoned me to him. 'Come on then.'

I sank gratefully into a hug. That smell: tobacco and beer. It reminded me of Dad, coming back from a boozy pub night while Sue babysat. No matter how tipsy Gerry got him, Dad always tiptoed into my room to give me a goodnight kiss before bed.

'Thanks, Uncle Gerry,' I murmured.

He smiled. 'I don't think you've called me uncle since your mam was alive.'

'Well. I need all the family I can get these days.' I drew back from the hug to look at him. 'You and Sue won't get divorced, will you?'

'Why would we get divorced?'

'You're always arguing.'

'Ah, that's just play. Love of my bloody life, that daft cow. Don't tell her though, eh?'

'Secret's safe with me,' I said, smiling.

'So what did I miss inside then? Please God, make it everything scone-related.'

'Just me having a breakdown.'

He examined my tear-stained face with concern. 'Go on, what happened?'

'Stewart didn't like my idea so I shouted at him.'

'Oh.' He nodded with satisfaction. 'Good. Serves him right for what he did to you last year.'

'He was still right though, what he said. I'm just an emotional wreck at the moment.'

'Course you are,' Gerry said gently. 'Want me to talk to him?'

'No, I need to do it. Much as it galls me, I owe him an apology.'

Speak of the devil. Just then Stewart poked his straw-blond head around the door, the rest of his athletic body quickly following.

'You OK, Lana?'

'Gerry, can you give us a minute?' I said. 'I need to talk to Stewart.'

Gerry shot a suspicious look at the younger man. 'All right, pet, if that's what you want.'

'You be gentle with her, sonny,' he muttered to Stewart as he passed him to go back into the pub.

'Sorry for shouting at you,' I said when Gerry had gone.

'Never mind about that, I was being a dick,' Stewart said, waving a dismissive hand. 'How're you doing?'

I sniffed. 'What's it look like?'

He came over, and for a minute I thought he was going to hug me. I flinched, but then he obviously thought better of it and his arms dropped awkwardly to his sides.

Stewart had changed in the last year; there was no getting away from it. The easy confidence I remembered was still there, but it felt forced somehow. And close up, his eyes... When we'd met a year ago they'd flashed with lazy fun, except when they'd softened just for me. Now, they were filled with something unspoken; something too familiar. Pain. I wondered how much the injury that had forced him out of professional cycling still hurt.

'I'm sorry, Lana. I was talking without engaging brain first, as usual,' he said. 'Tom was just telling me how important this viaduct plan was to your dad.'

'Not just to him,' I mumbled, but the words were gobbled up by sobs. Stewart was silent a moment while I struggled to get my tears under control.

'So I guess the viaduct means a lot to you, does it?' he asked when I was quiet.

'Yes. Yes. I need this.'

'Well, then I'll fight if you will.'

'Thought you said it was a rubbish idea,' I said, sniffing.

He smiled. 'Come on, I never said that. I just said there were issues to consider. We might be able to find a way.'

'You really think?'

'Don't get your hopes up too high, but yes. If it's not impossible that means it can be done, right? Let's just do a bit more research before we start picturing the TV helicopters.'

I laughed. 'I do tend to run away with myself a bit.'

'I'd noticed. It's sweet.'

Sweet. He was calling me sweet. I stared at him, suddenly remembering who I was talking to.

'Don't flirt with me, Stewart.'

'Didn't realise I was.'

'Why're you being nice to me anyway? I just gave you a right bollocking.'

'Because I upset you and now I feel bad. Anything wrong with that?'

'S'pose not,' I said warily. 'I mean it though, no flirting. Let's keep it professional.'

'We're friends though?'

'As good friends as ever we were.' I wiped the last of my tears away with my sleeve. 'Come on, let's go back in. We need to make a plan.'

13

Well, we made a plan. Which was why I found myself outside McLean's Machines a fortnight later, a document wallet under my arm and bitterness in my heart.

'You ready?' I asked when Stewart answered my knock.

'I was born ready.'

'Remind me again why you have to come with me.'

He shrugged. 'The others thought it might help if the council saw we had someone from the sporting world on board. And because you love me, obviously.'

I groaned. 'Please stop, I've just eaten.'

'Oh, come on, Lana, lighten up a bit,' he said, grinning. 'Only trying to make you smile. I know you can; I've seen you do it when you think I'm not looking.'

'Let's just get it over with. I might smile then.'

He leaned round to examine my face. 'Why so nervous, love?' he asked, dropping the teasing tone.

'I've got a lot invested in this, that's all.'

'I know you have.' He gave my shoulders a squeeze. I winced at the touch, and he hastily pulled his arm away. 'Try to relax. It won't help if you're on edge.'

'If there's funding up for grabs we need to make a good

impression.' I gestured to him. 'Hence you. So behave, all right?'

'Don't I always?'

'No.' I unlocked the car and nodded to the passenger side. 'In you get.'

All I knew about the man we were meeting was his name, Andy Chen, and that he was something called a communities liaison officer. I'd been expecting someone middle-aged, but the lad who took a seat opposite us in the town hall caf only looked early thirties. He was good-looking too, in a geeky, tousle-haired sort of way.

'Thanks for seeing us,' I said.

'Well, that's my job,' Andy said with a friendly smile. 'So I understand you're looking at getting the Egglethwaite Viaduct opened up?'

'That's the idea.'

'You're Phil Donati's daughter, aren't you? We were very sorry to hear about his passing on the council.'

I blinked in surprise. 'That's right. Did you know him?'

'My predecessor did, very well. Phil did a lot for Egglethwaite. He'll be missed.'

'He will,' I said, flushing. 'Oh.' I nodded to Stewart. 'This is Mr McLean. He's new to the village.'

'But he's very keen to help,' Stewart said, holding out his hand. 'Stewart.'

Andy shook the hand heartily. 'No introductions needed. I know who *you* are.'

'You follow cycling?'

'Of course.'

Stewart smiled. 'Pleased to hear it.'

Ugh. Cycling fanboy. I knew there'd be something wrong with him. Well, at least Stewart's ego was having a nice day out.

'So what's next from you?' Andy asked, his eyes shining. 'Are you in training for the Tour?'

I saw Stewart wince. 'No. No, I'm not competing now.'

'You're kidding! Why not? I would've put money on you being the next Bradley Wiggins this time last year.'

'Knee injury,' Stewart said, staring down at the table.

'Oh. Actually, yes, I remember reading about it,' Andy said. 'How long until you're back in the saddle then? Bet you can't wait to be on the road again.'

'It's… not the sort of injury you ever fully recover from. There's permanent cartilage damage, which means I can't cycle for extended periods without pain.' Stewart nodded at my paperwork on the table between us. 'So shall we talk about the viaduct?'

Andy looked surprised at the abrupt change of subject.

'If you like. Sorry, hope I didn't cause offence.'

'Not at all,' Stewart said, summoning a smile. 'Tough subject, that's all.'

'So is there any possibility of getting the viaduct opened up?' I asked, as much to rescue Stewart as anything. Even through the burning resentment I still harboured, I felt a twinge of sympathy. It must be tough, giving up something you loved that much.

'My dad started looking into it a few years ago,' I continued. 'Seems like there's nothing wrong with the structure.'

'Yes, I did some research,' Andy said. 'We have had

interest in opening it up before, it seems: not just from Phil. There was a charity who made enquiries, but when they found out the problem they dropped the idea.'

'I thought there weren't any structural problems,' Stewart said.

'The problem isn't structural, it's organic. Bats.'

'Right. Bats.' I frowned. 'Sorry – bats?'

'That's right. Barbastelle, the species is called: very rare. A colony were found roosting in one of the crevices. As soon as the charity found out they'd have wildlife protection groups up in arms, they decided it wasn't worth the effort.'

'Are you saying we can't do this?'

'No, it could be achievable,' he said cautiously. 'The bats could be relocated. But it'd need careful timing to fit round their hibernation cycle.'

'Could we do it in a year? Plus all the work?'

His eyes widened. 'In a *year*? Sorry, Lana, that'd be practically impossible.'

'Practically impossible means possible though, doesn't it?' Stewart said. 'Isn't there a hope?'

'But why the big hurry?'

'We were thinking if the viaduct was accessible to cyclists, the Grand Départ might consider running through Egglethwaite,' Stewart said. 'It'd certainly be a feature few other places could offer. Great TV, and great for our area's profile.'

Andy was silent a moment.

'I have to admire your determination,' he said at last.

'So are we wasting our time here, Andy?'

'The thing is, it's the money too. If Egglethwaite was part

of the national park it'd perhaps be a different story, but out here in no-man's land things're tight.'

'My dad costed it at fifty grand,' I said. 'Surely it's worth it?'

'When we've just halved our budget for community youth clubs thanks to government cuts? How would we explain to parents and kids that we'll be spending fifty grand on one little village's viaduct?'

'That's not how funding pots work, is it?'

'No. But it's how the public think they work. There'd be a lot of angry people once it got out.'

I looked at Stewart. 'Then it's hopeless.'

'Look, Andy. Couldn't you help us out?' Stewart said with one of his most winning smiles. 'This meant a lot to Lana's dad. We really want to try for it, in his memory.'

'It wouldn't have to be entirely council-funded,' I said. 'We could fundraise.'

Andy hesitated. 'I'll put it to the council for you, give it my best sell,' he said at last. 'But don't get your hopes up, guys.'

I flung him a grateful smile. 'Thanks, Andy. You've been brilliant.'

'That seemed to go well,' Stewart said as we drove home.

'As well as it could. Let's just hope he can help.'

'Keen, wasn't he?'

'Yeah, he was nice.'

I could see Stewart shooting me an appraising look in the rear-view mirror. 'You liked him. Didn't you?'

'None of your business.'

'Come on, Lana, don't prickle. I behaved, didn't I?'

I softened a little, remembering how helpful he'd been in the meeting and the pang of sympathy I'd felt when he'd talked about giving up cycling.

'Yes. You behaved.'

'So, did you?'

'He was all right,' I said at last.

'Why don't you ask him out?'

'All right, Stewart, that's enough. There's a line.'

'Sorry. Thought we were doing the friend bonding thing.'

'Well we weren't.'

'OK. Line well and truly noted.'

In the mirror, I met his grey eyes briefly.

'Look, thanks for today,' I said eventually. 'And thanks… for what you said about my dad. I didn't mean to snap.'

And so in the silence of a shaky alliance, we made our way back home.

14

I scrambled breathlessly up the ferny bank after a frisking Flash, watching the lightning-shaped patch of white on his tail disappear over the top.

'Come on,' I called to Tom. 'You know, you used to be able to do this faster before the three-times-a-week chip habit.'

'It's... twice a week,' he panted. 'I don't love him that much.'

'Three times last week.'

'All right, I do love him that much. Hey, he's started giving me free teacakes. You reckon that means something?'

'Yeah, it means you're his best customer.'

I pulled myself over the top of Pagans' Rock, earning a patronising well-done bark from Flash.

'OK, cheeky pup,' I said. 'Some of us have only got the two legs.'

Tom finally caught me up and leaned against my shoulder while he got his breath.

'Best view in the area... it may be, but it'll be the death of some poor bastard one day,' he puffed. 'And that poor bastard may well be one Tom Donati, RIP.'

'Worth it though,' I said quietly, gazing down at the toylike viaduct.

Given why we were there, I felt a sober gladness to find it looking its best. Even with the sunshine making only the briefest of appearances through the cloud, it was a magnificent spectacle. Delicate pastel pinks and blues melted together on the peaceful waters of the reservoir, sliced into segments by the reflected arches.

Let the other villages keep their steam railways and their canals. Dad was right: I wouldn't swap the view from Pagans' Rock for all of them.

'Erm, sis. Why is Flash's tongue that colour?' Tom said, pulling me out of my thoughts. The fluffy little sheepdog was panting in the heat, black-purple tongue dangling out of his mouth.

'Oh God. He's been at the bilberries.' I guided him away from the bush he'd discovered. 'Better get his lead on before he makes himself sick.'

'Oooh! Bilberries.' Tom kneeled down to gather some and started popping them into his mouth with relish. 'I'll tell Deano – he was on about it being nearly pie season. Me and him can come up for some before the village gets wise and clears out the bushes.'

I squinted at him. 'Are you taking Deano on a bilberrying man-date?'

He sighed, popping another plump purple berry in his gob. 'Closest I'm likely to get to a real date unless I can work up the nerve to ask Cameron out. Actually, me and Deano have got a pact. We made it on KP duty last week.'

'What pact?'

'To get married if I'm still single at forty. Always handy to have a backup plan, eh? At least I'll be well fed.'

'The bigamist git! He made that pact with me as well.' I patted Tom's elbow. 'Go on then, I'll let you have him.'

'Wow. Thanks.'

We were interrupted by the sound of muttered curses, and a second later Sue's peroxide perm appeared over the top of the rock.

'Get a shift on, old man!' she called down to Gerry.

'All right, keep your knickers on, love. I'm fifty-three, you know.'

'So am I, you don't hear me whinging.' She looked over at me and Tom. 'I swear this walk gets harder every year.'

'Still, you do all right for a big girl,' Gerry panted as he pulled himself up and went to give her bum a squeeze.

'You want a slap?'

Gerry shook his head at us. 'Can you believe it? Our time of life and the randy old cow's after getting me into the kinky stuff.'

Tom snorted. 'And the safety word is "Oh God, my hip!"'

'All right, old people, enough manky BDSM jokes,' I said. 'Come on, Gerry.'

Gerry threw off his rucksack and took out the small urn containing Dad's ashes. Sue came over to me and Tom and put an arm around each of us.

'Who wants to do it?' she asked.

Tom looked at me. 'Don't think I can. Lana?'

'You do it,' I said to Gerry. 'You were his best friend.'

'If that's what you kids want.'

Gerry opened the urn and scattered the contents into the

air. I followed the grey powder as it spiralled on the wind, over the edge of the rock and away towards the viaduct.

'Well, my loves, he's free now,' Sue said softly. 'No more pain. Just this.'

'Yes. No more pain.' I snuggled into the warmth of her shoulder, squeezing a tear into her fleece.

'Should we say something?' Gerry said.

'I don't want anything scripted. Let's just remember him.'

'Why did he love this view so much?' Sue asked.

'Something about the isolation of it, I think,' Tom said. 'Always feels like a lost world up here, doesn't it?'

'Plus he was a bit of a trainspotter,' I said with a smile. 'You should have heard him go on about that viaduct.' My eyes sparkled. 'God, just imagine if we can get it open for the Tour. Wouldn't he just've loved it?'

Tom shook his head at Sue. 'I don't know where the cycling fever has come from suddenly. She never gave a toss about any sport until a few weeks ago.'

'It's the young man,' Gerry said. 'That McLean. I wouldn't bother trying to impress him, petal. He already broke your heart once.'

I snorted. 'It bloody isn't the young man. The young man can take a flying jump. And he didn't break my heart, ta very much, Gerry, so I'll thank you not to start putting it about that he did.'

'All right, that's me told,' he muttered. 'So what is it then?'

'It's... well, it's Dad, isn't it?' I said. 'This could be a real memorial to him; a zillion times better than any bench. Something that'll showcase the village he loved in its best light, in the eyes of the whole world.'

'You know we'll do all we can, chicken,' Sue said, but

she had her worried mum voice on. 'Let's see how we go though, eh?'

See how we go. Don't get your hopes up. Why were people always saying that stuff to me?

'Yeah, OK,' I mumbled. 'Just want to give it my best shot, that's all.'

'Are we going down then?' Gerry asked. 'Roast's in, you two. The missus did your favourite for today: rosemary-roasted lamb.'

Tom glanced at me. 'You go down, guys. We'll meet you at the farm in half an hour.'

'Of course. Take as long as you need.' Sue gave our shoulders a last squeeze and the two of them disappeared over the bank.

When they were gone we were silent a moment, arms round each other's shoulders.

'Well, he's out there now,' I said at last. 'Part of nature.'

'Part of everything.'

'Yeah.'

Another silence. I leaned my head against Tom's shoulder. It was a sober moment, but there was a finality in it, a joy even, that we both needed.

'Always looks best in summer,' Tom said quietly, following my gaze to the viaduct.

'Mmm.' I shot it a resentful glare. 'Hope those bloody bats are enjoying it. Upside-down little hairy nocturnal bastards, with their fucking... sonar.'

He laughed. 'Don't be mean. They can't help being rare.'

'They could if they tried. They're not breeding hard enough. Lazy, I call it. If I was a rare bat I'd be doing it five times a night, minimum.'

Tom grimaced. 'Nice image. Thanks.'

My Adele ringtone went off and I yanked out my phone.

'Oh God, it's him,' I said in a hushed voice. 'Andy Chen, the bloke from the council.'

'Well, answer it then.'

I swiped at the screen. 'Andy. Hiya.'

'Hi, Lana. We just got out of the council meeting.'

'Shit, was it today? What's the verdict?'

'Depends if you want the good news or the bad.'

'There's bad?'

'Afraid so,' Andy said. 'It's the bats. I invited a representative from the local branch of the Bat Protection League and she wasn't a fan of getting them moved. I mean she *really* wasn't a fan. Not sure I've got the hearing back in my left ear yet.'

'Oh no, really?'

'Yep. She made it abundantly clear her group were ready to fight tooth and claw any attempt to have the bats relocated from their chosen habitat, even when I said we'd guarantee minimal loss of life.'

'That's terrible! Can the council overrule them?'

'Yes, but they wouldn't. Bad publicity. We have to try and talk them round.'

'Doesn't sound easy.'

'It won't be. But you haven't heard the good news yet,' he said, and I could tell he was smiling. 'The council loved your viaduct idea. When I told them we had a whole group of villagers ready to work for it, they were right behind you.'

'Really? That's wonderful!'

He laughed. 'Changeable, aren't you?'

'So is there funding?'

'Up to twenty-five grand if you meet the historic structures criteria, which I'm certain you do. If your committee thinks it can match that through fundraising and we can find a way out of this bat problem, we could be looking at a runner.'

'Arghh! That's brill, Andy! In time for the Tour, do you think?'

He hesitated. 'The councillors were keen for our area to be showcased, but…'

'But?'

'Well, you'd need the money in the bank by New Year to even have a shot at getting the work done. Plus the removal of the bats if we can talk round the wildlife people. And we'd have to do a safety survey; that might throw up some hitches.'

'But it's not impossible?'

'It's not as unlikely as I thought it would be,' he said cautiously. 'It'll be bloody difficult though.'

'All I wanted to hear. Thanks, Andy, you're amazing.'

He laughed. 'Sweet talk will get you everywhere. Anything else you want to know, Lana?'

I hesitated. I did like Andy. He was cute and smiley and not far off my age. He wasn't already in a committed relationship with a frying pan, and he didn't seem like the kind of bloke who'd disappear if you turned him down for sex on a first date. Plus I could swear he was flirting with me. Should I ask if he was single?

'No, I think that's everything,' I said after a pause. 'Thanks again.'

'Well?' Tom said as soon as I'd hung up.

I beamed at him. 'Andy reckons we can get twenty-five grand.'

'Really? That's brilliant!'

'Well, not all good news.' I glanced at the viaduct. 'The bats are still a problem, little buggers. Wildlife groups don't like the idea of us relocating them.'

'So what do we do?'

I shrugged. 'I think for now we just crack on with making money and hope we can talk them round. Maybe I could invite the chair of the Bat Preservation Society or whatever it was called to one of our meetings.'

'What's our next move then?'

'Basically a bucketload of fundraising. We need to match that twenty-five grand and we need to do it in the next five months to have any chance of getting the thing opened before the Tour, so get your ideas head on. I'm going to text the others.'

'Got one,' Tom said promptly as soon as I'd finished tapping out a message.

'Bloody hell, that was quick. Go on then.'

'Nude calendar.'

I rolled my eyes. 'Typical. Cameron joins the committee and within weeks you've found an excuse to get his kit off.'

'Come on, it'll be great. People love that stuff. Plus when they make our film, Helen Mirren can be in it. She's a hottie.'

'Since when is Mirren your type?' I said, laughing.

He shrugged. 'I'm gay, love, not dead.'

'Well, you can forget it,' I said. 'I'm not baring my bits for the village, good cause be damned. Much as he loved the viaduct, I hardly think Dad'd approve of pictures of my tits hanging up over the counter at the bakery.'

'No one'll see them. We'll get you a pair of cherry bakewells to hold up.'

I glanced down at my F-cups, jutting intrusively into my eyeline as usual. 'Couple of Sara Lee gateaux maybe. No, Tom, I'm too squishy.'

I jumped as my phone buzzed again.

It was a text from Stewart in reply to the round robin about the council meeting.

> Some good news from me too. Route's still being decided. I've arranged for committee to visit in September. Cross everything, Lana: this could be it.

15

'So. First on the agenda,' Sue said once we were all seated behind a drink at the Sooty Fox. As bossiest person in the cycling group, she'd elected herself de facto chair. 'Stewart's announcement.'

'Thanks, Sue,' Stewart said. 'OK, so as you know I got in touch with an old friend who knows someone on the inside and he was able to get us the dirt. The route's still very much under discussion, and although the focus is the Yorkshire Dales National Park, his contact told him they're amenable to bringing Stage 2 through our little bit of Airedale. Based on that I gave the decision-makers a ring, sold us pretty heavily, and they're coming to visit the first Thursday in September.'

'When the heather's in bloom,' I murmured. 'Good call.'

Stewart smiled at me. 'Yeah, that was my thinking. We want the old place dressed in its best, don't we?'

'Are they coming all the way from France?' Cameron asked.

'No, London. VisitBritain have appointed a group to make recommendations for the UK stages.'

'Good job,' Sue said with an approving nod. 'So what we

need to decide is, how're we going to impress them? We've got a lot to prove.'

'We should have a welcoming committee, shouldn't we?' Cameron said. 'A couple of us to show them round.'

'It'll be a working day for most of us,' Stewart said.

Sue turned to me and Tom. 'You two can do it, can't you? It's your show really.'

'S'pose,' I said. 'I'd be worried about cocking it up though.'

'Well, me and Gerry can come to support you.'

'How do we get them up to Pagans' Rock?' Tom asked. 'They'll only have little southern legs.'

'Good point,' Cameron said. 'Can't let them go without seeing that.'

Gerry shrugged. 'We've got my Land Rover. Off-road it up.'

'OK, that'll do. What else?' I said. 'Some sort of buffet in here?'

'Why not bring them to Flagons?' Stewart said.

I frowned. 'Why, you think they'll be into harpsichord music?'

'Bit of quirk, isn't it? All the villages they view'll have a pub or two but I bet none have got a medieval tavern.'

'Hmm. We'd have to close to the public.'

'Thursdays are quiet though,' Tom said. 'It's only one night, sis. And Stewart's right, it'd be something they'd remember.'

'Well… OK. I'll ask Deano if he'd be up for cooking.'

'So that's decided,' Yolanda said. 'Tour of the village, view from the rock, tea at the restaurant. The ladies and I can whizz out a few cakes for the buffet.'

'I'm doing scones,' Sue said quickly.

Yolanda waved a hand. 'Fine. You do the scones; I'll bring the indigestion salts.'

'And I'll bring a few gallons of Mother's Ruin to wash down those chalk-dry fairy cakes you always contribute.'

Yolanda opened her mouth to retort, but Cameron managed to get in first.

'So what's next on the agenda?' he said, wisely changing the subject before things got out of hand.

'Bats,' I said. 'Those bloody bats.'

'Do we have a plan for the bats?' Gerry asked.

'I thought we could invite the chair of the Bat Salvation Church to our next meeting; see if we can find a compromise.'

Cameron frowned. 'Sorry, what did you say the group was called?'

'Well it's something like that.'

'OK, Lana, we'll leave it with you.' Sue glanced at the beer mat she'd used to scribble out an agenda. 'And then the most important item: fundraising. Lana's filled out the paperwork for the council grant, but we still need to make twenty-five grand fast. Ideas?'

'I had one,' I said.

'OK, honey, amaze us,' Yolanda said. I tried to ignore the obvious sarcasm.

'Yarn-bombing.' I beamed round at them.

'Whatting?' Gerry said.

'You know, yarn-bombing. It's like urban graffiti with wool. Very trendy.'

'Oh yeah, I've heard of it,' Stewart said. 'Knitting scarves for lampposts, that type of thing. How would that work as a fundraiser?'

'It'd be more raising awareness really,' I said. 'Then we follow up with some sort of event.'

'But none of us knit, do we?' Sue said.

'I do.'

All eyes turned to Stewart, who shrugged. 'What, I can't have layers? It's therapeutic. Gave me something to do while I was recuperating from the knee injury.'

'Well aren't you just full of surprises?' Yolanda said, pawing nauseatingly at his upper arm. 'I do love a New Man.'

'One every bloody week,' Sue muttered.

I ignored them and carried on pitching my idea. 'So we get a load of knackered bikes, Stewart knits cosies for them, then we plant them around the village overnight and everyone wakes up to find the yarn bikes have taken over. I mean, photo op of the year, people! I bet we'd get a load of press coverage. We'd be...' I paused, trying to remember the line I'd jotted down when I'd had the idea '...combining the historic local industries of sheep farming and textile manufacture with a cycling theme. That's it.'

'Hmm. Not sure I can knit that fast,' Stewart said.

'Ladies Who Lunch must have a few knitters. Reckon you could pull us in some recruits, Yo-yo?'

'I don't know, darling,' she said. 'I'm sure I could, but it seems rather – well, naff. No offence. And I really think we should be making money.'

'I agree,' Stewart said. 'If we need twenty-five grand in the kitty by January we should be focusing on proper fundraisers; save the promotion for later. Sorry, Lana.' Yolanda sent a smug look my way.

I drooped a little. I'd been pretty pleased with my yarn-bombing idea and it was disheartening to have it rejected out of hand.

'Lovely thought though, chicken,' Sue said, giving my arm a comforting squeeze.

'So, any other ideas?' Gerry asked.

'I had one,' Tom said, trying not to look at Cameron.

'Don't you dare,' I whispered. But it was too late.

'Nude calendar. Cycling theme. That'd make money and get us some press.'

Cameron frowned. 'What, us lot?'

'Yeah, why not? Bit of cheeky fun. The village'd love it.'

'Well, Yo-yo?' Gerry said. 'This is your area. It's all jam-making in the buff with WIs these days, isn't it?'

'It's Ladies Who Lunch now, dear,' Yolanda said stiffly. 'And I do all my cooking nude actually.' She flashed a suggestive smile at Stewart. 'It's only natural, after all.'

'Ew,' Tom muttered.

'Visual?' I whispered back.

'Just thinking about that Victoria sponge I bought off her at the last cake sale.'

'Bit old hat, isn't it?' Sue said. 'It might've been original when that WI in Rylstone did it, but the world and his wife's doing nuddy calendars now.'

'With a cycling theme though?' Tom said. 'Anyway, it's more about it being a novelty round here than setting the world alight.'

'Oh, I think it's a wonderful idea!' Yolanda said, not taking her eyes off Stewart.

'You would,' Gerry muttered.

'After all, how many calendars have their own hunky

cycling celebrity? That would be a massive selling point,' Yolanda went on. 'You'll do it, won't you, Stewpot?'

'Christ, she's given him a nickname already,' I muttered to Tom.

'I'm more concerned about him slapping his massive selling point on the table for her,' he whispered.

Stewart shrugged. 'Yeah, why not? Always willing to get my kit off for a good cause.' He looked thoughtful. 'Hey. What if I could get us a real celebrity?'

'Oh God,' I whispered to Tom. 'He'd better not say what I think he's about to say.'

'I could get us Harper Brady.'

'Yep,' Tom muttered.

Yolanda's eyes were wide. 'You're not serious! You know Harper Brady? *The* Harper Brady?'

'Unfortunately,' Stewart said. 'He's my cousin.'

'Oh my goodness, really?' she practically squealed. 'I *love* him!'

'Yeah. You might want to meet him before you go too far down that route.'

Her gaze dwelt on his muscular arms. 'You must have excellent genes in your family, darling. Do you really think he'd do our little calendar?'

'Don't see why not. Harper loves taking his clothes off. I don't think he's had a TV role yet where he hasn't at least got his arse out. Anyway, he owes me a favour. I helped him with the research for *Soar*.'

Yolanda's eyes and mouth formed a teashop's worth of saucers.

'That drama about the soldier with PTSD? I've seen every episode! You didn't work on that?'

'Er, yeah, I gave a bit of advice on the cycling stuff. Not that Harper ever acknowledges it, but my name's in the credits.'

'I had no idea you were so important, darling,' she purred, resting her long fingernails on his arm.

'"Exploited" is the word I'd be tempted to use. But thanks.'

Yolanda was practically sitting in his lap now, and the name-dropping git was clearly loving every minute.

'Brady won't do it,' I said. 'He'll think it's beneath him.'

'Probably. But like I said, he owes me a favour.'

'All right, Stewart, go ahead and ask,' Tom said. 'It'd be good for sales, I guess. So, who else?' He glanced at Cameron. 'You?'

'What, like... you know, all of me?'

'If you want. Stewart can knit us all willy warmers to keep out the chill.' He turned to Stewart. 'How much wool've you got?'

'Not enough.'

'Pay no attention to them,' I said to Cameron. 'You won't have to full monty; it's not that sort of calendar. It'll be just the suggestion of nudity with the tiniest amount of flesh.'

Cameron still looked uncertain. 'Well, if all of you are doing it...'

'Not sure I will. I can be photographer or something.'

'Oh, come on, sis,' Tom said, nudging me. 'All for one and one for all. Like you said, we won't show anything. Just a bit of tummy and some arm or whatever.'

I glanced down at my tummy. I could feel it muffin-topping over my jeans as we spoke. Letting it all hang loose for the whole village to see wasn't exactly my idea of a good time.

'Absolutely not.' Gerry folded his arms. 'I won't have our Lana doing it. I was her dad's best friend, I stand in loco wotchacallit now he's not around.'

'Oh right, but you don't mind Tom doing it,' I said.

'That's different. He's a bloke. When women do it, it's…' he paused, fumbling for a word outside his usual vocabulary '…objectifying, that's it. You don't want every randy old bugger in the village ogling you in the altogether, do you?'

Sue snorted. 'Objectifying. He's been at my *Woman's Own* again.'

'Oh, no no no, it'll be empowering!' Yolanda said, her eyes glittering. The idea had clearly caught her imagination, in a way I sensed was nothing to do with WIs and everything to do with Yolanda Sommerville.

She came over and started prodding my arm and squeezing my hips like a prime cow on show.

'Ow! Geroff, Yo-yo!'

She ignored me. 'Oh yes, we can definitely work with this. New hair for the day – lose the frump, you know – I'll do your make-up; we'll give you something to keep this little tummy hidden. And of course we want to make as much as possible of these, don't we?' She gave my boobs a friendly pat.

'Yolanda, get OFF!' I batted her hand away, blushing furiously. 'Not appropriate, OK?'

She shrugged. 'All girls together, aren't we, darling? We've got the same parts. There's no need to be coy.' She turned to Stewart. 'What do you say, Stewpot? Don't you think our Lana would make a perfect Miss July?'

Stewart was still staring at my recently prodded chest. He blinked.

'Sorry, what? I was miles away.'

Yolanda flicked her eyebrows in my direction. 'Honestly, these boys. A hint of breast and they're away with the fairies.'

'OK, OK, I'll do it,' I said, mainly in the hope it might take the conversation away from my boobs. 'But I'm not showing my bits, top or bottom. I want to be completely covered.'

Yolanda looked disappointed. 'Well, I'm sure we can get you some props, if that's the way you must have it,' she said. 'I'll certainly show my tops and bottoms. It's for the village, after all.'

'We know, love,' Gerry said. 'Even when we were at school you'd get yours out for half a long fag and a bag of chips.' He turned to meet Sue's glare. 'Er, so I heard,' he said with a guilty smile.

Tom looked at Sue and Gerry. 'Well, suppose I have to ask. Are you in, old people?'

Gerry snorted. 'You what? You want me to chuck the wedding tackle over a bike saddle at my time of life? I thought we were trying to make money.'

Sue nodded. 'He's right, it's not a pretty sight. Reminds me of Christmas.'

I shot a warning look at Stewart, whose mouth was opening, but it was no good: he couldn't help himself.

'Go on, Sue, why Christmas?' he asked. 'Does he tie a little ribbon round it for you as a treat?'

'No,' she said. 'I was thinking more last turkey in the shop.'

I curled my lip. 'For God's sake, stop, or I'll have nightmares. Anyway, it'll be strictly pants on, thanks, Gerry. Just take your top off and sit in a tin bath or something.'

When we'd done as much planning as we could stomach and Yolanda and Stewart had gone on their merry way, Tom drained the last of his pint.

'Right, drink up, sis. Time to go home.'

'I'll walk with you. I'm going your way,' Cameron said.

'Er, yeah… actually, I'm just going to pop to the farm,' I said. 'I need food for the dog. You boys walk back.'

Gerry frowned. 'Eh? I sold you a big bag of biscuits last week.'

Sue nudged him in what after twenty-three years of marriage must be some pretty bruised ribs.

'Well, he's a growing puppy. Anyway, it does no harm to stock up.' She sent pointed side-eyes between her husband and Tom.

'Oh. Oh! Right.' Gerry stood up. 'OK, girls, come on. And on the way we can work out how to tell Roger Collingwood we need to book the Temp for the entire cycling group to take their clothes off.'

16

Iplonked the unnecessary bag of dog biscuits down in the hall, leaving Flash to give it a thorough sniffing, and joined Tom in the living room.

'So, how was your moonlit walk?' I asked, sitting down next to him.

His lips twitched at the corner. 'Not telling.'

I examined him through narrowed eyes. 'Ooooh. You got a snog tonight, didn't you?'

He let his mouth spread into a grin. 'Maybe.'

'Good lad! More to come?'

'Hopefully. We're going out for a drink next week.'

'Ha! I'm a genius. Told you inviting him on the committee was a great idea.'

He shrugged. 'Wasn't bad.'

'Say it. Say "Lana Donati is a genius".'

'All right, all right. Lana Donati is a genius.'

'Yes she bloody well is.' I grabbed him round the neck and rubbed his hair with my fist. 'Now say Peanuts.'

'Peanuts. Peanuts! Geroff, Lana!'

'That's right, Peanuts. And don't you forget it.' I let him go.

He smoothed his hair. 'OK, Lana Donati, self-proclaimed

genius. When're you going to leave my love life to self-destruct and sort your own out then?'

'How? You just bagsied the only decent lad under thirty-five in the village.'

'Come on, you're exaggerating.'

'Am I?' I put up a finger. 'Ryan Crooke, thirty-two. Lives with his mum, smells of Dairylea.' Another finger popped up. 'Scott Spen, twenty-six. Looks like a sheep, sounds like a sheep, may actually be part sheep.'

'Give over, he doesn't look that much like a sheep.'

'Yeah? Flash chased him down the street the other day.'

'You're making that up.'

'Maybe. Right, next. Graham Hobson, twenty-nine.' I curled my lip. 'Estate agent. Nothing more to say there. Matthew Cornwall, probably still a virgin at thirty-three; Jamie Collingwood, twenty-five, addicted to online porn; Olly Harrington, thirty-five, two ex-wives and a kid he never bothers to see; Johnny Southgate, twenty-eight, beard; Deano Teasdale, twenty-four, mad as a squirrel and still the best of a bad lot – need I go on?' I paused. 'Actually, I can't. That's it.'

'No it isn't. You missed one.'

'All right, fine. Stewart McLean, twenty-seven. Arrogant arse monkey, never wastes time with second dates if he doesn't get laid on the first one.'

'You really think that's why?'

I sighed. 'I don't know. I can't help remembering that he asked, I said no and that was the last I ever heard from him.'

'He fancies you, you know. He was staring at your boobs all night.'

'He fancied me a year ago. Yet, here we still are.'

'Hmm. You know, he had his accident around then. Maybe that had something to do with it.'

'For a whole year?' I shook my head. 'No, Tommy, he just forgot about me. Something that seemed pretty significant to me was obviously no big deal to him. I bet the man's shagged more women than you've had hot chips.' I scowled in the direction of the window looking out towards McLean's Machines. 'Thank God I didn't go back to his. The last thing I need is to be another notch on Stewart McLean's bike saddle.'

'Dunno. He doesn't seem like the kind of bloke to string women along to me.'

'Look, even if he does still fancy me, he's made it abundantly clear friendship's all he's interested in. Whatever ship me and him might've been on a year ago, it's well and truly sailed.' I shuffled round to look at him. 'Why're you defending him anyway?'

'I'm not really. Just playing devil's avocado.'

'You're on my side though, aren't you?'

'Course I am. You're my baby sister.' Tom gave my shoulder a squeeze. 'Forget him then. You've got options. There're more places in the world than Egglethwaite; you just need to put yourself out there.'

I thought about Andy Chen. 'No... not yet. I'm not in the boyfriend market right now. Too soon after Dad.'

'That excuse won't hold water forever, Lana. You know Dad wanted you to be happy.'

'Well, one of us at a time, eh?' I patted his leg. 'You've got a date next week. We have to get you ready.'

★

Tom looked in the mirror and shook his head.

'I'm not wearing it.'

'No, but come on, it'll be perfect!' Deano said, brushing a few Flash hairs off the shoulder. 'When he sees you in this he'll fall into your arms and you can crush him against your aching chest. It'll be well sexy.'

'For God's sake, Lana. Did you really have to ask the man whose last date was with a kitchen implement for style tips?'

I shrugged. 'Thought we needed the male perspective.'

Deano folded his arms. 'Look, do you two want my help or not?'

'No. Bye, Deano.' Tom nodded to the door.

'Don't listen to him – he's just nervous,' I said. 'Of course we want your help. You're our resident perfectionist.' I scanned Tom's outfit. 'Still. You seriously think bow tie, tweed jacket? He looks like a retired librarian.'

'Nah, it's ace,' Deano said. 'Very in with the hipster brigade. Bow ties are cool.'

'They most certainly are not cool.' Tom unfastened it and yanked it off his neck. 'Lana's right, I look about seventy-five.'

I could see Deano's brow gathering, the way it did when he'd been asked to cook something not on the menu.

'You're looking at it the wrong way, Deano,' I said in my best oil-on-troubled-waters tone. 'Imagine Tom's a meal you've been asked to prepare for a special occasion.'

'I'm not sure I like this analogy,' Tom said. 'Having Deano looking at me like a piece of meat.'

Deano broke into a grin. 'Yeah, you love it.'

I ignored them. 'So you've made the fanciest dish you can

imagine for the special occasion, truffles in blackcurrant jus or whatever.'

'And?'

'And it's a kids' party, and the little treasures all start crying for jelly and ice cream. Get me?'

'That's a bloody long way of saying you need to suit the clothes to the occasion, Lana,' Tom said.

'I thought he'd understand it better this way.' I slapped Deano's arm. 'So? Reckon you can make our Tom into jelly and ice cream before Cameron gets here?'

'S'pose,' he said sulkily. 'But you'll have to brief me. What's the date?'

'Just the pub,' Tom said. 'Thought I might function better in a crowd.'

'And what impression are you going for?'

'Well, sort of pale and interesting, the Byronic silent type. That way if I lose the power of speech he'll think I'm brooding rather than terrified.'

'Right you are. One Byronic jelly and ice cream coming up.'

Deano flung open Tom's cupboard and started chucking things on the bed.

'OK, black jeans, those'll do for starters. Keep the shirt you've got on, top button unfastened. Chuck this blazer over it.' He looked at Tom's bare toes. 'What trainers have you got? Any Converse?'

'What's Converse?'

Deano shook his head. 'If Jasmine hears you say that she'll give notice on the spot. Well, never mind, your usual ones'll do.'

Once Tom had changed, I had to admit the effect was

pretty good. He was tall and skinny, with a tendency to shrink himself by hunching, and as a result clothes tended to hang off his gangly frame like he was outgrowing last year's school uniform. But the ensemble Deano had put together suited his skinniness; sophisticated without being too dressy.

Deano examined him closely, then clicked his fingers. 'Ha! Still got it, right, guys?'

'Yeah, you've done well,' I said. 'Even I'll admit he's not entirely hideous.'

'Do I get a snog now then? You promised me one if I helped.'

'I did not!'

'Your eyes did. Go on, Lana-nana, just a little one.'

I pecked his cheek. 'There you go.'

He shrugged. 'Better than nothing. Right, I'd better get the pottage on. Enjoy your date, Tommy.'

'Enjoy is not the word,' Tom said when Deano had disappeared. He chewed anxiously on his thumbnail. 'If I can get through the night without him running away that'll be as much as I can hope for.'

'Oh, you'll be fine,' I said in what I hoped was a reassuring tone. 'You talk to him in our meetings, don't you? You even manage a bit of a flirt, sometimes.'

'It's different when there's other people though.'

'Still, you've already snogged. What can go wrong at this stage?'

'God, don't say that, it's a jinx. If there's a way to screw this up I'll find it, trust me.'

He jumped as a knock sounded at the hall door.

'*Cazzo*, he's bloody early!' he hissed. 'Stall him, Lana! If he sees me without socks I'll lose all mystique before we've even gone out.' He darted to his underwear drawer and started chucking out the contents in search of that elusive beast: the matching pair.

'Hi,' I said when I'd opened the door to Cameron, who was looking every bit as nervous as Tom.

'Hi. Um… is your brother playing out?'

I smiled. 'Yeah, he'll be with you in a sec.'

Flash picked that moment to come cannonballing into the hall and throw himself at Cameron, nearly knocking him back down the stairs. Cameron tickled his ears, laughing.

'God, I'm so sorry!' I said. 'He's just a baby; he's still learning good manners.' I wagged a finger at Flash. 'Naughty boy! You don't jump up at people.'

'Aww, no, he's lovely.' Cameron crouched down so Flash could give his cheek a bath. 'Aren't you, eh, little feller? What's his name, Lana?'

'Flash.'

'Ah-ahhh.'

I frowned. 'Sorry?'

'Like the song, right?' Cameron said, grinning. 'You know, from that cheesy old film? Come on, you must sing that every time you call him.'

'Well I'll have to now. Cheers, mate, I'm going to look a right tit down the park singing Queen songs at a sheepdog.'

There was the sound of a throat clearing behind my back, and I turned to find Tom blushing profusely in the doorway of his room. Cameron blinked, as if surprised to see him in something other than the usual T-shirt and jeans. Deano had certainly nailed the Cinderella effect.

'Your date, I think,' I said to Cameron. 'Have fun tonight, lads. Come on, Flash.'

I heard Cameron let out a last murmured 'ah-ahhh' as Tom followed him down the stairs.

When I'd finished locking up the restaurant, I found Tom back from his date and halfway through a bottle of red wine, staring blankly at a documentary about the Amazon rainforest.

'So, how was your evening?' I asked, switching the telly off.

He just groaned and took another gulp of wine.

I plonked myself down next to him. 'That bad, eh?'

'Worse,' he said. 'God, I proper cocked it, sis. I did this embarrassing thing… oh God. I can't even bear to say it.'

'Go on, I bet it wasn't that awful.'

'You weren't there. I was so nervous, I was jabbering any old rubbish. And he said… he said…'

'What?'

'I asked about films he liked and he said something about the new *Star Trek*. And I was panicking what to say back, trying to think of something funny and flirty…'

'Oh no. What was it?'

He groaned and buried his head in his hands. '"Set phasers to stunning."'

'Sweet Jesus.'

'I know, right? If he calls after that it'll be a miracle.'

I tried to rally. 'Maybe not. He might think it was cute. Everyone gets nervous on first dates.'

'And exponentially camper?'

I shrugged. 'Sometimes. Look, did he walk out?'

'No, he laughed. But he was just being polite.'

'You're paranoid, Tommy. Give him a ring tomorrow and see if he wants to go out again. I bet he'll say yes.'

'You must be joking! I'm entering a monastery tomorrow. Monks aren't allowed mobiles, right?'

'Well, you can't get out of it. You'll have to see him at the calendar shoot. In fact you might end up seeing quite a lot of him.'

'Shit! I will, won't I?' His eyes went wide. 'And he'll see quite a lot of me. Oh my God. That'll definitely be the end.'

'Don't be daft. I'm sure you've got the same bits as other blokes.'

'I might not have. What if they're the wrong shape or something? Oh God, what if I get them out and he cracks up laughing?'

'Come on, you've seen others.'

'Not for a while I haven't. And I wasn't paying that much attention to specifics, if I'm honest.' He turned to look at me. 'Hey, reckon I could get a second opinion?'

'Don't look at me, mate.'

'Not you. Deano.'

I frowned. 'Seriously, you want to flop your tackle out for Deano? I'm not sure looking at his boss's bits is covered in his staff contract, you know.'

'Favour to a mate. I just need to know if I'm a hideous mutant or not, help me determine the level of lighting needed if I ever get up the nerve to bring Cameron home.'

'God, you'd think you'd never taken your clothes off for a lad before.'

'It's different now. I'm older, I've got more dignity to lose,' he said. 'You think he would?'

'Knowing him, yeah. Just make sure you ask him before you pop it out, that's all. I don't fancy getting hauled off to an employment tribunal because you've been flashing the chef.'

17

I was propped on my elbow at the restaurant's front desk one exceptionally quiet Thursday when Gerry came in with a blank, distracted look in his eyes.

'God, you're not a customer, are you?' I said. 'Not sure I remember how to deal with them.'

'You have to say "Welcome to Here Be Flagons" and ask what name I booked under.'

'Yeah, all right, Gerry, I was actually joking. So are you? There's probably some of your sheep in the mutton pie if you fancy getting your teeth into a few old friends.'

'No,' he said, still with the strange, distant stare. 'Came to tell you about booking the Temp for the calendar shoot. Roger the Cabin Boy says we can have it a week Saturday.'

'Please don't call him that, it's disturbing. Will he be there to unlock it or do we need to fetch the key?'

'He'll unlock it.' He gazed over my shoulder. 'And he wants to be Mr August.'

'You're kidding me!'

'Wish I were. I've managed to live all my life in this village without seeing what should be for Mrs Collingwood's eyes only. Wouldn't have minded making it to retirement before he started popping the old chap out for everyone to have a look at.'

'Bloody hell, it's rife,' I muttered, thinking about Tom. 'What did you tell him?'

He shrugged. 'What could I tell him, when he knows we're all doing it? Had to agree, didn't I?'

'Holy Christ.' I summoned up an image of Roger in my mind's eye: white-haired, respectable Roger in his military-style band uniform. Then I tried to imagine the uniform away. My eyes went wide with horror.

The weirdest thing was, he was still holding his baton.

'Anyway, the missus sent me to ask if you can recruit anyone,' Gerry said. 'We still need another three models, assuming McLean can get this sauce lad, plus a photographer. Ideally lasses, if there's any you can ask. We've got half as many as blokes.'

I pondered for a minute. 'Well, Jasmine's too young and I know Deb wouldn't do it. I can ask Deano.'

'That's one. Anyone else?'

'Not that I can think of. Maybe Yo-yo can summon up a few lady-shaped people from the WI. Why don't you pop in and ask her on your way home?'

His eyes widened. 'What, go to Yo-yo's by myself?'

I laughed. 'You want to borrow some mace spray?'

'Actually, think I'll ring. Don't want Sue getting the wrong idea. Bye, love.'

He gave me a kiss on the cheek and turned to leave. Once he'd disappeared I headed to the kitchen to swap with Jasmine.

'Roast hog out in ten minutes,' Deano was saying as they bustled about.

'Yes, Chef.'

'Not a second longer or it'll be too dry.'

He looked up when Jasmine didn't answer. 'Did you hear me?'

'Yes, Chef. Not a second too long.'

I shook my head at him. 'Can you stop making her call you that? You're not Gordon Ramsay.'

He jutted his chin. 'It helps maintain a respectful distance between chef and staff.'

'It helps maintain your ego.' I smiled at Jasmine. 'Go on, love, you've done your time in hell's kitchen. I'll take over.'

She looked at Deano and blushed slightly. 'I don't mind doing a bit longer.'

'No, swap with Lana. I fancy a change in company,' Deano said without looking up.

Jasmine's face crumpled, and I gave Deano a subtle nudge. He glanced up.

'Good work tonight though, kid.'

The teenager's blush deepened. 'Thanks, Chef.'

'Well, if you're off duty you can call me Deano. Or the Shagmeister, whichever takes your fancy.'

Jasmine looked uncertain for a moment.

'Joke, Jaz,' Deano said patiently.

'Oh. Right. Bye then.' Still blushing, she left the kitchen.

'You'll have to do something about her,' I said to Deano when we were alone.

'Why, what's up with her?' he said absently, peering into the cooker to check his roast.

'Obvious, isn't it? She fancies you.'

He looked up with a surprised expression. 'The girl? Don't be daft. She's a little child.'

'She's seventeen, Deano. Not that much younger than you.'

'Yeah, if I had Yo-yo Sommerville's tastes.'

'Seven years isn't a lot really.'

'If we were ten years older it mightn't be. There's a massive gap between twenty-four and seventeen.' He nodded to Jasmine's shoulder bag, sitting under one of the work surfaces. 'Take a look at what she's written on that.'

I crouched down to look. 'JH hearts HS. Who's HS, someone from college?'

He shook his head. 'Nope. Harry Styles. You know, your lad from One Direction? She told me she's got a poster of him she kisses every night before bed. Probably trying to make me jealous.'

'OK, OK, point made,' I said, standing up again. 'What're you going to do about it then?'

'What can I do? Not exactly leading her on, am I?'

'No, you're mean as fuck when you're working.'

'Thanks. I try.'

I shook my head in sympathy. 'Poor lass. Well, I'll try to move shifts around so she's in the kitchen as little as possible. It's a bit awkward when she's too young to go on bar but I'll sort something.'

'Probably for the best.' He took his joint out of the oven and inhaled the steam coming off the juices deeply, like a muppet-haired Bisto kid. 'Smell that, Lana. I'm a bloody genius.'

'It does smell good.' I sighed. 'Shame there're so few customers in to appreciate it.'

'Well, more for us. You and Flash can have some for your tea.' He grabbed a ladle and started spooning off the juice to make gravy. 'So how's your Tour de France thingy going then?'

'Oh yeah, something I need to ask you actually.'

'Shoot.'

'Stewart's arranged for the Tour people to visit next month and we thought we'd put a buffet on here. Just a few things to get their tastebuds going. Can I count on you?'

'Am I getting paid?'

'No, sorry. This is a favour. Expenses only.'

'Well, since it's you,' he said. 'Don't get used to it though.'

I slapped his arm gratefully. 'Thanks, Deano, you're a good mate. Oh, there was one other thing.'

'What?'

'Will you come down the Temp a week Saturday and take all your clothes off?'

A lesser man might've been shocked, but this was Deano. He didn't even look up from his gravy.

'For this calendar thing Tom was telling me about?'

'That's it.'

'Yeah, why not?'

'The men I know are not normal,' I muttered.

'One condition though,' he said, glancing up to make eye contact. 'I want to be artistic director as well. Always fancied working with live nudes.'

'I bet you have.'

'Go on, Lana, I'll be awesome. And I'll bring the props and everything. Like you said, I'm our resident perfectionist.'

'You're our resident control freak.'

He shrugged. 'You say tomato...'

The door swung open and Jasmine came back in.

'How's the roast? Table 8 have been waiting twenty minutes.'

'Coming up,' Deano said. 'You can't rush genius, child.' He nudged me. 'Hey, Lana. Have you got a photographer for next Saturday?'

'Not yet, why?'

'Jaz is doing A-level photography. A charity nude calendar would be great for her portfolio.'

'We can't ask Jasmine.'

'Why not?' Jasmine said, looking offended. 'I'm not bad, you know.'

'Well, you're a…' I paused. 'You're a young adult,' I said after a second. 'And we're all crusty old fogies. Wouldn't you be embarrassed?'

She laughed as if the idea was absurd. 'Course not, it's only nudity. We have life models in class all the time.'

'Do you? God, school's changed since my day.'

'Did they have cameras back in the seventies though?'

'Ha! Funny girl. Get back to work.'

She grinned and grabbed the tray of gravy-sloshed hog Deano had served up. 'Think about it though? I'll do a fab job, Lana, honest.'

'All right, all right, I'll think about it. Go on, take that out before Table 8 starve to death.'

'What did you go and do that for?' I hissed when she'd gone. 'Inviting her to take pics of you in your birthday suit is hardly the best way to cure her of a crush.'

'You wouldn't say that if you'd seen me naked.'

I raised an eyebrow. 'Scary, is it?'

'More… intimidating,' he said with a grin.

'Seriously though, Deano. You can't think this'll help.'

He patted my bum reassuringly. 'Don't you worry, Lanasaurus, all part of my plan. She's a kid; it's all windswept kisses and true love when you're that age. Once someone gets their clothes off, all the mystery evaporates. I bet even Harry Styles looks a right prat with the old meat and two veg swinging about between his legs.'

I curled my lip. 'Yeah. Actually, could you forget about saving me any hog? Sudden loss of appetite.'

'Right, that's your lot, sugarplum,' Deano said at the end of the night, pulling off his stripy apron. 'Think you can switch everything off here while I change out of my whites?'

'Yeah, go on. I'll see you tomorrow.'

It took me fifteen minutes to put away the ingredients and turn off the equipment. By the time I emerged, the restaurant was dark except for the always-on Fire Exit signs, their green glow bouncing menacingly off Galahad, the decorative suit of armour we kept propped in a comedy position at the bar.

'Tom?' I called.

No answer. He must've gone up to bed.

I popped into the Ladies to check the light was off, then knocked gently on the door of the Gents to make sure Deano was definitely gone. There was no reply, so I shouldered it open and barged in.

I was met by Tom's back. He was facing away from me holding his waistband out with both thumbs, Deano peering curiously into his pants at the contents.

'Looks perfectly normal to me, mate,' Deano was saying.

'Does yours look like that then?'

'Yeah, give or take. There aren't really that many different models, know what I mean?'

'And you're one hundred per cent positive he won't laugh?'

I cleared my throat, and the two men jumped. Tom's waistband bounced back into place with a comedy twang.

'What, if he hears about you getting it out in restaurants for the chef to have a look at?' I said. 'He'll laugh or scream, one or the other.'

'Busted,' Deano muttered.

Tom frowned. 'Oi. Can't you read, sis? This is a private gentlemen's room. For gentlemen.'

'And yet there's only you two oiks here.' I glared at Deano. 'What did you think you were doing?'

He shrugged. 'Looking at Tom's knob.'

'I could see that. I meant, what for?'

'Well, because he asked me to. He is half the boss, you know.' He glanced down at my breasts. 'Always happy to extend you the same courtesy, by the way.'

'I bet.' I jerked my head towards the door. 'Go on, bugger off home.'

Deano shot me a last grin as he left.

'When you said you were going to ask him, I didn't think you meant at work!' I hissed to Tom. 'What if a customer had come in?'

'Don't be daft, we're closed. The last one left half an hour ago.'

'So are you happy now?'

'Dunno. It was kind of reassuring. But then it might look weird when I've got the rest of my kit off, mightn't it?'

'It's meant to look like that though. All boys look weird with their clothes off.'

Tom snorted. 'Ta very much. Like your lot look so great.'

'Well, you'll find out what Cameron thinks a week Saturday.' I hooked my arm through his and guided him out of the loo. 'Gerry's booked the Temp for us. It's hammertime, Tommy.'

18

With a bathrobe under my arm and my heart in my ears, I walked with Deano and Tom to the Temp for the calendar shoot.

'Oh my God oh my God oh my God,' Tom muttered. 'Whose bright idea was this?'

'Yours. Thanks a sodding bunch, bruv.'

'Give over, it'll be great,' Deano said, hugging his box of props. He was fiercely guarding the contents until we got to the shoot. 'This might lead to a whole new career for us.' He wiggled his hips slightly, as if his jeans were uncomfortable.

'What's up with you?' I asked.

'I'm commando. Got a chafing issue going on.' He shrugged as both sets of eyes turned to him. 'What? Seemed a waste of time finding clean undies if I was just going to take them off again.'

I snorted. 'You are one classy bastard.'

'And you are well sexist, Lana Donati,' he said, slapping his superior face on. 'You're supposed to find it arousing. Boys do when girls don't wear pants.'

'Ahem,' Tom said.

'Present company excepted.'

'Well, boys are weird,' I said. The door of the Temp

loomed large before us like the gateway to hell, or at least the gateway to uncomfortable public nudity. 'OK, lads. No backing out now.'

In the meeting room, the other models were milling about, chatting: our five committee members, plus Roger Collingwood and a handful of the more adventurous Ladies Who Lunch to redress the male/female balance. Yolanda was already in her dressing gown: a very short pink kimono with little hearts all over it.

I made my way over to Stewart.

'Where's your cousin?' I asked. 'He is coming, isn't he?'

'He'll be here. Harper's always fashionably late.'

I glanced up into his face. He looked like he'd had a sleepless night or three, his eyes puffy and tired against pale skin.

'You OK?' I asked.

'Fine. I'm fine,' he said absently. 'See you later, Lana.' Before I could say anything else, he'd wandered off to stand on his own by the window.

I'd been noticing it more and more: the change in him since he'd turned up in my life again. There were still flashes of the old Stewart – that laid-back, wry humour that had first drawn me to him; the warm smile that, hard as I tried, had a nasty habit of making various bits of me flutter. But there were other times, like today, when he seemed morose and tired. When he ended conversations abruptly, or sat in brooding silence, staring into the distance. Sometimes, even, when from the state of his eyes I'd swear he'd been crying. He usually managed to pull himself out of it when people started to notice, but I could tell it was an effort.

In spite of everything, I couldn't help feeling for the lad. Quitting cycling had obviously broken him up a lot more than he was willing to let on.

'So what now, guys?' Tom asked the room at large, jerking me out of my Stewart musings.

'We're just waiting for Mr Brady, then we can make a start,' Roger said, taking over in typical businesslike fashion. I was starting to think the man had been a closet naturist for years. It was true what they said: it was always the quiet ones.

'Young Jasmine is in the main hall setting up,' he continued, 'and we can use the shower room to change.'

'So, Deano, what've you brought?' I said.

'Aha. I'm very glad you asked. First our Miss July 2014 – one Lana Donati...' He rummaged in his box of tricks and pulled out a couple of bicycle horns: the big, old-fashioned kind with a brass trumpet and black rubber bulb on one end. 'For you.'

I cast a puzzled look at them. 'To do what with?'

'To hold in front of your boobs so I can put the caption "nice hooters" underneath.'

I shook my head. 'Oh, no. Not a chance, mate.'

'"A honking good pair"?'

'Absolutely not. I thought this calendar was supposed to be tasteful, not a *Carry On* throwback.'

'And I thought it was supposed to be funny.'

I looked at Tom. 'It was your idea. Tasteful or funny?'

'I think funny'll sell better,' he said with an apologetic grimace. 'We're not trying to rival Spencer Tunick, are we? It's about giving the village a laugh.'

'Traitor.' I folded my arms. 'Well the village aren't having a laugh at my honking good pair, thanks very much. I told you: completely covered or I'm not doing it.'

'But you can't be, can you?' Deano said. 'It's a nude calendar.'

'You know what I mean. All the important bits.'

He waved a hand impatiently. 'All right, we'll come back to you.' He nodded to Yolanda. 'Yo-yo, or should I say Miss May: a couple of smaller ones for you.' He handed Yolanda a pair of ordinary bike bells.

'And what will my caption be?' Yolanda asked.

'How about "village bike"?' Sue said brightly from a nearby table where she was drinking tea with Gerry and Cameron. Yolanda shot her a dirty look.

'For a lady like you it has to be "ding-dong", of course,' Deano said, his smile dripping charm.

She giggled. 'Oh, I love it! Thank you, darling.'

'What about the bottom bit then?' I asked.

'What about it?' Deano said. 'Yo-yo's a modern, enlightened woman. I'm sure she doesn't mind the village seeing her bottom bits.'

'Especially as most of the village has already seen them,' Sue muttered.

'But it's no good covering boobs then putting everything else on display, is it?' I said.

'Aha!' Deano lifted a finger in the air. 'There, my dear Lana, you have hit on my cup de grass. My arc de triomphe. My piece of the resistance.'

'Which is?'

'Wait a minute. I'll just go fetch it.'

He disappeared, coming back a second later carrying a huge bit of topiary in the shape of a bike.

'Jean at the florist's made it for us,' he panted as he put it down. 'To protect the ladies' modesty. I've got bike pumps and helmets for us lads.' He winked at Yolanda. 'In a range of sizes.'

I squinted suspiciously at him. 'Did you get that so you could use the caption "cracking bush"?'

He drew himself up. 'Do you mind? I have got some class, you know.'

'Did you though?'

'I did, yeah.'

'Sorry, but I'm not catching a word of this,' Roger said. 'What is that fearful row outside?'

He was right, a terrible racket had sprung up while we'd been talking: raised voices and some sort of repetitive clicking sound. By the window, Stewart flicked back a curtain to investigate.

He jerked it hurriedly back into place.

'Shit, there's a load of photographers!' he said. 'It's like Cup Final day at Valley Parade out there. What the hell's going on?'

I just shrugged, looking bewildered. The same look of bewilderment was reflected on every face in the room.

Every face except one.

'Ah. Yes. I had been meaning to say something,' Yolanda said with a guilty smile. 'I may have been rather naughty.'

'So come on, Yolanda,' Stewart said patiently. 'What exactly did you do?'

'I just sent out a teensy press release on behalf of the group, that's all,' she said, flushing under his gaze.

'But what did the press release say?' he demanded. 'You don't get photographers turning up in these numbers for a village's poxy nude calendar. A royal visit, maybe.'

'I said we were doing it to raise money for the viaduct. The human-interest angle, you know?'

He leaned towards her. 'And you said something else. Didn't you?'

'I said… you'd be in it.'

'And?'

'And… and Harper Brady.' She looked up to meet our accusing stares. 'Well, what would be the point having a famous TV star here if we didn't publicise it?'

'The publicity comes *after*, Yo-yo!' I snapped. 'God, once they find out Brady's in some tiny village hall with his clothes off they'll break down the door. That must be story of the year.'

Stewart groaned. 'He'll bolt when he sees that lot.'

I turned to Roger. 'Could we sneak him in the bottom way, through the cellar?'

'He'd be rather recognisable coming through the village,' Roger said.

Deano had been looking thoughtful throughout the conversation. Now he spoke up.

'I may have a typically genius Deano Teasdale plan hatching. Stewart, can you text your cousin and tell him you'll meet him just outside Egglethwaite?'

'Why?'

He reached into his box and pulled out a green clown wig and red nose. 'I brought these for a circus-themed shoot I'm planning for August.' He nodded to Yolanda. 'And we'll need that kimono off you, Yo-yo.'

She looked hesitant. 'But I'll be cold.'

'Oh right. Now she gets coy,' Sue muttered. 'Come on, Yo-yo, get it off. This is all your fault.'

'Fine.' She wriggled out of her robe and handed it to Deano, then sank back into her chair and started examining her nails in a state of completely unembarrassed nakedness. I shot her an envious glance. It must be nice to feel that comfortable in nothing but your own skin.

'So what's your plan, Deano?' Tom asked.

'Stewart's going to dress Brady up in these,' he said, shoving the pile of assorted disguise into Stewart's arms. 'Then they're going to jog back here and come in the cellar way. If anyone asks, they're a fun runner and his coach.'

I lifted my eyebrows. 'Hey, that's not bad.'

'Thanks. I'll claim my reward snog later.'

'No you won't.' I paused. 'But go on, I'll hold up the bike horns. Yo-yo's inspiring me.'

Deano grinned. 'Good girl. Off you go then, Stewart. We'll start the shoot.'

Twenty minutes later a breathless Stewart was back, closely followed by a seriously pissed-off clown in a sexy kimono.

'...never been so humiliated in my life,' the clown panted, obviously rounding off a much longer bollocking. 'You seriously owe me for this, Stew.'

'Suits you, Harper,' I said with a grin.

He blinked at me over the top of his big red nose. 'Do I know you?'

'Only from when I haunt your dreams, clown boy.'

'Why am I picturing you in a leather corset?' Harper's

eyes widened. 'You're not that dominatrix from Kyle's after-party, are you? Look, I was really pissed or I wouldn't normally be into that, and I meant to return the whip, I swear—'

'No I bloody well am not.' I hastily changed the subject. 'Who's next, Deano? We'd better rush this through before the press outside realise we've done the dirty on them.'

'You can be then,' he said, fishing the humongous bike horns back out of his props box and giving them a couple of comedy parps.

I winced. 'Do I have to?'

'Course you have to. We can't take July out of next year just to save your modesty, treacle.' He patted my arm. 'Don't worry, it's only me and Jaz.'

'Yep. Only two-thirds of my staff staring at me in the buff. Jim Dandy then, eh?'

After I'd nipped into the shower room to discard my clothes and put on my bathrobe, I tiptoed back into the main hall. Jasmine was fiddling with her tripod in front of the bike hedge, a big white screen behind it. Assorted bike-shaped shadows from out of Stewart's hire stock lurked around the room. The lighting was low, but everything was still far too visible for my liking.

'Hi, boss,' Jasmine said with a bright smile. 'You all right?'

'Not in the mood for small talk, Jaz. I just want to get this over with, OK?'

'Oh, no need to be nervous,' she said. 'Trust me, I do this all the time. Just chuck your robe over the chair there.'

The door swung open and Deano came in, just as I'd discarded my robe and was trying to simultaneously hide my naughty bits and my wobbly bits behind his cracking bush.

'Er, hi.' I blushed deeply, covering my breasts with both hands. Unfortunately the hands weren't really up to the job and there was quite a bit of flesh spillage round the fingers.

'Hi yourself.' He grinned. 'Just how I imagined them. Right, let's get on with it.'

He came round behind me and put one hand on my bare hip. My eyes shot wide open and I jumped forward about a foot.

'Deano, get your hands off me!'

'Just putting you in position,' he said in a surprised tone. 'None of the others complained.'

'Well you don't work for them, do you?' I hissed. 'Just tell me how you want me: no touching. And you can get out from behind me as well. I don't want you looking at my backside.'

And just as I removed my hands from my bare breasts to push him away, in strode a de-clowned Harper Brady.

'Look, this is taking ages. Can I go next?' he demanded. 'I've got places to—'

He stopped short, staring at my uncovered breasts. I'd always thought dropping jaws were something you only found in books, but I could swear Harper's chin actually hit the floor.

I clapped my hands over my nipples, wincing in embarrassment.

'Are those real?' he asked in a hushed, reverent voice.

'None of your business, mate! What the hell do you think you're doing? Get out!'

'Doesn't matter. They are; I can tell.'

'Funnily enough, yes,' I snapped. 'Restaurant salaries don't tend to cover major cosmetic enhancement, you might be surprised to learn.'

'Restaurant... hey!' He pointed at me. 'I do know you! That waitress from the weird place with all the pigs' heads, right? You pretended you didn't know who I was and I pretended to be a pain in the arse.' He grinned at the memory.

I turned to Deano. 'Why the fuck is he still talking to me?' I muttered. 'Get him out, can you? I feel vulnerable enough as it is.'

Deano marched forward and grabbed Harper by the arm. 'Come on, mate. No coming in while the ladies are exhibiting, eh?'

'Yeah, yeah,' Harper said, jerking his arm away. He was still staring as if hypnotised at my breasts. 'I'm just talking.'

'No, you're just leaving.' Deano grabbed his arm again and guided him forcefully to the door. 'You can chat when everyone's got their clothes on.'

'Bye – er, waitress,' Harper called as Deano ejected him, waving to me over his shoulder.

Jasmine was gazing at Deano with worshipful admiration. 'That was amazing,' she breathed.

'Thanks.' He frowned. 'What was?'

'The way you defended her honour. Like a knight from the olden days, all strong and chivalrous.'

'Oh Jesus,' he muttered. 'You spend too much time in the Middle Ages, Jaz. Let's get on with it, eh?' He handed me my horns. 'Here's your honkers, Lana. Just smile seductively and try not to slouch.'

*

When I was done, I went back into the meeting room and nodded to Harper, who was chatting to Stewart.

'OK, pervert, you're up.'

'Right. Er, hey, what was your name again?'

'Never you mind.'

Harper frowned for a second. 'I know! It's Lana, right? Lana... Italian.'

I smiled. 'Nice try.'

'Why did you call him a pervert?' Stewart asked when Harper had gone to disrobe.

'Because he barged into the hall while I was starkers and stared at my breasts for a full ten minutes.'

Stewart winced. 'Oh God, he didn't.'

'He bloody did; I was there. I remember because it was the first time I'd had my arse on display in that hall since a split leotard incident at a ballet recital when I was five.'

'Tell me he didn't ask if they were real.'

I frowned. 'He did actually. Why, does he make a habit of this sort of thing?'

'No, he's just got a... you might call it a fetish.'

'For big boobs? Him and every heterosexual bloke in the known world, mate.'

'All right, not a fetish then. I guess he just sees a lot of implants in his line of work, so he's built up a thing about the... you know, ones like yours. Sorry.'

He was blushing beetroot now. I was quite enjoying it.

'And what's your preferred size, Stewart?' I asked with a teasing grin. I couldn't help myself. Getting my kit off in the Temp had obviously been liberating.

He managed a smile through his blushes. 'All depends who they're attached to.'

Fifteen minutes later Harper came back in and jerked his head at the door.

'You're next, Stew. Mr December apparently.' He chucked Stewart a Santa hat. 'The lad said you'll be needing this.'

'Cheers,' Stewart said, placing the hat on his head.

'I don't think that's where he wants you to put it.'

'Ah. I see.' Stewart took the hat off again and stretched it. 'In that case, we're going to need a bigger hat.'

There was a muttered 'oi' in my ear. I turned to find Tom lurking behind me.

'Oi what?'

'Did I hear you doing boob-related flirting with Stewart McLean not so long ago?'

'No,' I said, colouring. 'I was just winding him up. He managed to turn it into flirting.'

'I thought you didn't like him.'

I watched Stewart's broad back leaving the room. 'I don't.'

'Well, he seems to have lost his other fan anyway,' Tom said, nodding to Yolanda. She'd reassumed her kimono and was clustered around Harper Brady with the other women from Ladies Who Lunch, hanging on his every word.

'You didn't really go to the front lines to research *Soar*, Mr Brady?' one of the women was saying.

'Yes. It was dangerous, of course, but nothing compared to what our troops face every day.' Harper shook his head. 'Those courageous men and women.'

'Oh, you're so brave,' Yolanda breathed, practically elbowing the other ladies aside so she could shuffle closer.

'Ugh.' I turned away and nodded to Cameron, still chatting to Gerry and Sue. For Tom's sake they seemed to be making a special effort to take the lad under their wing. 'So, did you talk to him?'

He flushed. 'Briefly. He wants to know when we can go out again.'

'Ha! Told you.'

Once everyone had done their shoot, with a final joint one for Stewart and Harper to go on the cover – star appeal, Yolanda reckoned – it was time to leave.

'Sorry, Yo-yo, we'll be needing your kimono again,' Stewart said. 'There's still a few photographers. I'll have to sneak Harper out the way he came.'

'Not a problem, darling,' a now fully dressed Yolanda said, handing it to him from the back of her chair. She lowered her voice. 'Feel free to hang on to it if you'd like, Mr Brady.'

Harper's lip curled slightly. 'It's OK. Stew can bring it back.'

'I bet she'll never wash it again,' Tom muttered in my ear.

'Er, hey. Lana,' Harper said. 'Can I have a word?'

'If you must. What?'

He took my elbow and guided me out of earshot of the others.

'You're a bit different, you know that?' he said when we were in semi-privacy.

'Are you on about my boobs again?'

'Not just them.' He dipped his head to look into my face. 'You don't like me much, do you?'

'Hard to believe, right?'

'Look, I'm sorry about that night in the restaurant. I was being a prick. It was uncalled for and I apologise.'

I blinked. 'Oh. Er, OK. Thanks.'

'So now we've got that out the way, I thought me and you could maybe go for a drink some time. What do you say?'

I frowned. 'Sorry – you think I don't like you so you want me to go for a drink with you?'

'Yeah. It gets sickening, everyone blowing smoke up your arse 24/7. You're not like that, it's sort of refreshing.' He grinned. 'And I bet I could get you to like me. Love a challenge.'

'I don't think so, Harper.'

'Why not? Apologised, didn't I?'

'And I accepted. It doesn't mean I'm obligated to go out with you.'

He glanced down at my chest again. He seemed to find it hard to pull his eyes away now he'd seen it in all its uncovered wobbly glory. 'Go on, love, don't be a mug. I am Harper Brady. You know... rich? Famous? Borderline national treasure?'

'You just asked me out because I don't care. Now you want me to go out with you because I should?' I shook my head. 'You're a weird bloke.'

'Think about it, OK?' He pressed a business card into my hand. 'Give me a call when you come to your senses.'

'I wouldn't hold your breath.'

'You will though.' He turned to Stewart. 'Right. Where's that sodding clown wig then?'

19

The next meeting was at Flagons. Debbie was off sick so Tom and I wanted to be on hand in case we were needed. It felt daft putting our serious faces on and talking bats with the lady from the wildlife group in our medieval get-up, but such was life. My life anyway.

Stewart was the last group member to arrive.

'Evening, fellow naturists,' he said with a grin as he sank into his seat. 'Any news on Egglethwaite's first foray into the soft porn market?'

'Apart from Gerry's youthful career as an adult film star, but we don't talk about that,' Tom said.

Cameron laughed. 'I wondered about the moustache.'

Gerry glared at them. 'Oi. Watch it, kids, or I'll set my missus on you.'

'Keep your voices down,' I hissed. 'The customers can hear. I don't need a reputation as a porn star on top of this corset, thanks.'

'You going to go medieval on our asses?' Stewart said.

'Funny.'

'So have the calendars arrived?' he asked in a lower voice.

'Not yet,' Tom said. 'Jasmine's picking them up from the printer's this week.'

'I can't wait to see how I look,' Yolanda breathed, her eyes glittering with girlish excitement. 'Oh, and the rest of you, of course.'

'No one's talking to you, Yo-yo,' Sue said. 'You made a right hash of things with the papers, didn't you?'

In spite of our best efforts sneaking him in and out, one of the photographers had somehow managed to snap a long-lens pic of Harper in his ridiculous kimono-and-clown outfit. It appeared next day in one of the larger regionals, along with the full story leaked by Yolanda and a caption that said 'Running away to join the circus, Mr Brady?' The day after, the photo – minus the calendar story – was in most of the nationals as well.

'Nonsense, Susan,' Yolanda said, waving a hand. 'Everyone knows there's no such thing as bad publicity.'

'I can tell you on good authority Harper doesn't,' Stewart said, rubbing his ear. 'I nearly went deaf when he rang.'

'She's right though,' said Gerry, who'd been appointed group treasurer. 'I had a load of advance orders after that photo came out. Ladies after a pic of your sauce man mostly, much as I'd like to claim credit myself.'

'How much have we made so far then?' Cameron asked.

He looked down at a sheet of paper. 'At £7.99 a pop... about £600 after print costs.'

'Bloody hell!' Tom said. 'That's not bad, is it?'

'So. I think someone owes someone an apology, don't they?' Yolanda said, sending Sue a smug look.

'Don't push it, Yo-yo.'

'While £600's good for starters, it's a long way off twenty-five grand,' I said. 'We'd better get planning the next fundraiser if we're going to be quids in by January. And we need to get everyone in the village on board, organising coffee mornings and that. We'll never make that sort of money on our own.'

'First things first.' Stewart nodded to a woman scanning the tables for us. 'I think our guest's here.'

I suppose in the back of my mind I'd expected Batwoman to be some sort of ecowarrior stereotype, all dreadlocks and no deodorant. But the person heading towards us looked like any other thirty-something, apart from one thing: she was clearly seven holy shades of pissed off.

'God, she looks terrifying,' Tom whispered. 'What're these bats called again? Barbie dolls?'

'Barbastelles, pillock.'

'Have you got a plan then?'

'Don't be daft. When do I ever have a plan? Er, hi,' I said with a sheepish grimace as Batwoman reached our table. 'Sienna, is it? Lana Donati. I think Andy filled you in.'

She grabbed the hand I offered and shook it vigorously: almost aggressively, in fact.

'Ms Edge. Let's save first names for if or when we're all friends, shall we?'

With that she sank into a seat and folded her arms. I could see her sneering at my corset and cap.

'Oh. Yes. Sorry about the gear,' I said. 'My brother and I had to come dressed for work, just in case we're needed.'

'It seems to me that if this issue really mattered to you, you'd have taken the night off.'

'Well, we've got a staff member off sick, you see,' Tom mumbled, flushing with anxiety. I saw Cameron give his knee a reassuring squeeze under the table.

'So, Ms Edge,' Stewart said. 'We hear you like bats. Er, we also think bats rock. They can... see in the dark.'

I shot him a look.

'What he means is, we're all really big on bats here,' I said, smiling ingratiatingly. 'There's nothing we'd like more than to give them what they need so we can get what we need. I'm sure we can find a solution that makes everyone happy: bats and people.'

'Pffft. People,' Sienna snapped. 'What're people? Just another animal. And yet they think they own the earth: lords of all creation.'

I blinked. 'Well, no, I don't think we—'

She leaned forward to stare into my face. 'Have you ever held a motherless baby bat, Miss Donati?'

'Er, no. I mean, I would. You know, if it was lonely...'

'I have. Beautiful, empathic creatures. They can read your heart.'

'Um, they're certainly great, but that does seem a bit unlikely. We've never even met.'

She scowled. 'You don't care about the barbastelles at all, do you?'

'We do, promise!' Cameron said. 'Honestly, I know this matters. I was conservation officer for my students' union.'

Tom blinked. 'Were you?'

'Yeah. I'm a zoology graduate, aren't I?' He turned an earnest gaze on Batwoman. 'But people matter too, Ms Edge. This community matters. We can't just close this off because it's a bit of rock out of thousands of bits of rock the bats could call home.'

'They chose this home. Who are we to tell them they're wrong?' Sienna Edge leaned across the table to glare at him, but Cameron didn't flinch. 'Typical human arrogance,' she breathed. 'We have to stop thinking we outrank every species on earth.'

'You're right, of course you're right,' Cameron said. The rest of us just sat back, speechless with admiration, as his eyes fired with passion. 'But what built the viaduct? Human arrogance. It's not about rank, it's about living together and sharing what we have. Fighting for the greatest good for the greatest number of people. Anyway, that's what I believe.'

'Jesus Christ,' I muttered to Tom. 'Your boyfriend's amazing.'

He blinked. 'He is a bit, isn't he?'

'Bats are people too,' Sienna snapped.

'No they're *not*! They're bloody bats!' Cameron sighed. 'Not that that means they shouldn't have rights. God knows, I've fought for it myself. But we need some perspective here.'

'So it's the usual colonial bastard response, is it? Wipe them out and move in?'

'Why shouldn't we move them?' Cameron demanded. 'We've been told translocation can be done with minimal loss of life.'

'Because minimal means some. That species is endangered: every life is precious.'

Customers had started to turn now, noticing the raised voices.

'Cam,' Tom said quietly.

'Let's calm down,' Cameron said to Sienna, leaning back in his chair. 'I'd like us to be on the same side.'

Batwoman sneered. 'The side of the greater good, right? The greater good for Man, as usual.'

'The greater good for all,' Cameron said patiently. 'Why

did you come tonight, Ms Edge? To tell us off or to find a way forward?'

'To talk you out of it, clearly.'

'Well, that's not an option, clearly,' he said, sweeping a hand around the table. 'We want to do right by the bats. But a man called Phil Donati who's not here any more cared a lot about this, and a lot of people who are still here, still do. So it's compromise or a fight. And I think I'm speaking for everyone when I say I'd prefer the former.'

'And I wouldn't,' Sienna said, jumping to her feet. 'I came here to help you see sense. Well, you had your chance. You'll be hearing from me.' She kicked back her chair and stormed out.

Stewart blinked. 'Well that escalated.'

Cameron pushed back his floppy hair, slightly breathless. 'Yeah, sorry, guys. Really hope I haven't cocked it up for us. It's just an issue I get a bit exercised about, you know?'

'No, you were fab,' I said. 'Better arguments than we'd have made.'

'Sexiest thing I ever saw,' Tom muttered.

Cameron grinned. 'Well there's more to me than chips, you know.'

'Hey, if you're not doing anything important right now, how about that second date?'

'We're not done, are we?'

'Nope, you two're done,' I said, giving Tom's back a pat. 'I'll fill you in on anything important tomorrow. Oh, and there's a bottle of chianti in the kitchenette. I won't miss it if you want to help yourselves.'

'If you're sure we're not needed.' Cameron was barely looking at us, his eyes fixed on Tom. 'Night then.'

When they'd disappeared upstairs, Stewart grinned at me.

'Those crazy kids.'

'I know. Suckers for bat-related foreplay.'

Sue elbowed Gerry. 'Oi. Stop looking disapproving, you miserable old fogey.'

'I wasn't!'

'Yes you were. Times've changed, Gerry Lightowler. Young Tom deserves his share of love, same as we all do.'

'I know.' He sighed. 'Well, he's a good lad, that Cameron. I don't disapprove; I've just got that sort of face.'

Sue nodded. 'Melted bulldog. We had noticed.' She nudged Yolanda on her other side. 'Another one bites the dust, eh?'.

Yolanda shrugged. 'Plenty more fish.' She shot Stewart a suggestive grin. 'Still, he should really have given my elderflower gin a try.'

I waved a hand. 'Never mind them. What about fundraisers?'

'But we don't know what Batwoman's going to do yet,' Stewart said.

I frowned. 'How did you know that's what I call her?'

'I didn't. That's just what I call her.'

'Oh. Right. Well, I don't think that should stop us planning. She's not much more than a gob on legs at the moment, is she?'

Gerry nodded. 'Lana's right. We've got a lot of money to make in the next few months.'

'I think our group should be looking at big moneymakers and encouraging the village to plan smaller ones,' Yolanda said. 'Ladies Who Lunch will do something, of course.'

'And I'm sure the band will,' I said. 'What about your morris men, Gerry? Sponsored pub crawl?'

Gerry looked offended. 'We're not all about drinking, you know.'

'Why, what else is there?'

'Sometimes we go watch the rugby.' He shrugged. 'OK, we'll do something. What about this group though? Any ideas?'

'I wondered about a Halloween event,' I said. 'We could call it The Boneshaker. Like an old bike, see?'

Stewart nodded approvingly. 'I like that. Hey, not just a pretty face, are you?'

I blushed. 'Thanks. You think it could work then?'

'I do. What's more, my shop'll sponsor it. How does all your publicity materials covered and a £1000 donation to the viaduct sound?'

'Really, Stew?'

'Really.' He flashed me a warm smile, and I blushed deeper when I realised what I'd just called him.

'And you could be the face of it, couldn't you, darling?' Yolanda said, resting her hand on his arm.

He hesitated. 'I'm not sure about that, Yo-yo. I don't cycle now.'

'You're well-known among people who follow the sport though.'

'To an extent,' he said. 'But I've never been comfortable in the limelight. Maybe I can get us someone else.'

I groaned. 'If you say Harper Brady I'm going to need a drink.'

'No, not Harper,' he said. 'I was thinking someone from the cycling world.'

'But what will the event be?' Sue said.

'Let's all go away and have a brainstorm,' I said. 'I'm sure we can come up with something.'

20

'Where's Cam?' I asked Tom next morning when he joined me on the sofa, yawning.

'Asleep. All tuckered out, poor little chap.'

I smiled. 'Not surprised. So he didn't laugh then?'

'Nope. If anything he seemed quite impressed.'

'See? Told you you were worrying over nothing.'

He drew himself up. 'You watch what you're calling nothing. No way to talk about a love god's equipment.'

'All right, that's enough. Some equipment little sisters don't need to think about.' I nodded to four square envelopes on the coffee table. 'Speaking of, look what came while you were in bed. Models' advance copies.'

'The calendars! Did you have a look?'.

'No. I was waiting for moral support.'

'Why are there four?'

'One each for me, you, Cameron and Stewart. Jasmine asked if we could bob his over when he's up.'

'Well go on then, open one.'

I grimaced. 'Don't think I can bear it. You do it.'

'Hang on, let me fetch Cam first,' Tom said. 'This is worth waking him up for.'

Ten minutes later, the pair of them joined me, Cameron

in an old dressing gown of Tom's with his floppy hair adorably rumpled. I smiled when I noticed them holding hands.

'Morning, Lana,' Cameron said with a little blush. 'Hope you didn't mind me staying over.'

'Don't be daft. You know you're always welcome.' I shuffled up on the sofa to make room for them both.

Flash was curled in his bed, unconvincingly pretending to be asleep, but his ears pricked when he heard Cameron's voice. As soon as the lads sat down, he sprang into Cam's lap to lick his face.

'You've got a friend there,' I said, laughing. 'He must sense you're an animal lover. Flash can smell opportunities to get himself spoilt.'

'Well, he's come to the right man.' Cameron gave him a rough jiggle and the little dog wagged his tail vigorously. 'I'll spoil him rotten.'

'Do you have pets?'

'No, my mum reckons they're unhygienic. Me and my sister must've wasted half our childhoods begging for something fur-bearing and the best we got was a bloody stick insect. Larry.'

'You'd better not just like me for my dog, Cam,' Tom said, slinging an arm around his boyfriend's shoulders.

'He is a very nice dog.' Cameron leaned over to give Tom a kiss. 'But you're not bad either.'

'So which of you soppy gits wants to open these calendars?' I asked.

'I would but there's a dog on me,' Cameron said. 'I'd hate to disturb him.'

'Oh, very convenient.' Tom grabbed one of the envelopes.

'All right, cowards, I'll do it. The only person I was worried about seeing me naked has had the worst; the rest of the village are welcome to a perve.'

Cam shook his head. 'Those lucky bastards.'

'I know, right?' Tom ripped across the envelope and yanked out the calendar, covering his eyes with his other hand. 'So, is it bad?'

'Depends what you think of Harper Brady in his birthday suit,' I said.

The cover showed Harper and Stewart appearing to push a bike each up a cobbled hill like they were in a nuddy Hovis bread ad. Both were starkers apart from Stewart's helmet and Harper's army cap – a nod to his role in *Soar*, I assumed – with a bike-mounted water bottle each to protect their modesties. Still, they weren't leaving much to the imagination. One knock to those bottles...

'What happened to "tasteful, just a hint of flesh"?' Cameron asked.

'We put Deano in charge.' I snatched the calendar off Tom. 'Honestly, lads, would you look at them. It's not natural, that, is it?'

'What?' Cameron said.

'Well, six packs. You'd think they hadn't even heard of Toblerone. Freakish, I call it.'

'And yet you're still staring,' Tom said.

'I know, I don't know what's wrong with me. It's like I can't look away.'

He grabbed the calendar back. 'Give us that. You can perve at Stewart later. We've twelve months to get through yet.' He handed it to Cameron. 'You do it. It'll be less traumatic for you.'

Cameron opened it at random and peered tentatively inside, then hastily closed it again.

'Oh God. It's Yolanda.'

'Worse than we thought?' I said.

'Let's just say whoever taught Jasmine Photoshop has a lot to answer for.' He flung open the calendar and held it up.

'It's... very clever,' Tom said hoarsely when we'd scooped our jaws from our laps.

'Amazing what computers can do nowadays,' I mumbled.

'Would you say there were maybe one or two more flamingoes than there needed to be though?' Cameron said.

'The flamingoes aren't so bad,' Tom said. 'The unicorn: maybe a shade too far.'

'Hey. You remember that panto where she sang "Nobody Loves a Fairy When She's Forty" in a glittery tutu while dangling from the Temp roof?' I asked Tom. 'Getting a few flashbacks.'

The photo was certainly very... Yolanda. Jasmine had taken Yo-yo's hair as a starting point and superimposed her on the pinkest of fantasy scenes, rife with flamingoes, rainbows, cherry blossom trees and – for some reason – a unicorn.

Yolanda herself, much as I hated to admit it, looked great in her fairy wings and tiara. She was flashing some cheeky bum and side boob as she cycled away on a sparkly pink bike, giving a suggestive wink back over her shoulder.

'Perky, isn't she?' I said. 'Hope I look like that from behind when I'm her age.'

'Oh God, enough, please,' Cam said with a groan. 'She was my sister's Brownie leader. Come on, who's next?'

'Let's save ourselves till last,' Tom said. 'Once we've seen what a tit everyone else looks, it'll soften the blow.'

'Agreed,' I said. 'Find Roger, that should be good for a laugh.'

Cameron flicked through to August and held it up.

'Bloody hell! He's not above letting it all hang out,' Tom said, eyes wide.

Cameron peered round to look. 'They've only got little handlebars, them unicycles, haven't they?'

Roger was in the green wig that had so suited Harper Brady. Under his face paint he looked just as stern and pompous as ever, almost like he'd forgotten he was done up as a unicycling sex clown and thought he was chairing a meeting. Jasmine had superimposed him on a big top scene, where a lion was eyeing his backside quizzically. Underneath was the caption 'Show us your red nose, Rodge!'

'Well I don't think band practice will ever be the same,' I said after a minute.

'Or a trip to the circus,' Cameron said. 'Just when I'd finally got over my childhood fear of clowns...'

'You'd better hope he never forgets his baton, Lana,' Tom said. 'God knows what he'd whip out to conduct with.'

I shook my head. 'Upstanding community member Roger Collingwood. Who knew, eh?'

Cam flinched. 'Please don't say upstanding member. My eyes are burning.'

'Hey, sis, you going to have a look at December?' Tom said with a grin.

'Who was December again?'

'Like you don't remember.' Tom nudged Cameron. 'Lana's got a thing for Stewart McLean.'

'Yeah, I'd noticed,' Cam said.

'I have not!' I paused. 'Wait. What do you mean, you'd noticed?'

'Come on, Lana, everyone's noticed. You're always blushing at him.'

'That is not true. I never blush at him. I'm not even sure I like him half the time.'

'You fancy him though.'

'I don't. Shut up or I'm taking my dog back.'

Tom was peeping into the calendar. 'So you won't want to see December then, Lana. Since you don't fancy him.'

I attempted a casual shrug. 'I could take it or leave it.'

'You can see his bum in it.'

Sighing, I held out my hand. 'Give.'

You could see quite a lot of his bum. Actually you could see quite a lot of all of him. Deano had got him crouching down pretending to pump up a tyre in the snow, one knee raised to hide the essentials but with pretty much everything else on show. I couldn't help staring at the firm, muscular buttocks; imagining them shifting enticingly under the taut flesh as he cycled…

Oh, and a typical Deano caption to cheapen it: 'Nice pump action.'

'So can we take it from the drool all that not fancying Stewart McLean stuff was bollocks then?' Tom said.

'I'm not drooling.'

'Please. If we weren't here you'd be licking the page.'

'All right, so I can't help it,' I said, still staring. 'I'm genetically programmed to look at fit hunter-gatherers' bums. That's just evolution. It doesn't mean anything.'

Tom turned to Cameron and raised his eyebrows.

'Deluded.'

Cameron nodded. 'Sad really. Poor sexually frustrated Lana.'

'Right. No more puppy cuddles for you.' I reached for Flash and half-coaxed, half-dragged him on to my knee. 'I miss the old days when I only had one knobhead taking the piss out of me in the morning. Just because you two are flush with the glow of having just had it off.'

'Oh right, take all the romance out of it,' Tom said. 'So what're you going to do about your crush on Stew then?'

'I don't know. Ignore it till it goes away, I suppose.'

'Great job so far.' He snatched away the calendar I was still transfixed by. 'Here, give us that. I know how to cure you.' He flicked through until he found Gerry and Sue, who'd done a joint shoot, and held it up in front of me. 'There.'

'Yurgh.'

'Yurgh indeed,' he said, leaning round for a look.

It was a gardening scene behind Deano's bike bush. Gerry had his hairy chest on display and was eyeing his shears with a look of unmitigated disgust, and Sue, arms folded across her humongous bosom, was fixing him with a disapproving stare. I couldn't tell if the photo had been staged or Deano had just waited till they had a barney. Their record for staying civil stood at just under two minutes.

'At least he ditched the "cracking bush" caption,' Tom said.

Cameron squinted at the picture. 'Yeah, but I'm not sure "get your privets out" is really an improvement.'

'Sue's lucky Harper didn't walk in on her,' I said. 'If he'd got a look at those mothers, Gerry would've had to fight him off with the shears.'

Cameron raised his eyebrows. 'Why, did he walk in on you?'

'Oh God, I don't want to talk about it. He's got a thing for my boobs, OK?'

'Bloody hell, how many men has your sister got on the go?' Cameron asked Tom.

'I know. She'll be challenging Yo-yo for village floozy status soon.' Tom shot me an evil grin. 'Go on, Cam, show her July.'

I folded my arms on top of Flash. 'Why is everyone picking on me?'

'Keeps your ego in check now you've got all these suitors.' Tom leaned over Cameron's shoulder to get a look at my shot. 'Hang on. Weren't you behind the bike hedge thing too?'

'Yes. Why?'

'Well, it's… gone.'

My eyes widened. 'Gone? How can it be gone? Give me that.'

I grabbed the calendar off Cameron and stared at my photo.

I don't know how Jaz had done it, but the boys were right: the cracking bush had disappeared, replaced by a miniature penny farthing.

'Matches your nice hooters, Lana,' Cameron said.

I examined the picture more closely. I was in a street, looking faintly startled while Victorian folk milled about, not apparently as shocked by the naked woman in their midst as they would've been by an uncovered piano leg. I couldn't shake the feeling there was something wrong.

'Hang on,' I said slowly. 'Those can't be my legs through the spokes. Mine were covered by the bush.' I stared at the boys. 'Bloody Jasmine! She's given me new legs!'

'They're very nice legs though,' Cameron said gallantly.

'Yeah, because they're not mine!' I glared at the fake legs. 'Look at those skinny things. They'd buckle under the weight of my boobs.'

'Not going to shout at her, are you?' Tom said.

'Maybe.' I jutted my chin. 'I don't see why people should go round taking liberties with my limbs. My legs've maintained the appropriate distance between my arse and the floor for many years and I have nothing but the greatest respect for them.'

'I don't think your legs ought to take it personally, sis. Jaz probably felt she couldn't get away with using the bike bush twice.'

'She's still getting a bollocking. Replacing my legs after I'd shaved them specially.' A thought suddenly occurred. 'Hey, how's Deano's shoot? It was supposed to be part of his plan for curing Jaz of her crush.'

Tom flicked to the appropriate month and laughed. 'Ha! Gent and a scholar. I take back everything I ever said about him.' He shoved the calendar under my nose.

There was no cycling theme this time. Deano was in a room all too familiar, filled with rudely fashioned oak tables heavy on the candles and goblets.

'The restaurant!' I laughed too. 'The devious sod, sneaking in a plug.'

Deano was leaning against Galahad, our suit of armour,

as if they were out on a drinking session, a chef's hat on his head and a skillet on his... well, you know.

I curled my lip. 'Hope that's not one of our pans.'

'Not his special one, is it?' Tom asked.

'Katie? No. Maybe he thought it'd be demeaning for her.'

Tom squinted at the photo. 'I don't reckon that's Photoshopped, you know. Him and Jaz took that in the restaurant.'

'Bloody hell, you're right! I'm going to have to have words with our staff about getting their cocks out at work.'

'Hey, one time, OK?'

Cameron raised his eyebrows at Tom. 'Anything you want to tell me?'

'I was worried you'd think my bits looked weird so I gave Deano an advance preview.'

'Oh.' Cameron gave a bemused shrug. 'I guess that's... sweet. Also, bizarre.'

'That about sums me up.' Tom turned to me. 'Bit confused how this is supposed to get Jaz over her crush, Lana.'

'Deano reckons lovestruck teenage girls'll balk at the sight of their adored with everything hanging out. Takes away that certain *je ne sais quoi*, you know?'

'Have I still got that French thing now you've seen me with everything hanging out?' Cameron asked Tom.

'Dunno. Did you have it before?'

Cam shook his head. 'I knew you wouldn't respect me in the morning.'

'Hey, don't hold it against me just because I don't speak French.' Tom leaned over to give him a kiss. 'Have that.'

'Very nice. I wouldn't mind a bit of breakfast to go with it though.'

'God. High maintenance or what?' Tom sighed. 'Fine, I'll do fried eggs and sausages when we've seen the rest of the calendar.'

'Not sure I fancy any breakfast,' I said, my gaze still fixed on a nude Deano. 'I've seen too many of my nearest and dearest bollock-naked this morning to work up an appetite. And sausages are right out.'

Tom grinned. 'You want another look at Mr December's pump action to take the taste away?'

'No. I want a look at your boyfriend,' I said, quickly moving the calendar to one side before he could grab it. 'February, is it, Cam?'

When we'd checked out their months, it seemed to me Tom and Cam had got off pretty lightly. They were well covered by pump and helmet respectively, and what's more they had all their own limbs. Tom was blushing so much he looked like a nude red-skinned supervillain, but other than that...

'How much did you have to bribe Deano for that sort of special treatment?' I demanded.

Tom shrugged. 'He always did love me best.'

'Well, that's everybody. Suppose it could be worse. You get the breakfast on, Tommy. I'm going to drop Stewart's round.'

'Try not to shag him!' Tom called after me as I grabbed my coat.

There was no answer when I rang the bell of McLean's Machines.

It was after ten. Stew couldn't be in bed. I tried again. When there was still no answer I fished out my mobile.

'You in?' I said when he picked up. 'I've got your calendar.'

'Yeah, sorry, just been in the shower. I'll buzz you up.'

I wasn't sure why I felt nervous as I climbed the stairs to Stewart's flat. Something about being alone with him after Tom's jokey comment seemed to be giving me butterflies. I pushed them down with a stern telling-off.

Stewart was in a bathrobe in the living room, towelling his shower-tousled hair.

'Morning, calendar girl.'

It was a modern, open-plan front room. Tasteful. Lots of moody-looking moorland paintings. And I was definitely looking at the decor. Anyone who accused me of slyly checking out Stewart's athletic legs – definitely all his own – would have to prove it in a court of law.

'Nice decor,' I observed, a touch defensively.

'Thanks,' he said. 'Thought it might be a bit light on the antlers for your tastes. You want a drink?'

'Coffee, please.' I took a seat.

'How did Tom and Cameron's date go?' he asked from the kitchen area while he spooned out a couple of coffees.

'They've spent all morning flirting and taking the piss out of me, so I'm thinking well. Definitely an item now.'

Stewart smiled. 'Glad to hear it. They suit each other. Sugar?'

'Just milk, thanks.'

'I'm sensing your brother's on the shy side when it comes to relationships.'

I laughed. 'Yeah. Unfortunately I got the gob for both of us.'

'I'd noticed.' He handed me a steaming mug and took a seat next to me. 'You all right, Lana?'

'Course. Why wouldn't I be?'

'You've got jiggle-foot, that's all.'

'I've got what?'

'Jiggle-foot.' He nodded to the foot wobbling on the end of my crossed legs. 'My mum does that when she's nervous.'

'I'm not nervous. Why would I be nervous?'

He put his coffee down on the table. 'Look, are you sure you're OK?'

I flinched when he twisted to face me. The wet-look hair really did suit him. What was it with Stewart McLean? Whether he was driving me crazy or... well, driving me crazy, he was just the most confusing man.

'I'm fine,' I lied. 'Just got a bit anxious about the calendar. We're not all as confident in the buff as you.'

Oh, well done, Lana. Move the conversation on to his naked body. That'll help...

'What, you think I'm not self-conscious?'

'Not like me.' I flicked my gaze over him. 'It's all right for you. I bet you could go nude trampolining and nothing would even move.'

He grinned. 'Some things would.'

I flinched at the visual. This was going to be one of those mornings.

'Only the bits that're supposed to,' I managed at last. 'Trust me when I say that's not the case for me.'

His eyes darted down my body, and I shifted uncomfortably in my seat.

'Doesn't mean I don't worry about my bare flesh being scrutinised,' he said. 'Suppose I forced myself to deal with the worst of the body anxiety when I realised there was Lycra in my future though. That stuff doesn't forgive, especially when you've got a TV camera trained on your backside. You might as well be naked.'

Ugh. Now I had that picture to go with nude trampolining and his nice pump action. God, I needed to get out of there.

'Right, I'd better get off,' I said, dumping my still-full mug on the table and standing up.

He frowned. 'But you've barely touched your coffee.'

'Bit strong for me. Anyway, lots to do before the restaurant opens.'

'Hey. Before you go.' He put one hand on my wrist and looked up into my face. 'I wanted to say well done on all this. I know it's tough when you're still grieving.'

'Oh. Cheers,' I said, dropping my gaze. 'It kind of helps actually. You... cry less, I think, when you've got something to focus on.'

'Do you cry a lot?' he asked quietly.

'At bedtime. I... I can't sleep unless I cry at bedtime.'

He stood and took my shoulders in his hands. 'You know, your dad'd be proud as anything. That calendar shoot took a lot of guts, kid.'

I smiled. 'He'd go spare, more like. But thanks, Stewart.'

'Call me Stew. I like it.' He dipped his head to my level, and before I knew what was happening he'd planted a little kiss on my cheek. Gentle, brief: just the softest touch of his lips.

'That's for you,' he said. 'You're a brave lady, Lana Donati. And for what it's worth, I thought you looked beautiful. Even with the fake legs.'

'You've seen it already?'

'Yeah, sorry. Yolanda popped in twenty minutes ago to show me her Miss May shoot. Very... flamingoey.'

My face was burning scarlet now, the blush seeming to spread from the place his lips had brushed my cheek. With a mumbled something – a thanks, or a sorry, possibly – I floated in a confused daze back to the restaurant.

21

Over the next month, even as we prepared for the Tour people's visit, our fundraising really kicked into gear.

Plans for The Boneshaker – which, we'd decided, would be a sort of autumn fete with spooky cycling theme – were progressing well. Roger organised a Hits from the Shows concert for Egglethwaite Silver at the Temp; Ladies Who Lunch held coffee mornings and cocktail evenings like their lives depended on it; and even the morris men's curry and quiz night was packed out, despite them insisting on a longsword dancing display.

And our enthusiasm seemed to be catching. The school, nursery, Scouts, Guides, pub, churches – practically every group and business in the village, in fact – all organised events to get the cash rolling in. By the end of August we were nearly halfway to our twenty-five grand total. I couldn't walk past the big thermometer outside the Temp without a grin.

To my mingled delight and dismay, the calendars were selling brilliantly too. We had to do a second print run, then a third. Every village shop was flogging them over the counter and Cameron set us up a website to sell them online as well.

Purchasers seemed to fall into two camps: randy women who wanted to see Harper Brady with his kit off, and the sort of rubberneckers who probably stared at car crashes, desperate through some sort of sick curiosity to see what Roger Collingwood looked like as a nude unicycling clown.

'We're all looking forward to next July, Lana,' Billy said when me and Tom stopped off in the Fox one night after band practice.

'I wouldn't make any big plans for the Départ just yet. We're still waiting on the decision.'

'Not that.' He held up his copy of the calendar. 'This. We'll have one up behind the bar, of course.'

I groaned. 'God, do you have to?'

'Are you kidding, lass? With the Tour hopefully in town and a juicy pair of good-cause knockers to lure people in, it could be my most successful month ever.'

My eyes went wide.

'Shit!' I hissed to Tom when we'd paid for our drinks and were making our way to a table. 'The Tour! The Tour's in July!'

'So?'

'So, if we're successful the village'll be packed.'

'I know, brilliant.'

'I *mean*, the village'll be bursting with offcumdens and every single shop and business is going to have a picture of my tits up with the caption "nice hooters" underneath!'

'Ha! You're right. That's hilarious.'

'It bloody isn't! There'll be TV cameras and everything.' I shook my head. 'Yo-yo planned this, didn't she? I knew there must a reason she wanted me to be Miss July.'

'Nah,' Tom said. 'This is Yo-yo. If she'd thought there

was a chance of getting some tits on telly, she'd have bagsied July herself.'

'Oh. Good point.'

We claimed a recently vacated table, pushing the previous occupants' empty glasses and *Yorkshire Post* to the edge.

'Sort of appropriate though, you being pin-up for Tour month,' Tom said. 'This was your idea.'

'Yeah. Worst I ever had.'

'Give over, you're loving it. Don't try to deny it.'

'It does feel good to be doing something positive,' I admitted. 'I can see what Dad used to get out of stuff like this.'

'Looks like the council are well on with the safety survey. There was a gang of lads in high-vis up on the viaduct when me and Cam walked Flash this afternoon.'

I snorted. 'Well I hope they don't disturb the bats. Barbastelles can read their souls, you know.'

'Yeah, she's gone quiet, hasn't she?'

'Suspiciously quiet.' I nodded to the *Yorkshire Post* perching on the edge of the table. 'Chuck us that then. Let's see what's going on in the world outside Egglethwaite.'

Tom's eyes widened. 'There's a world outside Egglethwaite? Why wasn't I informed?'

'Oh, it's nothing to shout about. Drinks're overpriced.' I started flicking through the paper he passed me. 'Some Tour news here. One of the first British Yellow Jersey holders has donated a load of money to a kids' cycling club in Mirfield.' I pointed to a photo of a kind-faced old man surrounded by children on bikes.

Tom took a gulp of his pint. 'Wish he was from round here; he might donate to the viaduct.'

'Yeah. Can't see our local millionaire spending his hard-inherited champagne fund on it, can you?'

'You rung him yet? Maybe you can shag him into a donation.'

I snorted. 'The day I get that desperate, I may as well marry Deano.'

I was still flicking absently through the paper. Suddenly Tom's hand shot out to stop me.

'Go back!' he hissed. 'Thought I saw something.'

I turned to the previous page and blinked in shock. It was our viaduct: a massive photo spanning a double page.

The council surveyors were on top, neon yellow and ant-like, and Sienna Edge at the base with a gang of others. They were all wearing 'Save the Barbastelles' T-shirts and doing a thumbs-down, under the headline *Viaduct plan is 'batty', claim wildlife group*. Inset was a baby barbastelle, looking sad and disgustingly cute.

'*Cazzo!* I knew she was up to something!' I skimmed the article. 'Listen to what she says, Tommy. "The Egglethwaite cycling group is acting with typical human callousness towards the barbastelle colony that has made the viaduct its home, putting their own greed and self-interest before the needs of these gracious creatures." Oh, and then she gets fucking personal. "I went to meet the group, all successful owners of large businesses—" large businesses! A struggling restaurant, a farm and a cycle shop, Jesus. And then she has a go at Stew. "One of them, Stewart McLean, a bike shop owner who I believe had some limited success as a pro cyclist, in particular stands to gain financially if the group is successful in opening the viaduct as a cycle path. And while they are fundraising through such crass and undignified means as a nude calendar, the barbastelles, once evicted from their home, will very likely die from the shock."'

'Ooooh!' Tom said. 'She's got a nerve. The bats wouldn't die; we'd rehome them.'

'"Greed and self-interest".' I snorted. 'Who the hell does she think she is? She doesn't even mention Dad.'

'So what do we do?'

'We have to respond, don't we? Especially as we haven't got that grant in the kitty yet. The council are sensitive to bad publicity. It could jeopardise the application.'

'If we write to the paper it'll just turn into a slanging match,' Tom said. 'She writes back, we write back, et cetera. They'll keep campaigning, and we'll look guilty and defensive by engaging. Doesn't move us forward bat-wise, does it?'

I paused to think. 'She wanted a fight. Let's fight,' I said at last. 'I'll write a response stating our case. Just once: if she comes back after that we'll be the bigger person and ignore her. Then we need to humanely sort out these bloody Barbie dolls.'

'How though?'

'Take it to a higher power.'

'I don't think praying's going to help us much, sis. I'm sure if there's a man upstairs, he's got bigger fish to fry than unwanted bats.'

I grinned. 'The Lord helps those who help themselves, Sue always says. We'll write to Harold Fitch.'

'Who?'

I shook my head. 'Don't you follow politics at all? He's been our local MP for three years.'

'Oh. Yeah, I knew that.'

'The council won't intervene because they're worried about losing face with the public, but if we can get Fitch to, Sienna Edge won't have a leg to stand on.'

22

Coming home from Holyfield Farm one evening, I discovered Stewart outside his shop, topping up the black paint with an equally black look on his face.

'Doing up the place already?' I called.

'Thanks to bloody Sienna Edge.' He nodded to a patch of red he was giving a vicious rollering to. 'Nice of her to single me out in the paper. Some prick vandalised my shop last night.'

'Oh my God!' I went to join him. 'Did you report it?'

'Yeah, I couldn't paint over it until the police and insurance people had taken photos. It's been there all day for everyone to see.' He scowled at the paint. 'Whoever it was sloshed "Save the Barbastelles" across the shop in red paint. Probably supposed to represent the bloody murder of innocent bats by us evil capitalist tycoons.'

'Bastards!'

'My thoughts exactly,' he said. 'You're lucky they didn't target the restaurant too.'

'God, yes. We'd never have sorted it in time for opening. A whole night's takings lost.'

He snorted. 'We can afford it, according to Sienna.'

'So you want a hand, love?'

'No, I'm OK. Got reinforcements on the way.' He turned to me. 'We need to get this bat thing sorted though, Lana. I can't have this happen again.'

'I know, we're running out of time. I wrote to Harold Fitch last week making our case. I'll do a letter to the paper correcting what Batwoman said now.'

'You want me to do anything?'

'If you're offering. You can help me get a petition out supporting the viaduct plan; show the public's on our side.'

'How will that help with the bats though?'

I tapped the side of my head. 'Public support equals public votes equals a sympathetic MP. *Capisci*?'

He grinned. 'Pretty cynical for a youngster, aren't you?'

'It's one of my more endearing qualities.' I looked at the ugly graffiti and shook my head. 'I'm sorry about this, Stew. It's not fair you were singled out when it was my idea.'

'Belongs to all of us now though, doesn't it?'

'S'pose it does. See you later.'

In the restaurant, I said a quick hello to Tom on the front desk and jogged upstairs.

Flash immediately bounded up and threw himself against my legs in welcome. He didn't seem to realise he wasn't puppy-sized any more, acting like the same tiny, fluffy rocket he'd been when we'd adopted him seven months ago. I bent down to pat him and he gave my cheek a rough lick.

'Right, doggy features. Me and you have got work to do.'

As soon as we'd set up camp in a corner of the sofa, I grabbed my netbook to write a response to Sienna Edge.

What was it she'd said? Greed and self-interest. Yeah, that'd been bloody irritating.

I started tapping away and after ten minutes or so, I had this:

Sir. In your issue of Thursday last, you included an interview with Ms Sienna Edge regarding plans for the reopening of Egglethwaite Viaduct as a public right of way. In particular, Ms Edge raised a number of concerns relating to the colony of rare barbastelle bats resident there. As spokesperson for the campaign group seeking the reopening, I would like to state that the council have assured us the bats can be translocated with minimal loss of life, thus ensuring a future for both the colony and the viaduct.

Yep, that sounded good. What else? I thought about Dad and felt my anger rising.

Ms Edge also accuses the group of self-interest. While several of us are indeed business owners – albeit small village enterprises rather than the mega-industrialists she paints us as – our primary interest is as local residents.

My late father, Filippo Donati, had a vision for the viaduct. He believed it could be opened up for the enjoyment of everyone. As a memorial to him, it is our intention to fight for this.

We have nothing but the greatest respect for Ms Edge and her colleagues, nor do we wish to act inhumanely to any wildlife resident in the viaduct. We remain open to future dialogue with the bat protection group, especially if it can help us find a mutually acceptable way forward. But we won't stop fighting. We owe it to my dad and to local people to make the viaduct useful once again.

Faithfully,
Lana Donati

I wondered if I should mention Stewart and the graffiti too, but decided against it. It might sound defensive, and I wanted the tone to be calm and businesslike compared with the over-the-top rhetoric of Sienna's statement.

My Adele ringtone fired up and I grabbed my phone from the table.

'Hi, Lana. Andy Chen.'

'Let me guess. Good news and bad news, right?' This was the third time he'd rung me, and he always opened the conversation the same way.

'You know me too well,' he said, laughing. 'Don't worry, it's not *bad* bad news. Just ringing about your grant.'

I felt a stab of panic. 'The council didn't reject it?'

'No, but there's been a hold-up processing the application while they check you definitely fit the criteria for a historic structure grant. Nothing to worry about. With an amount like that they need to be extra cautious, that's all.'

'So what's the good news?' I asked.

'The workmen finished the safety survey today.'

'Oh. Right.' I frowned. 'That's good news?'

'It's not just that. Look, I shouldn't really be telling you this before the official report, but it sounds like the 2001 survey still stands: everything structural is fine. In terms of making it safe, it's just a case of clearing out the plant and animal life, getting the old rails up and having the thing resurfaced. No new problems.'

'Oh my God, really?' I almost squealed. 'Andy, I think I love you.'

He laughed. 'Then you'll be naming the wedding date in a minute.'

'What, is there more?'

'Yep.' He lowered his voice. 'Lana, you have to promise this goes no further than you and me for now, OK?'

I hesitated. 'Not even my brother?'

'Well, you can tell your committee if you trust them to keep it in confidence. But no one else.'

'I'll be careful. Go on.'

'You wrote to Harold Fitch, didn't you?'

'Yes,' I admitted. 'Sorry, I wasn't trying to go over your head or anything. I was just running out of ideas for moving things forward.'

'It's fine, honestly. Anyway, he contacted the council demanding to know more. Said the viaduct plan was obviously polarising his constituents and he was taking a personal interest.' I could tell he was grinning.

'What did you do, Andy?' I said, smiling.

'I convinced him to send a wildlife expert up with the survey team. I can't announce anything yet, but... well, there's a good chance there might not be any barbastelles. The expert thinks they might've died out or moved on since the 2001 survey.'

'You're kidding!'

'Nope. He'll have to analyse all his photos and make an official report, but it could be problem solved. Keep schtum for now though, OK? Remember, this conversation never happened.'

'As long as my mobile isn't going to self-destruct.'

'I'm afraid the council don't have the budget for that level of espionage. You'll just have to eat it.'

I laughed. 'Well, thanks, Andy. You know, you're getting to be my favourite person.'

'No problem. Oh, nice calendar shoot by the way,' he said just before he hung up.

I winced. So our calendar had found its way to the council, had it? Another group of people I could never look in the face again without blushing.

But even that thought couldn't bring me down. Our biggest problem, seemingly unconquerable just a few minutes ago, gone! No more Sienna Edge, no more nasty letters in the paper, no more graffiti. I felt like I'd burst if I didn't tell someone.

I almost skipped down to the restaurant, where Jasmine was on the front desk.

'Where's Tom?' I demanded.

'Popped out. Cameron came in to say hi after work; your brother's walking him home.'

Damn it! Who else could I tell? Andy had said only to talk to committee members I could trust. That ruled out Yolanda for a start. I wasn't even sure about Sue. Deny it as she might, she liked a good gossip.

I thought of Stewart. Surely he deserved to know. The barbastelles had just cost him an afternoon's work.

'If Tom comes in, tell him I've just bobbed over the road,' I said to Jasmine.

When I got to Stewart's shop, the front door was open. I barged straight in and jogged up his stairs two at a time.

I pounded at the door of his flat. 'Stew! Guess who's got news?'

He answered a minute later, in his bathrobe again, holding a tumbler of something that smelt sweet and alcoholic.

'Is it... Lana Donati?'

'Yep!' I beamed at him. 'I just spoke to Andy. You can't tell anyone yet, but—' I stopped, detecting a distinctly feminine floral smell that couldn't be his aftershave. 'Oh, sorry. Did you have company?'

'Who is it, Stewpot?' a voice called from the living room.

'It's Lana,' Stewart called back. 'She's got news, apparently.'

My eyes saucered as Yolanda appeared behind him, clutching another tumbler. She was in the little kimono she'd worn to the calendar shoot, her pink hair turbaned in a towel.

'Hello, darling,' she said with a slightly smug smile. 'We were just having a post-shower drinky-poo. Care to join us?'

'Erm, no,' I mumbled, backing away. 'Sorry, didn't realise you were – I just came to tell Stewart something.'

'About the viaduct?'

'Yes. The viaduct.'

'Then come in and tell us both,' she said, waving her tumbler in the direction of Stewart's living room. 'I'm sure we can rummage out a third glass, can't we, Stewpot?'

'Of course.' His eyes looked searchingly into mine. 'If you'd like to, Lana.'

'No, I... you're obviously busy. Anyway, I've got a shift in an hour. I'd better go.'

'But what about the news?' Stewart said.

'Oh. The news.' I shot a wary look at Yolanda. 'Actually, I got a bit overexcited. It's sort of secret at the moment. I probably shouldn't say anything.'

'You can't just leave it like that, darling,' Yolanda said, laughing. 'The suspense might kill us.'

'I'm sure you'll find a way to console yourselves,' I muttered as I headed back down the stairs.

In the living room, Tom was back from seeing Cameron home, snuggled up with Flash watching TV.

'Stew OK?' he asked, switching the telly off.

'He's plenty OK.'

'I read your letter. Hope you don't mind but you left it open. It's good, sis. That'll tell Sienna Edge and her gang, eh?'

'Yeah. Tell Sienna Gang and her hedge.'

He frowned. 'Are you all right?'

'I'm... fine,' I answered absently, sitting down next to him.

He waved a hand in front of my eyes. 'You want a cuppa then, zombieface?'

I shook my head to free it of the cloying fog. 'Coffee. Ta.'

Tom dislodged Flash and went to make drinks, floating back what seemed like seconds later with a mug of something hot. I was still staring ahead, unblinking, as he put it in my hands and closed my fingers around it.

'Tom?' I said as he reclaimed his seat.

'What?'

'Think I just caught Stewart McLean and Yolanda Sommerville having a post-shag nightcap.'

'*What?* Don't be daft!'

I jerked my head in the direction of Stewart's shop. 'She's there now. Drinking something that smells suspiciously like elderflower gin.'

'Doesn't necessarily mean they've been at it, does it?'

'She was in her kimono. With him in his bathrobe. And unless I'm sorely mistaken, not a right lot underneath.'

Tom hesitated.

'OK, that does seem pretty damning,' he said after a minute. 'Yo-yo though! She's twice his age. It's not like Stew can go short of offers.'

'But she's very available,' I said. 'And much as I hate to admit it, Yo-yo's an attractive woman. An experienced one too. Maybe he's got a Mrs Robinson complex.'

'Yeah, but age gap aside, she's so... well, full-on.'

'Terrifying, you mean?'

'That's the word. She'll eat him alive.' Tom shook his head. 'That elderflower gin must be stronger than I thought.'

I scowled as the anger finally clawed through my daze and bit me in the spleen. 'Stewart *bloody* McLean! Just when I'd started to think he might not be so bad, just when I was actually thinking about forgiving him, he's off shagging Yolanda!'

'Does he know you like him?' Tom asked.

'I don't like him. I hate him. I really, really *hate* that guy.' I put my coffee down. 'Right. Where's my phone?'

'Erm, sis. What're you up to?' Tom said, sounding

worried. 'You're not ringing him, are you? At least wait till you're calmer.'

'Nope. I'm ringing Andy Chen. Got some revenge dating to do.'

'Don't, Lana. It's not nice. You won't enjoy it.'

'Who says I won't? Andy's a lovely guy. And he's been flirting with me, I'm sure.'

'Yeah, but you like Stew.'

'I *don't*.' As if to prove the point, I yanked my phone out and dialled Andy's number.

'Hello?' a feminine voice said.

'Oh. Hi. I was after Andy.'

'He's just in the bath. This is Melanie, his fiancée. Can I take a message?'

Well, that answered one question.

'It's Lana from the cycling group,' I said. 'I was… speaking to him about something earlier, but it's not important. No need to ring me back.'

'Girlfriend?' Tom said when I'd ended the call.

'Fiancée.'

'Good. That'll stop you making that daft mistake then.'

'Hmm.' I paused to consider an idea I'd just had. 'Tommy, I'm about to do something you'll find hard to understand. Just remember I'm your sister and I love you, OK?'

'Oh God. What?'

'Pass me Harper Brady's business card.'

23

I arranged to meet Harper in the restaurant on Wednesday, which – by complete coincidence – was also the night Stewart had started coming in regularly for his tea. Also by coincidence, I accidentally reserved us the window table looking out to McLean's Machines.

Whoops.

Harper had suggested some fancy bistro in York, but there didn't seem much point in a revenge date if the person you were getting revenge on couldn't see you. I'd told him I'd rather stay close to home, which to my surprise he'd agreed to instantly. I'd been expecting a mini tantrum at least.

I was in my best boot-cut jeans and a green silk blouse, all but the top button fastened. The last thing I wanted was my date salivating into my décolletage all night.

When Harper arrived, I'd already grabbed us a bottle of pinot and taken my seat. At least, I assumed it was Harper. It was hard to tell with what he was wearing.

I snorted when he came to join me.

'Who're you, the Man from Del Monte?'

He tipped his Panama hat further down his face. 'I'm incognito. You might remember last time I came to this bloody village, some twat snapped a picture of me dressed as a clown and flogged it to the nationals. I don't fancy them following it up with a photo of me on a date with a waitress.'

I shook my head. 'You're all charm, aren't you?'

'Oh, don't be offended,' he said, sitting down opposite. 'I just meant it'd be news. It's not that I'm ashamed to be seen with you or anything.'

'Gee, thanks.'

'Cheers for asking me out anyway.' He grinned. 'Told you you'd come round.'

'Er, yeah. Well, you were right, because... here I am. On a date. A real one.' I glanced at the front desk. No sign of Stewart yet.

He patted the side of his seat. 'How about you pull your chair over and make this a bit cosier, babe?'

'How about you take that daft hat off?'

He smiled. 'Go on, tell me off; I love it. Hardly anyone insults me but you.'

His eyes were already fixed on my chest, which meant he couldn't see the way my lip was curling.

Just then I noticed Tom's voice at the front desk.

'No, she's not working tonight,' he was saying. 'Usual table?'

'Isn't she?' Stewart sounded surprised. 'How come?'

'She's got a date,' Tom said. 'She's over there with your cousin.'

I froze, then fixed on a seductive simper for Harper.

'So tell me about a typical day in the life of a megastar,' I purred, trying not to focus on the Stewart-shaped blur heading our way.

'Oh, same old.' Harper gave a dismissive flick of his wrist. 'Filming for this drama about saving the elephants or some shit. The director's been up my arse all day about – oh. Hi, Stew. What're you doing here?'

Stewart rolled his eyes. 'And it's this again. I live across the road, mate.'

'Hey, that's right, I forgot.' He nodded to me. 'Do you know Lana?'

'You know I know her. We were all at the calendar shoot, remember?'

'So we were,' he said, staring at my chest as if it brought back memories. 'Yeah. That was your thing, wasn't it?'

'For God's sake,' Stewart groaned. 'I know we all look like ants from your lofty position in the stars, Harper, but try to keep a loose grip on the world outside your ego, eh?'

Harper grinned at me. 'See? He insults me too. I let you do it because it turns me on and I let him because he's family.'

Stewart finally turned to me, looking embarrassed. 'Hi, Lana,' he said. 'Um… so. You're on a date. With Harper. Who's wearing a weird hat, for some reason.'

'He's incognito.' I shot Stewart my best ice-cold glare. 'How's Yolanda?'

He blinked. 'Er, OK, I guess.'

'Sorry, who the hell's Yolanda?' Harper said.

'She's the one whose kimono you borrowed.'

Harper's eyes went wide. 'Oh God, that one. She's not here, is she?'

Stewart grinned. 'No, you're safe.' He turned back to me. 'Right, I'll get off then. I actually just popped in to let you know I wouldn't be eating tonight. Yo-yo offered to cook for me.'

'I bet she did,' I muttered.

'Sorry, what?'

'Nothing.'

'And you,' Stewart said to Harper with a stern jab between the shoulder blades. 'Try to be a gentleman. This one's not like the usual girls you go out with.'

'I know she isn't. She's meaner.' Harper sent what he probably thought was a winning smile in my direction. 'That's why I asked her out.'

'Are you going to want somewhere to crash when you're leathered later? I can make up the spare room for you.'

'No thanks. I'll be staying with Lana.'

'*What?*' I exploded.

Harper shrugged. 'That is why you wanted to eat here, right? I know when I'm on a promise, love.'

'You bloody well are not—' I stopped, glancing up at Stewart. So he was getting his tea cooked by Yolanda, was he? Viagra-laced oysters and champagne, no doubt.

I fixed my face into a provocative smile for Harper. 'I mean, we'll see how it goes, OK... er, honey pie?' I wasn't good with impromptu endearments.

'Ah.' Harper winked. 'Don't want me to think you're easy. No worries. We'll just "see how it goes" then.' He actually did the air quotes too. The man could redefine obtuse.

'Right. I didn't realise you'd made... arrangements,' Stewart said. 'Well, night then, guys. Oh, Lana: your blouse is undone, by the way.'

I glanced down and hurriedly fastened the button that had popped open to expose the broadest part of my cleavage.

'You could've bloody said something!' I hissed to Harper when Stewart had gone.

He grinned. 'What, and ruin the view?'

'...so Bernice, my agent, thinks I've got a shot at a BAFTA nomination for *Soar*. I mean, it's always rigged. That's why I've been overlooked so far – old school tie network, right?' Harper paused for an acknowledgement.

'Mmm,' I said, chin propped on my fist. If I'd learned one thing over the past hour of listening to Harper talk about himself, it was that an 'mmm' was all the acknowledgement his ego needed.

'But yeah, feeling next year's my year. Bernice is going to buy a few drinks, hump a few legs, see what she can—' He broke off when Tom approached. 'Another bottle of wine here, mate.'

'Actually, I need to talk to your date.'

Harper frowned. I think he'd managed to forget this was mine and Tom's restaurant and thought he had an uppity waiter on his hands.

'My brother.' I turned to Tom. 'What's up?'

'It's Jaz. I can't find her anywhere,' he said. 'She went to the loo and just vanished. Deb checked the Ladies – she's not in there. Sorry, sis, I know it's your night off, but we're seriously short without her. Can you lend a hand?'

'Oh God, yes,' I said with a sigh of relief. 'Er, I mean, if it's an emergency.' I turned to Harper. 'You mind if we postpone this conversation? Missing waitress crisis.'

'Will you come back after?' he asked, shooting a resentful look at Tom. 'I can wait at the bar.'

'I'll be too tired for nightcaps after work, Harper. Or for... anything else. Maybe another time.'

'Right,' Harper said, getting to his feet. But he didn't leave. 'I'll call you, babe, OK?'

I winced. 'Please don't call me that. I sound like a talking pig.'

He laughed. 'You're funny, aren't you?'

'I'm a riot.'

'Well, thanks for tonight, Lana. It's been laughs.' Before I knew what was going on, he'd leaned across the table and planted a wet kiss right on my lips.

I pushed him away. 'Jesus, Harper! Bit of warning might be nice.'

He clicked his tongue. 'You're a lucky lady. You know how many women dream of that every night?'

'Amazingly, no.'

'Well, it's lots. Bernice tallies up the fan letters that mention sexual fantasies for me.'

'Oh God,' I groaned. 'I bet that's not even a joke, is it?'

'Might be, might not,' he said, winking. 'Toodles, babe – er, honey. Speak soon.'

He blew me a last kiss over his shoulder as he sauntered to the exit, daft Panama hat still perched on the back of his head.

When he'd gone I turned, wide-eyed, to Tom.

'Harper Brady just tried to slip me the tongue.'

'Yeah, I saw. Well, congratulations, sis.' He grabbed my hand and gave it a shake. 'You are now officially one of the most envied women in the country. How's it feel?'

'I can tell you how it tastes. Fried fish and garlic. He had the herb-crusted trout.' I knocked back the last of my wine to get the Harper Brady flavour out of my mouth. 'Right, I'd better get into my costume.'

'No need. Jaz was on kitchen duty all night. Just stick a pinny on.'

I frowned. 'So she was in with Deano, was she?'

'Yeah, why?'

'Did you text her? It's not like her to take off without letting one of us know.'

'I tried ringing. No answer.'

'Hmm. OK, let me try. You go back to the front desk; there's customers waiting.'

I pulled up Jasmine's number as I headed towards the kitchen. Three rings, four... no answer.

Just as I passed the toilets, I paused. There was a very faint sound, like a tinny... was it One Direction?

Jasmine's ringtone. But Tom said Debbie had checked the loos.

My eyes lighted on the little cleaner's cupboard. So that was it. Quietly, I opened the door and slid myself inside.

I fumbled for the light switch. Jasmine was sitting under a shelf laden with bleach and antibacterial spray, hugging her knees and sobbing.

'How'd you find me, boss?'

'First rule of hide-and-seek, Jaz: always put your phone on silent. Tough one for a teenage girl, I know.' I sat down and put an arm round her. 'Want to talk about it, love?'

'No.'

'Fibber.'

She buried her head in my shoulder while she squeezed out a few more tears.

'Did Deano say something to you?' I said gently.

'Yes. He said don't overcook the mutton, kid. He said check there're no lumps in the mashed turnip, kid. He said make sure your hands are cold before you make the pastry, kid. That's all he ever says. And I say yes, Chef; no, Chef; three bags full, Chef – like a pathetic bleating sheep.' She stifled another sob. 'No wonder he only ever notices you.'

'Come on, that's not true. He's very fond of you.'

'Yeah, like a pet hamster or something. It's you he fancies.'

I shook my head. 'It isn't like that.'

'And I know why,' she said, ignoring me. 'Because you're all relaxed and jokey with him, like I wish I could be. When I'm with a boy I like, I say so many stupid things I want the ground to eat me.'

'So do I,' I said. 'Tom's worse, and he's twenty-eight. Everyone feels like that: it's part of getting to know someone.'

'You're not like that with Deano,' she said, blowing her nose quietly on the tissue I handed her.

'No. Know why? Because I don't fancy Deano. And he doesn't fancy me. We're friends, that's all.'

'You're always flirting though.'

I shrugged. 'Oh, that's just mucking about. Friends do that.'

'He never mucks about like that with me.'

'You're… younger,' I said diplomatically. 'He probably thinks it's not appropriate.'

'Yeah, I know what he thinks. What you all think. You think I'm a child, don't you?'

'Well you are a child. You know, technically.'

'I'm old enough to know what I feel.' She flushed and looked down at her knees. 'To fall in love.'

'Oh, Jaz…' I sighed. 'You poor kid.'

'And don't tell me I don't love him,' she said, suddenly fierce. 'Older people always think they know better.'

'No one's saying that, sweetie.' I gave in to whatever maternal instinct was guiding me and reached up to stroke her hair. 'But it won't help. Deano thinks you're too young for him, and, well, he's right really.'

'No he isn't. My stepdad's six years older than my mum and they've been married years.'

'And how old was your mum when they met?'

'Twenty-seven.'

'Well, there you go. Twenty-seven and thirty-three is a lot different than seventeen and twenty-four. There's a whole world to find in the next few years.'

She pulled herself up a little. 'No there's not. I'm dead mature for my age, everyone says. And I can do commitment for the right guy; I've had loads of long-term relationships. One was, like, six months.'

I managed to suppress a smile. 'What happened to him?'

She sniffed. 'He wanted me to wear a promise ring. I said it was too soon. You're only young once, right?'

'Exactly.' I gave her a comforting squeeze. 'What's brought this on, eh?'

'This.' She fumbled in her bag for a piece of paper. 'I've been offered a place studying design and photography at the University of East London.'

'Oh my God, Jaz! That's amazing!' I blinked at the letter she'd handed me. 'Unconditional offer too. They must think a lot of your portfolio.'

'I haven't accepted yet.'

'What?' I looked up at her. 'Are you mad? Bite their hand off, love.'

'But it's London. It's so far away from…' she bit her lip '…from him. And when I told him, he just congratulated me like he… like he wouldn't even miss me.' She gave way to sobs again.

'What, so you're just going to stay working at this dive all your life in the hope Deano'll eventually notice you?' I said. 'He'll meet someone one day – unless they change the law and let him marry that bloody frying pan – and you'll have to see it and it'll hurt like hell. Get out, while you still can.'

I was frowning at my hands, and when I looked up I found her blinking at me.

'Why do you sound so angry about it?'

'I'm not angry. I'm just…' I sighed. 'Look, I never told anyone this. Not even my brother, so you have to keep it secret, OK?'

Her eyes were like dinner plates. 'I promise.'

'Well, just before Dad got sick I was applying to unis too. I got an offer to study cosmology, but he was diagnosed before I accepted. So I turned it down.'

'And now you regret it?'

I paused. 'No,' I said at last. 'I don't regret a minute I spent with Dad – they were all precious. But I can't help wondering what if things had been different, you know?'

'Why don't you go now?'

'Oh, it's too late for me,' I said with a sad smile. 'I'd feel daft surrounded by kids. Anyway, my life's here: Tom, Sue, Gerry. This place.'

'And that famous man you like, right?'

I laughed. 'Harper Brady? I wouldn't miss a bus for that guy.'

'Not him,' Jasmine said with a knowing smile. 'That famous cyclist from the bike shop.'

'Oh.' I glared at a mop that was giving me evils. 'Him.'

'You like him, don't you?'

'Sometimes. When he's not driving me insane.' I turned to her. 'But I didn't like him when I was seventeen. I liked a lad in my year called Scott Spen. You know him?'

She frowned. 'That man who looks like a sheep?'

'Yep. And if I'd given up on going to uni because I'd stayed around here for him, I can tell you I'd regret it like nobody's business.' I patted her shoulder. 'Don't make that mistake, eh?'

'This is different. I love him.'

'And I loved Scott. Made a little sheep-faced shrine to him with a photo I'd stolen from somewhere and an old pencil he'd left behind in Maths. That's the thing about love when you're seventeen. It can be real as hell. Doesn't make it forever.'

'Mine is,' Jasmine said fervently. 'I won't forget him, Lana. Not ever.'

I pushed myself to my feet. 'Right. Then you'll just have to impress him. Accept that uni place and become the best designer in the world, then he'll have to notice you.'

'You think?'

'He recommended you for the calendar, didn't he? And you did a bloody good job too – everyone's been saying.'

She managed a wan smile. 'I did, didn't I?'

'Plus when you're finished with uni, you'll be twenty-one. Twenty-one and twenty-eight doesn't sound such a big gap, does it?'

She looked thoughtful. 'No. It really doesn't.'

'And if Deano still doesn't notice you, there's always Harry Styles. Come on.' I grabbed her hand and pulled her to her feet. 'You get on home and let them know you'll take that place. I'll tell Deano you went off sick.'

'Thanks, Lana.' She wiped her eyes and pushed open the cupboard door. 'You're the best boss. I hope it works out with you and the bike shop man.'

'Honestly, Jaz, there is no me and...' I sighed. She'd already gone. 'Never mind. Just... never mind.'

24

Our next cycling group meeting was the last before the Tour people came to visit. When we met at the pub, everyone was in a state of high anxiety.

'I just wish we knew what they were looking for,' Cameron said for about the fourth or fifth time.

'We can take a fair guess,' Stewart said. 'Stuff that makes good telly. Scenery, history...'

Gerry drained the last of his pint. 'What I wish we knew is how far to sell them on the viaduct. We can't guarantee it'll be open for the Tour.'

'I think we should just go for it,' Stewart said. 'We don't need to mention the bats, do we?'

'Oh, they'll know all about it, darling,' Yolanda said in her usual affected drawl. She had her chair so close to Stewart's, she might as well just climb up on his lap. 'It's been in the newspaper, hasn't it? I'm sure these people do their homework.'

Stewart shrugged. 'We can mention it as a possibility anyway. It's a waste not to capitalise on it after all our fundraising.'

Tom and I were silent. We were still waiting for the report on the viaduct's barbastelle population and until we got it, we'd decided it was best to keep quiet. Just in case we got everyone's hopes up only for there to be a last-minute hitch.

'Right,' Gerry said. 'I'm off to get another round in.'

'No, it's my turn,' I said, standing. 'Same again, everyone?'

There was a hum of agreement and I headed to the bar. I'd just put our order in for the usual when I felt a tap on my arm.

'Come to give you a hand,' Stewart said.

'No need. Billy'll sort me a tray.'

'Well, thought you might like some company.' He went silent for a minute, watching Billy pouring Yolanda's G&T. 'Good date the other night?'

'Er, yeah. Jasmine went home ill though so I had to end it early and cover her shift.'

He laughed. 'So that's why Harper was on my doorstep at nine demanding booze and a listening ear for an in-depth analysis of his BAFTA prospects.'

'You were home then?' I said, trying to sound casual. 'Thought you'd gone to Yo-yo's.'

'I didn't stay long. She was heading out so I took my shepherd's pie back to the flat.'

'Oh. I thought you two were having a meal.'

'No, she just cooks for me sometimes. I think she likes having someone to look after.' He leaned round to look into my face. 'Did I do something to annoy you, Lana? You seem a bit off with me lately.'

'We're fine. Same as always.'

He looked awkward, like he was struggling to put something into words.

'Look, is this about the other day?' he said after a second.

'What other day?'

'At the flat. You know, when the shop got vandalised. I was wondering if you might've maybe... got the wrong idea. About me and Yo-yo.'

I shrugged. 'Why should I care who you have in your flat?'

'I'd hate for you to think – she only came over to help me with the painting.'

'Right. Painting the shower, were you?'

'We had a shower afterwards, yeah. Got a bit dirty. One each, I might add.'

'You expect me to believe that?'

His lips curved into a half-smile. 'OK, so I'd be lying if I said she didn't take a whack at it. I was a bit suspicious when she had a bottle of gin and her dressing gown stashed in her handbag. But come on – Yolanda? You can't think I'd go for her.'

'Why not?' I felt illogically offended on Yolanda's behalf even as I felt pissed off at her for putting the moves on Stewart. 'Yo-yo's a good-looking woman. Trust me, she's always done all right for herself.'

'It's nothing personal. Yo-yo's lovely – in her way – but she's old enough to be my mum.' He shuddered. 'She looks a bit like my mum too. We're on safer ground with shepherd's pie.'

'Hmm.'

'Would it've bothered you if there'd been more to it?' he asked, in the familiar fake-casual tone I recognised from my own voice.

'No. Why should it?'

'Well, absolutely. You've got Harper now, right?'

'Um, yeah.' Stewart didn't need to know I'd spent the last few days not taking Harper's calls.

'He's filthy rich, you know,' Stewart observed nonchalantly.

'So he tells me.'

'And handsome.'

'Lots of women seem to think so.'

'Did he show you his Rear of the Year award?'

My mouth started to quirk into a smile and I willed it back into deadpan mode. 'Not yet. We have to save something for the second date.'

'Well, I'm happy for you. He's… some catch.' Stewart's face was a picture of studied sincerity. 'Funny though, I got the impression at the calendar shoot you weren't a fan.'

'He grows on you.'

'Come on,' he said, smiling. 'Let's stop messing about, Lana. I think you know I—'

'Cheers, Billy,' I said to the landlord as he dumped the last drink on the bar. 'Perfect timing. Stick it on our tab, yeah?'

After grabbing the tray, I hurried back to our table. I badly needed time to think and process before I could respond to what I suspected Stewart might've been about to say.

'About time,' Gerry grumbled as I handed drinks round. Stew slid back into his seat, shooting me a meaningful look I pointedly ignored.

'What've you two been chatting about?' Sue whispered when I'd sat back down. 'Your head looks like a radish.'

'We'll talk later, OK?' I whispered back. 'Stewart's being confusing. He's good at that.'

'Right,' Sue said when we'd finalised arrangements for the Tour people's visit. 'Me and Lana are going to get off so we can talk about you all. You lads stay and have another drink. I'm sure Yo-yo can provide female company for the three of us.'

I glared at her as we made our way to the exit. 'Did you have to say that? Stew might not know it's a joke.'

'Good. Let him think we're talking about him. First rule of keeping men on their toes, lass: always make sure they feel nervous. Once they know what you're thinking they get complacent.'

She shouldered open the door and we made our way into the night. It was a balmy early autumn evening, or as balmy as it ever was this many feet above sea level: warm with a warning tang. The Dales liked to remind you that, however far you'd lapsed into a false sense of security, it was never wise to go out without a coat.

'God, Sue, you're like the talking 1950s,' I said. 'Don't you tell Gerry what you're thinking? You've been married a trillion years.'

'If I did he'd have left me yonks ago.' She slipped her arm into mine as we started making our way up the cobbles. 'So. We've all noticed you making cow eyes at Stewart McLean.'

I frowned. 'I don't make cow eyes. Cows make cow eyes. I make... lady eyes.'

'Trust me: as someone who spends most of her day with

farm animals, those're cow eyes. Thought I'd give you a few weeks to get over it, but since you seem to be getting worse it's time we had some girl talk.'

I sighed. 'He's just confusing. He's a confusing man. An irritating, confusing man.'

'Hunky though,' she said, watching my face carefully.

I shrugged. 'He's all right. I could take him or leave him.'

'Good. Because trust me, when all that's heading south, all you're left with is the pillock underneath.' She gave my arm a squeeze. 'He hurt you before, chicken. Buggered if he'll do it again on my watch.'

'That's what's so confusing,' I said. 'Every time I start to warm to him, I remember how upset I was when he disappeared out of my life before. Then I think, is it safe to let myself get close?' I sighed. 'I'm... fragile, just at the moment. And this is strictly between us, but he actually did break my heart just the littlest bit.'

'I know he did,' she said gently.

'I can't put myself in that position again, Sue. Not after everything I've been through in the last six months.'

'Does Stewart know any of this?'

'What, you mean did I tell him that after one date I was in pieces because he didn't call, like a pathetic schoolgirl? Course he doesn't know.'

Sue skimmed my body approvingly. 'Still, at least you're losing weight.'

I frowned. For a big woman she didn't half take a lot of interest in my figure.

She must've read the thought in my eyes. 'Well, when you get to my age you can afford it,' she said with a smile. 'So what did Stewart say before to turn you all radishy?'

'He... well, nothing, I ran away before he could finish. But I think he was going to tell me he likes me.'

'Been seeing a lot of him lately, haven't you?' she said quietly.

Sue would've made a great counsellor. She always gave just the right prompts, getting you to spill exactly what was bothering you before you even properly knew what it was.

I had been seeing a lot of him. More than I realised, now I thought about it. Apart from the last week, when I'd suspected him of having a fling with Yolanda and gone out of my way to avoid him, I'd actually seen him most days: either outside his shop, at the group meetings or in the restaurant when he came in to eat. Sometimes, when Tom was out with Cam and I was feeling particularly lonely, I'd even called at his flat and invited him to walk Flash with me. Slowly, gradually, I'd got used to Stewart McLean being there when I needed someone.

'Yes,' I said at last. 'Hard not to when he's right in front of me.'

'Do you like him a lot, my love?'

'I... think about him a lot,' I admitted. 'All the time.'

'So you're falling for him.'

She was very matter-of-fact, but the words sent a jolt through my stomach.

'No,' I said, my brow lowering. 'I can't let myself do that.'

'Then why spend time with him?'

'He makes me laugh. He's kind when I need someone to be kind, and funny when I need someone to be funny. I guess it all comes down to...'

'Your dad?' she said in the same quiet voice.

'Yes.' I was speaking half to myself now. 'I get lonely. And now Tom's with Cameron… it feels like it'd be nice, you know? To have what they've got.'

'Not jealous of your brother, are you?'

'Course not, I'm happy for him. But…' I sighed. 'It must be wonderful to have something like that. To fall in love.'

'And you never have, have you? Not properly.'

I looked at her in surprise. 'How did you know that?'

She shrugged. 'Worked it out. You were only a lass when your dad got sick, and it's not like you've made much time for boys since then.' She took her arm out of mine and nodded to the restaurant door. 'This is you.'

I was home. I wasn't even sure how we'd got there. It felt like I'd been in a trance.

Sue kissed my cheek. 'Don't fall in love because you're lonely, chicken,' she said gently. 'Fall in love because he's worth it.'

'I'll try. Thanks, Mum.'

'Give us a hug then.' She threw her arms around me, crushing me against her comforting bulk. 'Shame really, he seems a nice lad otherwise. But who could do that to our little girl, eh?' She gave my back a hearty slap. 'Call me or the old man whenever you're lonely, all right? The sooner you free yourself of Stewart McLean, the better.'

25

The following Thursday I woke with a strange feeling in my tummy.

I swung myself out of bed and flicked open the curtains. It looked like any other late summer day: sunnier than some, colder than others. Stewart's shop looked the same as usual, apart from the string of yellow and blue bunting across the front. But it wasn't the same. It was far, far scarier, because today the Tour people were coming.

I felt oddly calm. We'd planned everything to within an inch of our lives, with a detailed itinerary for everyone. This was the abridged version:

2pm: committee met at bottom of village by Lana, Tom, Gerry, Sue

2.15pm: tour of village

3.15pm: coffee and cakes at café

4pm: rest of tour

5pm: Pagans' Rock

6pm: buffet at Here Be Flagons. Everyone gets pissed.

That bit was highlighted. We were all really, really looking forward to that bit.

It was a working day for most of the others, but Yolanda had arranged for cakes at the caf where she worked, Cam had promised to do a bike-themed display in the chippy window and Stew said he'd have something special ready too.

'So you definitely know what you're doing?' I asked Tom over lunch.

He rolled his eyes. 'Yes, Lana, we've been over it, like, fifty times. Take them round the village, give them the history, generally show them a good time. Remind me again: do I have to sleep with any of them?'

'Only if things get desperate. Have you learned your patter?'

'Well I practically memorised that book of Roger Collingwood's. *Egglethwaite: One Thousand Years of Bugger All.*'

'Come on, that's not what it's called.'

'No, but it might as well be. Community spirit it may have, but this place isn't half bloody boring.'

'So what will you say then?'

'Don't worry, I'll sex it up a bit,' he said, grinning. 'Leave it to Tommy.'

'You just behave yourself, that's all. I don't want any surprises today.' I got to my feet. 'Right. I'm going to see how Deano's getting on with the food.'

In the kitchen, a pleasant smell of frying shallots and fresh herbs assaulted my nostrils.

'Deano, how're you—' I stopped short when he turned to grin at me. 'Jesus, what the hell are you wearing?'

'Ace, isn't it? I got it online.'

He was in a white T-shirt, emblazoned with the legend:

I'm a Yorkshireman, born and bred: strong in t'arm and good in bed.

'Hang on,' I said. 'It's "weak in t'head", isn't it?'

'I liked this version better.'

'Why's it so tight?'

'Bought an extra small.' He patted his little cotton-hugged belly. 'No harm giving them the goods, right?'

I shook my head. 'No, Deano. You are not putting the moves on my committee. You'll have to change.'

'Oh, what? You're not my real mum.'

'I am today. I'll get Tom to lend you a shirt.'

'That lanky git?' He glanced down at his round tummy. 'I'll pop all the buttons.'

'You'll be fine. Suck in.' I scanned the bowls and plates covering every surface. 'So what've you got for us then?'

'All sorts. Those lucky bastards. If we don't get the route after this I'm hanging up my whites.'

I picked up a bowl of something black and held it to my nose. 'What's this, anchovy paste?'

'Don't do that!' Deano grabbed the bowl off me and set it down reverently. 'That's caviar, you daft cow!'

'Caviar?' My eyes went wide. 'Shit, Deano! We haven't got the budget for caviar!'

'It's fine, I sourced it off a mate from college. Owed me a favour.'

I cast a worried glance over the rest of the hors d'oeuvres. They all looked a bit... dainty.

'Haven't you got anything proper?'

'What you on about? This is proper.' He pointed to a plate of something that looked vaguely potatoey. 'Look. Garlic rissoles.'

'I mean, anything local?'

'It's all local. I got the ingredients from the farm shop, same as always.'

'Local as in local dishes. You know, mini Yorkshire puds, rhubarb tarts, that sort of thing.'

I could see his brow lowering.

'Not that all this French stuff doesn't look great,' I said quickly. 'But you can whip up a few more things to go with it, can't you?'

'Absolutely not. I've spent hours on this lot.'

'I'll let you wear the T-shirt.'

He folded his arms. 'Nope. Not good enough.'

'Come on, Deano,' I said in my best pleading tone. 'It'll be a challenge. This could be your crowning achievement.'

'Hmm.'

'You can snog me.'

'Right.' He grabbed his apron and pulled it over his head. 'Let's get cooking.'

He drizzled Katie the pan with olive oil, his brow furrowing in concentration. 'I'll need more eggs,' he said over his shoulder. 'Oh, and some double cream, red onions and a bottle of Henderson's Relish.'

'On it.'

'And get red wine!' he called as I pushed open the door.

'Right.' I frowned. 'What for, gravy?'

'No, me. This is going to be thirsty work.'

When I'd finished at the farm shop Gerry was outside, leaning against his Land Rover smoking a roll-up.

'Hiya,' I said. 'Picking up or dropping off?'

'Dropping off. They ordered some eggs.' He nodded at the bags in my hand. 'What've you got there?'

'Supplies for Deano.'

'You're all set then?'

'Think so. Hard to know what they'll expect when they get here really.'

'These are Londoners, petal. They'll probably expect to find us worshipping Satan and boffing our sisters.'

'Then we'll just have to keep your morris men in for the day,' I said. 'You're still able to give us a lift up to Pagans' Rock, aren't you?'

'Yup.' The shadow of a grin flitted across his face. 'Got something special for them up at the farm.'

'What is it?'

'It's a surprise. You'll see.'

'Don't you be springing surprises on me at this stage, Gerry,' I said, wagging a warning finger. 'Does Sue know about it?'

'It was her idea. One of her better ones, although I'd appreciate it if you didn't tell her.'

'Hm.'

'Oh, don't worry,' he said, giving my shoulder a slap. 'They'll love it, I promise. See you outside the Methodist in an hour, eh?'

'They're late,' I hissed to Tom as we waited outside the Methodist church with Gerry and Sue. 'They're going to ruin my lovely itinerary.'

'Awww. And after you coloured it in and everything.'

'I know. Inconsiderate bastards.'

'Calm down, petal,' Gerry said. 'They aren't late yet. They just aren't early.'

'Oh God, what if they're not coming? What if they read that Sienna Edge thing in the paper and blackballed us? I knew it'd all go wrong.'

'Yeah?' Tom pointed to a couple of large taxis creeping towards us. 'Who's that then?'

'*Merda*, they're here! Are they here? They are, aren't they?'

'Oi.' Sue flicked my ear. 'You might've got away with swearing in Italian when you were teenagers. Don't think I'm not wise to it by now.'

I smiled. 'Sorry, Mum.'

Tom gave my elbow a reassuring squeeze. 'Try not to panic, OK, sis? I'm ready for them.'

'You're uncharacteristically confident.'

'Yeah, Cam's been coaching me in bed. I play me and he plays the Tour de France people.'

I shook my head. 'Epic sexy role-play fail, Tommy.'

'Helped though. I could do this village tour with my eyes closed.'

'Hmm. Rehearsal didn't help much at the Class Four Nativity.'

'Well, I'm all grown up now. Just as long as they don't ask if there's room at the B&B.'

We plastered on a matching set of toothy smiles as the taxi pulled up and the Tour people piled out.

There were ten of them, more than we'd expected. The woman whose body language said she was every inch in charge was a thin, St Trinian's-looking lady of sixty-something, with one of those faces whose default expression was disapproval. There was only one other woman: the rest were men.

'Hi,' I said, shaking the headmistressy lady's hand enthusiastically. 'I'm assuming you're our people. I mean, er, the VisitBritain people. Um, so… welcome to Egglethwaite, I guess.'

One of the nondescript men in suits had a little smile hovering about his lips. I wondered if he was laughing at my accent or my embarrassment.

'Good afternoon,' the woman said. 'Ms Donati, is it? Vanessa Christmas. Mrs.'

'Vanessa… Christmas.' I tried not to look surprised. 'That's an unusual surname.'

'I assure you, in my late husband's family it was very common. They've been passing it down for generations.'

Was that a joke? I wondered whether it was OK to laugh. Vanessa Christmas was either the queen of deadpan or she had no sense of humour at all.

'You'd think with a name like that she'd be a bit jollier,' I heard Sue whisper to Gerry. I shot her a look.

'Will Mr McLean be joining us?' Vanessa asked, peering over my shoulder to see if there was anyone behind.

'Not right now. We'll see him later.' I gestured to the others. 'This is my brother Tom, and Sue and Gerry Lightowler. They own a farm just outside the village.'

Vanessa looked a little disappointed Stewart wasn't there to meet her, but she shook hands all round. When we'd been introduced to the rest of the committee, we started making our way up the cobbles.

I fell into step beside Vanessa.

'So are you seeing a lot of other places while you're up?' I asked.

'Oh yes, at least fifty.'

My eyes widened. '*Fifty*? Shi – I mean, gosh. That's a lot.'

'Well, with the eyes of the world upon us we need to show our best side, don't we? This is a splendid opportunity, not just for Yorkshire but for the country. The value to tourism is inestimable.' She flashed me a withering smile. 'If you'll excuse the pun, there's a lot riding on us getting this right.'

So many other places in the running! I wondered if Stewart knew.

'And when will the route be announced?' I asked.

'The organisers will be announcing the stages in October, but it's likely to be January before they make the full itinerary available.'

'So we won't know whether we've been selected until next year?'

'I'm afraid not.'

'What made you consider us?' Sue asked.

'Your Mr McLean was full of the area's suitability – the challenging nature of the terrain, how photogenic the scenery was. And of course, he's a man who would know.' She cast an underwhelmed look around the terrace-lined main street. 'We came prepared to be impressed.'

'Bollocks!' I muttered to Tom. 'Bloody Stew, he's oversold us. Do they think we've got a life-size Taj Mahal in Lego waiting at the top or something?'

'Got them here, didn't he?' Tom muttered back.

'They've got another fifty places to see as well though. Go on, try your patter.'

'Right.' Tom stepped forward with a determined, slightly kamikaze look on his face. 'Um, allow me to tell you a little about the village, Mrs Christmas.' I saw him grimace when he said the name, trying not to laugh. If he could just stay off the James Bond one-liners...

'Certainly,' Vanessa said with a gracious nod.

'Well, Egglethwaite has always been a hive of industry,' Tom began, in a tone that sounded like he was channelling Jeremy Paxman. 'In Victorian times most people were employed in the worsted mill or on farms, but nowadays villagers do all sorts. We have a number of shops, as you can see. Florist's, newsagent's, chemist, butcher's...' He gestured round the street.

'Mmm,' Vanessa said with a polite-but-vague nod. If we weren't the first village on their list, they'd probably heard a dozen stories like that already.

'You're losing them,' I whispered to Tom in Italian. 'Something more unusual.'

'Er...' I saw Tom hesitate while he fumbled for anything vaguely interesting from that godawful book of Roger Collingwood's. 'Oh!' He pointed to the caf where Yolanda worked. 'And that's The Peach Tree, one of the oldest surviving buildings in the village. A few hundred years ago, it was an unlicensed alehouse whose landlady was notorious for giving shelter to wanted poachers. It's believed peach is a corruption of poach, and tree refers to the gallows – a reminder of where the lawbreakers could end up if they didn't mend their ways.'

Vanessa and the committee examined the café with interest.

'Could we see inside?' one of them asked.

'We'll be popping in later for tea and cakes,' Sue said. 'Our friend is a waitress there.'

'That's more like it,' I muttered to Tom. 'Got anything else like that?'

'No. That was the only interesting bit of history in the book. Don't worry though, got a plan.'

'Oh God. Please, Tommy, no plans.'

'Just trust me, OK?'

He cleared his throat as we stopped outside the Temp. 'So here we have the village stocks,' he said, gesturing to the rotting wood-and-rust construction. 'Some of the oldest in the country, it's believed.'

My eyebrows shot up. Tom knew as well as every Egglethwaiter that the stocks were a replica. Even if they'd been the originals, they'd be far from the oldest in a ten-mile radius, let alone the country.

Tom ignored my dirty look and carried on. He nodded to the Temp, its sandstone façade jet black now from centuries of mill smoke.

'This is the old temperance hall, which serves as our community hub,' he said. 'It was once dedicated to fighting the demon drink, that curse of the working classes. Fully licensed for weddings, christenings and bar mitzvahs. Funded by, er, Branwell Brontë back in 18...' He coughed loudly. 'Sorry, something in my throat. So yeah, back in the 1800s. He was a frequent visitor to the village.'

One of the men stared at him. 'Are you trying to tell us Branwell Brontë paid for a temperance hall to be built here?'

Tom shrugged. 'Yeah, why not?'

'But wasn't he the most frightful alcoholic?'

Tom didn't miss a beat. 'Absolutely correct,' he said. 'This was in one of his sober periods. The repentant sinner, you know?' He shook his head mournfully. 'So sad it didn't last.'

There was a hum among the committee members. I just gaped.

'Actually, when he was off the wagon he often went drinking over there,' Tom said, pointing to the Fox. 'Er, yeah, with his sisters; they used to come pub crawling over the moors from Haworth. Charlotte, Emily and... the other one.'

'Anne,' I muttered from behind a fixed smile.

'Anne,' he added smoothly.

'But surely in those days women from their social background wouldn't be found in an alehouse?' Judy, the other female committee member, said.

'No. No, that's right, I remember now: the girls used to wait in the beer garden to carry Branwell home when he staggered out trolleyed off his tits. All good research for *The Tenant of Wuthering Heights* and, um, their other books.'

Vanessa shook her head. 'Unbelievable.'

'Unfortunately they had to bar Branwell in the end,' Tom said. 'Outstanding debt.'

'Didn't pay his bonus ball,' Gerry said brightly. I threw him a look.

'And they say Turner stayed there too, when it was a coaching inn,' Tom went on. I shook my head slightly, but he paid me no attention. 'Yep, Turner. You know, the sculptor.'

'You mean JMW Turner, the landscape painter?' one of the men said.

'The very same.'

He squinted one eye suspiciously. 'But you said sculptor.'

'Sometimes, sometimes, when the mood struck. I think

there're still some of his clay figurines in the church hall actually. "Woman with suggestively placed oranges" is a local favourite.'

Vanessa laughed, for the first time that day. At least she was finding it entertaining.

'Actually, there's an interesting story behind the pub name,' I said, jumping in before Tom pointed out the toadstool where the Cottingley fairies used to hang out, or whatever semi-local celebrity it occurred to him to draft in next.

'Oh yes?' Judy said. She didn't exactly sound intrigued, but I ploughed on.

'Yes, a local legend. There was a Londoner who fell on hard times, so he went in search of a better life. By the time he made it here he was starving. He found himself lost on the moors, no civilisation in sight, but just as he took off his pack to lie down in the snow and wait for the end, he noticed a trail of dirty black pawprints. Followed them to the village, where a local farmer cared for him. When he was well he became an innkeeper and named the place in honour of the animal that'd saved his life. Sooty Fox, see?'

Vanessa looked impressed. 'What a sweet tale. Is it true?'

'Yes.' I shot a look at Tom. 'That actually is true.'

'Well, thank you, Mr Donati,' Vanessa said to Tom. 'We've been on many village tours more factual, but few more entertaining, I promise you.'

Tom grinned. 'Rumbled.'

She flashed him a rare smile. 'I wrote my MA thesis on the Brontës. I'm afraid you picked the wrong subject to fake expertise on. But it was certainly amusing.'

'OK, what the hell was that bit of improv all about?' I

muttered to Tom as we walked on. 'You didn't think you'd get away with laying it on that thick, did you?'

'Course not. Trying to make her laugh, wasn't I?'

'And give me a bloody coronary in the process?'

'Look, Lana, we have to go for broke here. There's fifty other places in the running; it's Vegas or bust.'

Vanessa was walking a little ahead, talking in a low voice to the other committee members. She turned to me, interrupting our whispered conversation.

'So does the village have any real history?' she asked.

'Not that you'd call illustrious,' I admitted. 'But it's an incredible community. Everyone's very invested in next year's event, as you can see.' I pointed to Your Plaice or Mine, Cam's chip shop. He'd created a cycle-themed diorama in the window using fish-tank toys and blue cellophane: little divers in old-fashioned metal helmets riding bikes while a puzzled octopus looked on.

'A trifle premature, perhaps,' Vanessa said. 'Still, it's good to see some enthusiasm locally. In the last place we viewed, we were taken to task by a rather rude farmer who was adamant the Tour would upset his animals.'

Gerry broke into a loud fit of coughing and Sue slapped him heavily on the back.

'Well that's certainly not the case here,' she said, smiling sweetly. 'We've been right behind the idea from the start. Haven't we, dear?'

26

Sensing that it might be the way to the committee's hearts, I waxed lyrical about community spirit all the way round the village. I managed to keep it going over tea in The Peach Tree, where even Yolanda was on her best behaviour, but by the time we were approaching Stewart's shop I'd done the subject to death.

'…and it's been truly amazing, seeing village groups and businesses get behind the Tour,' I waffled for about the third time as the shop came into focus. 'It's been inspiring to see… to… to see… oh my *God*, bums!'

The committee members stopped dead, wide-eyed and agape, like newborn deer blinking at the full moon, or proverbial rabbits caught in some proverbial headlights, or Queen Victoria on her wedding night. They were staring, horror-struck, at the fibreglass constructions that had appeared outside McLean's Machines.

There were six of them, or twelve if you counted buttock by buttock. Six large, shining, pink backsides, each wearing a thong painted the colours of the Tour jerseys. Above them, a banner proclaimed: 'Need somewhere to park your bike?'

'Christ, what the hell is he playing at?' I muttered to Tom.

Tom just shrugged, looking as flabbergasted as the rest of them. I shot Vanessa an apologetic smile.

'I'm so sorry about this, Mrs Christmas. Stewart's idea of a joke.' I nudged Tom, whose mouth had started to twitch. 'Don't you bloody dare laugh, Tom Donati,' I whispered. 'Look, tell them he's the local maniac and we'll keep him locked up for race day or whatever. I'm off to have a word.'

I barged in and gave the bell on the counter an angry ring.

'Get down here, you bastard, and start explaining why you thought mooning my committee was a good idea!' I called out.

Stewart came jogging down from upstairs, breaking into a wide grin when he saw who it was.

'Classic, right?' he said. 'Custom bike stands, I had them made specially. I bet none of the other villages thought of that.'

'No, because they're not off their heads!' I hissed. 'What the fuck, Stew?'

He blinked in surprise. 'You don't like it? I thought it'd be good to do something a bit quirky, put us on the map.'

'What, the village with the weird arses? I'll say it'll put us on the bloody map! They'll put a giant pin on the map with a note saying "insane pervert village, steer well clear". What were you *thinking*?'

His face fell. 'It's only like the calendars, isn't it? A bit of cheeky humour. I thought you'd think it was funny.'

The door opened and in came Vanessa.

'Mr McLean?' she said, fixing him in a stern gaze.

'Er, yes?'

'Vanessa Christmas. We spoke on the phone.' Her face

relaxed into a smile. 'I just wanted to say, what a unique idea. The best giggle I've had in ages. You know, that one second from left... reminds me of my husband doing the weeding, God rest him.' She came over to give his hand a vigorous shake. 'We're all big fans, by the way. Such a shame you had to retire prematurely. All that wasted potential.'

Stewart just blinked. 'Oh. Thank you.'

She nodded to a stack of calendars on the counter. 'So this is your new career, is it?'

Vanessa definitely had a deadpan sense of humour, I'd decided. Her face never even twitched.

Stewart smiled. 'More of a sideline,' he said, handing one to her. 'It's a fundraiser for—' He caught the warning look I flashed him and stopped. We were saving the viaduct for a big unveiling at the end. 'Um, for a local project.'

'It's certainly very... revealing,' Vanessa said, staring at the cover photo. 'Is that Harper Brady with you?'

'That's right. He's my cousin.'

'Is he really?' She squinted at the picture more closely. 'Well. You learn something new every day. Actually, there is a resemblance.'

'You think so?' Stewart said. 'Most people say I look more like my dad's side.'

'I wasn't referring to a facial resemblance,' Vanessa said, casting her eyes over Stewart's toned thighs and stomach.

'Ah. I see. Well, can I interest you? It's £7.99, all for a good cause.'

I'd just about managed to recover the power of speech by then. 'If you like the cover, Mrs Christmas, you'll love December,' I said. 'Er, not a joke about your name.'

Vanessa flicked through to December and I saw her eyes widen.

'Goodness me! Suddenly your bike racks seem rather tame, Mr McLean.' She fished in her handbag and handed over a tenner. 'Keep the change, please. I hope we'll be seeing more of you later?'

'Absolutely.' Stewart grinned. 'Well, not as much of me as you've just seen. But I'll be popping over to the restaurant as soon as I close up.'

'So am I forgiven?' he muttered to me as Vanessa turned to leave.

'No. It was a bloody stupid thing to do.'

'Worked, didn't it?'

'You got lucky. Don't dare spring anything like that on me again, Stew. We'll be having words.' I followed Vanessa back out to the others.

'How did you sort it then?' Tom whispered as we carried on past the restaurant and into open countryside.

'Stewart did. Turns out Vanessa Christmas is kind of a perve.'

'Really?' He examined her back with surprise. 'Just goes to show, you never can tell. So what did Stew say then?'

'Flirted a bit and sold her a calendar. She well fancies him.'

'Her too, eh?' He nudged me. 'There's getting to be quite a queue for Stewart McLean.'

'Shut up.'

The next stop was Holyfield Farm for a trip up to

Pagans' Rock in Gerry's Land Rover. Then it was back to the restaurant, and a boozy buffet to round the day off.

As we approached the farm, I fell back to talk to Sue and Gerry.

'So what's the big surprise, guys?'

'Oh. That,' Gerry said. 'Have to say, when I planned it I didn't realise I'd have McLean's arses to follow.'

'It better not be anything awful, that's all. Between Tom's bullshit history lessons and Stewart's kinky bike racks, I've had at least three mini heart attacks today.'

'Nothing like that.' Gerry pointed as the farm came into view. 'There it is.'

'Your yarn-bombing suggestion gave us the idea,' Sue said. 'Only we thought it'd be better if we left the wool on the sheep.'

I couldn't help laughing. Gerry's Swaledales were grazing in their field as usual, placidly oblivious to how silly they looked. There were six or seven yellow ones, a handful of red spotty ones and a couple of green ones, their fleeces dyed the colours of the Tour jerseys. The star was Gerry's old tup Rambo, in the red, white and blue stripes of the French Tricolore.

'You daft old sods.'

'You like it then?' Sue said.

'I love it. Must've taken you ages.' I gave her a kiss on the cheek. 'Can't help feeling sorry for the sheep though.'

'Never mind them, stops the yows getting vain,' Gerry said. 'They're getting clipped next week anyway.'

I planted a kiss on his cheek too. 'Thanks, Uncle Gerry. I know you were never a fan of the Tour idea. Means a lot, you doing all this just for us.'

'Well,' he said with the hint of a blush. 'If it's important to you and Tom, that's good enough for this grumpy old git. Been a tough year for you.'

'Oh! Isn't that wonderful?' Vanessa exclaimed when she clocked the Tour sheep. 'Is this your farm, Mr Lightowler?'

'No, it's my farm,' Sue said. 'But them're his sheep.'

Vanessa laughed. 'It's very here, isn't it?'

Gerry grinned. 'Yep. We're funny buggers this side of the Pennines.'

Vanessa shook her head. 'Not Yorkshire. I mean it's very *here*. Very Egglethwaite.'

Tom raised an eyebrow at me and I gave a slight nod. So she thought we had a character all of our own. That had to be a good sign.

Vanessa was full of beans now she'd had her nudey Stewart McLean fix but the rest of the committee seemed to be flagging. Some of the men were slowing down, and Judy was stopping every few minutes to rub her feet.

'Nearly done,' I said brightly. 'Just one more thing to see.'

'Um, petal?' Gerry said in a low voice. 'What's your plan for getting this lot up? I didn't think there'd be so many.'

It was a point. Ten of them, plus me, Tom, Sue and Gerry... that meant three trips in the Land Rover. It'd take ages.

'There's one other option for off-roading.' Sue nodded to the big blue tractor outside the farmhouse. 'Hook up the wagon, get them there on that.'

Gerry snorted. 'Don't be daft, our lass. These aren't bloody heifers.'

'Better than spending the next hour ferrying folk up and down, isn't it?'

'Sue's right, it's the fastest way,' I said. 'If we're lucky, Vanessa Christmas'll think riding round on cattle wagons is very "here" too.'

She did as well. Some of the others looked sceptical when I suggested transport by tractor, but Vanessa practically giggled.

We hoisted up a few hay bales for something soft to sit on, Gerry got into the front with Sue, and the other twelve of us clambered onto the wagon.

'I feel like a rabbit,' Judy said, shuffling her bum against the scratchy hay. 'I say, doesn't it smell funny?'

'Nonsense,' Vanessa said. 'That's the countryside, my dear. My grandmother always told me to breathe country air deep and it would stop me taking cold.'

'Where are we going, Miss Donati?' one of the men asked.

'Local beauty spot,' I said. 'Last stop before Beer O'Clock, I promise.'

The man's expression told me that in his opinion it'd been Beer O'Clock for at least half an hour, but he didn't say anything. And it was worth it to see the look on their faces when we came to a stop at the top of the dirt track that led onto Pagans' Rock.

I jumped down and beckoned them to follow me. There was a muttered 'oooh' as they absorbed the view.

'Gosh!' Vanessa said in a hushed voice, casting her eyes over the viaduct's imposing loops; the heather-purpled moors; the sun-soaked sparkle of the reservoir. 'Now isn't that something?'

'This was our dad's favourite spot,' Tom said. 'We scattered his ashes here.'

Vanessa turned to look at him. 'Recently?'

'Few months ago.'

'Oh, I am sorry.'

'What do they call this place?' one of the others asked.

'Pagans' Rock,' Tom said. 'It's actually a sort of folly. Local squire a few hundred years ago had a big rock towed up here then gave it a fancy romantic name to impress his guests. He liked to pretend the Druids used it as a sacrificial altar.'

Vanessa narrowed one eye. 'True story, Mr Donati?'

'Trust me, if it wasn't I'd have something much better for you. Possibly involving naked virgins and witches' covens.'

'Of course, the view was a little different then,' I said. 'The landowner probably put it here so he could keep an eye on his tenants down in Moorcroft. That was Egglethwaite's neighbouring hamlet.'

Vanessa squinted into the distance. 'I don't see a hamlet.'

'No.' I nodded to the peaceful waters of the reservoir. 'It's under there. They submerged it in the forties.'

'How terribly exciting!' Judy said. 'Your own Atlantis. Are there any ghost stories?'

Tom shrugged. 'Not really. All the residents were relocated.'

Judy looked disappointed. I glared at Tom. Apparently when it came to him and history, it was all or nothing.

'There are more than four hundred souls in Moorcroft Cemetery though,' I said. 'After a dry season, you can sometimes see the ruined church spire peeping over the water.'

'Oooh!' Judy breathed, her eyes shining. 'I'd love to see that.'

And now it was time. The big finish.

'Is that a working viaduct?' Vanessa asked, almost as if she could read my thoughts.

'Not yet.' I nodded to the calendar under her arm. 'Look at the back.'

She blinked as she read about our viaduct plans.

'That sounds ambitious,' she said when she'd finished.

'Ambitious but achievable,' Tom said. 'The council have already guaranteed us half the funding we need, and we're well on the way to the other half. We're hoping resurfacing work can begin in the new year.'

I put on my earnest face. 'Mrs Christmas. Is there any possibility... if the viaduct was available in time for the Grand Départ, would that affect your recommendation?'

Vanessa looked serious for a moment. 'It could certainly be a factor,' she said at last. 'It would add excellent texture to the live broadcast.'

'It sounds a very tight schedule for getting it reopened though,' one of the faceless suits chipped in. 'Could you guarantee its availability?'

Tom opened his mouth to answer, but I jumped in first.

'Absolutely,' I said. 'One hundred per cent.'

Our last stop was Here Be Flagons, closed to the public for one night only. When we got there, we discovered Yolanda, Cameron and Stewart already propping up the bar along with Deano and Jasmine, plus Roger Collingwood, who'd invited himself because he didn't like being left out. Under Deano's instruction, they'd pushed furniture to the edges to create a sort of mingle area, the buffet tables slicing it into a couple of aisles.

Foodwise, Deano had really risen to the occasion. Along with his dainty French nibbles, he'd managed Yorkshire pud canapés with roast beef, cocktail sticks with cubes of Christmas cake and Wensleydale on them – not very seasonal but certainly local – fat rascals, parkin slices, and an impressive centrepiece of a sponge cake iced with sugar white roses, a little Yorkshire flag and Tricolore crossed on top. The Tour committee, hungry after their walk in the fresh moorland air, lost no time tucking in.

Vanessa eventually managed to peel herself off Stewart, who she'd attached herself to almost immediately – much to the disgust of Yolanda, forced to get her flirting fix off Deano instead – and came to find me at the bar.

'What an unusual place, my dear,' she said, scanning the

restaurant's oak-and-armour decor. 'How on earth did a bright young thing like you end up here?'

'It was my dad's.'

'It can't be making money though. These novelty places are all very well for the city, but in the middle of nowhere…'

'We manage,' I said, a trifle defensively. 'We've got a very talented chef.'

I could see our very talented chef out of the corner of my eye, helping himself to a double whisky while beatboxing Jame Blunt's 'You're Beautiful' under his breath. I crossed my fingers, hoping Vanessa wouldn't ask to be introduced.

'The food is excellent.' She picked up a cocktail stick from the paper plate she was holding. 'Fruitcake and cheese. What a bizarre combination.'

'Round here we like it like that.'

'Yes, it does seem to work.' And she popped it in her mouth.

'Well, Miss Donati,' she said when she'd finished. 'It's been an odd day. We won't forget it in a hurry, I assure you.'

'When will we hear from you?'

'I'm afraid I can't tell you anything officially until the schedule is released in January.' She lowered her voice. 'But between ourselves, you have nothing to worry about. It's a wonderful little place, isn't it? And your viaduct – spectacular. I'll be giving my very highest recommendation.' Giving my arm a pat, she wandered off in search of Stew.

Cameron spotted me staring after her and came over, leaving Tom to entertain Judy from the committee.

'You OK, Lana?' he said, waving a hand in front of my face. 'You look kind of stoned.'

'Yeah.' I shook my head, blinking. 'We got it.'

'What?'

'We got the route. A half-cut Vanessa Christmas just came over and she said some stuff about restaurants and Wensleydale and… and she said we got it.'

'Oh my God!'

'It worked.' I threw my arms round him and squeezed. 'Arghh! It worked, Cam! All Tom's bullshitting and Stewart's bums and Gerry's sheep – it was just the right amount of weird.'

'Brilliant!' he said, hugging me back. 'Can we tell the others?'

'Better wait till the committee's gone. It's sort of unofficial until January. But she definitely seemed to be saying it was a done deal, as long as we can get the viaduct sorted.'

'And what if we can't?' Cam said. 'Sienna Edge could still chuck us a spanner, couldn't she?'

'Maybe.' I lowered my voice to a whisper. 'There could be good news on that front too though. This is top secret, but our man on the council says there might not even be any barbastelles. Not any more.'

'Did he? Wow, that's huge!' He held me back to grin at me. 'Some day, eh?'

'You can say that again. I'm knackered.'

'Better let me go now, love,' Cameron said, glancing round the room. 'Me and Tom aren't officially an item yet. People might get the wrong idea.'

I untangled myself from the hug. 'But everyone knows, don't they?'

'Our group does. No one else.' He looked dejected. 'Your brother wants to keep it quiet.'

I hopped up on a bar stool and patted the one next to me for Cam. 'You don't though, right?'

'I hate secrets,' he said, climbing on to the stool. 'And I don't see the point of this one. Not exactly an illicit liaison, is it?'

'But it is early days. You want to take things slowly.'

'Still. When he doesn't even want to hold hands in case people see... it's hard not to feel he's ashamed of me.'

I shook my head. 'That's not it at all. He's just shy. He hates the idea of people talking.'

Cameron frowned. 'Why would they? There's not a lot of homophobia here, is there?'

'No, but there aren't a lot of same-sex couples either,' I said. 'Not much happens in Egglethwaite. People'll gossip about anything out of the ordinary.'

He shrugged. 'Let them, if they lead such quiet lives. I'm not fussed.'

'But Tom is. Suppose it goes back to our dad really.'

'What, he had a problem with Tom being gay?'

'Sort of, but not like you might think,' I said, flinching. It was hard, remembering Dad as anything less than perfect. 'When Tom came out Dad just went quiet for a bit, then said he didn't understand it personally but he wanted his kids to be happy. Gave him a hug and told him not to worry about it.'

'So what was the issue?' Cameron asked. 'Sounds like everyone's dream come-out.'

'Because Dad really didn't understand, and that bothered our Tom. He never said anything, but I know it did. Something that seemed to him like the most uncomplicated thing in the world being questioned. Gerry's the same.

He doesn't disapprove exactly, but heterosexual is always default.' I sighed. 'And then there was this distinction Dad made, between the two of us.'

'He treated you differently than Tom?'

'He would've said he didn't. I don't think he even noticed he was doing it. But it was there, all the same. If he liked my boyfriends, he'd invite them for tea, shake hands, all that stuff. He never did that with Tom's boyfriends. Oh, he'd have them over if Tom invited them – cook all his best dishes for them, almost like he was overcompensating. But he never asked.'

'And then you felt guilty.'

'Yes,' I said in a small voice. 'It felt like I was taking Dad away from Tom.'

'It wasn't your fault, Lana,' Cam said, rubbing my back. 'Tom says you're a great sister. His best friend too.'

I sent a fond smile in Tom's direction. 'Well, back at him. Not that we ever say it to each other.'

'Seems like you don't need to.'

'So how about you?' I asked. 'Are your parents fine with it?'

'Ha! Yeah, funny story. I spent years worrying about telling them, then one day it was getting serious with a lad from uni so I sat them down to break the news. They looked worried sick. Then when I told them I was bi, my mum just looked super-relieved and said, "Oh, we know *that*." Thought I was going to say I'd got hooked on Class-As or something.'

I laughed.

'Anyway, softened the blow before I told them about my crystal meth habit,' Cameron said, grinning.

'Can I ask something personal, Cam?'

'If you like.'

'I was just wondering – well, you've got a zoology degree,' I said. 'How come you work in a chip shop?'

'What's wrong with working in a chip shop?'

'Nothing. Just all the fish are sort of... dead. Couldn't you be doing something with less batter and more, you know, zoology?'

He sighed. 'I don't know, Lana. It was the family business; a stopgap after uni. And a year became two, and three... There's jobs enough down south, but this place – gets under your skin, doesn't it?'

'I know what you mean.'

'I could ask you the same,' he said, glancing at the painted coat of arms behind the bar. 'You're a clever girl, Lana Donati. What're you doing trapped here in the Dark Ages?'

I shrugged. 'Same really. I always had this thing when I was young, about astronomy. And I said it was Dad's illness that stopped me following it. But now he's gone, I just think, where can you see the Milky Way better than the moors on a clear night?'

'Yeah. It does feel like everywhere else is trading down.'

I patted his knee. 'Well, for Tom's sake I'm glad you stuck around. You two go perfect together.'

'Wish he thought so,' Cameron said, casting a morose look at Tom laughing with Sue and Judy by the buffet table.

'He does. He's probably just scared that if he rushes things, he'll mess it up. Talk to him if you're worried about it.' I pushed back my stool. 'Right, buffet's done, I think. I'd better let Deano know he can shut everything down in the kitchen.'

I was assuming the kitchen was where Deano was hiding, since I couldn't see him. I found him taking a time out, leaning against the cooker sipping his stolen whisky.

'Helping yourself to my booze, you cheeky get?'

He shrugged. 'I earned it. You've had enough free labour out of me today.'

'Give us some then.' I took the whisky off him and downed a swig.

'Come to congratulate me?' he said.

'You did do well on the buffet. Nice idea with the fruitcake.'

'Cheers. So what do you reckon to our chances?'

I grinned. 'Well we got it.'

'Shit! They told you already?'

'Sort of off the record, but yeah. Turns out the viaduct plus Stew in the buff is a winning combination.'

Deano squinted at me. 'Speaking of, what's with you and Stew?'

'Nothing,' I said, hiding my face in the whisky tumbler. 'There's nothing with us.'

He didn't say anything. He just examined my face with a cross-eyed look, like he was reading my soul. The man must be part barbastelle.

'All right,' he said at last.

'Is that it, "all right"?'

He shrugged. 'Why, what else do you want?'

'Normally when people grill me on Stewart McLean, they start dishing out free advice all over the shop.'

'You can have some advice if you want it.'

'Yeah, go on,' I said with a resigned sigh. 'I'm starting a collection.'

'Well, you're in love with him, so based on that my advice is go for it.'

I actually staggered backwards. 'Say that again.'

'I said go for it.'

'Not that bit. The first bit.'

'Oh, right. Yeah, I said you're in love with him.'

'No I'm not.' I managed a pretty obvious fake laugh. 'Don't be daft, Deano.'

'All right.'

'Can you stop saying "all right"?'

'All right.' He took the half-forgotten whisky out of my hand and finished it. 'Anyway, lie to yourself if you like, that's your business. Just don't forget you owe me a snog. You can't get out of it this time, Lanasaurus, you promised.'

I groaned. 'I did, didn't I? OK, pucker up then. No tongues, mind.'

And just as I planted a smacker right on his lips, I heard the door swing open.

'Oh my God, I knew it!' came a distraught whisper from behind us.

It was Jasmine.

28

'Your friend's here,' Tom said the following evening when I went to relieve his shift. I followed his gaze to Stewart, sitting at his usual table examining the menu.

'Again? That's the third time this week.'

'He is in more and more these days, isn't he?'

'Must be a fan of Deano's cooking.'

'Hmm.'

'Hmm what?' I demanded. 'Come on, you've got that face on.'

'Well, who's that big on medieval cuisine?' Tom said. 'We're a novelty night out, sis. Once a month at best.'

'What're you getting at?'

'Just a theory I've got. I'll tell you another time.' He nudged me. 'Take his order then.'

'Can't you do it?'

'Nope.' Tom yanked his daft feathered hat off. 'As of right now I'm on my break. Off you go.'

I sighed and made my way to Stewart's table.

'So, is it true?' he asked when I reached him.

'Is what true?'

'What Deano told me when I bumped into him this morning.'

My stomach tightened. Not that it wasn't complete bollocks, obviously, but if Deano had told Stewart I was in love with him... He wouldn't do that to me, would he? He wasn't exactly a dab hand at judging the appropriate boundaries of social interaction.

'Well?' Stewart said. 'Did we get it?'

I breathed a sigh of relief. The Tour. It was just the Tour.

'Yeah, we got it,' I said. 'Thanks to one enormous arse.'

'Six, technically.'

'I stand by my original statement.' I flashed him a grudging smile. 'Still... not that it wasn't a gamble, but I'm sorry I snapped at you. I was a bit tense yesterday; you probably noticed.'

He looked taken aback. 'Wait. Did you just admit I was right about something?'

'Very nearly.'

'And that consequently, you, Lana Donati, must've been – I think the word is, "wrong"?'

'All right, all right. Don't gloat or I'll take it back.'

'Nuh-uh, no take-backsies. You said it and it's forever engraved on my heart.' He patted the seat next to him. 'Fancy joining me for a bit?'

I sighed. Apart from one elderly couple, he was the only customer in. I'd been avoiding him a bit lately, after my heart-to-heart with Sue... Still, he did seem inviting when he was being all smiley and funny.

'OK, since you did so well flirting with Mrs Santa Claus yesterday,' I said, sitting down. 'Five minutes then I have to get back to work.'

'You're not really still mad at me, are you?' he asked with a winning smile.

'Little bit.' I grinned. 'But it was bloody funny.'

'I am widely acknowledged to be the master of the prop gag.' He handed me his goblet of wine. 'Here you go. This'll get me into your good books.'

I took a sip. I really shouldn't while I was working, but...

'Admit it,' Stewart said. 'Sometimes you think I'm all right. Sometimes you're even quite fond of me.'

'OK, I admit it,' I said, smiling. 'But only sometimes.'

'Ah, there's the old Lana. Was starting to think you'd forgotten how to smile.'

'I smile.'

'Not as much as you used to,' he said. 'What happened to you, kid? When we met you laughed all the time. Now you're nearly always on edge.'

He reached over to cover my hand.

'You know what happened to me. A year of caring for a sick man happened. Watching him hurt and not being able to do anything about it. Knowing what was waiting at the end. It... changes you.'

'I know.' He sighed. 'Lana...'

'Hmm?'

'I wanted to... I mean, last year. Pagans' Rock.'

Ugh. And we'd been getting along so well.

'I told you, forget about it. I have.'

'Come on. We both know that isn't true.'

I pulled my fingers away from his touch, annoyed by the self-assurance in his tone.

'You really think I've spent the last year and a bit pining over bloody Stewart McLean?' I snapped. 'It was one date, that's all. Not true love.'

'No! That's not what I meant at all.' He pushed his fingers

into his hair. 'God, you're hard to talk to when you get like this.'

'And you don't half think a lot of yourself.' I pushed back my chair. 'I need to get back to work.'

'Lana, I'm trying to tell you something here. Can you cut the wounded pride act and just listen a sec?'

'Fine.' I sat back. 'One minute then I have to go.'

'I meant to call you, OK? Honestly.'

'So you said. But something came up, right?'

'Yeah.'

'Like the fact I wouldn't go to bed with you?'

He shook his head. 'You can't really think that was it. You know me.'

'What then? Was it Dad? That I was so committed to his care I might not have time to do the boyfriend thing properly?'

'What? No! Lana, come on.' He took my hand again and gave my fingers an impatient squeeze. 'It was the accident, all right?'

'It was a year, Stew. Accidents don't last a year. And I was... There were other things going on that made it worse.' That was the closest I'd ever come to admitting to him just how much he'd hurt me.

'I know,' he said, his head drooping slightly. 'I was a mess too. Afterwards, I mean.'

His face contorted with a spasm of pain as he went through it again in his memory.

'What happened?' I asked in a gentler voice.

'I was training. Came off my bike going over a cattle grid. Head-first into a puddle.' He laughed bleakly. 'It was actually sort of comical, me sitting there with mud all over my face while a puzzled sheep blinked at me. Didn't realise at the time I'd just ruined my life.'

'Did it hurt a lot?'

'That's the thing. There was a twinge, and I knew I'd twisted my knee, but it wasn't agony. I even finished my ride. It was only when I saw my physio next day, the look in her eyes, that I realised it was bad. And then she said the words all athletes have nightmares about.'

'What words?'

'"This doesn't look good." Everyone knows what that means.' He shook his head. 'When I found out I had to quit for good... Jesus. The bottom just dropped out of my world.'

His features twitched as he stared down into his wine.

'I'm sorry,' I said, forgetting about everything except that he was so obviously in pain. I pressed his hand gently. 'You've had a tough time of it, haven't you?'

'So've you.'

Tom appeared at foot of the stairs, scanning the restaurant for me. I yanked my fingers away from Stewart's before he noticed.

'Um, guys,' Tom said when he reached our table, his voice radiating anxiety. 'News.'

I frowned. 'Bad?'

'Well it's not good.' He passed me his mobile.

On screen was our local paper's website, a new story added that afternoon. The headline was *Tour de Farce*, emblazoned over a big photo of Stewart's ridiculous bike racks.

'I don't know who sent it but they've obviously got it in for us,' Tom said.

I skimmed the article. 'Bringing the area into disrepute. Juvenile… oh for fuck's sake! All that's missing is "won't somebody think of the children?"' My brow lowered. 'Sienna Edge. Her and her cronies'll be behind this.'

Stewart took the phone so he could have a read.

'Hmm. Probably true. She seems to have it in for me particularly.'

I glared at him. 'I told you it was a stupid thing to do.'

'Doesn't matter now though, does it?' Tom said. 'Vanessa Christmas liked them, that's the main thing.'

'It might matter to the council. You know how they are about bad publicity, and we haven't got our grant yet.' I shook my head at Stewart. 'For God's sake, Stew! What the hell were you thinking?'

His eyebrows shot up. 'Me? Ten minutes ago you were saying what a great idea it'd turned out to be!'

'That was then. This is now.'

'It's not my fault, is it?'

'Yes it's your fault! You can't keep going behind the backs of the committee with stuff like this.'

'Come on, sis, that's a bit harsh,' Tom said. 'It did get us the route.'

'Let's just hope it hasn't cost us our grant, that's all,' I muttered darkly. 'Without the viaduct open in time, we're screwed.'

'Lana, please,' Stewart said. 'I'm sorry, OK? You know I didn't mean to—'

'You didn't mean to. Right,' I snapped. 'You never *mean* to do anything, do you, Stew? It just happens. Maybe one day you'll be a big enough boy to understand actions always have consequences.' I glanced at the door. 'Jasmine's here. I'm taking my break. Tommy, I'll see you upstairs.'

I went to speak to Jasmine by the counter.

'I'm knocking off for an hour. Can you handle things down here for a bit?'

'I'll be fine.'

I couldn't help noticing the way she avoided eye contact.

'Jaz... we're still friends, aren't we?'

'Why wouldn't we be?'

'Look, about yesterday, there wasn't anything – me and Deano were just messing about. I didn't know you were there.'

'Clearly. I don't want to talk about it, OK? I'm going to get changed.' And she stomped off to the Ladies.

I sighed and headed upstairs, where I found Tom on the sofa. He looked a bit down.

'Look, there's no point worrying about the story now,' I said, plonking myself next to him. 'I'll give Andy a ring tomorrow and try to smooth things over. Let's just hope the council see the funny side.'

'It's not that,' he said, sighing. 'Man trouble.'

'God, tell me about it.'

He shot me a look. 'You and Stew looked like you were getting cosy downstairs.'

'Till he ruined it with his stupid bums.'

'You were being a bit unfair then, you know.'

'He needs to think before he does stuff, that's all. We're supposed to be a team, not The Stewart McLean Show.'

'This isn't really about those bike racks, is it?' he asked quietly.

'Maybe not. Dunno.'

'Think you'll ever forgive him?'

'I'd like to.' I swallowed, feeling the rise of a sob. 'I just don't know if I can trust him. It... hurt, Tommy.'

'I know it did,' Tom said gently. He slung an arm round me. 'We have no luck, do we?'

'Come on then, tell us your man trouble.'

'Cam's mad at me.'

'What's up, did you have a row?'

'Not exactly. He wants me to meet his parents,' he said with a low groan. 'I said it was too soon for that so he's sulking. Says he's not but I can tell.'

'Is it too soon or are you just hiding in your comfort zone?'

'All right, the second one,' he admitted. 'I just need to psych myself up a bit first. It's a big thing, isn't it? I want them to like me.'

'Have you told Cam that?'

'Sort of. I tried to, but... well, you know what I'm like. Words hate me. I probably made it worse.'

I managed a smile. 'You're a bit keen on this one, aren't you, bruv?'

He dropped his gaze. 'I am. More than keen.'

'I know.' I patted his knee. 'Want me to talk to him for you?'

'No,' he said with a sigh. 'I'm a big lad, I have to fix these things myself. I'll ask him over while you're at the dentist's on Wednesday, have another go at talking it out.'

I winced. With everything that'd been going on, I'd forgotten I was booked in to have my wisdom teeth removed.

'God, that's all I need after the last few days: a nice dose of painful dentistry,' I said. 'Will you be able to pick me up? The nurse said I could be a bit out of it from the anaesthetic.'

'Don't worry, I won't forget.' He squeezed my shoulders. 'We'll get you home no matter how high you are.'

29

'She'll need to stay in for at least the next twelve hours, Mr Donati,' the snowman behind the reception desk said to Tom. He was a very serious snowman. All his mouth currants were in a straight line.

I giggled. 'Snowman.'

The snowman shot me a cold look. Well, technically all his looks were cold, being made of frozen water, but this one was particularly chilling.

'How long till the drugs wear off?' Tom asked. His voice sounded weird and bubbly, like he was underwater.

'An hour or so, but she could be quite groggy for a while afterwards. Make sure there are no hazards around her, and it goes without saying she mustn't drive or operate machinery.'

'Hey. He said that without moving his currants,' I whispered super-duper quietly to Tom.

He winced. 'All right, druggie, no need to shout.'

Everyone in reception had turned to look at me. I gave them a friendly wave. One of them looked just like Flash.

'Hiya, Flash!' I shouted. I thought of Cameron and giggled. 'Ah-ahh! Good doggy.'

'Oh God. This is going to be a rough trip,' Tom groaned.

I leaned heavily against him as he guided me to his car. The world seemed to have gone a bit spinny.

'Like them Teacups in Morecambe,' I told Tom. 'You were sick on Dad. Ha! Loser.'

Back at home, he put me to bed. The ceiling was spinning and I could see right through to the stars, just like a whirlpool. All the constellations, and the moon and the aurora borealis, twisting and whirling kaleidoscope-like... I gazed up at it, hypnotised.

'You OK, Lana?' Tom asked softly when he'd tucked me in. 'How're your teeth, do they hurt?'

'Stars.' I pointed to the ceiling.

He sighed. 'Course they don't hurt, do they? You've got more drugs in you than Keith Richards.'

'See all the colours? Beautiful.'

'Um, yeah. Pretty stars.' He patted my head. 'Get some sleep, crazy girl. I've taken everything out you could hurt yourself on. As soon as Jaz gets here I'll come sit with you.'

'Will you read to me like you do to Dad?' I asked sleepily.

He smiled. 'If you want.'

'He's... gone, isn't he?'

'Yes, sis,' Tom said gently. 'He's gone now.'

'But you're not?'

'No. I'll try to always be right where you need me. Rest now, eh?'

''K. Thanks, Tommy. Love... you.'

The stars went dark. When I opened my eyes Tom was gone and there was a fuzzy black budgie sitting on top of the telescope Dad had given me for my eighteenth.

I glared at it. 'Oi. No birds in my room. Go 'way.'

It didn't move. I examined it more closely.

'Oooh. You're not a budgie, are you? You're a Barbie doll.' I jabbed a finger in its direction. 'Don't you be going back to the viaduct, batface. S'mine. You and your mates find somewhere else to live.'

The little bat fluttered to the door. Sienna thingy was right, it was sort of cute. I didn't like the expression on its face though. Looked like a trouble-maker.

'Hey! Where you going?' I called after it. 'Are you going to my viaduct, you bat?'

With an effort, I swung my legs over the bed and followed it unsteadily through the door.

I tiptoed barefoot down the stairs, feeling my way along the banister. I could see Tom in the restaurant, taking an order from one of Yolanda's calendar flamingoes.

'Shh!' I put a finger to my lips. 'Don't you go making any noise, Mr Bat, or he'll send us to bed.'

I opened the front door and tiptoed ever so sneakily after the bat as it fluttered across to Stewart's shop.

Stewart was with another giant flamingo that'd escaped from the calendar. He was showing it a Harley Davidson with big feathery wings, hovering just off the floor.

'...yeah, new in,' I heard him say as I pushed open the door. My little bat flapped forward and landed on his head, but he didn't seem to notice. 'Very lightweight, ideal for road cycling and it'll take some off-roading if it's nothing too heavy. What is it you're wanting it for?'

'Wahhh-wah,' the flamingo said. 'Wah-wah-wah.'

'Oh right, well if it's just for band practice it'll manage the cobbles—'

'Setts.'

Stewart turned when he heard me speak. 'Lana, Jesus!

Why the hell are you in your pyjamas? Where're your shoes?'

I giggled. 'There's a bat on you.'

He frowned. 'Sorry, what?'

'Bat. On your head. Looks well funny.'

'Are you drunk?'

The bat jiggled its wings as if it was laughing. As I watched, all the colour drained out of its body until it was albino-white. Then it fluttered up and disappeared through the ceiling.

'S'a ghost now,' I told Stew matter-of-factly.

'Oh God.' He came over to slip an arm around me and I leaned affably against him. 'Today was your wisdom teeth op, wasn't it?'

'Yep.' I opened my mouth wide so he could see. 'Ahhh!'

'So sorry about this, Rodge,' he said to the flamingo as he guided me out. 'They must've given her something pretty potent. Can you mind the shop for ten minutes while I get her home?'

'Wah-waaah,' the flamingo said with a bob of its beak.

'Hey, you should totally take the Harley,' I called back to it. 'It flies and everything. That is some kind of awesome, Pinky.'

'Bloody hell, what did they give you, LSD?' Stewart panted as he struggled across the road with me.

'Dunno. Ask the snowman.'

'The snowman. Right.'

'Hey.' I wiggled free of his grip and tottered backwards. 'Why're you holding me? Not OK. Don't listen to what Deano said before, that's trollops.'

'Because if I don't you'll fall down.' He put a hand out

just in time to stop me staggering over. 'What's trollops, Lana?'

'You are. I don't even love you one bit.'

'Er, OK,' he panted as he manoeuvred me through the door of the restaurant. 'Tom! You've lost something.'

'Oh my God! How did she get out?' Tom said, darting from behind the bar.

'No idea, she just turned up in the shop talking gibberish. I don't know what they gave her at the dentist's but it must have some impressive street value.'

'Laughing gas, among other things. She got so anxious over the operation, they really dosed her up.'

I giggled. 'Laughing gas. It's called that coz it's funny.'

'Can't you keep an eye on her?' Stewart asked. 'She's not safe like this.'

'I safety-proofed her room and waited till she fell asleep,' Tom said. 'Thought that was her done for the night to be honest, the state she was in. Can you get her upstairs and sit with her till Jaz gets here? She's due any minute.'

Stewart looked hesitant. 'Bit awkward. I left Roger looking after the shop.'

'He won't mind,' Tom said. 'Please, Stew, it won't be for long. I can't leave the restaurant, there's a stag do in. We opened early for them.' He nodded to a table of mead-supping Alsatians in rugby shirts.

'Well... all right. Text Rodge for me, will you? Tell him I'll be back soon as I can.'

'Ta, mate. Up the stairs, first on the right.'

The Alsatians let out a barky cheer as Stewart guided me past, and I gave them a friendly wave.

'I like dogs. Do you like dogs?' I asked Stewart as he

almost carried me up the stairs. 'Oi, are you coming to my room?'

'Yes, I like dogs. And yes, just for a bit.'

'Boys aren't allowed in my bedroom 'less I say.' I wagged a finger at him. 'No funny business, you.'

'I'll try to restrain myself,' he panted. 'Come on, Trippy the Bush Kangaroo.'

In my room, he helped me back into bed. I frowned at the ceiling.

'Stars've gone. Where'd you put them?'

'Maybe they went to sleep. Or maybe your drugs are wearing off.' He sank wearily into the chair by my bed. 'Well that's my exercise for the day. Bloody hell, girl.'

'Am I heavy?'

'When you're a dead weight you are. My arm's gone numb.'

I looked at his arms. They looked like bags of... sexy walnuts. Or something.

'You've got all them muscles though,' I said. 'Hey, can I have a stroke of them?'

'Sorry, no energy left for foreplay.' He squinted at my jaw. 'Looks pretty swollen,' he said in a softer voice. 'Is it hurting you, kid?'

'Don't feel a thing.' I blinked sleepily. 'Why're you here, Stewpot?'

'Because I'm looking after you till your brother gets off work.'

'Why?'

'Don't you know?'

'Nopey.'

He sighed. 'Well, I might as well talk to you while you're too out of it to get all pissed off at me. I bet you think I'm a cartoon platypus or something.'

I giggled. 'Silly.'

'Oh God, Lana,' he said, squeezing his eyes closed. 'I made a right mess of things, didn't I?'

'Yeah.' I jabbed a finger at him from under the covers. 'You said you'd call me. And I waited and waited and waited and waited and… and you didn't.' I frowned. 'Why didn't you?'

'If you'd seen me then, you'd get it.' He let out a sound that was half sigh, half groan. 'I know it was only the one date, Lana, but I could tell there was something special about you. Then I moved here, got to know you better, and I knew I'd been right. That just made it so much worse, knowing I'd blown my shot.'

I blinked hard. Stewart was getting blurry, but I fought back. He was saying stuff. Stuff I had to remember.

'Then you should've rung me like what you said,' I managed to slur.

'I couldn't,' he said, going red. 'After the crash, I – it was the week after. Everything seemed so bleak, so hopeless… I couldn't face it. I couldn't face anything.'

'Pffft,' I snorted. 'Couldn't face it. S'only a phone.'

'You have to understand. After the accident, I wasn't the guy you met that night in the restaurant. Not for a long time.'

'Because your knee hurt?'

'Because I had to quit. I was depressed for the longest time when they told me I wouldn't compete again. I didn't leave the house for four months.'

I blinked the blurry Stewart back into focus, or as close as I could manage.

'Why'd you join my cycling committee, Stewart McLean?'

'Because I thought I could help. I was still coming out of it then. It seemed like just what I needed. And maybe...' He flushed. 'Maybe I thought if we were working together you might stop being pissed off at me and like me again. One day.' He dipped his head to look into my barely open eyes. 'I'm sorry, Lana. I hurt you and I hate myself for it. I don't deserve to have someone like you look twice at me, and I'm a selfish bastard to still be trying to get you to. And yet... I can't help it.'

'Why can't you?'

'Because of how I feel about you,' he said softly. He pulled his chair closer to the bed and leaned down to kiss my hair, brushing his lips lightly against the point where it parted. 'Because there's no one like you; not to me. You know what I'm trying to tell you here, right?'

'That felt nice,' I said, letting my eyes fall closed. 'Do it again, Stew.'

'OK. But no funny business, remember?' He kissed my hair again, then started stroking it softly with his fingertips. It felt so comforting, I didn't want him to ever go away.

'You can get in bed if you want,' I mumbled. 'Cuddles are nice.'

'I think your brother might have something to say about that when he gets here.'

'Been a long time since a boy was in my bed.' I waved my hand. 'Yeeeeears.'

He smiled. 'I'd better forget you told me that. You'll be swallowing your fist about it tomorrow.'

'There was never anyone I wanted to… never time…' I whispered as the black closed in.

'I know, kid,' he said gently, his fingers still playing in my hair.

I yawned heavily. 'Stew?'

'That's me.'

'I like you really, you know.'

'Do you?'

''S,' I managed with the last of my speech. 'Lots. But shush, secret.'

'I like you too, Lana. More than…' were the final words I heard as the last of my consciousness drifted away.

30

The first thing I felt when I woke was pain, searing through my jaw and into my brain. My head was aching like I'd downed ten pints and gone a few rounds with Mike Tyson in his prime.

I checked my phone and groaned: 12.30pm. I'd slept half the day away.

There were strange images floating around my brain. Memories... dreams? The only things I could see clearly were a bat and a pissed-off snowman.

That and Stewart. Had he been in my room? Or was that a dream too?

I swung myself out of bed, massaging my swollen jaw with one hand, and staggered through the door.

There was a man's coat hanging in the hallway when I passed. Cameron must've stayed over.

'Morning,' I said to Tom, who was watching football in the living room. I yawned, then clutched my jaw. 'Fuckcakes, that hurts!'

'If you're inventing new ways to swear then I'm guessing your drugs have worn off.'

'Feel like I've been kicked in the head by a premenstrual rhino. What happened yesterday?'

'Don't you remember?'

'I remember... a talking snowman.'

He grinned. 'Yeah, you spent the afternoon tripping off your tits.'

'Didn't do anything embarrassing, did I?'

'God, yes,' he said. 'It was comedy gold. Next time you have dental surgery it's going straight on YouTube.'

'If it does you're dead. Where's Cam, still in bed?'

'No, he's at work.'

'Oh. Yeah, forgot it was afternoon. Does he know he left his coat?'

Tom shook his head. 'Not his.'

'Whose is it then?'

'Mine,' Stewart said, poking his head round the door of the kitchenette. 'Afternoon, drugface. You want coffee? Kettle's just boiled.'

I glared at him. 'What're you doing here?'

'Thought I'd use my lunch break to pop over and see how you were feeling,' he said, coming into the living room.

'We've been watching the footie while we waited for you to wake up,' Tom told me with guilty smile.

I shook my head. 'If you two're boy-bonding I'm doomed. What do you want, Stew?'

'Just to see if you're feeling better. You were in a real state yesterday afternoon.'

I groaned. 'Then you were here.'

'Yep. You came to see me in your pyjamas and I helped you to bed. It was all very sexy.' He turned to Tom. 'Can you give us a minute, mate? Me and your sister need to have some words.'

'If Lana's OK with it,' he said, glancing at me.

'S'pose,' I muttered. I had a vague idea I was supposed to be annoyed with Stew about something but it'd disappeared in the fog of pain and drugs.

Oh yeah, the bike racks – that was it. Going behind the backs of the committee, getting us yet more bad press. But being annoyed with Stew felt like hard work today, for some reason.

'I'll pop downstairs then,' Tom said. 'Update the specials board or something.' He flashed an anxious look back at us as he pushed open the door.

Stewart took a seat in the armchair and Flash, the treacherous hellhound, slithered out of his bed to weave himself round the warmth of Stew's calves.

'So, what words do you think we need to have?' I asked.

'Well, there's an apology coming. And I need to tell you some news.'

'News?' I said, instantly alert. I'd learned to dread that word over the last few months. 'You haven't heard from the council? Ow!' I clutched at my jaw. The sudden panic was making my gums vibrate.

'Calm down, it's nothing bad. Look, can I do my apology first?'

'If you must. What're you apologising for today?'

He looked at me keenly. 'Don't you remember any of yesterday?'

'Not really, no.'

He lapsed into thoughtful silence for a moment.

'I'm sorry about the bike racks,' he said at last. 'You're right: I should've run it past the committee. Wanted to surprise you, that's all. I genuinely thought you'd think it was funny.'

'Hmm. OK.'

'It never occurred to me it was all grist to the mill for Sienna Edge. I'm sorry, Lana.'

'Suppose you weren't to know,' I said, relenting at last. It was hard to stay mad at him with that earnest, pleading look in his eyes. 'It's the council's reaction that worries me. You know how they are about anything that could reflect badly on them.'

Stewart smiled. 'Then I should probably tell you my news.'

'Go on,' I said, frowning.

'Only if you promise not to have a go at me about doing things behind your back. I caused this and I wanted to sort it.'

'Sort it how?'

'Look, I know you like to keep Andy all to yourself, but I gave him a ring this morning to tell him what'd happened,' he said. 'I thought it'd be better coming from us. Anyway, he didn't seem to think it was a problem. We had a good laugh about it.'

'Really?'

'Yeah. I don't think the council are as prudish as we thought. We got ourselves all worked up over nothing.'

I flushed. 'You mean I did.'

'Well. The viaduct project's your baby, isn't it? Of course you're protective of it,' he said. 'Anyway, I was just as bad. I was scared stiff I might've jeopardised the whole thing.'

His expression was serious, but there was an amused glint in his eye. What wasn't he telling me?

'OK, what?' I said, my mouth twitching with a smile. 'Out with it.'

'Nothing,' he said, casting his eyes to the ceiling.

'I know you, Stewart. Come on, what else?'

He nodded to the window. 'See for yourself.'

I stood up, massaging my jaw as another spasm shot through it, and twitched open the curtains.

There was a little gaggle of teenagers clustered around Stewart's bike racks, giggling as they took photos of each other posing with the bums. One lad was laid across a pair of buttocks, pouting provocatively as his snickering girlfriend took a pic on her phone, while another crouched in a position that made it look like the huge backside was his own.

'We've gone viral,' Stew said. 'There's a whole Facebook group set up for fans of what they're calling The Arses of Egglethwaite. People've been coming from all over to take pictures with them.'

'Bloody hell! They've only been there a week.'

'Yep, and already a landmark. The best thing is, I put a donations box up by them for the viaduct. We've made nearly a hundred quid.'

I fixed him with an impressed gaze. 'In a week? That's amazing!'

'Isn't it? It's been bringing in a good bit of business for the shop too. Hope you don't mind, but I pinched a few of your Flagons business cards to put on the counter. Thought it might get you some knock-on trade.'

'Did you?' I said, blinking. 'Thanks, Stew. That was a nice thought.' I laughed. 'Sienna'll just love the fact she's boosted trade for us, won't she?'

'So am I properly forgiven this time?'

'You're forgiven. I'm sorry. Overreacted, didn't I?'

'No, you were right. It was reckless and I should've thought it through.' His eyes darted over my face. 'You mean it this time? Because I actually came over to offer to resign. If you wanted me to.'

'Resign from the cycling group? Why?'

'You seemed so pissed off with me the other day in the restaurant. I can't be in meetings if you don't want me there, Lana.'

'I do want you there.' I flushed. 'I mean, we all do. You're the cycling expert, aren't you? Can't do without you.'

'Hoped you'd say that.' He stood up. 'Right, I'd better get back to the shop. See you later, kid.'

And he was gone, leaving me as confused as ever. That did seem to be the lingering aftertaste of a chat with Stewart McLean.

'Well, we made friends again,' I told Tom when he came back up. 'Sort of.'

'What, you've forgiven him?'

'For the bike rack thing, yeah.'

'And the not calling you thing?'

'Not that. Not yet.' I massaged my jaw again. 'Be a while before that one stops hurting.'

'Hmm.'

I turned to glare at him. 'Why're you always saying "hmm"? If you've got something to say, just come on out with it.'

'You sure you want to hear it?'

'I'm a big girl, I can take it. Je*sus*!' I grabbed my jaw as another spasm shot through it. 'Go on, tell me while I'm in pain. Might make it easier to digest.'

'Well, I've got this theory.' He paused. 'You sure you want to hear?'

'Oh for God's sake, get on with it.'

'All right. I reckon Stew's in love with you.'

I frowned. 'Have you been talking to Deano?'

'No, why?'

'He said… only…' I shook my head. 'Never mind. You're both wrong.'

'I don't think so.' He started counting on his fingers. 'He's been coming into the restaurant more and more. He's always staring at your boobs. He flirts like mad with you. Looks after you when you're on drugs.'

'That's just fancying someone though.'

'Yeah. It's the looks he gives you that were the clincher.'

'What looks?'

'The soft ones with the love-light in his eyes. The ones that seem to say "Ooooh, Lana, hold me close against your ginormous bosoms and whisper sweet nothings to me for ever and ever".'

I shook my head. 'You watch too many films.'

'I'm serious,' he said. 'He does look all soppy at you. Plus he calls you "kid".'

'I know, patronising git.'

'He only does it sometimes though. When he's worried about you, like he feels protective. And he touches you inappropriately.'

'He does not!'

'All right, he touches you appropriately then. Patting your hand and stuff. When you mention Dad, mostly.'

I blinked. 'You noticed all that? I didn't.'

'No, well you're as bad.' He sighed. 'You know, I can't help liking him. Wish it was all straightforward for you, sis.'

'Me too.' My brow lowered. 'But it isn't, is it?'

'Did he tell you why he did it?'

'He told me he was depressed after he had to quit cycling. The bottom dropped out of his world – that's how he described it last week in the restaurant.'

'And you're not happy with that.'

'That I can understand. It's the fact he left it a whole bloody year. A year, and not a word.' I scowled. 'And then he just turns up out of the blue, grinning obliviously like it'd meant nothing, asking if we can be friends... ugh.'

'Why did he do that?'

'God knows.' A single tear slid down my cheek. 'Wish I could just hate him, Tommy,' I whispered.

He guided my head to his shoulder. 'Hard work, these relationship things, eh?'

'They make my jaw hurt.' I snuffled wet eyes on his T-shirt. 'How'd it go talking to Cam?'

'Well, I'm meeting the parents now,' he said with a grimace. 'He sulked me into it in the end.'

'Did you tell him what you were scared of?'

'Not sure I got my point across too well.' He clicked his tongue and Flash went bounding up for a stroke. 'I thought I'd said absolutely no way to the parent thing, but apparently I agreed unreservedly. So he tells me anyway.'

'When is it?'

He groaned. 'Next month, week after The Boneshaker. Hey, reckon your dentist'd sell me some drugs? If Cam's parents were animated snowmen I bet they'd be a lot easier to handle.'

31

I had genuinely forgiven Stew for The Great Bum Rack Debacle. Still, I don't know what it was: after our latest falling-out-and-making-up, something seemed to change between us.

We were matey enough, but I felt strangely awkward in his company, especially on the rare occasions it was just the two of us. And although he was his usual funny, flirty self, there was a certain... I don't know, keenness. I often caught him looking at me when he thought I wasn't paying attention, then quickly averting his eyes.

I tried my best to ignore it, throwing myself into planning for The Boneshaker with gusto. If ever I found myself thinking about what Deano had said the day the committee visited, I pushed it to the bottom of my mind.

At least the viaduct fundraising was straightforward, an antidote to my confused and confusing feelings about Stew. I'd been working really hard – promoting the calendars, encouraging groups to set up their own events, roping in volunteers for The Boneshaker – and the thermometer outside the Temp had shot up to eighteen grand. We were still waiting on the council grant, but Andy sounded confident the delays were just paperwork.

Added to that was the excitement of finally seeing the route map, which was released by the Le Tour organisers in late October. We still had to wait until January for the official announcement that Egglethwaite would be included, but for now just looking at the wiggly Stage 2 line running between York and Sheffield gave me a buzz.

The Boneshaker was to be a sort of autumn fete-cum-community trick or treat with a spooky cycling theme, something a bit different than the usual vegetable shows and harvest festivals. Practically everyone in the village had been roped into getting involved one way or another.

The kids had been decorating their bikes for a costume procession down the main street, with a prize for the scariest bike and owner. We had over thirty themed stalls and pocket-money games in and outside the Temp, where a wide cobbled yard served as our village green, and Billy was setting up a beer tent for thirsty grown-ups at one end.

For entertainment we had Gerry's morris men, who were down to dance a Welsh border morris – spookier than their usual ribbons-and-hankies prancing, apparently – and Roger had had the band rehearsing a selection of Halloween music. You haven't lived until you've heard 'Werewolves of London' arranged for brass.

Me, Tom, Sue and Gerry arrived at the yard, lantern-lit for the occasion, shortly before kick-off.

'Right, I'd better go get changed,' Gerry said.

'Where's your kit?' Tom asked. 'You'll have to dance in your vest and pants if you've forgotten it, you know.'

He grinned. 'Jim's bringing it. Bit different than the usual clobber. Wait and see.'

I glanced down at my uniform as Gerry dashed off ahead to the Temp. At least with the morris men performing, the band wouldn't be the most ridiculously dressed people there for a change.

Speaking of which…

I nudged Tom and pointed to where Yolanda was waiting for us. 'Check out Audrey Hepburn's big sister.'

'Jesus. Has she raided Jasmine's wardrobe?'

Yolanda had abandoned her usual shawls in favour of some oversized designer sunglasses and a big floppy hat. It was the low-cut and oh-so-very skintight little black dress that really disturbed me though.

Sue snorted. 'Oi, mutton dressed as lamb,' she called as we approached. 'What's with the get-up?'

Yolanda turned to give her what I recognised as a pretty filthy look, despite the sunglasses.

'Well, you should know, Old McDonald. You're the sheep expert.'

'Don't come the class warfare line with me, sweetheart,' Sue said. 'What've you done with your two A levels that's so amazing? And everyone knew you only got those because you were having it off with Mr Gallagher in exchange for private tuition.'

'I was not!' Yolanda lowered her voice. 'It was Mr Boswell. And my God, was he worth it.'

'Bloody hell. No wonder the poor sod died of a heart attack.'

'Just because you didn't lose your virginity until you were twenty-one, Susan.'

Tom shook his head. 'I did not need to know that.'

'Enough,' I said, holding up a hand for quiet. 'No bitching

today, please, ladies. This is supposed to be a jolly village event, not an episode of *Dynasty*.'

'She started it,' Yolanda muttered.

'And I'm finishing it. Behave, Yo-yo, or I'm sending you to your room.' I glanced at Tom, the nearest man of her preferred age within grabbing distance. 'Alone.'

'Spoilsport.'

'Why aren't you in fancy dress then, Yo-yo?' Tom asked. He gestured down at his zombie cyclist costume. 'We were expecting group members to set a good example.'

'Oh but I am,' Yolanda said. 'Ladies Who Lunch decided on a Witches of Eastwick dress code for our stall, to add a bit of glamour. Spooky buns and tarot card reading. We're calling ourselves The Cupcake Clairvoyants.'

'You'd better not be got up like a dog's dinner for the benefit of some poor lad, that's all,' Sue said.

Yolanda scanned Sue's high-vis vest with disdain. 'And what're you supposed to be, the planet Saturn? It clashes dreadfully with your hair, you know.'

'I'm marshalling the kiddies' procession,' Sue said. 'But of course, with your psychic powers you already knew that.'

'Of course.'

Sue put two fingers on each temple. 'OK, what am I thinking now?'

Yolanda grinned. 'Language, Susan Lightowler.'

Sue laughed and slapped her on the back. 'All right, love, that's enough fun for one afternoon. Come help me get the little dears in position.'

When they'd gone, I shook my head. 'I'll never get those two. Have you ever seen a friendship built entirely on out-insulting each other before?'

'Well, if Gerry and Sue managed to build a marriage on it...' Tom said with a shrug. 'You'd better go find Roger. He'll panic if you're late, and you know that makes him go extra pompous.'

'Where's Stew?' I asked casually as we made our way to the band's marquee. 'He is still running our cycling group stall, isn't he?'

'Hmm.'

I nudged him in the ribs. 'Oi. Can you cut out the Stew-related hmming, just for today?'

'Hmm. Well, all right.' He gestured to the tables around the edges of the courtyard. 'Me, Stew and Cam are supposed to be stallholder liaisons. I'd better go find them actually.'

'All right, see you later.' I gave his elbow a goodbye pat and nipped under the marquee.

'Afternoon, fellers,' I said to the band, squeezing down the second row to my seat. '"Abide With Me" on standby in case it all goes tits up, yeah?'

All my nightmares for weeks that hadn't been about giant flamingoes and mead-supping Alsatians had involved no one turning up for this event. We'd really put all our eggs in one basket by going for a single big fundraiser rather than a lot of smaller ones, and we were counting on a healthy five-grand profit.

After about ten minutes, a crowd had started to gather. I breathed a sigh of relief.

Roger struck us up for a bit of creepy background music: the *Star Wars* imperial march. It was an old favourite and I knew the part by heart, so I was free to keep one eye on the growing crowd.

Nearly all the kids and quite a few adults were in fancy

dress. There was a scythe-wielding Grim Reaper in black Lycra, a ghost rattling bike chains, a witch with a bike-mounted broomstick... the theme had obviously captured Egglethwaite's imagination.

I tried not to look at a giant vampire bat in a cycling helmet. It reminded me of the barbastelles.

Sienna Edge had been doing her damnedest to get us into a war of words in the press, upping the heartstring-tugging with every letter she wrote, but I'd kept my word to Tom and refused to engage. She was still painting us as the heartless millionaire capitalists intent on wiping out a colony of innocent baby bats, like a bloody Disney film from the eighties. What's worse, other letters were starting to appear. Letters of support for her.

Whenever I nagged Andy for the wildlife report, the answer was the same one I got when I asked about our loan: paperwork delay. But his warm, reassuring tone always left me feeling things were in safe hands.

Suddenly I noticed Roger glaring at me, waving his baton emphatically, and realised I'd raced ahead a few bars while my thoughts wandered. Luckily the kids' procession was about to start so no one was paying us much attention.

I couldn't help smiling as I watched the children getting ready, their faces shining with excitement and mischief. Some of the cutest little witches, werewolves and monsters you ever saw, pushing bikes covered in everything from mummies' bandages to real homemade slime. They each had a trick-or-treat basket attached to the front, the idea being that villagers would throw sweeties into them as they went by. The cycling celebrity Stew had got for us – a former Tour de France winner turned coach called Harry

Croston, apparently pretty big if you followed that sort of thing – was to judge best costume.

I could see Stewart in the crowd too. He was with someone else: a tall, well-built vampire with his face painted deathly white.

That costume – tailored and expensive-looking, not the usual tatty wear-once clobber people bought for these events. And that disdainful lip curl, the swaggering gait…

Ugh. Harper Brady, trying to be incognito again. I'd been avoiding his calls ever since our disastrous fake date.

The band had a special number lined up to accompany the bike parade: 'Time Warp' from *The Rocky Horror Picture Show*, with cornet solo. A bloody cornet solo. In 'Time Warp'. When Harry Croston gave the word, the kids started wheeling their bikes down the hill to the mellifluous sound of a brass band murdering a school disco favourite.

Harry eventually selected a tiny girl of about four as the costume prize winner. She and her bike were dressed all in yellow with a load of grey cardboard triangles attached, and when Harry asked what scary thing she was meant to be, she whispered shyly that she was 'shark-infested custard'. I was guessing it wasn't a gag she'd supplied herself, but it got a laugh out of Harry and she attached the blue rosette proudly to her onesie.

After that it was another five numbers from us, then a break while Gerry's morris men took over. Abandoning my trombone, I went to talk to Sue.

'Will you look at that?' she said when I joined her. I followed her gaze to the beer tent, where a gang of pint-nursing morris men in various stages of drunkenness were huddled.

'Bloody hell, what're they wearing?' I said, goggling.

'It's not what they're wearing that worries me, love.' She nodded to Gerry. 'It's that second pint he's just glugged.'

'To be fair, I can see why he needs a drink. Is that what border morris dancers wear then?'

She shrugged. 'So his lordship tells me. Tragic, isn't it?'

Egglethwaite Morris Men were a familiar sight at village events in the traditional white bloomers and bells, but today's get-up was radically different. Knee-length smocks covered in red and orange rag-ribbons and battered top hats stuck with feathers, faces painted with swirly black patterns – they looked like fire demons or something. They also looked ridiculous, but being morris men they were presumably used to that.

'Suppose it is spookier than the usual gear,' I said.

'You know, we were twenty when I first let him take me out. Thought he looked like Martin Kemp without the eyeliner.' She sighed. 'Now look what I'm married to.'

'Ah, give over. You love him to bits.'

'I do, sadly. Although I might change my mind in a minute when he starts titting about like Fairy bloody Snowdrop.'

I felt a jab in the back, and turned to find Tom and Deano behind me.

'You two coming for a wander or did you want to stay for Gerry's dance?' Tom asked.

'Better not,' I said. 'Might hurt his feelings if I descend into fits of uncontrollable laughter.'

'Again.'

'I'll stay,' Sue said. 'He'll only sulk if one of us isn't here for moral support. See you in a bit, kids.'

32

I took an arm each of the two lads and we started meandering through the crowd, looking at the stalls.

'No Cam?' I asked Tom.

He flushed. 'No. I'm avoiding him a bit, to be honest. This meet the parents thing's still sore. The closer it gets, the more terrified I get, and he won't let me out of it.'

'Just talk to him about it, mate,' Deano said.

'Easy for you,' Tom said, glaring at him. 'You just say whatever pops into your head with no worries, don't you? I have talked to him. He always seems to end up more confused than before.'

'Write to him then,' I suggested. 'Might be easier to explain your chronic shyness by letter.'

He looked thoughtful. 'That's not a bad idea actually.' He nodded to Stewart on our cycling group stall. 'Come on, we'd better show our faces over there. Curious to see what he's doing.'

'Don't you two know what's on your own stall?' Deano asked as we weaved through the crowd.

'We couldn't think of anything good in the planning meeting,' I told him. 'Stew said to leave it with him.'

I frowned when we reached our table. Apart from a stack

of calendars for sale there was nothing on it at all: just a sign shaped like a pair of lips with £1 written on. Stewart saluted when he saw me, like he always did when I was in my band uniform.

'You'd better be flogging homemade lip balm, McLean.'

He grinned. 'Guess again.'

I shook my head. 'Selling kisses – seriously? That is so tacky.'

'Bit of fun, isn't it?' he said, shrugging. 'I'm having a great afternoon.'

'Oh, I bet you are. Hope you get a cold sore.'

'I meant takings-wise.' He shook his bowl of coins. 'Why, Lana, jealous?'

'Um, let me think… no. What's soft-core prostitution got to do with Halloween then? Or cycling?'

'Well, I was a cyclist. And the kisses are pretty spine-tingling.' He waggled his eyebrows. 'Fancy a free sample? I don't usually do try before you buy, but for you…'

'This wasn't Yo-yo's idea, by any chance?' Tom asked.

'How'd you guess?' Stew nodded to the cash bowl. 'About a fiver of that came from her. She's my best customer.'

'You astound me,' I muttered.

'Go on, I'll take one.' Deano chucked a quid in Stewart's bowl and leaned over the table to plant a big kiss on his lips.

'Er, whew. Thanks, Deano.' Stewart rubbed under his nose. 'You shaved today, mate?'

'No.'

'I can tell.'

Tom shook his head. 'Straight guys are weird.'

'What is it with you and personal space?' I asked Deano.

He shrugged. 'I had a very lonely childhood.'

'Where's Harper?' I said to Stewart. 'I saw him creeping about in his vampire costume.'

'He's around somewhere. Probably bragging about how he was first choice to play Edward Cullen in *Twilight*.'

Tom's eyebrows shot up. 'Bloody hell, was he?'

'Nah, don't be daft. That's just what he tells girls.'

'Did you have to invite him?' I said. 'You already got us a celeb; we don't need Harper Brady's unique brand of star appeal.'

'I didn't. He just turned up. Must've seen my plug on Facebook. He's been following me round like a puppy lately. Don't know what's up with him.'

There was a queue building behind us: a gang of girls about my age whispering together and giggling. Stewart had become a bit of a local heartthrob lately, and I'd noticed a steady increase in the number of women popping into McLean's Machines. They never seemed to come out with a bike, although quite a few emerged clutching calendars.

'How much do you think he charges to do it with his shirt off?' I heard one girl mutter to her friend.

'So, Lana?' Stewart said. 'Last chance. I've got customers waiting.'

'If it'll shut you up.' Something about the girls seemed to have brought out my recessive jealous gene. For some reason, I didn't want to go without them seeing Stewart give me a kiss.

'On the cheek,' I said as I leaned over the table. But it was too late. He'd already taken my chin in his palm and the next second his lips were on mine.

If I thought I'd put our kiss that night at Pagans' Rock behind me, well, I was wrong. As soon as our lips met, it came rushing back: the rightness of it, the unleavable security of his arms. I could feel my body waking for him, just as it had then – just as it sometimes did in the dreams I'd never admit to.

And yet this kiss was chaste as anything on the surface. There was no searching tongue, no urgency, no bodies pressed close. It was gentle and lingering, his thumb just caressing the tip of my ear as he held his lips against mine. The purity of it, the sweet, beautiful simplicity of his touch, was what caught me off guard. God, it was sexy.

'Lana…' he whispered when he drew back, his eyes holding mine.

I cleared my throat. 'Right. Thanks for that.' I managed what I hoped was an unconcerned smile as I chucked a pound in his bowl. 'For a good cause, right?'

'Bloody hell, was that really only a quid's worth?' I heard one of the girls whisper as I marched away. 'Wonder what I could get for a tenner.'

'And you can both stop looking at me like that,' I said to the boys when we were out of earshot.

'She hates that guy, you know,' Tom said to Deano.

'Oh, yeah. Obvious. I often kiss tenderly with people I hate while they stroke my ears.'

I shot him an accusing glare. 'You kissed him too.'

'Not like that I didn't. That was out of *Casablanca* or something.'

'Come on, sis,' Tom said quietly. 'Why not stop kidding yourself, eh?'

I sighed. 'I'm not kidding myself. I mean, I'm trying to, but… well, it's not working, is it?'

'You can say that again.'

'OK, so I like him,' I admitted. 'More than I've liked anyone in a long while. Ever, probably. And you two going on about it all the time is hardly helping.'

'Why don't you do something about it then?' Deano asked.

'Such as?'

'Well, maybe I'm being too scientific about this, but if I like someone and I think being with them might make us both happy, I be with them. You know, in the biblical sense. With genitals.'

'Even if they'd hurt you once before?'

'I admit that's never come up,' he confessed.

I looked at Tom. 'What do you think?'

He sighed. 'I don't know. I want you to be happy, and he seems to make you happy – sometimes, anyway. But he hurt you, and I don't want you to be hurt. I'm a simple person, Lana. To be honest I'm a bit out of my depth.'

Deano pointed to where Yolanda was doing her cupcakes and clairvoyancy. 'You could try professional help. Maybe your future's in the cards.'

I snorted. 'What, Mystic Yo-yo? I don't think so.'

'Go on. Might cheer you up, at least.'

He guided me to Yolanda's stall. She'd spread a red-and-white-checked tablecloth over it, a crystal ball stuck in the middle next to a pack of tarot cards. The whole display was, rather bizarrely, surrounded by gravestone cupcakes on little silver stands.

'Evening, gorgeous,' Deano said to Yolanda with a wink. 'Brought you a customer.'

'How much are the cupcakes?' I asked.

Deano shook his head. 'Don't let her get out of it,

Yo-yo. Lana needs some advice on her love life from the spirit world.'

Yolanda tutted. 'Tarot has nothing to do with the spirit world, darling. It's all about channelling your own latent energy. The cards are merely a guide to help you clear the blockages you've created for yourself.'

Deano nodded. 'I get it. Roughage for the soul.'

'Well yes, if you must put it that way.'

'Where do you get all this New Age guff, Yo-yo?' Tom asked.

'There was a feature on it in *Perfect Homes*.' She picked up her tarot pack and held it out to me. 'OK, Lana, I'm going to ask you to cut the deck in three places for past, present and future. All the time you must be focusing on the question you want answered.'

'You don't really believe in all this, do you?' I said.

'But of course, hun,' she said, eyes wide at the mere suggestion. 'There are more things in heaven and earth and so forth. You should try opening your mind a little.'

I took the cards from her with a resigned sigh.

As I shuffled them, I tried to focus on the question I wanted to ask. What was it? Something to do with Stewart. Why was he so annoying? No, that wasn't it. Why did he have to keep popping up in my life to make things all confusing? How did he get his hair so perfect?

'Try to keep your energy positive, dear, or you may get a bad reading,' Yolanda said.

'I am positive.'

'Are you? You look angry to me.'

I lifted my frown and forced my face into something a bit more neutral. The question I eventually focused on as I cut the deck three times and handed the cards to Yolanda was simple. What the fuck do I do now?

Yolanda laid the three cards I'd selected face down on the tablecloth.

'OK, let's see what we have. The first card represents something from your past that's colouring your life in the present. Something that still needs closure.'

She turned it over and looked up at me with sympathy in her eyes. 'Oh, darling, I am sorry.'

The picture was of a heart, pierced with three swords.

'What's it mean then?' I said, my tone carefully nonchalant.

'The Three of Swords means just what it looks like. Heartbreak. Pain or loss in your romantic life.'

Deano nudged me. 'See? It works.'

'It can't work. It's random, isn't it?'

Yolanda drew herself up. 'It most certainly is not random, young lady. And if you're not taking it seriously I may decide not to do the rest of the reading. Honestly, typical Aries.'

'Sorry, Yo-yo,' I said with an apologetic smile. 'Go on, please. What's in my present?'

She turned the next card, which showed a grinning moron in motley. I didn't need to be a tarot expert to guess this one was called The Fool. Anyway, it was printed underneath.

'Oh, very nice,' I said, folding my arms.

'Ha!' Tom leaned round me to talk to Deano. 'You're right, it does work.'

'No, no, you're misinterpreting the card,' Yolanda said. 'The Fool doesn't represent literal foolishness. It can signify new beginnings, a freeing of the spirit.' She squinted at it through her sunglasses. 'Only...'

'Only what?' I said.

'Well, it's upside down. A reversed Fool means something different. Naivety, wilful blindness...' She looked up at me. 'Is there anything in your life you've been avoiding facing up to, Lana?'

'No,' I mumbled.

'You would say that though, wouldn't you?' Deano shook his head. 'This is uncanny. Do the last one, Yo-yo.'

She flipped the last card, and despite my lack of faith I instinctively recoiled. It was the one card in the tarot everyone knows and fears. Death.

'Now, don't worry,' Yolanda said quickly. 'Death doesn't mean what people think. It's a positive card, especially for the future.'

'What does it mean?' Tom asked. He looked frightened too. Perhaps after losing Dad we were more superstitious than we realised.

'Change or rebirth; an upsetting of the status quo, perhaps. Not always for the better, but that very much depends on the individual. The energy for change is there; it just needs to be channelled.'

'Well, Lana?' Deano said. 'Reckon you're ready to align your chakras and do some channelling?'

'I reckon I'm ready for a cupcake.'

When we'd paid Yolanda for the reading and a bun each, we wandered away to watch the end of Gerry's dance. The morris men were still skipping about bashing sticks together, although Sue had wisely sidled off to the beer tent.

'How weird was that?' Deano said. 'It's like the cards knew all about you, Lana. Heartbreak, hiding, change... we might have to burn Yo-yo as a witch.'

'Don't be daft,' I said through a mouthful of crumbs. 'She could've picked any three cards and we would've made them about Stew. You see what you want to see; that's how it works.'

Still, the whole incident had left me jittery, if only because it'd forced me to think about Stewart. Our history, how I felt about him now, and... future. Did we have any future?

I wished I hadn't let Deano talk me into it.

'Right,' Tom said when he'd finished his bun. 'I'd better go find Cam. Don't want him to think I'm sulking.'

'I'm going back to Yo-yo's,' Deano said. 'Quite fancy a go on the tarots myself. You coming, Lana?'

'No, the band'll be back on soon. I'll wait here till Rodge needs me.' I didn't want to watch Deano getting his cards read. The pictures on those things creeped me out.

33

A few minutes later someone tapped me on the shoulder. I turned to find a well-groomed vampire grinning at me.

'Sexy outfit,' Harper said. 'Have you got the pompoms to go with it?'

'Ugh. You and Stew really are cousins, aren't you?'

'Can't believe you play in a brass band. Is it supposed to be ironic or what?'

'Er, no. I enjoy it.'

He laughed. 'You are the strangest girl. Hey, did you get a new phone, babe? Keep ringing you and there's no answer.'

Of course. Obviously it wouldn't occur to Harper Brady I just didn't want to talk to him.

I sighed. 'Harper, listen, I'm sorry. I've been ignoring your calls.'

'Why would you do that?'

I shook my head. 'Do you really not know what it means when a girl you've been out with doesn't take your calls?'

'Can't say it's ever happened before.'

'Look, I didn't want to hurt your feelings, but – well, I never should've gone out with you when I knew you

309

weren't my type. It wasn't fair and I'm sorry. Let's just leave it at that, shall we?'

He frowned. 'You mean you still don't like me?'

Bloody eureka…

'You're not as bad as I once thought,' I admitted. 'But I don't *like* you like you. Sorry. And I'm not in a great place to be dating right now, to be honest. I lost my dad earlier this year.'

'Did you? I didn't know that.'

'Well, no. You wouldn't, would you?' I glared at him. 'Tell me one thing you do know about me, Harper. Just one.'

'Why?'

'Humour me.'

'OK, well, you…' He hesitated, scanning my body for clues. 'You play in a band?'

'What instrument?'

'Er, trumpet?'

'Wrong. Anything else?'

'You're at least an E-cup?'

I shook my head. 'Typical. OK, my turn. Your mum's called Sonia. She patented the upside-down squeezy sauce bottle, raised you alone and died when you were eighteen. You've got an agent, Bernice, and you reckon you'll get a BAFTA nomination next year. You won Rear of the Year 2013 and you're excessively proud of the fact. Your favourite colour's duck-egg blue, your favourite animal's an armadillo and you take a size eleven shoe – shall I go on?'

'Bloody hell,' Harper said, blinking. 'You know all that about me?'

'I could probably reel off your inside leg measurement, mate,' I said. 'Know why? Because when we went out, you spent over an hour talking about yourself and didn't ask me a thing.'

'Come on, that's not fair.'

'I'm telling you, Harper. Not a single, solitary thing,' I said. 'Look, I'll see you later, OK?'

I turned to head back to the band marquee. There was ten minutes yet, but Roger was there arranging his music and it seemed as good a way to escape as any.

'Lana, wait.' Harper put one hand on my shoulder. 'Don't go yet. Let me say one last thing.'

'OK, what?'

'Look, women don't say no to me. That doesn't happen.'

'Well, it just did, so...'

His brow knit into a puzzled frown. 'OK, suppose it did. But it's pretty rare.'

'Where are you headed with this, Harper?' I demanded. 'You're not going *Indecent Proposal* on me, are you? Because I can promise you, I don't need the money that badly.'

'No. I'm apologising, aren't I?'

'Are you?' I shook my head. 'You must be seriously out of practice.'

He smiled. 'I am a bit. What's the usual way?'

'You'd start with a sorry, usually. A brag about being irresistible to women: less common.'

'OK, then I'm sorry,' he said. 'I'm sorry for being like I am, and I'm sorry you didn't have a nice time when we went out. I know I'm hard work – Stew tells me all the time. I can't help it.'

'Course you can help it. That's just an excuse.'

'You have to understand, Lana. Nearly all my life I've been told exactly what I want to hear. If I wanted something, I just took it... until you came along.' He dipped his head to look into my eyes. 'I – well, the truth is I keep thinking about you. Since we went out you're in my head, all the time, and I don't know what to do about it.'

'Because I'm something you can't have.'

'No. Because you treat me like a real person. Because you're different from anyone else in my life. I want to keep you in it.'

I shook my head. 'I'm sorry. I do like you – sort of. Sometimes. But you're not right for me and that's an end of it.'

'I could change. With someone like you to show me how I could.'

'But that's not good enough, is it? I'm not a prop for you, Harper. I've got my own life. I wasn't put on this earth to show you how to live yours.'

'Won't you just go out with me again?' he said, his blue eyes pleading. 'This time I want to hear all about you, babe: every little thing.'

'No, Harper. Look, I've got to go.'

'Come on, just once to make it up to you. I'll take you to Venice.'

I snorted. 'That better be the name of a cocktail bar.'

'Seriously. I know this adorable little place on the water. I can fly us out there; it'll be romantic.'

'See, this is exactly what I mean,' I said, shaking my head. 'Big, showy gestures like flying to Venice aren't a substitute for genuine interest in the other person, Harper.'

'But I am interested, promise. Won't you? It doesn't have to be Venice. You can pick the place; anywhere you want.'

'I told you, no. I just don't see you that way, I'm sorry. I have to go now. My conductor's staring at me.'

'All right, bye then,' he muttered, looking dejected under his white face paint. 'You've got my number if you change your mind.'

'Oh, and Lana?' he said as I turned to go.

I glanced over my shoulder. 'What now?'

'I'm sorry about your dad. I know what it's like to lose a parent too young.' He smiled: a warm, sneer-free smile different than his usual lip curl. Suddenly he looked a lot more like Stew. 'It does get easier, I promise.'

I blinked. 'That's... well, thanks, Harper. See you around, I guess.'

It was dark by the time we finished playing, and most of the crowd had disappeared.

The plan was for volunteers to get everything tidied away then head to the Fox for a post-fundraiser pint. When I eventually made it over, I found all our group except Cameron already there, a bottle of Prosecco in a cooler between them.

'Are we celebrating?' I asked, claiming a seat next to Tom and helping myself to a glass.

'Yep.' Stewart shot me a warm smile. I dropped eye contact, remembering our kiss earlier. 'Ask Gerry why.'

'You haven't counted up already, Gerry?'

Gerry grinned. 'Not all of it, but I can give you the estimated profit.'

'Oh my God!' I said, clocking his triumphant expression. 'We hit target?'

'And then some. Looking like we made eight grand.'

'We never! From a little village event? That's incredible!'

'It's not all from stalls,' Tom said. He looked a little down, I couldn't help noticing. 'There was a three-grand donation as well. Mr Squeezy Sauce. He gave Stew a cheque before he left.'

I frowned. 'Did he now?'

'Yeah,' Stewart said. 'Maybe he thought that Grim Reaper bloke was the Ghost of Christmas Yet to Come or something. Suddenly he's riddled with charitable feelings towards his fellow man.'

'Hmm.' I took a meditative sip of my wine. The fizzy stuff tended to go straight to my head, and I made a mental note to take it slow. 'I'm not sure we should accept it.'

'Why not, chicken?' Sue asked.

'Well…' I hesitated, wondering how much I wanted to tell them. 'OK, this might sound weird, but I think he's trying to impress me.'

Yolanda laughed. 'You? Don't be silly.'

I glared at her. 'And what's so incredible about that, Yo-yo?'

'Oh, I didn't mean to insult you,' she said. 'It's just that he's Harper Brady, isn't he? His last girlfriend was Ava Dubois – you know, the supermodel? I saw a photoshoot with them in *Hello!* earlier this year. I mean, no offence in the world, Lana. You're very pretty when you make the effort, but…'

She trailed off, the words 'you're no supermodel' hanging unsaid in the air.

'That thing with Ava was a PR stunt,' Stewart said. 'His agent set it up to build some publicity for *Soar* and her new perfume range.'

'Good God! Really?' Yolanda looked as if her whole world had been rocked. I mean, if you couldn't even trust *Hello!*, what hope was there for humanity?

'Not that Harper doesn't do all right for himself, for some unknown reason.' Stew sent me a look, one I couldn't quite interpret. 'He does seem keen on our Lana though.'

'But why?' Yolanda said.

'Well, Yo-yo, maybe, just maybe, he appreciates my many sterling qualities and sparkling personality.' I sighed. 'Plus he's got a thing for my boobs.'

'Oh.' Yolanda shot them an envious glance. 'Well, if he likes it that obvious...'

'Lana's a beautiful girl,' Stewart said, taking a casual gulp of Prosecco. 'Harper's a lot of things but he's not stupid.'

'Um, thanks,' I mumbled. From the corner of my eye I saw Sue fix me with an appraising stare.

'So do you think we should take the money, Stew?' Tom asked. 'I don't want to repair the viaduct if it means pimping out my sister.'

'Absolutely we should take it,' Stewart said firmly. 'Three grand's spare change to Harper. He's probably already forgotten he donated it. About time he started spending on good causes instead of fast cars.'

'Lana?' Tom said.

'I don't know,' I said. 'Doesn't feel right, somehow.'

'How did it come about, Stewart?' Sue asked.

'Harper asked what we were raising money for so I told

him all about the viaduct. Your dad,' he said, nodding to me and Tom. 'And he said he wanted to make a donation.'

'Did he mention me?' I said.

'He said he'd been talking to you. Said he was a selfish bastard and it was about time he started thinking about other people a bit.' He shook his head. 'I think he might be ill.'

'Are we keeping it then?' Gerry was looking panicked at the idea of giving back money.

'Yes,' I said at last. 'If that's what he said.' I laughed. 'Hey, this'll be the first Grand Départ fuelled by ketchup.'

Gerry breathed a sigh of relief. 'Champion. I'll send him a thank-you letter from the group.'

'Can't believe we made target.' I topped up my Prosecco. 'Where's Cam? He should be here for this.'

Tom flushed. 'Not coming. We had another row.'

'Oh no, Tommy. Not the parent thing again.'

'Yeah. Told him I'm not going and that's final, so he stormed off.'

'Why don't you just go meet them?' Gerry said. 'I know his dad. Top bloke, Danny Finn. He's on the darts team.'

'It's not that though, is it? You only get one chance to make a first impression. I just want to wait till we've been together a bit longer.' Tom swiftly changed the subject. 'You seen who's serving food tonight, Lana?'

I followed his gaze to the waitress taking someone's order at a nearby table. 'Jaz?'

'Yeah, Billy's offered her some work. She's trying to get a bit of money saved up before uni.'

I smiled. 'She took that place then.'

'Yep. Looks like we'll be advertising for a new waitress next summer.'

34

An hour or so in, our 'swift half' had turned into a bit of a session, for me anyway. After the stress of the day, the Prosecco was slipping down far too easily. Sue had taken a tipsy Gerry home for an ear-bending, Yolanda had disappeared, so there was just me, Tom and Stewart left.

'Right,' Tom said, getting to his feet. 'I can't sit here drowning my sorrows with you losers all night. I'm going home to ring Cam, see if I can wheedle my way back into his good graces.'

I blinked groggily at him. 'You're not leaving me?'

He shrugged. 'You're a big girl. Anyway, Stew can see you home. And by "see" I do mean "carry".'

I glanced at Stewart, who was leaning on one elbow looking at me, his eyes soft just like after we kissed. Only blurrier, because for some reason my vision had gone a bit funny.

'Unless you're ready to go now?' Tom said.

'No, I'll finish this one, I think,' I said after a pause. 'If Stew's staying.'

He smiled. 'I am if you are.'

When Tom had gone, Stewart shuffled his chair round to mine.

'Why're you drinking so fast, Lana?' he asked in that gentle voice I hated because it confused the hell out of me.

'None of your business.'

'Come on. You're not going to be all prickly at me, are you?'

I giggled. 'Like a hedgehog. Hedgehogs are awesome.'

He nodded. 'Hedgehogs are awesome. Hey, is that your sixth Prosecco?'

'Dunno. Stopped counting.'

'Did Harper upset you today?'

'Not him. Yo-yo.'

'Oh, ignore her,' Stewart said, flicking a hand. 'You know what she's like. Trust me, you're ten times sexier than Ava Dubois.'

'Not then. Before. With the… cards.' I tried to focus on his face. 'You kissed me.'

'Best quid I ever earned.'

I bobbed my head fuzzily at him. 'Do it again.'

He hesitated. 'You're asking me to kiss you?'

'Yeah. Don't you want to?'

'God, yes, course I do. But when I imagined it, I always thought you'd be more—' He squinted into my face. 'Well, I thought you might have your eyes open properly for a start.'

'This is an experiment kiss though. Go on.'

He leaned forward, and I lifted my lips to him. But at the last minute he pulled away.

'No, Lana, I can't. You don't know what you're saying.'

I snorted. 'Patronising.'

'What's the experiment for?' he asked.

'Trying to work out if you're Death.'

'Right.' He frowned. 'Are you calling me names, Miss Donati? Didn't have you down as one of those fighty drunks.'

'Ahhh,' I said, waving a finger at him. 'But that's the classic mistake. Death doesn't mean death. It means... happy. Or something.'

'Not making much sense tonight, are you?' He slung an arm around me and squeezed me against him. 'I still like you though.'

'Kiss me then.'

'Well, just a little one. But you owe the viaduct fund another quid.'

He leaned round and planted the lightest, gentlest kiss on my mouth. My eyes fell closed and a little 'ah' escaped from between my lips.

'So? How was the experiment?' he asked softly.

'Tasted of wine.' I tilted my lips up. 'Need to try again. For... control or whatever.'

'No, love, not tonight.' He smiled. 'Hey, should I be worried you only fancy me when you're on some mind-altering substance?'

'Nuh-uh. I fancy you all the time. Just don't want you to know.' I blinked. 'Did I say that out loud?'

'Yep.'

'Bollocks.'

He sighed. 'Will you ever forgive me properly, Lana? I said I was sorry.'

'Well sorry doesn't cut it, Johnny Cheekbones.' I downed the dregs of my Prosecco. 'You know your problem? You're an ostrich.'

'Right. Um, what?'

'You're physically incapabubble of facing up to things. First sign of trouble, that stupid blond head goes straight in the sand.'

'You know they don't actually do that, right? It's an urban myth.'

'I don't care if they do it,' I said, pouring the last of the fizzy wine. 'You do it, you ostrichy bastard.'

'OK. Someone's had enough booze for one night, I think.'

He reached out to draw my wine away but I clung to it protectively.

'No! Mine. Get your own ostrich drink, ostrich.'

'Can you stop calling me an ostrich?'

'Stop being an ostrich and I'll stop calling you one. Ostrich.' My face crumpled as I took another gulp of wine. 'Want to know why you're an ostrich?'

'Oh God yes, please share so we can move on from the ostrich thing.'

'One year and some months ago we went out on a date.' I pointed an accusing finger. 'Go on, deny it.'

'I can't, can I?'

'The one thing that happened to vary the monotonotony, the one bright spot in a life filled with someone else's pain. Someone I loved. And then you went and hid your head in the sand, and everything was greyer than it was the day before.' I glared at him. 'I never knew what it meant to be miserable until you came along with your bloody... contrast.'

'Lana...' He reached for my hand, but I jerked it away. 'Is that really how it felt for you?'

'No. It felt fucking worse. And then you swan back here, grinning away and going on about being friends like it was all just nothing. Well not to me it wasn't, mate. Not to me.' I gave in and let the sobs overwhelm me. 'It might've been just one night in your whole glamorous, telly-star-hobnobbing existence to you, McLean, but for me it was... hope. And you snatched it back as quickly as you brought it. You could just've texted to say you weren't interested... oh God.'

'But I was interested,' he said softly. 'I never meant to hurt you, Lana. I'm sorry, I really am.'

'So you keep saying. And yet here we are.' I wobbled slightly on my stool and made an effort to pull myself straight.

'Come on.' Stewart stood and guided me to my feet. 'I spend a lot of my time these days helping you home when you're out of it, don't I? But you're worth it.'

'Are we going?' I mumbled.

'Yes, kid. You need your bed now.' He supported me to the door, sending an apologetic smile to Jasmine clearing tables as we passed.

Outside, I almost tripped over a snogging couple pressing each other up against the wall.

'Sorry.'

I squinted at the pair as they separated. There was a shocking clash of colour. If people would insist on dyeing their hair like that, there should at least be some sort of system to make them harmonise. Red and pink, it made your eyes water.

Suddenly, Stewart burst out laughing. He slapped the lad heartily on the back.

'Good for you, mate.'

'Cheers, Stew.'

Deano. But that wasn't the worst of it.

'Hello, darling,' Yolanda said, patting her ruffled hair back into place. 'Did we overdo it a little on the Prosecco?'

I tried to focus on anything but the dizzying haze of hair colour.

'Deano?' I mumbled. 'What're you doing out here?'

'Er, getting off with Yo-yo.' He squinted at me. 'You OK, Lanasaurus? You look well hammered.'

I glared at him. 'What, Jaz is too young but Yo-yo's all right? She's old enough to be your mum.'

He shrugged. 'So? It's just a bit of fun. Anyway, it was in my cards. The Lovers.'

From the corner of one bleary eye I thought I saw someone at the door of the pub, but when I glanced round there was no one there.

'We're both adults, aren't we, darling?' Yolanda said to me. 'I don't know why you need to be so judgemental; it's really none of your business.' She was smirking like the cat that got the cheese, or whatever the phrase is.

'Well, excuse us, guys,' Stewart said. 'I've got a drunk lady I need to deliver to her brother. Have a good night, eh? Go easy on the elderflower gin, Deano – it packs a wallop.' He winked at Yolanda. 'As someone who got a snog off him earlier, trust me, you're in for a treat.'

'Oh God. Jaz'll be devastated,' I mumbled as Stewart guided me away.

35

One monster hangover and six working days later, it was the first Sunday in November. A layer of crunchy leaves on the cobbles and a winter-is-coming tang in the air took pains to remind me autumn was on its way out.

The restaurant didn't usually open Sundays, but that afternoon we had a wedding reception booked so it was all hands on deck, me and Jaz waitressing and Deb on bar while Tom helped Deano in the kitchen. I was still limiting Jasmine's kitchen shifts in the hope it might make the upcoming separation from her one true love a little easier.

'You're in a good mood,' I said to her after we'd served the last table and were taking a time out by the front desk. She'd been humming to herself all afternoon.

'Yeah. Got my student loan approved last week.' She squeezed my arm. 'It's really happening, Lana! Me and Mum are going to look at my halls on Thursday.'

I smiled. 'Well, I'm very jealous. Good for you, love.'

Her face fell. 'Oh, I'm sorry. I didn't mean… I know you wanted to go.'

'Talk about it as much as you like. Don't mind me,' I said. 'I'm just worried about finding another waitress who'll work as hard. Will you want shifts in the holidays?'

'Oh, could I? Yes please.'

'Thought you'd need the beer money. You, er… you still working for Billy?'

'Yeah, he's given me a few hours a week till after Christmas. Don't worry, I won't let it interfere with my shifts here.'

I hesitated. Deano and Yolanda were still fooling around, and if Jaz was working in the pub it was only a matter of time until she got to hear about it.

'I'm glad you're excited about going to uni,' I said, trying to sound casual. 'I thought you might miss… someone.'

'Who?'

'Well, Deano.' I sighed. 'Look, Jaz, this is going to be hard for you to hear, but—'

'He's sleeping with that old lady from the WI? Yeah, I know.'

'*What?* How do you know?'

She shrugged. 'I saw them snogging at the pub. That night the bike shop guy had to help you home? I followed you out to see if you were OK. Anyway, everyone's been talking about it.'

'And you're not upset?'

'Not as much as I thought. It's weird, but actually, soon as I saw them… it's like, before, I thought there was something wrong with me when he wasn't interested. But now it sort of feels like it's his problem. Know what I mean?'

'Kind of.' I blinked, bewildered at the dizzying speed of teenage attachments. 'I thought you loved him.'

'I do. But it's not the same.' She grimaced. 'I mean, she's like the same age as my nan. I can't find him sexy after that.'

I smiled. 'Well, I don't think she's quite that old. What age is your nan?'

'Fifty-nine.'

'Oh. Yeah, that's not far off actually.' I shook my head. 'God, you're young. So you're going to be OK?'

'Think so. It's sad, losing that feeling, but he just isn't the person I thought he was.'

'Really? He's exactly the person I thought he was.'

'I thought it was you he liked. That's what was tough, because you're so pretty and funny and... and nice. It made me feel rubbish, thinking I couldn't compete. But someone like that Yolanda – it all looks different now.'

'Aww. You're sweet.' I gave her arm a pat. 'I'm sorry I made you feel bad. I told you, there never was anything with me and him. Just mates.'

'Yeah, I get that now. Sorry for being jealous.'

'So do you think you're OK to go back on KP duty?'

'I'm fine,' she said. 'Might be nice to spend some time with Deano actually, now my head's sorted. I hope we'll still be friends.'

'Thank God,' I said with a sigh of relief. 'Staff schedules are a nightmare when you're in love.'

She laughed and kissed my cheek. 'Well, thanks for looking out for me. You're a good boss. And a good friend.'

There didn't seem anything to add to that. I just beamed and gave her arm another pat.

Someone tapped my shoulder. I turned to find a glum-looking Cameron behind me.

'Hi, Lana. Didn't think you'd be open.'

'We're not. Private function.'

'Oh. Your brother's not around then?'

'Sorry, he's on kitchen duty. I'm just about to take an hour's break though, if you fancy a cuppa?'

'Yeah, sounds nice. Thanks.'

Upstairs, I flipped the kettle on while Cameron made himself comfy with his old friend Flash.

'Guessing Tommy told you about us reaching target,' I called through the kitchenette door. 'Great news, right? Looks like as soon as our grant goes through, it'll be plain sailing viaduct-wise. Hey, still tea for you?'

No answer. I poked my head round the door. Cam was petting Flash blankly.

'You OK?'

'Yeah.' He shook his head. 'Sorry, did you ask me something?'

'Just if you wanted tea.'

'Oh. Yes, please.'

He looked tired. I abandoned tea-making and sank down next to him.

'Upset, love?' I said gently.

'A bit. Did Tom tell you we had a row?'

'Yeah. I thought you'd made up.'

'We did, but it's still...' He sighed. 'There's this thing with my parents.'

'I know, he's been racked with angst about it. Why's it so important to you that he meets them?'

'It's them more than me.' He gave Flash an absent tickle between the ears. 'I told them I was seeing someone and it was sort of serious, and they've been nagging me about bringing him round ever since. And now it's even worse, with Christmas coming up. Mum keeps asking if I'm bringing him to our family dinner on Boxing Day. My grandparents are flying over from the States, and my sister'll be up from London... pretty big deal.'

It certainly was. I could just imagine Tom's panic when Cam had sprung that one on him.

'Maybe you told them too soon,' I said.

'Maybe. I was excited, you know? That I'd finally met someone who might be...' He flushed. 'Well, you know.'

I curled an arm around his shoulders and gave them a scrunch. 'Yeah, I know.'

'And it's been two months now. That's not really early days any more, is it?'

'Did you tell Tom all this?'

'He doesn't get it. Whenever I bring it up he changes the subject.' He sighed. 'And it's not just Mum and Dad, it is me as well. Feels symbolic, meeting the family. That it'll show he thinks we're properly committed.'

'He does think that, honestly. He really likes you, Cam. I mean, *really* likes you.'

'He tell you that?'

'Yeah.'

He was silent a minute. 'Then how come he doesn't tell me?'

'Worried about scaring you, I guess,' I said. 'Worrying's kind of his thing.'

'Has he had a lot of boyfriends?'

I frowned. 'Not sure it's for me to say. Why don't you ask him?'

'I don't want him to think I'm obsessed with his past or anything. Just curious if he's been through this before, that's all.'

I hesitated.

'No,' I said at last. 'A few, but nothing really long-term. He'll kill me for telling you, but this is probably his longest relationship.'

'Really?' He blinked in surprise. 'How come?'

I shrugged. 'We've neither of us been dating much, the last few years. And it's harder for Tom, shy as he is and gay too. It's not like there's loads of options round here.'

'He could go out on the scene. Online dating maybe.'

I laughed. 'What, you don't know him better than that by now?'

'Yeah, all right,' he admitted. 'Not very Tom, I guess.'

'He's always happier hiding in his comfort zone than forcing himself into terrifying social situations. Tommy's a romantic at heart: too many Disney films when we were kids. Thought if he waited long enough, the perfect lad'd land in his lap.' I gave his shoulder a pat. 'And he was right, see? He's dead picky. You should be flattered you pass muster.'

He smiled. 'I am. I just wish we could be a real couple. Do the hand-holding in public, the family parties, all the usual stuff.'

'Give it time.'

'I'd give it time if I knew how much. Tom keeps saying it's too early, and when I press him he shuts down the conversation. I need to know if we're going somewhere, before… I don't want to get my heart broken, Lana.'

'You won't. Not by Tom. Oh! That reminds me.' I went to the coffee table and rummaged in the drawer. 'He won't mind me giving you this. Saves him bringing it round.'

Cameron took the envelope I handed him, frowning. 'What is it?'

'Just a letter. Nothing scary, promise. Tom had something he wanted to say in writing.'

'Shall I open it now?'

'I think he wants you to do it when you're alone. It's sort of personal.'

'Hmm. OK.' He stashed it in his jeans pocket.

If I was hoping my pep talk might've bucked him up, I was wrong. He looked more depressed than when he'd arrived.

'Let me get your tea.' I handed him the TV remote. 'Here you go, find a cartoon to cheer yourself up. Back in a sec.'

Actually I was back in half a sec. I was no sooner in the kitchenette than Cameron called to me.

'Lana! Quick!'

I went back into the living room. He was staring in horror at the TV.

'What is it, Cam?'

'It's the viaduct,' he whispered. 'Local news are there. Look.'

I glanced at the telly, and my eyes widened. There was Sienna Edge and a load of people with placards and megaphones, a giant *Save the Barbastelles* banner stretched across the viaduct's arches.

36

I stared, transfixed, at the screen.

'Oh my God! What the hell's she doing?'

'I thought you said there weren't any bats,' Cameron said.

'Yeah, but she doesn't know that. We can't announce it till we get the official report.' I examined the crowd. 'Shit, there must be fifty protesters! We have to get down there, Cam.'

'Us? What can we do?'

'I don't know. I just know we have to get down there.'

I grabbed my coat and flew down to the restaurant, Cameron hot on my heels.

'Jaz, Deb, there's been an emergency,' I panted when I caught up with them at the bar. 'Can you manage without me for an hour?'

Debbie frowned. 'Well no, not really. We've got all the tables to clear when this lot finish eating.'

'Oh, don't be such a drama queen, Deb, there's only a few,' Jasmine said. 'Go on, Lana, if it's urgent.'

I smiled gratefully. 'Cheers, Jaz. Me and Cameron need to get to the viaduct. Tell our Tom where we've gone, will you?'

'She's always doing this lately,' I heard Deb mutter as we headed out. 'That viaduct's a distraction. No wonder business is bad.'

'Be nice,' Jaz whispered back. 'She misses her dad.'

It was only a ten-minute walk to the viaduct. When we got there, we discovered it was worse than we thought.

What had looked like fifty people on the TV was at least seventy-five, maybe a hundred, plus a shedload of TV cameras and photographers. Sienna must've rallied every wildlife activist in the area. She might be fanatical to the point of madness when it came to bats, but she wasn't half press-savvy.

There were some pretty gruesome placards to go with the giant banner. 'Stop this cruelty!' one screamed. 'Hands off our home!' said another, presumably written by a highly literate bat. One simply said 'Murderers'. So that was nice.

'Oh God, this is awful,' Cameron muttered. 'What do we do, Lana?'

'We have to get to Batwoman. God knows what she's saying to those cameras.'

We barged through the crowd to Sienna Edge, who was at the front talking to a news presenter.

'…and the disdain of the Egglethwaite viaduct campaign group has been nothing short of staggering,' I heard her saying as we approached. 'Despite many letters in the local press expressing our concerns, and my repeated invitations to them to respond, they have totally ignored us while steaming blindly ahead with their plans. This has been typical of their behaviour from the start.'

'Which is sort of ironic, isn't it?' the young reporter said.

Sienna frowned. 'I'm sorry?'

'Well, you know. Steaming blindly ahead. Bats, as in blind as a?' He grinned nervously. I was sensing this might be his first big assignment.

Sienna glared at him. 'That's a myth. Some bat breeds have eyesight three times as good as ours. But of course, human arrogance knows no bounds when it comes to dismissing other species as inferior.'

The lad looked sheepish. 'Do they? I didn't know that.'

'Of course you didn't. You never bothered to find out, did you?' Sienna clocked Cameron and me as we made it to the front, and her face spread into a smug smile. 'Speaking of the viaduct group, here's one of their spokespeople now.' She gestured to me. 'Perhaps you'd like to ask this person for a comment, Ivan? In the interests of balance.'

'Of course.' Ivan turned to look at me. 'Oh. You mean this lady?'

'I do.'

He beckoned me in front of the camera, looking faintly puzzled. I glanced down and winced when I realised I was still wearing my medieval costume. So that's why Sienna had picked on me and not Cameron. She'd spotted another opportunity to humiliate us.

'Why are you in fancy dress?' Ivan asked.

I snatched the mob cap off my head and stuffed it hastily into my skirt band. 'It's my work uniform. I own a theme restaurant.'

'Oh. How odd. So would you care to give us your statement, Miss…?'

'Donati. Lana Donati. Yes, Ivan, I'd be happy to.' I smiled sweetly at him, then glared at Sienna. 'She's bloody insane, that's my statement.'

I could see Cameron in the crowd. He shook his head, a warning, but I ignored him.

Ivan put one hand over his mic. 'We're live, Miss Donutty,' he muttered. 'Could you please modify your language? Otherwise we'll get letters.'

'Donati. And I hope you do.' I lifted my frown with an effort. 'OK. Sorry, I know you're just doing your job.'

'So I'm insane, am I?' Sienna sneered. I could tell she was looking forward to this.

'You're more than insane,' I snapped. 'You're a blood—blinking zealot, love. We tried to find a compromise, didn't we?'

She snorted. 'Compromise? What compromise can there be?'

Behind the camera I noticed Stewart, newly arrived and whispering to a worried-looking Cameron.

'We offered to rehome the bats,' I said to Sienna. 'Absolute minimum loss of life.'

'Not good enough. Barbastelle is a highly endangered species; every one is precious.' Sienna rummaged in a file and held a laminated photograph up to the TV camera. 'Look. This is what they'll be sacrificing in pursuit of sordid, dirty profit.'

The picture showed a baby barbastelle, its tiny pug face staring appealingly into the camera while it snuggled into its wings like a blanket. It was adorable. Little bugger.

'Aww,' Ivan said, simpering.

'Aren't you supposed to be impartial?' I demanded.

'Sorry. Reflex.' He cleared his throat, making an effort to knit his brow into serious newsman face. 'Perhaps we can move on from hyperbole and get to some hard facts.

Can you explain your group's plans for the viaduct, Miss Donut— er, Donati?'

'We want to open it as a right of way.' I blinked into the camera, suddenly aware that the world – or at least large parts of West and North Yorkshire – was watching. 'My late father pioneered the idea, and we're continuing with it in his memory.'

'You said pursuit of profit, Ms Edge,' Ivan said to Sienna. 'Can you expand?'

'That's right. That's what this is really about, whatever they say.' Sienna spun to face me. 'Oh, don't think I haven't done my homework, Lana. I know all about *you*. I know your ridiculous medieval restaurant's struggling. I know you plan to use the viaduct to lure the Grand Départ through your nonentity of a village, and I know that in the end it's all about money, money, money. It makes my stomach churn, hearing you pretend it's for your dead father.'

'*What?*' I felt tears prickle in my eyes. 'How… dare you! Who the bloody hell do you think you are? I've never pretended anything about my dad.'

'Language,' Ivan muttered.

'Oh, sod your language, Ivan,' I snapped. The lad blinked in shock, but he didn't cut the mike. In the back of my mind, it occurred to me we were probably making for some pretty gripping telly.

'You deny this is about bringing in customers then, do you?' Sienna demanded.

I hesitated. 'I won't deny a boost in trade would be appreciated, by a lot of local businesses. But there's a bit more to it than that.'

'*Aha*! So you admit it.'

I scowled at her. 'It's not a crime to make a living, Sienna. Just what're you trying to say? Out with it.'

'What I'm saying is that you're a fraud.' Her eyes narrowed unpleasantly. 'That you're using phoney grief to promote your business.'

'God, you're... you're sick! He's not been dead six months and you...' I blinked back angry tears. 'Do you think I'm some kind of monster?'

'I don't know,' she snapped. 'Maybe we should ask the bats you want to murder.'

I couldn't hold back any more. I burst into tears.

'There *are* no fucking bats, Sienna!' I yelled.

'Oh my God,' Ivan muttered as he realised I'd just dropped the f-bomb live on air. But he still didn't cut the mike.

Sienna blinked in shock. 'What did you say?'

'You... heard,' I sobbed. 'The barbastelle colony's gone. Dead. That or moved on.'

'Don't be ridiculous. I would've been told.'

I couldn't reply. My voice was lost in tears.

I felt a strong, comforting arm go round me. 'Come on,' a gentle voice whispered. 'Let's get you away from here, kid.'

I went limp against Stew, my body drained. 'But... I'm not... finished.'

'Yes you are.' Cameron had materialised on the other side of me. He gave my arm a pat. 'Go with Stew, Lana. I'll stay to represent the group.'

I let Stewart guide me through the crowd, people staring as I sobbed through their ranks, until we reached the reservoir. There was a hidden spot overlooking the water, sheltered by a twisted yew. When we reached it, Stew took his coat off and spread it on the ground.

'Sit,' he said, nodding to it. 'And try to calm down.'

'Do you – did you hear what she—'

'I heard,' he said quietly, sinking down next to me. 'It was out of order. Come here, love.'

I snuggled gratefully against him.

'So you think I was right?'

'Normally, yes. That was an awful thing to accuse you of. But...'

'...but it was live on TV?'

'Yeah,' he said with a sigh. 'It won't help us, Lana. We need people on our side.'

'I'm sorry. Let you all down, didn't I?'

'Don't be silly,' he said, kissing my hair. 'You're our glorious leader. It's only because of you we've come this far.'

I managed a soggy smile. 'Thanks.'

'So is it true then?'

'About the bats? Yes. Andy sent an expert up and he said they were all gone.' I wiped damp eyes on my sleeve. 'I wasn't supposed to say anything until we'd had the official report though. I've really fucked up, Stew.'

I jumped when I felt my phone buzz.

'It's him,' I whispered when I'd fished it out of my boobs. 'Andy Chen. You think he saw me on TV?'

'If he didn't then I'm sure someone's filled him in by now. Want me to talk to him?'

'No; I need to clean up my own mess. But thanks for offering.' I swiped to answer the call.

'Good news and bad news, right?' I said to Andy, trying to keep my voice steady.

'No. Just bad.' He sounded angry. 'What the hell was that about, Lana?'

'I'm sorry. I just – you heard what she said about my dad. I lost it. I couldn't help it.'

'For Christ's sake! Why did you have to talk to her at all?'

'Well she was… everyone was watching. Taking her side.'

'I told you not to mention the bats till we had the report. God, it'll be finalised next week, then Sienna would've been out of your hair. Could you not have ignored her till then?'

I choked on another sob. 'Sorry, Andy. I didn't mean to. You saw, she got me all worked up.'

'Of course she did. That's how she operates. You know that.' He sighed. 'Never mind. It's too late now.'

'Listen, I said I was—' I stopped. 'What do you mean, too late?'

'I just got off the phone to our chairman: he wasn't impressed with your little medieval meltdown. He says bats or not, the council doesn't need that sort of publicity.' He hesitated. 'Look, I tried to talk him out of it but it's no good. I'm sorry, Lana. He's vetoed your grant.'

37

'Lana? Lana!' Andy's voice was urgent.

Silently, I took the phone from my ear and hung up.

'You remember a minute ago when I said I'd really fucked up?' I said to Stewart in a hushed voice.

'I know it's not great, but let's stay positive. We've still got everything we had before, and the bats aren't a problem now. We just need to go on a charm offensive, that's all.'

'We haven't got everything we had before,' I mumbled. 'Not... everything.'

He took one look at my expression and his brow lowered. 'Oh no. Not the grant.'

'Yes.' I gasped, almost gagging with the effort, my throat was so dry from crying. 'We lost it, Stew. I lost it for us.'

'What did Andy say?'

I let out a wet snort. 'Apparently the council don't want to be associated with potty-mouthed tavern wenches who lose it on daytime TV.'

'But what can we do? We'd have to start work in January to have any chance of getting the viaduct open for the Départ.'

'I know. And Vanessa Christmas as good as told me no viaduct meant no place on the route.' I buried my head in my hands and groaned. 'Oh God. Six weeks. Where will we find twenty-five grand in six weeks?'

'There must be other funding sources. Charities.'

'Not that could approve us in six weeks. And it'd take ages to raise that amount through fundraising. The original £25,000 total was a tall order as it was.'

Stew stared morosely over the reservoir. 'Then we're screwed.'

'I could... resign from the group,' I said hesitantly. 'Maybe if you told the council the scary sweary medieval lady was gone, they'd reverse the decision.'

'Absolutely not. This is your project.'

'But you—'

'I said no. We won't let you.' He gave me a squeeze. 'You're for keeps, kid.'

I blushed, wondering whether he was still talking about the cycling group.

'There has to be another way,' he said. 'We've come so far...'

I shook my head. I felt deflated from the ground up, my eyes sandy with crying.

'No. This is it. I've ruined everything. Oh God, and after I had such a go at you about the bike racks too. I'm sorry, Stew, I'm so sorry.' I turned wide eyes up to him. 'How will I tell the others? We've got a meeting tomorrow.'

He sighed. 'I don't know. I'm sorry, I wish I had a better answer.' He gave my shoulders a last press and stood up. 'Come on, you'd better get back to work. Let's sleep on it and see what we can come up with.'

★

I don't know how I got through my shift. I was floating about in a daze the rest of the evening, eyes swollen with crying. Only autopilot guided me through the motions of clearing up and tending bar until the wedding guests had gone.

When I'd locked up, I dragged my poor tired body upstairs. Tom was on the sofa, surrounded by empty packets of chocolate buttons and half embalmed in rioja fumes.

'So how was your day?' he asked without looking round.

I chucked myself down next to him. 'Had a meltdown live on TV. Got called a murderous fraud. Said "fuck" to around a million people. Reckon you can top that?'

'Yeah.' He put down his glass of wine and choked back a sob. 'Cam dumped me.'

'*What?* Oh my God!' I threw an arm around him. 'What happened? Did you have another row?'

'No. He read my letter, rang me, told me calmly he wanted to take a break and hung up.'

'Jesus, Tom! What the hell did you write?'

'I don't know,' he said, burying his hands in his hair. 'I didn't think it was anything bad. I just said I was grateful for the time we'd spent together, I really liked him, but I wasn't ready to meet his family and I didn't appreciate him putting me under pressure. Oh, and I said I hoped he wouldn't be mad at me. I specifically remember saying that.'

'Bloody hell, you wrote that? In those words?'

'Pretty much. Don't you think I explained it properly?'

'You sound like you're rejecting him for a job, you muppet! No wonder he's pissed off. I bet you signed it "sincerely", didn't you?'

'No. "Regards".'

'Sweet Jesus.' I shook my head. 'Poor Cam. You've just confirmed everything he was worried about.'

'What was he worried about?'

'What, you don't know? He said he'd told you all about it.'

'Maybe he did. But when he tells me off I start to panic, and then I just nod until I can get out of the conversation without having an anxiety attack. You know I'm not good with conflict.'

'He thinks you're not ready to commit. That you don't see a future for the two of you.'

'But I do see that.'

'Then you should've put it in the letter, you plank.' I sighed. 'Well, maybe it'll be OK. "Take a break" doesn't necessarily mean "break up"; he might just want time to think. Anyway, you'll see him tomorrow at the meeting.'

'No I won't. He's resigning. Asked me to pass it on to you.'

'Oh no. Not that too.'

'Yep. He doesn't want to be around me, Lana. I've ruined everything, like I always knew I would.' He let out a choked sob. 'Just when I'd realised something as well.'

'What's that?'

'Love him, don't I?'

I patted his head fondly. 'Poor little donkey. Yeah, I know.'

'What do I do, sis?'

'Just give him a bit of space,' I said. 'Maybe he'll come to you. He must've guessed how you feel about him, even if you do write a crap letter. Everyone else has.'

'God, I hope so.' He looked up from the crook of my

shoulder. 'So what was your thing? Did you say you had bad news?'

I hesitated. 'No,' I said at last. 'Nothing you need to worry about.'

'Evening, petal,' Gerry said when I got to the pub the following night, a bag of nerves as I worried how to break the news about our grant. 'Where's your brother?'

'He's sent apologies,' I said, sinking into a seat next to Stew. 'Sudden rush at the restaurant so one of us had to work.'

That was a fib. Tom was still moping, wondering what to do about Cam.

'So we're just waiting on Cameron then,' Sue said.

'Nope. Cam's resigned. Er, personal reasons.'

'Has he now?' Sue shot me a searching look, and I shook my head to let her know I'd explain later.

'Resigned? Before we've finished the project?' Yolanda pursed her lips. 'Well I must say, I think that is most untoward. Certainly not the way I was brought up.'

Seriously, she'd been given childhood lessons in village committee etiquette? My parents' teachings on good manners had basically boiled down to 'Say please and thank you and don't wipe your nose on your sleeve'.

'You were brought up?' Stew said to Yolanda. 'I thought you were raised by a herd of wild drag queens in the Australian outback.' Gerry snorted, then hastily turned it into a cough.

'So does anyone have any news?' Sue said. 'Apart from our Lana using naughty words on the telly, but we'll get to that.'

I cast Stew a nervous glance, and he grabbed my hand under the table for support.

'Yes, I—'

But before I could finish, Gerry interrupted me.

'Some important news from your treasurer,' he said. 'The council grant came in today. That means work on the viaduct can start ASAP, assuming we've sorted this bat issue.'

I stared at him. 'No. It can't have.'

Gerry shot me a puzzled look. 'Don't see why not, love.'

'But we... they would've notified us. We haven't had approval yet.'

'Well it showed up in our bank account this morning: £25,000, payer BPL. I'm assuming that's the grant-awarding body.'

Stewart's hand was still in mine – it hadn't occurred to me to drop it, somehow – and I felt him jerk when Gerry read out the initials.

'Oh, wonderful,' Yolanda said, beaming. 'Then we made it.'

I lifted a palm to my forehead. 'You know what, guys? I'm actually feeling a bit iffy tonight. Think I might have a touch of the bug that's going round. Is there any way we can reschedule? We're a bit thin on the ground without Tom and Cam as it is.'

Sue was examining me with concern. 'Of course, chicken, if you're poorly. You do look pale.'

'Thanks, Sue. Really think I ought to go to bed.' I stood and looked down at Stew. 'Walk me back?'

Yolanda sent me a knowing look. 'I see. It's that sort of bug, is it?'

I glared at her. 'You do not see, Mrs Smirkychops. I'm feeling a bit faint, that's all.'

'Mmm. Weak at the knees, are we, darling?'

'Enough, Yo-yo,' Stew said. 'Come on, Lana. Let's get you to bed.'

I tried to ignore Yolanda's snort as Stewart and I left the pub.

'You know something about this. Don't you?' I demanded when we were outside.

'Yes. I think so.'

'Where's the money from, Stew?'

'Well, you work it out. Who's got money like that?'

My eyes widened. 'Harper?'

'Yes. BPL, that's the production company he set up. He must've paid it through them.'

'But why? How would he even know we needed it?'

Stewart flushed. 'I mentioned it on the phone last night. He's been ringing me a lot lately.'

'You asked him for money?'

'Are you kidding? I've never asked him for money in my life. I just said we were screwed, by way of a general unburdening. Amazingly, it sounds like for once he was actually listening.'

My brow knotted. 'Bastard! This is all about me!' I looked up at Stew. 'Isn't it?'

'Could be,' he admitted. 'He asks about you a lot. I thought it was just some weird infatuation at first because you knocked him back, but now... well, I don't know what you said to him but he's been acting pretty oddly since The Boneshaker.'

'Take me round to his place.'

'What?'

'Harper's. I need to have this out with him, right now.'

38

I blinked as Stewart's car pulled up in a country lane somewhere outside Halifax.

'This is where he lives?'

'Yep. My Aunty Sonia bought it before she died. Daft, isn't it?'

I gazed up at the huge white mansion that was apparently Harper Brady's humble home. There were at least eight bedrooms, three floors... one resident.

'What does he do with the space?'

'Fills it with expensive rubbish, these days. When we were kids we used to play football down the corridors.'

He got out of the car and pressed the intercom by the spiky iron gate.

'Harper, it's me. Can you let us in?'

'Us? Who'd you bring, Stew?'

'Lana. She wants a word.'

There was a buzz, and the gates swung open. Stewart drove us up to the front door and parked next to a couple of Ferraris.

A *couple* of Ferraris. I mean, bloody hell.

Harper was waiting on the step. He beamed when he saw me.

'Hi, Lana. Thought I might be hearing from you.'

I shook my head at the pillared front of his tacky house. 'Nice place. What's it called, Dunsqueezin?'

Stewart laughed. Harper just looked puzzled.

'No. Arncliffe House.' He nodded to the door. 'You coming in then? I'm assuming you got my present.'

'Yeah, we got it,' I said as I followed him in. 'What're you playing at, Harper? You know we can't take that.'

'Course you can. This way.'

He ushered us into a large white-walled room, where a glass of something fizzy was sitting on a white coffee table next to what looked like a script.

'Just learning some lines,' he said. 'Champagne?'

I cocked an eyebrow. 'Seriously?'

'Er, yeah. There's a bottle open in the fridge.'

'I'll take a tea, thanks.'

'All right.' He turned to his cousin. 'Can you do it, Stew?'

'I'm not running round after you, Harper. You're the host; you make the tea.'

'Go on, please. There's something personal I need to discuss with Lana.'

'Hmm.' Stewart cast him a suspicious look. 'Well, OK. Don't touch her up.'

'Take your time,' Harper called as Stew left the room.

He took a seat on the sofa and patted the cushion next to him. I ignored him and parked myself in the seat opposite.

'How much of that stuff do you drink?' I said, nodding to the champagne.

'Not much. Four or five bottles a week.'

'Sounds expensive.'

He shrugged. 'I can afford it.'

'I'd noticed,' I said dryly. 'So come on, Harper, what was that money all about? If you think you can buy me, you're going to find not everything in your life's for sale.'

'It's not that.' His eyes had latched on to my chest again. He seemed to have a real problem looking away from that whole area whenever we were together. 'I mean, I do really like you, but that's not why I sent the money. I knew that wouldn't impress you.'

'Then why?'

'Dunno, it was weird,' he explained to my boobs. 'I saw you on TV, and that woman was such a bitch about your dad, and it... it made me feel sorry for you, I guess.'

I stared at him. 'What, you've discovered empathy?'

'I didn't like seeing you upset. Then when Stew told me what'd happened with your grant, I felt like I wanted to fix it. And I could, so... I did.'

'Because you want a feel of my boobs, right?'

'God, yes. I'd love a feel of your boobs.' With an effort he dragged his gaze to my face. 'I mean, academically speaking. That's nothing to do with the money. I just wanted you to stop crying. If anyone had said that stuff about my mum...' His brow knit into a frown. 'It's not fair you should lose your grant over a stupid thing like that.'

'That's... um, wow,' I said, blinking with surprise. 'Thank you.'

He patted the sofa. 'Will you sit by me now, babe?'

'Please don't call me that.'

'Sorry. Lana.'

'All right. Strictly platonic, mind.' I went to sit next to him. 'And try not to keep staring at my breasts, will you? It's unnerving.'

He grinned. 'I'm making no promises. So you'll take the money?'

'You know I can't. It's twenty-five grand, Harper. I appreciate the gesture, but you shouldn't be chucking that kind of money around just to cheer people up.'

He shrugged. 'Why not? Twenty-five grand isn't much.'

'Are you kidding? That's more than I earn in a year, mate!'

His eyes widened. 'Shit, really? How do you live?'

'Oh, you know, a few cuts here and there. Had to get rid of my eight-bedroom mansion and five-bottle-a-week Bolly habit, but it's amazing how you adjust.'

He shot me a puzzled smile. 'Was that a joke?'

'Yes, it was a joke,' I said, smiling back. 'You get used to the sarcasm when you've known me a while.'

'Please keep the money, Lana. It's not just for you. It's for Stew as well.'

I frowned. 'Stew? Why do you want to give him money?'

'Because he's entitled to it. Mum would've left him some, but she died thingy – intestate. She was only thirty-eight; probably never occurred to her to make a will. The whole lot went to me.'

'What other relatives have you got?'

'None close. Just Mum's sister, Aunty Heather – that's Stew's mum. I tried to fix it when I got a bit older, but his parents are sort of proud. Wouldn't take a penny.'

I remembered Stewart's boast that he'd never asked Harper for money. For all his laid-back attitude to life, I knew he could be a stubborn bugger when he thought he was in the right.

'But he's always nagging me to do stuff for charity,'

Harper said. 'And here's something he cares about. It's not like I'll miss the money.'

'Can you stop saying things like that? I feel like a Dickensian street urchin next to you.'

'Sorry,' he said, smiling. 'You don't hate me too much, do you?'

'No. Not now.'

'Ha! Knew I could get you to like me.'

I shook my head. 'I thought you were such a brat when I met you, but you're actually... you really are fond of your cousin, aren't you?'

'Course. He's the best friend I've got. And somehow I appreciate him more, these days.' He took my hand in both his, looking earnestly into my face. 'I meet a lot of phoney people in my line of work, Lana. Stew's about the only person I trust. And you.'

I laughed. 'You've only met me a few times.'

'Yep. And you've insulted me every time,' he said with a grin. 'That's why I trust you. I'm sick to death of flattery.'

'That's... sweet. Thanks, Harper.'

'Friends then?'

I cleared my throat. 'Up here, mate.'

'Oh. Sorry,' he said, pulling his gaze away from my chest. It'd drifted down again.

'Yes. I think we're friends.'

'And you'll keep the money? I'll be very offended if you try to give it back.'

I hesitated. 'Is it really about Stew?'

'No. It's about both of you. Your daft viaduct as well. I guess if you both care about it then it must be important.' He smiled. 'Come on, this might be the first thing I've done for someone else my whole life. Don't screw it up for me, eh?'

'I think... we'll take it,' I said at last. 'Here. Since we're friends you can have a hug. Mind the boobs though.' I chucked my arms around him and gave him a squeeze.

'Thanks very much. I like them where I can feel them.' He raised his voice. 'Stew! You can come back now. I'm just getting off with your girl.'

'No change there then.' Stew came back in with a couple of very tasteful mugs, steaming with what was probably expensive, posh-sounding tea. He dumped them on the coffee table. 'You've been taking girls off me since you were sixteen.'

'Well, now you can get your own back and take this one off me,' Harper said, letting me go. 'From what I've seen I don't think she'll object.'

God, even Harper Brady, the world's most unobservant man, was making with the me-and-Stew teasing. This was getting embarrassing.

'Are we sorted then, Lana?' Stew said.

'Yes.' I smiled at Harper. 'I think we're on the same wavelength.'

'And are we... what about the viaduct?'

'Lana's happy to keep the money if you are,' Harper said. 'And I told her you are because I'm the oldest.' His eyes fell on the mugs of tea. 'For Christ's sake, Stew, coasters! That table cost two grand.' He grabbed a couple and slid them underneath.

Stewart shook his head. 'Have you been bodysnatched or something? You're being weirdly nice lately.'

'Nope.'

'Oh! I know. This is research for a role as a wealthy philanthropist, right?'

Harper smiled. 'Not that either.

'Flying champagne cork to the head?'

'Maybe I'm just growing up, Stew.'

'Yeah. You are twenty-eight though.'

'According to my Equity card I'm twenty-six, so you can keep your bloody mouth shut,' Harper said. 'Go on, get out: I know you don't really want my Lapsang Souchong. Go tell your little viaduct buddies the good news. I've got to finish learning these lines for tomorrow.'

I leaned over to plant a kiss on his cheek.

'Thanks, Harper. You're a good man.'

'We won't forget this,' Stewart said, shaking his cousin's hand vigorously.

We left, abandoning the fancy stinky tea steaming on its coasters.

39

My favourite band gig of the year was definitely Egglethwaite Temperance Hall's senior citizens' Christmas party in early December. In a massive yah-boo-sucks to the hall's founding fathers there was always free-flowing wine and a full bar, and it made me swell with pride, watching our old folk stagger home afterwards. Plus it gave me the chance to get my slide around a juicy little solo in 'Frosty the Snowman' that was off limits outside the festive season.

Tom met me from the concert – Dad used to do that once the nights got dark, even though, knicker theft aside, the crime rate in Egglethwaite was virtually non-existent – and we walked back to the restaurant.

'So did the old folk have fun?' he asked.

'Till they were under the table. I swear the pensioners round here get lairier every year.'

He laughed. 'Give it twenty years or so and you'll have Yo-yo to contend with too.'

I grimaced. 'Yeesh. When it turns into an all-out orgy they can find themselves another First Trombone. So what've you been up to this afternoon?'

'Me and Flash went down the viaduct. Looks like they've started work. There was a hell of a racket.'

'Brilliant. I'll ring Andy tomorrow, see if he knows when they'll be done.'

Despite our split with the council, Andy was doing his best to be helpful in a personal capacity. I was sensing he felt guilty for the loss of our grant. We'd finally got the wildlife report proving there were no barbastelles, and he'd helped us organise workmen to get the resurfacing done.

'Any word from Cam?' I asked.

'No,' Tom said glumly. 'Still not taking my calls. He did reply to a text I sent him, so that's something.'

'What did it say?'

'Said he's not ready to talk yet.'

'But that's good though,' I said, trying to sound encouraging. '"Yet" means he will be ready eventually, right?'

'Hope so. I'm sick of being a miserable bastard.' He nodded to McLean's Machines, which was blazing with light. 'Stew's working late. If I'd known he was up I'd have dropped off that book he lent me.'

'You two are getting pretty chumsome these days, aren't you?' I said. 'Book lending's bromance territory, you know. You'll be singing along to *Frozen* and having boy sleepovers next.'

'Sorry,' he said with a guilty smile. 'I know it's the big brother's job to resent the guy who done you wrong, but you have to admit he's a hard man not to like.'

I sighed. 'He is, isn't he? Well, I'm glad you're mates. You could do with a few more, Shyey McShyface.'

'Have you forgiven him finally then?'

'I'm... getting there.'

I cast a worried glance over my shoulder as we crossed the road.

'Can you take my trombone in?' I asked Tom. 'I'll just pop back and check everything's OK. Ten o'clock's late to be oiling chains or whatever. Stew might've gone to bed without realising he's left the lights on.'

'All right, Lana. Want me to do you a hot water bottle?'

I smiled. 'You know, you don't have to baby me just because Dad used to. I'm twenty-six; I can make one if I want one.'

He smiled back. 'Sorry. I just want to make sure our first Christmas without him is still the same old Christmas, you know?'

'I know you do.' I stood on tiptoes to plant a kiss on his cheek. 'You're a good little donkey, Tommy Donati.'

I handed Tom the trombone case and headed back across the road. The bell over the door jingled merrily as I walked into Stewart's shop.

But the Stewart inside was far from merry. He was leaning against the counter on both elbows, staring straight ahead. His fists digging into his cheeks made him look like a grumpy bulldog pup with great hair.

'What's up, Stew? Everything OK?'

'No, Captain Shiny-Buttons, everything's not OK. It's been a long time since everything's been OK.'

Despite the crack about my band uniform, he didn't sound his usual jokey self at all. His voice was thick, and I'd never seen such a dark look on his face.

'Been drinking, love?' I asked gently.

'Might've had a couple.'

He was still staring, and I turned to follow his gaze. It was fixed on a bike against the back wall, half-covered in colourful knitwear.

'My yarn-bombing idea! You did it?'

'Yes, for the Départ. Was going to put it in the window. I thought you'd like to see it from the restaurant.'

He was still speaking in the same flat, slurred voice, slightly muffled by his fists in his cheeks.

'Why am I here, Lana?' he burst out. 'Why the fuck am I here?'

I blinked. 'What, like, why do you exist?'

'Probably.' He jumped up and kicked the bike nearest him. 'What the hell was I thinking, opening a bloody bike shop? Dozens of the bastards, right where I can't get away from them.' He pointed at the partially yarn-bombed bike. 'And he's the worst.'

'He?'

'Yes. Herbert. The anthropo— doing that anthro thing helps me hate him.' He blinked hard. 'Sorry. I did actually have quite a few drinks.'

I'd been tiptoeing towards him all the time he'd been speaking. Now I reached him, and rested a calming hand on his arm.

'What's Herbert done, Stew?' I asked softly.

'He just sits there, judging me. Mocking me because I'm not taking part in the Tour next year. Or any year. Or any competition, ever again. I'm just a waste-of-space businessman hidden in some nowheresville in the back of sodding beyond.' He aimed another savage kick at a nearby mountain bike, which fell from its stand and clattered to the floor. 'Ow! And now I've hurt my bad leg on that fucking pedal. I told you the bastards had it in for me.'

'I don't think you're a waste of space.'

He snorted. 'Please. You think I'm the biggest waste of space of everyone. And I don't blame you for hating me either, after the way I treated you.'

'Here.' I guided him to the bench behind the counter and took a seat next to him. 'I don't hate you, Stew – not any more. I mean, I'd be lying if I said I wasn't still a bit sore. But Tom was right, you're a hard man not to like.'

'Tom said that?'

'Yeah. Mind you, he hasn't seen you taking your drunken anger out on an innocent pushbike.'

He let out a damp laugh. 'Taught it a lesson, didn't I?'

'Yep. Sort of caveman and sexy, the way you stuck it to the bad old bike.' I slipped one arm around him. 'So you want to tell me what's brought this on?'

He sniffed and rested his head on my shoulder. 'Phone call from my friend who's competing with Team Sky next year. It was nice to catch up, but he was so full of his training, all excited about the Tour... just reminded me how much I miss it.'

'Can't you cycle at all now?'

'A little. Maybe an hour's gentle riding before it starts to hurt. But I can't race or time-trial, and cross-country's out of the question.'

I paused, seeking out a memory.

'The night we went out, you told me when you fell in love with the sport it wasn't about competing,' I said. 'You just loved the freedom. Like you were flying – that's what you said.'

He turned a wan smile on me. 'You remember that?'

'Every word.' I sighed. 'How come you never called, Stew? Go on, the whole story.'

'Like I said. I was planning to, then...' He stopped to swallow a sob. 'My injury came less than a week later, and I was distracted by that, getting it seen to. Then when they told me I wouldn't race again – God, worst time in my life. It felt like there was nothing left for me.'

'So you forgot me.'

'Maybe at first,' he admitted. 'Not forgot, but it felt like there was... It's hard to explain. Like you were part of a potential future that couldn't exist for me any more. All I saw was the miserable present, and everything beyond that, all my dreams and desires, were swallowed up in this fog of hopelessness. Know what I mean?'

I thought back to when we'd found out Dad had cancer, and later when they'd told us the chemo hadn't worked and it was only a matter of time. Every day, then, had felt like tomorrow might not happen. I hadn't cared if it happened or not.

'Yes,' I said quietly. 'I know what you mean.'

He brushed away a little tear that had started to trickle down my cheek. 'Course you do.' He sighed. 'I'm a selfish bastard, Lana. Still to have my youth, my health, and to sit there feeling sorry for myself like the world was ending. You and Tom, everything you've lost, and there's Stewart McLean with his poorly fucking knee.'

'Depression isn't that simple, love,' I said, giving his shoulders a gentle squeeze. 'And me and Tom had each other to get us through. Who did you have?'

He laughed. 'Harper.'

'You're kidding!'

'He was great actually,' Stewart said. 'Oh, I know he can be arrogant, vain, self-absorbed. But when I needed him, he really came through.'

'He's not a bad lad at heart, is he?'

'No. Just spoilt by an overindulgent mother and too much money, too young. For all his faults, he's the closest I've got to a brother.'

'So it was Harper who helped you out of it?'

'Him and my physio, Shiloh. She got me into knitting. Reckoned having something productive to do would keep my mind occupied. And she was right: five holey scarves later I'd started to realise there could be a future for me, even without cycling, if I just went and found it.' He glanced up. 'And sometimes I thought about this girl I'd met before it all happened: a pretty girl with laughing, sad brown eyes and a sarky lopsided grin. Wondered if she was still single. If she'd want to know me now I was nobody.'

'You could never be nobody,' I said with a warmth that surprised me. 'Why didn't you just call her and ask? That's the part I don't get.'

'I told you. Ashamed,' he said, dropping his gaze. 'How do you ring someone after seven months and say "Hi, sorry about the delay, hurt my knee a bit. If you didn't go and get married, how about that dinner?"'

'If you'd just explained—'

He shook his head. 'You don't know what it was like – what I was like. It was cycling that'd always given my life meaning. Without that I just felt so completely worthless, you know? Even after I finally started to come out of the worst of the depression, I didn't dare believe someone like you could be interested in someone like me.'

'You really think I would've cared you'd had to give up cycling?'

'I don't mean that, I mean me. The man I'd become,' he said. 'I was a state, Lana. Seriously, you didn't want to know that self-pitying bastard. I certainly didn't.' He snorted. 'I had a beard.'

I couldn't help smiling. 'I could fancy you with a beard.'

'Not this beard. Put it this way: you ever wondered what Captain Birdseye would've looked like if he'd fallen on hard times?'

'What, selling sexual favours to get his golden breadcrumbs fix?'

He laughed. 'Yeah. That was me.'

'You could've talked to me when you moved here, instead of feeding me all that "let's just be friends" bollocks,' I said. 'I honestly thought the whole thing had meant nothing to you. Do you know how much that hurt?'

'I'm sorry, Lana. I wasn't trying to be a dick. I was still in such a dark place, and you were dealing with losing your dad. I didn't dare hope for anything more than friendship from you. Not then.' He shook his head. 'God, you must've thought I was pathetic.'

'Now come on. You know I did no such thing. I hated you for a good while, but I never thought you were pathetic.'

'You should've. I did.'

'Don't talk like that. Here.' I put a finger under his chin to bring his eyes to mine. 'You could've told me you'd won fifty Grand Tours the night we met and it wouldn't have impressed me. *You* impressed me, Stewart. You made me laugh, and you made me feel safe and comfortable and happy, and you...' I flushed. 'You were different, I guess. Not because of your job, because of you. That's why it hurt so much when you never called. I thought we had a connection, and then you disappeared, just like that. Whoosh.'

'I missed you, Lana,' he said softly, eyes shining with tears and drink. 'The way you smile and scowl and joke. The way you randomly say "whoosh". Even when I was at my lowest, I used to think about you.'

'Really?'

'Really. I was so excited, that night at the meeting when I saw you again. It was a real effort not to let it show.'

'Is that why you got the shop? Because of me?'

'Not exactly. I was looking for premises to start a business and suddenly there it was: shop and flat to let in Egglethwaite, available immediately. And when I discovered it was right across the road from you – seemed like fate or something.'

I shook my head. 'You should have talked to me, Stew. I would've understood.'

'Would you?'

'Yeah. I know what it is to resent the future.'

'You're right, I should. I'm sorry.' He summoned a slightly tipsy grin. 'Mind you, you were kind of sexy when you were always telling me off. Like a scary but erotic medieval headmistress.'

'Well, I'm sure I can still tell you off if you enjoy it so much,' I said, smiling back.

'Will you wear the corset?'

'Don't push it, McLean. The corset costs extra.'

'So can I have a hug now then?'

'Go on. Since you're upset.'

I put both arms round him and pulled him close, feeling his damp cheek meet mine. He smelled so real as he sank into me: aftershave and sweat and wine, just as he'd smelled that night up at Pagans' Rock.

'You smell good, Lana. Like... kiwi fruit,' I heard him whisper in the ear he was tickling with his hot breath. 'Can I kiss you?'

I paused before answering.

'No, lamb. Not just now. You get to bed and sober up, OK? I'll see you soon, triple promise.'

'If you definitely triple promise. Thanks for looking after me, kiddo.'

'Well, someone has to,' I said as I drew back from the hug.

'And I'm forgiven?'

'Yes, Stew. This time you're really forgiven.' I planted a little kiss on top of his curls. 'Night night, my love. Take care of yourself.'

40

I gave Stewart a day's grace to struggle through his hangover, but the Sunday following his little meltdown I was on his doorstep.

The shop was closed so I rang the bell. After a couple of seconds I rang it again. I needed to get off the street, ASAP.

'Hi, Lana,' Stewart said when he answered. 'What's with the long mac? Have you joined the French Resistance?'

'I'm going to show you something in a minute, Stewart McLean, and if you dare laugh you can stick Herbert the bike where the sun doesn't shine.'

'What, Barnsley?'

'Very funny. Let me in, can you?'

He held open the door and I sidled past him into the shop.

'Right,' I said. 'You're about to see something pretty wobbly and if you so much as titter—'

'—I can try wedging a bike handlebar-first right up the Barnsley. Got it.' His eyes widened. 'You're not naked under there, are you?'

'Worse.' I scrunched my eyes closed and yanked the mac open like a comedy seventies flasher. 'It's Lycra.'

After a second, I risked opening one eye. Stewart wasn't

laughing, but he was certainly having a good stare. It'd been a long time since I'd donned cycling shorts for a session on the gym exercise bike, but I had tried to tuck away the most stare-worthy of my jiggly parts before going over.

'What?' I said, looking down at my Lycra-hugged body.

'Nothing.' He shook his head. 'God, never knew that stuff could bear the strain.'

I rubbed my palm along the thigh of my shorts. It wasn't that bad, was it?

Stewart grinned when he clocked my offended expression. 'Not the bottom half, love.'

'Oh,' I said, glancing at the bosom stretching my top alarmingly. 'All right, it is on the tight side. Still, I think it'll survive the afternoon.' I nodded to the stairs. 'Off you go then.'

'Right.' He frowned. 'Um, where am I going? Is this some kinky role-play thing I agreed to when I was drunk the other night? Because if so, brilliant, obviously, but you might have to fill me in on any pre-designated safety words.'

'You wish. Nope, we're going cycling up Cockcroft Hill. I can't have you here moping when you could be out on a bike. I want to see you Lycra-clad in ten minutes with a couple of helmets and whatever hire stock you think can cope with us. On the double, McLean.'

'What? But, Lana, it's been ages since—'

I raised an imperious finger. 'I believe I said on the double, young man. I'm not used to repeating myself.'

'God. Did I ever mention you scare the bejesus out of me?'

'Then you'd better obey me, hadn't you?'

'All right. But you really shouldn't turn me on when I'm about to get into Lycra.'

'Pfft, pfft!' I made an impatient motion towards the stairs, and he shot me a last grin as he took them two at a time.

'Here you go. Picked you out a nice lady bike,' Stewart said through the door of the shop, beckoning to me.

I went to examine the bike he was holding, trying hard not to let my gaze linger on his Lycra-clad body. The cycling gear clung to every muscle and sinew like a second skin. It was very distracting.

I ran my hand along the sleek metal frame. 'Why do they make girls' bikes with diagonal crossbars, Stew? I've always wondered.'

'In the olden days it was to stop your petticoats riding up. God forbid we shock the neighbourhood with a flash of your bloomers.'

I laughed. 'At least the Egglethwaite knicker thief would get a kick out of it. Come on, let's go. And no taking the piss if I have to get off and push.'

It wasn't long into our ride before that joke came back to bite me on the arse. I think my record for staying on the bloody thing was about half a mile.

'Who... designed... this bastard county?' I panted as I made a valiant effort to get up Cockcroft Hill.

Stew chucked me a smile over his shoulder. 'What, you're not having fun?'

'I think my legs dropped off half an hour ago. Also at least one of my buttocks.'

He laughed. 'We can stop for dinner in the White Cross

when we get to the top. I need to rest my knee up a bit anyway.'

Knee injury or not, he didn't seem to be having any trouble. I shot him an envious glance as I finally gave in and clambered off to push. Stew made getting up the hill look like the easiest thing in the world: those fluid movements, perfect unity of man and machine. He even had enough spare breath to whistle.

I sniggered.

'What?' he said, looking round.

'You're like a bike centaur.'

'Bike centaur. Right,' he said, laughing. 'Hey, reckon you can manage this last bit? You'll appreciate your pub lunch more.'

'Ugh. OK.' I threw my leg over the saddle with a groan.

Seeing him on a bike, I could understand why Stew loved all this. He was a natural. No wonder finding out he had to give up had broken him.

Plus he looked really good in Lycra. I mean, *really* good. The way the firm, silken muscles in his buttocks shifted as he pedalled was so hypnotic I kept swerving my bike. It'd be pretty ironic if I got hit by a tractor on my first proper cycling outing, cause of death: sexy bum cheeks.

It was a relief to finally reach the pub.

'What're you doing?' Stew asked when we'd chained up our bikes.

I rummaged in the little rucksack I'd brought. 'Putting my mac on. I can't go in like this.'

He nodded soberly. 'Good point. You might give some poor old feller a heart attack.' He came up behind me and squeezed my hips. 'You look lovely. Come on, kid.'

I flushed at his touch. I hadn't really thought about it when I'd gone round; I'd just wanted to cheer him up, but... did Stew think this was a date?

Maybe it was. There'd certainly been plenty of flirting.

After we'd had a drink and a sandwich, Stew leaned back in his chair with a contented sigh.

'Thanks for bringing me out, Lana.'

'Enjoying it?'

'I am. Didn't realise how much I'd missed it: cycling with no pressure to win.' He grinned. 'Still beat you though.'

'I wouldn't be too proud of that one,' I said, smiling. 'Hey, you ever think of getting back into it as a coach or something? Me and Tom were reading about this youth cycling programme over in Mirfield. I don't see why we couldn't start something like that here.'

'Not stopping until Egglethwaite's the cycling hub of the western world, are you?'

'Nope,' I said, draining the last of my wine. 'I'm serious though, Stew, you'd be great. Think about it.'

'Maybe I will,' he said. 'So how about you? Enjoying yourself?'

'Yeah, it's been fun – despite the, you know, excruciating pain through my whole body. How's your knee?'

'Fine now I've had a rest. Ready to go again when you are.'

I reached into my rucksack for my purse, but Stew shook his head. 'Nope. Dinner's on me. Least I can do after you dragged me out of my misery pit.'

'Oh no, I couldn't let you—'

'It wasn't a suggestion.' He smiled at the look on my face. 'Don't worry, I won't offend your feminist sensibilities. You can pick up the bill next time.'

Next time? OK, tally two for this being a date…

'So now it's time for the best bit,' he said after he'd paid.

'Is it?'

'Let's just say it wasn't uphill climbs that made me fall in love with cycling. Come on.'

I gaped at the view in front of me. If Cockcroft Hill had seemed steep on the way up, that was nothing to how it looked from the top. It reminded me of the first time I'd been tall enough to ride the rollercoaster at Blackpool Pleasure Beach. Top of the biggest ascent, the other kids screaming happily and waving their arms, and little me gripping the rail in white-knuckled terror.

'You don't really expect me to ride down there?' I said to Stew. He was mounted next to me, eyes sparkling like this was the treat of his life.

'No, I expect you to coast down there,' he said. 'If you want to love cycling, you have to love it like a kid does. Like nothing can hold you back.'

'But what if I go into the wall?'

'You won't if you keep the handlebars steady. Come on, live a little.' And he pushed with his feet to go sailing down the hill.

I took a deep breath, kicked the bike forward and felt myself lose control as it propelled me rocket-like down the hill.

'Let go of the brakes!' Stew shouted back.

'I can't!'

'Come on, you're missing out if you don't! You trust me, don't you?'

Sucking in another mouthful of rushing air, I let my fingers ease off the brakes and felt a sudden jolt as the bike picked up speed.

It was incredible: like sitting on the nose of a fighter jet. My hair flew out behind me, eyes stinging, as the frost-crusted fields blurred into a haze of green and silver.

'Arghhhhh!'

'Good, yeah?' Stewart yelled back.

'It's amazing! Oh God, Stew, I think I might be sick...'

At the bottom, I braked and dismounted breathlessly.

'So?' Stew panted. His cheeks were pink, eyes shining with exhilaration. 'Tell me you didn't love it. Bet you a million pounds you can't.'

I laughed. 'If you were Harper, I'd be worried that wasn't a figure of speech.'

'Did you though?'

'Yes,' I said, smiling at the boyish excitement he seemed so desperate for me to share in. 'It was an incredible feeling.'

When we'd cycled home, I got off my bike and leaned it against the wall of McLean's Machines.

'I'll take this one out of the hire stock,' Stew said. 'It's yours now. It can live in the back for whenever you want it.'

I pinkened. 'Oh. Thanks, that's thoughtful.'

'Well, cheers for today, Lana. Let me know when you want to do it again.'

I shook my head. 'Nope. Your turn to ask me out to play next time.'

'OK. I'll look forward to it.'

He moved closer, and his eyes had that searching expression in them... I felt a sudden panic as I realised a kiss was heading my way. A proper one, with tongues and arms and everything that followed. I definitely needed more thinking time before we got into kissing territory. The one he'd given me at Halloween had thrown me totally off balance, and there'd been a table between us then.

I turned my face to one side so his lips landed on my hot cheek instead.

'Right,' he said, looking bashful as he drew back. 'I'll see you later then. Thanks again.'

There wasn't much time for thinking about Stew-related issues at the restaurant. We had another afternoon function, a Dungeons and Dragons group's Christmas party, and I only had half an hour to get ready before relieving Jasmine in the kitchen.

'Liver casserole out in five,' Deano was saying when I pushed open the door.

'All right, Granny Shagger, keep your apron on,' Jasmine said, rolling her eyes.

Deano turned to face me. 'When is she going?' he demanded. 'She's got a proper gob on her lately.'

'Well, about time she got her own back after all the years you've been picking on her.' I nodded to the door. 'Go on, Jaz. I'll take over, you can get off home.'

'OK. Thanks, Lana.'

'I take it the constant abuse means she's cured,' Deano said when she'd gone.

'Yep. Somehow you're less alluring as a teen idol when you're having it off with someone nearly the same age as her nan.'

'Haha. All part of my plan.'

I frowned. 'Really? You shagged Yo-yo to help Jaz get over her crush?'

'No, I shagged Yo-yo because I was randy and she was up for it. But that's a convenient side effect.'

I shook my head. 'Can't believe you're sleeping with her. You know, when you're forty, she'll be...' I did a quick calculation '...old. Like, bus-pass old.'

'Yeah. We weren't thinking of anything that long-term, to be honest.'

'It's still going on then?'

'When the mood takes us.' He leaned down to peer in at his casserole. 'Which in her case is most nights and a fair few mornings. Surprised I can still walk.'

I curled my lip. 'Thanks for that.'

'And what about your love life?' he asked.

I blushed. 'It's... dunno. Might be progressing.'

'You and Stew sorted things out?'

'We're kind of just good friends at the moment. Still need time to think.'

'Oh, get on with it, you daft cow,' he said, straightening up again. 'You haven't had sex for, like, three years.'

My eyes widened. 'How the hell did you know that?'

He grinned. 'Lucky guess. But thanks for the confirmation.'

'Look, you can't rush these things.'

'Rush it? For God's sake, you've been dancing around each other for months,' he said. 'Go on, go for it. At least you'll get a shag.'

'There's more to life than getting laid, Deano.'

'Nah, I'd have heard,' he said. 'So what do you think you'll do then?'

I sighed. 'Take it slow, I guess. I've forgiven him, but... well, the whole thing's left me a bit cautious.'

'Really hurt you, didn't he?' Deano said in a softer voice.

'It's not something I can easily forget about, let's put it that way,' I admitted. 'I'll just see how it goes.'

41

It was a funny old Christmas Day. Bittersweet. Gerry and Sue had invited us to the farm for dinner, but we'd decided we wanted to be alone with one another and our thoughts while we ate. Merriment wasn't really on the cards, with an empty chair at the head of the table.

'Thanks for the jumper, sis,' Tom said when we'd had dinner. Dad had always made us wait until after we'd eaten to exchange presents. As kids it'd driven us mad, but we'd secretly enjoyed our toys more for the anticipation.

Tom pulled his new jumper, a novelty Fair Isle with a picture of Darth Vader and the legend 'I find your lack of cheer disturbing', over his head.

'You're welcome. Ta for the book,' I said, flicking through it. It was called *F**k: A History of the F-Word*. Now everything with the viaduct was sorted, my little outburst at Sienna had become something of a family joke.

'No worries,' he said with a grin. 'At least next time you start chucking obscenities about on telly you'll be well informed.'

'Dad'd give you a right telling-off for that.' I sighed. 'Weird just us, isn't it?'

Tom smiled as Flash came bounding in from the kitchenette and nearly cannoned into one of K&M Garden Centre's finest Norwegian spruces. 'Not just us. This is Flash's first Christmas, don't forget.'

'Wish it was a jollier one for him.' I grimaced as he jumped up to lick my face. 'Ew. Turkey breath.'

'He still tries to get into Dad's room. Funny how they remember people.'

'I know.' I gave Flash a hug. 'He's a good dog.'

'Keeps trying to drag me off to the chip shop too.' Tom sighed. 'Six weeks now.'

'Don't give up yet,' I said, patting his knee. 'Let's just get through Christmas, then… well, we'll think of something.' I pushed Flash off my knee and stood up. 'Right. Dad wouldn't want us moping. I'll sort a couple of sherries and we'll have a game of Scrabble, how does that sound?'

'Perfect. You're prepared for an arse-kicking though, yeah?'

'Please. You've never, ever beaten me. Ever.'

'Ah, but this is my year. Flash and me are going to form a boys' superteam. No mere girl can beat us.'

I frowned when I heard the intercom buzz to tell us someone was outside the restaurant.

'Who's that?' I asked Tom.

He shrugged. 'Dunno. Not expecting anyone.'

I went into the hall and pressed the intercom button.

'Hello?'

'It's Stew. Can I come up?'

'Oh. Course, we'd love to see you.' I pressed the button to unlock the door.

'What?' I said to Tom, who was standing in the living

374

room doorway grinning at me. 'We would love to see him, wouldn't we?'

'One of us would.'

I opened the hallway door and Stew came in. He gave me a hug and a kiss on the cheek.

'Happy Christmas, love.'

'You too,' I said with a little blush.

He gave Tom a hug too. 'Liking the jumper, Tommy.'

'Thanks. I do think the flashing light sabre brings out my eyes. Had a good day?'

'Not bad. Just back from Christmas dinner at Mum and Dad's. Lucky Harper's abandoned that living foodist stuff or I think Mum might've had a nervous breakdown cooking for him.'

'You want to stay for a sherry? We were just about to play Scrabble.' Tom lowered his voice. 'You have to watch Lana though – she cheats.'

Stew frowned. 'Did you two not get the message?'

'Eh?' Tom said. 'What message?'

I slapped my palm against my head. 'Sorry, Tommy, totally forgot. Gerry and Sue invited us for afternoon drinks with some people from the village.' I shot him an apologetic smile. 'I did say we'd go. You don't mind, do you?'

'Course not, sounds nice. I'll just grab a fleece.'

He ducked into his bedroom, and Stew shot me a knowing grin.

'All set?' I asked him.

'Yep. Everyone's in place. You sure he—'

But he was interrupted by Tom coming back out in his winter coat and beanie.

Stew cleared his throat. 'Right. Let's go.'

'Happy Christmas, you three,' Gerry said when we knocked at the farmhouse. It looked very festive, the roof salted with frost and a jolly wreath on the door in stark contrast to Gerry's black 'Bah Humbug' Santa hat.

'How long have you had that hat, Gerry?' I said, presenting my cheek for a kiss. 'I remember you wearing it when we were at primary.'

'Brand new, this is. The missus treated me to another this year. Said the old one had fleas.'

He beckoned us inside. We followed him into the living room, where Sue had arranged a table of festive nibbles. There were various people milling around: Yolanda and Deano, thankfully managing to keep their hands off each other for five minutes; Roger Collingwood scoffing a mince pie; Billy from the pub; a load of Gerry's morris men mates...

'Where is he?' I muttered to Gerry.

'Helping Sue in the kitchen.' Gerry raised his voice. 'Er, let me get the three of you a drink. Beer for you lads?'

'Yeah, cheers,' Tom said.

'Can I not have a beer?' I asked.

Stew grinned at me. 'Nope. Your uncle says you have to drink wine with your little finger stuck out like a proper lady. He is from the olden days, to be fair.'

Gerry laughed. 'Well, I can probably find a Guinness, since it's Christmas. You'll still have to stick your little finger out though, Lana.'

He disappeared off into the kitchen to get our drinks.

'There's Deano,' Tom said. 'Shall we—' He stopped as the kitchen door opened. 'What's he doing here?'

'Surprise,' I said, smiling. 'This is your real present; the jumper was just a sweetener.'

Cameron's eyebrows shot up when he caught sight of Tom.

'What's he doing here?' he demanded of Sue, dumping his tray of sherries down on the piano.

'That's what I just said,' Tom said.

Cameron glared at him. 'I didn't ask you.' He turned back to Sue. 'You told me him and Lana couldn't make it.'

'Well, I lied,' she said with a shrug.

'What for?'

'I'll tell you what for, young Cameron. Because I've known Tom Donati since he thought the main purpose of his willy was playing fireman in the garden...'

Tom grimaced. 'Thanks for that.'

'...and I know him too well not to know what he's feeling,' Sue went on, ignoring him. 'Oh, he can be a right pillock. He stutters and stumbles and talks a load of old rubbish...'

Tom turned to me. 'Is this a family intervention? Because no offence but so far it royally sucks.'

'Give her a minute. She's just getting into her stride,' I whispered.

'...but those are just words,' Sue said. 'He's not good with words but he's good with feelings. And he loves you.'

Cameron's eyes went wide. 'Bloody hell, does he?'

Gerry nodded. 'Yep.'

'Yep,' I said.

'Yep,' Deano called from the buffet table.

Stew smiled. 'Everyone knows but you, Cam.'

Tom glared at us. 'Why're you lot talking about me like I'm not here?'

I gave him a little push forward. 'Go on then, bruv. We've said our bit. The floor's all yours.'

He walked hesitantly towards Cameron.

'Looks like they set us up,' Tom said quietly.

'I know. Soppy gits.' Cameron looked him up and down. 'Nice jumper.'

'Thanks. Christmas present.'

'So do you, Tommy?'

'Yeah. You?'

'Yeah.'

'Come here then.' Tom bent to plant a kiss on Cameron's lips and the two melted into a hug.

'Missed you,' I heard Cam whisper. 'Sorry I wouldn't talk to you. I thought you didn't... you know.'

'Missed you too,' Tom said. 'Sorry I was daft about your parents. I'd be proud to meet them. Just be prepared for them to hate me.'

'Give over, they'll love you.'

'Well, I love you.'

'Me too. Happy Christmas, Tommy.'

I elbowed Stew as we watched them embrace. 'It's a Christmas miracle, eh?'

'They just needed a nudge. These shy people are a nightmare to get talking.'

I turned to face him. 'Well, thanks for helping.'

'Anything to see them happy. Oh.' He handed me a small gift-wrapped parcel from his jacket pocket. 'For you.'

I eyed it quizzically. 'You didn't have to get me anything.'

'I wanted to though. Go on, open it.'

I tore off the paper. Inside was a box, which I opened to find a pretty silver bracelet with four tiny charms attached: a bat, a train, a trombone and a bike.

'One for all the times you've done something amazing this year,' Stew said. 'Like bringing the Tour here, and getting the viaduct reopened – that's the little train. Maybe by next Christmas it'll be full.'

I blinked as my eyes filled with tears. 'It's beautiful,' I whispered. 'What made you think of it?'

'It's what your dad said in his eulogy, isn't it? I wanted you to have something to mark every time you make the world better.'

The eulogy... how did he know about that?

He smiled at the look on my face. 'Tom told me. I knew it'd be a difficult Christmas for you.'

'Thank you,' I mumbled. 'I feel awful for not getting you anything.'

'There is one thing I'd like very much,' he said softly. 'Can I?'

My eyes were fixed on his, and the rest of the room seemed to have fuzzed into nothing.

'Yes,' I whispered. 'Yes please.'

His face was moving towards mine, and if he'd kissed me then I'd gladly have melted into his arms forever, caution be damned. But before our lips could meet, Roger Collingwood came barging over with his stupid size twelve clown feet and the room came back into focus.

'Hello, you two,' he said, beaming. 'Any news on the viaduct?'

Stew turned to glare at him. 'No. It's fallen down.'

Roger looked puzzled. 'Was that a joke?'

He sighed. 'Yes. Sorry, Rodge.'

'I'm not interrupting, am I?'

'Not at all.' Stewart summoned a polite smile. 'Go on, please. We can finish this later.'

42

There was no time for snuggling under the duvet with a post-Christmas hangover on Boxing Day. Not while Roger Collingwood was still conductor of Egglethwaite Silver.

Rodge was a popular village leader because he combined tireless hard work with shrewd business sense. Which was why every 26th December, he booked us to play outside Bilby's department store in town: catch the Boxing Day sales crowd.

I couldn't argue there was a healthy chink as shoppers chucked coins into our bucket. But it was also bloody freezing. It only took until our third number, 'Carol of the Bells' – the world's creepiest Christmas tune – for my gloved fingers to lose all feeling.

'I think my slide's seized up,' I muttered to the euphonium player, Nathan.

'Tell me about it,' Nathan whispered back. 'My lips nearly froze to the mouthpiece for that one. He's not really going to make us do the full three hours, is he?'

Of course he was. He was Roger Collingwood. By the time we finished our set – ironically, with 'Let It Snow' – there was about three inches of white powder on the ground.

And things were about to get worse. When I got back to my car, I discovered the damn thing had thrown a tantrum at being left in the cold and was refusing to start. I pulled my phone out to ring Gerry, see if he could fetch me in the Land Rover.

No answer. Bollocks. I tried Tom instead.

'Hiya, Lana,' Cameron said when he answered.

'Hi, Cam. Is our Tom there?'

'Yeah, he's helping my mum with the washing-up. What's up?'

'I'm stuck at Bilby's in this bloody snow. Can you ask him to pop round Gerry's, see if he can fetch me? Sorry to be a pain when you're with your family but I can't get hold of him.'

'No worries, we'll both go. Could use a walk.'

'Thanks, love.'

I stashed my trombone in the boot and headed back to the front of the shop, abandoning the car until I could get back next day with warm clothing and jump leads.

Fifteen minutes later I was still staring into the road, freezing my jollies off while the mufflered bargain-hunters bustled around me. My thin nylon band blazer was soaked through and there'd been no word from Tom. I only hoped the lack of contact meant Gerry was on his way.

But I blinked in surprise when instead of Gerry, Stewart hoved into view, riding a bike through the crusting of snow. And not just any bike either. This was a whole lot of bike. Two saddles, four pedals...

He braked beside me and rang the bell.

'Evening, soldier. Need a ride?'

I laughed. 'You daft bugger. What the hell are you doing on that?'

'What does it look like?' He jerked his head to the back of the tandem. 'I'm picking you up. Your brother stopped by to say Gerry wasn't in. Best snow-friendly transport I could manage at short notice.'

'You seriously expect me to ride that thing?'

'It's only a few miles. Come on, it'll be fun.' He dismounted and rummaged in the pannier bag for an enormous fleece and a helmet. 'Brought you these.'

I pulled the lovely warm fleece over my blazer and cuddled into it gratefully.

'How does this work then?' I asked, examining the tandem.

'Like any bike. You get your own handlebars and pedals. We just need to find a rhythm that works for us both.' He grinned. 'Possibly a euphemism, I'll leave it up to you.'

I didn't like it at all when we got going. My handlebars were there to grip, but they couldn't set direction or brake: all the control was at Stewart's end. Every time we turned a corner, my stomach lurched.

But after ten minutes, I started to relax. It was actually quite pleasant once you got used to it. I could look around me, enjoy the bonny snow-blanketed scenery, trusting Stew to keep us safe. I'd even feel secure letting him coast us down Cockcroft Hill – almost.

I frowned as we rounded a corner to Holyfield Farm. Gerry's Land Rover was parked outside, and the light was on in the window.

'I thought our Tom said he was out.'

Stewart blinked at the farmhouse. 'He did.'

'The sneaky git,' I muttered.

'Hey, let's stop a minute,' Stewart said. 'Someone's not doing her share of the pedalling and my knee needs a rest.'

'So why would your brother say Gerry wasn't in?' he asked when we'd propped the bike against a drystone wall.

'Subterfuge. I think it's revenge for that intervention we pulled on him and Cameron.'

'Revenge?'

'Yeah. Tom's got this theory. About... about me and you. You know.'

I turned my burning cheeks to the ground and peeked up at Stewart through my eyelashes. There was a little smile at the corner of his mouth.

'You must be cold,' he said at last. 'Come here to me.'

I let him pull me into his arms and sighed against his chest. There didn't seem any point fighting. I wanted to be in his arms so why not be in them? Suddenly it was all very simple.

'Tell me about these stars then, skywatcher,' he said softly.

'You remember that?'

'I remember. Couldn't forget the sparkly look in your eyes when you told me.' He ran a gentle finger along my cheek. 'They are very pretty eyes.'

It was a sharp, clear evening now the snow had stopped, with a bleach-white gibbous moon. When a thin cloud passed over, it shone through to make a little halo of rainbow.

I pointed to a cluster of stars against the inky black, tracing them with my finger. 'Well, that sort of W-shape, that's Cassiopeia. The Romans believed she was a queen, cast into the night sky for being vain of her beauty.'

Stew laughed. 'Someone should warn Harper.'

'I bet he'd like it. Then he could be the biggest star of all.' I pointed out another constellation. 'And that stickman one's Orion. See, you can just make out his sword belt. Thirteen hundred light years away, can you believe it?' I shook my head. 'Always amazes me the Romans could look at that and see a man. They must've been smoking something pretty hardcore.'

'Which star's your favourite?'

'Oh, the brightest,' I said dreamily. 'First one I ever learned: Venus.'

'Is that a star?'

'No. But when I was little Dad used to tell me the brightest star was Venus. Maybe he thought it sounded poetic – the goddess of love.' I laughed. 'Or maybe he just picked a random planet because he didn't want to admit not knowing the names.'

Stewart's fingers were playing in my hair. I could feel his heart throbbing hard against my cheek.

'You're remarkable, you know,' he murmured.

'Thanks,' I said with a little blush. 'Most people go with "strange".'

'Can I have my Christmas kiss now, Lana?'

'Yes,' I whispered. 'You know you can.'

He took my cheek in his palm and touched his lips to mine. His other hand slid down my back, pressing me closer, but he kept the kiss gentle. It felt like he was waiting. Waiting for me to show him what I wanted.

I parted my lips a little. The next second his tongue was in my mouth and all at once the kiss became hungry and intense, our long-suppressed feelings shooting out in a frenzy.

'Oh, Lana, Lana,' Stew breathed as he peppered kisses into my neck. 'Is it happening?'

'God, yes,' I murmured, tilting my head so his eager lips could find as much flesh as possible under the collar of the fleece. 'Yes, it's happening.'

'You'll come home with me?'

I hesitated, then gasped as his mouth found its way to my earlobe. 'Well, it is Christmas.'

I think we might've set a new land speed record for tandem, getting the thing back to McLean's Machines. When we got there, Stew practically dragged me to his bedroom, slamming the door behind us.

We fumbled off our helmets and he pulled me on to his lips, wasting no time picking up where we'd left off. I shivered as he feverishly stripped me of the chunky fleece.

'You OK?' he panted, calming his passion a little when he felt me tremble.

'I'm OK.' I smiled bashfully. 'Cold.'

'Course you are. You're wet through.' He nodded to the bed. 'Get your clothes off and get in.'

I laughed. 'You old romantic.'

'All right, get your clothes off romantically,' he said with a grin. 'You need to warm up.'

I kicked off my soaked pumps and crawled into his bed.

'Not undressing?' he asked.

'Under the covers. I don't want you to see.'

'Right.' He frowned. 'Why not? Unless I've seriously misread the signals, I had assumed we were about to have sex.'

'Yeah, in the dark.'

He laughed. 'Is this Lana Donati speaking? Siren-like star of nude calendars and my more erotic dreams?'

'This is different,' I said, thrashing the duvet as I struggled out of my damp blazer. 'Please, Stew, look the other way. I'm shy.'

'If it makes you feel more comfortable.' He turned to face the door.

'Do you really dream about me?' I asked, sliding out of my trousers.

'Sometimes. Don't you?'

I blushed. 'Sometimes.'

I could only see the back of his head, but I could tell he was smiling.

'I'll put on some music,' he said at last.

While I was unfettering my overly ample bosom, Stew plonked his phone into a speaker dock on the chest of drawers.

'Kirsty MacColl, right?' he said as 'Fairytale of New York' started up. 'Something seasonal for you.'

I smiled as I removed my last item of clothing. 'How'd you know that?'

'You told me. One year and—' he counted on his fingers '—six months ago.' He glanced at the little pile of clothes by the bed. 'Did you just take your knickers off?'

'Yup.'

He rubbed his hands. 'Right. Budge up.'

'Not until you strip off. You might catch cold or whatever made-up thing you just said.'

'What, I'm not allowed to do it under the covers? I might be shy.'

'The hell you are. Go on, McLean, get it off.'

He shook his head. 'First time I've stripteased to "Fairytale of New York".'

He pulled off his chunky aran jumper to reveal the toned stomach I remembered from the calendar, then his shoes, socks and jeans.

'Your legs are ridiculous,' I said, running my gaze over them. 'They look like boiled eggs in a sock.'

'Er, thanks. Not sure you've quite got the hang of sexy small talk.' He nodded to the bed. 'Can I get in?'

'You've still got your boxers on.'

He slid under the covers. 'Got to save you one Christmas present to unwrap.'

'You didn't just say that.'

'Let's pretend I didn't. Then maybe it'll never have happened.'

He pulled me close; close enough to smell him. Then he tucked a strand of hair behind my ear with one finger. It was a tiny gesture but so light, so intimate, it thrilled me. His hot, short breaths were against my neck; the solid mass of his erection on my hip.

'Let me look at you,' he whispered.

'But—'

'Let me look at you, Lana.'

He tweaked the duvet so he could dip his head underneath. For a minute, he didn't say a word.

'You are so beautiful,' he murmured at last. 'How can you not know?'

'No one ever told me before.'

'Then they didn't deserve to touch you.'

He rolled on top of me and kissed softly along my neck.

If he'd seemed frantic out in the snow, he was taking it slow now, and I was glad. I needed this to last.

'Stew?' I whispered as he drew tender fingertips over the curve of my waist. 'Have you... have you been with lots of girls?'

'Is it important?'

'It's just... I haven't...' I gasped as his other hand glided to my breast. 'It's been a while.'

I sucked in my breath as he ran his tongue-tip around an erect nipple. My whole nervous system was blossoming into flame for him, like a – what was that flower? A poinsettia. Although that could be the Christmas talking.

'You trust me, don't you?' Stew whispered.

'Course I do. I—' I bit my lip. 'I'm just scared of getting it wrong.'

'There is no wrong, Lana. Just us.' He moved his hot mouth to my other nipple, and I gave a little moan as he lapped at it with his rough, wet tongue. My hips had started to rise and fall under him, my body instinctively seeking his.

'You know how I feel about you, don't you?' he murmured between licks.

'Tell me.'

He smiled. 'You're really going to make me go first?'

'I... need you to. Ah!' I flinched with pleasure as he took my nipple between his teeth and bit lightly, pushing under my shoulder blades to bring me closer to his mouth.

'I love you,' he whispered against my breast. 'Come on, you know that. Everyone else seems to. We're even less of a secret than Tom and Cam.'

'Stew... you mean it?'

'I do. There's no one like you, Lana Donati.' He looked up into my face. 'You know, politeness dictates you really should say it back now you've got your hands in my pants. I wouldn't want to feel cheap.'

He was right, my hands seemed to have their own sweet agenda. They'd slipped into his boxers and were having a grand time caressing the sleek, enticing muscles of his buttocks.

'You know I do,' I murmured.

'Say it for me.'

'I love you, Stew.'

He shuddered. 'Now say it in Italian.'

'*Ti amo*. What for?'

'Dunno, it's kind of sexy.'

I sucked at my lip as he slipped one finger inside me, his thumb-tip gliding around the wet heat between my legs. He groaned into my skin at the touch.

'Ah! Stew?'

'Chatty, aren't you?'

'There's just... what we said, just now. Need you to know. I never said it before, not in – God! – not in English or Italian. You're the first.'

He stopped the delicious movement of his hand for a second and blinked up at me.

'You're serious?'

'Yes. There were boyfriends, but... well, I never felt it so I never said it. It seemed too important to chuck about.'

He reached up to stroke my face. 'Then I'm honoured,' he said softly. 'Relax now, Lana.'

Relax. He wanted me to relax. Those adventurous fingers were dipping rhythmically between my legs as his mouth played around the full, plump flesh of my breasts. Relaxed was the last thing I felt.

I could feel my sex-starved body getting more and more turned on at the noises we made while we explored each other – as much from the whispered, needy sounds escaping my own lips as Stew's throaty groans. I tried to keep quiet at first, embarrassed by my own arousal, but Stew murmured to go on and I could tell it was getting him excited, so I gave in and was just as loud as came naturally.

Finally, I ran my fingertips along his rippling back to the waistband of his boxers and peeled them off.

'Oh God,' I whispered as my fingers found their way to his erection. He gasped as I massaged both hands along its length. 'Oh God, Stew, you feel… I'm ready now, love.'

'You sure?'

'Yes. Get on with it.'

He looked up from my breasts to grin. 'You know what it does to me when you go all schoolmistressy.'

'Have you got protection?'

'Somewhere.' He leaned over me to his bedside cabinet and fumbled in the drawer for a condom packet. 'Er, cinnamon flavour,' he said, squinting at it. 'Hope that's OK with you.'

I laughed breathlessly. 'Cinnamon?'

'It's not been all that recent for me either,' he said with an embarrassed smile. 'Might've had this a while.'

'And there I was thinking you were such a sex god.'

'Oh, I am. But only on special occasions.' He rolled on top of me. 'And since it's Christmas and there's a gorgeous woman naked in my bed…'

He ripped open the foil, filling the air with a sweet scent

almost entirely unlike cinnamon, and reached down to roll on the condom. The noise he made when our bodies joined was choked, like a sob.

'Oh Lana,' he breathed as he thrust gently into me. He nuzzled into my hair, dropping hot kisses against any bit of skin he could find. 'Oh God, Lana...'

I loved the way he said my name, sliding each syllable over his tongue like melting ice cream. It sounded like he was claiming me, every time a new declaration of love.

'Does it hurt?' Stew whispered when he heard me suck in my breath.

It did feel slightly uncomfortable as my body adjusted to his. After three years, it was almost like my first time all over again.

'No,' I said. 'Just... long time. Don't stop, Stew, please.'

'Want to swap round? Then you can be in control.'

'Will you turn the light out?'

'I will not. You're beautiful and I want to see you.' He drew the back of his fingernail gently along my cheek. 'No need to be nervous, Lana. It's only me.'

I flushed. 'Well... OK.'

He guided me round so I was straddling him, shuffled into a sitting position and eased himself inside me again.

'Lean back,' he murmured. 'Trust me.'

I did as he said, flexing against the strong hands holding my shoulder blades. God, it felt incredible in that position; every pulse so deep and thrilling. I clutched his thick thighs and pushed him into me, over and over, discomfort evaporating as my body moulded itself naturally to his.

Stewart buried his head between my breasts, plunging kisses into them and groaning something that might've been my name. He met me greedily, thrust for delicious thrust, and my senses responded like they never had to anyone else. And I didn't care, by then, what parts of me he saw, because I felt beautiful and sexy and in love, and I didn't even care how much we punished his headboard, which was banging the wall alarmingly. I only cared that I loved him, and I loved his relentless body snug and firm inside mine, and I was about to have the most shattering orgasm of my life.

And then I did, the whole thing catching me by surprise. Stew sucked hard at my nipple, and I pushed myself against him and I moaned, and then I *really* moaned as something broke and my body shot into a sudden fever of trembling. My hips stilled while the unfamiliar throbs paralysed me, Stew bucking under me the only motion I was aware of. A second later he let out a long, low groan, clasping me tightly, and he whispered I love you, I love you until it was over for him too and we fell back against the bed, panting.

'That was... different,' he said breathlessly.

I nodded. 'Cinnamony.'

'Can you stay over? Don't want you to leave me.'

'I can stay. Tom knows where I am.' I snuggled against him, wrapping both my legs around one of his, and planted a soft kiss on the tip of his nose. 'Did I tell you already that I love you?'

'You might've mentioned it in passing.' His fingers traced the waves of my hair, so gently I was only barely aware he was touching me.

'I'm so happy, Stew,' I mumbled as my eyes grew heavy. 'Everything's... OK now.'

'Me too. I'm happy too,' were the last words I heard before I drifted into sleep.

43

'Come on, red or blue?' I demanded, holding two cocktail dresses up for Tom to examine.

He shrugged. 'What am I, Gok Wan?'

'Ugh. You are so useless.' I shoved both dresses back in the cupboard. 'On second thoughts, think I'll try the silver again. Chuck it to me, will you?'

Tom grabbed the dress from my bed and threw it to me. I held it up, eyeing it critically in the mirror.

'Nope. Too cleavagey.'

'Just relax, it's only Stew,' Tom said. 'We're having a couple of New Year's Eve drinks in front of the telly; he's not taking you to the Savoy.'

'But it's our first proper, official date since, you know, the very first one. I want it to be perfect.' I looked round to smile at him. 'Never thought this time last year we'd be double-dating on New Year's Eve. It seemed pretty unlikely this time two weeks ago, to be honest.'

'And yet it was there in your tarot cards as far back as Halloween,' Tom said with a grin.

'Right.' I reached into the cupboard for the red and blue dresses. 'Sorry, Tommy, but I need some advice from a man who's heterosexual and unrelated. See you in a bit.'

We weren't open, but Deano – who refused to go out on the 31st due to his oft-stated belief that New Year was 'the bastard that kills Christmas' – had asked if he could borrow the kitchen to test a few dishes for our 2014 menu. When I got there, he was squinting at some sort of omelette.

'Quails' eggs,' he was muttering to himself. 'Why didn't I get the bloody quails' eggs? Hi, Lana.'

How did he *do* that? He hadn't even looked round.

'I can smell you,' he said, once again demonstrating an uncanny ability to read my mind. 'Tom never smells of kiwi fruit.'

'Er, all right. That's not creepy.' I held up the two dresses. 'Deano, what's a sexy thing to wear for a date?'

'Man's shirt, no knickers,' he answered instantly, not looking up from his pan.

I tutted. 'Not that sexy, it's a double date. Look at these.'

He gave whatever was in the pan a last jab and turned around.

'Both look good to me,' he said with a shrug. 'I'm sure Stew'll think you look hump-worthy whatever.'

'Go on, pick. I'm running out of time.'

'The red pencil thing then,' he said. 'It'll make you look all hourglassy. Plus it matches my hair.'

I punched his arm. 'Thanks. So you coming up for a drink later?'

'All right. But you're not making me sing "Auld Lang Syne".'

I needn't have worried about running out of time. Half an hour after Stew was due, there was still no sign of him.

'Where the hell is he?' I demanded of Tom and Cameron, who were snuggled with Flash between them, supping Prosecco and watching telly. 'He's only coming from across the road.'

'Calm down, sis. Stop pacing,' Tom said impatiently. 'He's probably just trying to decide between the red and the blue boxers.'

'You're not still paranoid about what happened last year, are you?' Cameron asked.

I glared at Tom. 'Have you been telling your boyfriend about my love life failures?'

He shrugged. 'Whiles away the hours.'

'Are you though, Lana?' Cam said.

'Listen, mate. Just because my dog thinks you're his long-lost bollocks, don't think I'm up for sharing my most intimate, humiliating secrets.'

'Definitely paranoid,' Tom said to Cam.

'All right, so I am.' I threw myself down in the armchair. 'I just can't help remembering that he disappeared out of my life once before.'

'Under very specific circumstances.'

'I worry about losing him, that's all.' I sighed. 'Chuck us my phone, Tom.'

There was no text, and no answer to my call when I rang. I stood to look out of the window.

'Hmm. All dark over there.'

'Gone out for a bottle maybe,' Tom said.

'Maybe.'

An hour later, it was nearly nine. Deano had joined us, bearing assorted plates of medieval tapas, but there was still no sign of Stew. No lights on in the flat, no answer to my calls...

'Where the hell is he? Where the *hell* is he?'

'Ask as many times as you like, Lanasaurus. The answer'll still be "we don't know",' Deano said. He nodded to the plates on the coffee table. 'Try some of this game pie – it's delish. Going to be our big seller for Tour weekend.'

'I don't want game pie. I want to know where Stew is.' My eyes went wide. 'Oh God, what if he's had an accident? He might be lying in a ditch somewhere. And we're all here, gobbling pie and swigging Prosecco like the bastards we are.'

'There'll be an explanation, you'll see,' Tom said.

'There'd bloody better be.' I got to my feet. 'I need a drink. Let's get another bottle open.'

Uncorking the Prosecco made me think of Harper, probably tucking into his second bottle of Dom Perignon by now while us lowly proles made do with the £7.99 stuff from Sainsbury's. And that made me think about Stew again, and the night we'd first met. Where *was* he?

'Lana!' Tom called from the living room. 'It's Stew!'

I felt a surge of relief. He was here. Thank God.

I went into the living room and glanced around. 'Where's Stew? Didn't you buzz him up?'

'Not here.' Tom nodded at the TV screen. 'There.'

I looked at the telly. A choir were performing a bit of Handel's 'Messiah' outside a manor house twenty miles away, Monkton Hall.

'You what?'

'He's in the crowd,' Deano said. 'We just saw him.'

My eyebrows shot up. 'He stood me up so he could go watch bloody *Songs of Praise*? I'll kill him!'

'It's not *Songs of Praise*,' Tom said.

'What is it?'

He snorted. 'Your mate. *The Harper Brady Live NYE Extravaganza*.'

'Oh God, is he a presenter now?'

'Apparently.'

The choir finished and Harper appeared on screen, smiling his most charming smile.

'Beverley Minster Choir there,' he said. 'Coming up we've got a chimney sweep whose services as a bringer of luck are always in demand at New Year, and a couple who shared their first kiss as the bells chimed in 1946.' His face set into an earnest expression. 'But first, there's something important I need to talk to you about.'

I shook my head. 'I don't believe it. He's good at this too.'

He had a very natural presenting style, easy and conversational, as if everyone in the audience was his best mate. Whatever lucky star Harper Brady had been born under, it clearly had a wicked sense of humour.

'These sort of shows are so cheesy, aren't they?' Cameron said. 'It's always the same sentimental crap: couples celebrating golden anniversaries and that.'

'Stew, can you come on over?' the telly Harper said. A second later Stewart had edged into view, grinning nervously under a thick beanie.

I frowned. 'All right, lads, what the heck is going on?'

Tom looked as bewildered as I felt. 'Don't ask us.'

'This is my cousin, Stewart McLean,' Harper told the cameras. 'Say hi, Stew.'

'Hi, Stew.'

'Ugh. That joke is ancient,' Deano groaned.

'Give him a break,' Cam said. 'He's obviously nervous.'

'Some of you will remember him as a demon in the saddle back in his cycling days,' Harper went on. He held up the microphone to Stewart. 'So. Busy year for you. Want to tell us about it?'

'Thanks, Harper.' Stewart's voice was trembling, but he fixed the cameras with a determined look that seemed to be aimed straight at me. 'It has been a busy year. Sadly, I was forced to give up professional cycling eighteen months ago due to injury. Since then I've made my living running a bike shop in a wonderful little village called Egglethwaite.' He paused to take a deep breath. 'A group of us have worked hard this year to get our viaduct reopened as a right of way.' The programme cut to a picture of the viaduct, but we could still hear Stew's voice over the top. 'This project was very dear to a village resident who passed away recently, Phil Donati.' I felt a jolt as the viaduct faded into a photo of Dad, grinning happily – and slightly tipsily – at the bar of the Sooty Fox. He was in a battered top hat and shabby suit, back in the days when Egglethwaite Players were still in existence and Dad was their star turn.

The picture cut back to Stewart and Harper.

'Sounds a lot of work,' Harper said smoothly.

'In a very short time. In six months, we raised over £50,000.'

'Why so quickly?'

Stew seized the prompt gratefully. 'Because our ultimate aim, as a memorial to Phil, was to bring next year's Grand Départ route through Egglethwaite. We felt the viaduct would be our unique selling point, and a lasting legacy for local people.'

'Did it work?'

'We were told so.' Stew looked sober now. 'The lady in charge, Vanessa Christmas, promised we'd be recommended for inclusion on the route.'

'But?' Harper prompted.

'But last night I spoke to a friend who'd seen an advance copy of the Stage 2 York to Sheffield schedule. It passes within five miles of Egglethwaite – but it doesn't pass through.' His eyes seemed to be looking right at me. 'We're not getting the Tour.'

44

I clapped my hand to my mouth. 'Oh my God! No. No, that can't be true.'

'It has to be.' Cam shook his head in disbelief. 'So it's all been for nothing. All our hard work – wasted.'

'It's not fair. It's just… not fair,' I whispered.

'But why would they do it?' Tom demanded of no one in particular. 'We did everything they wanted. The viaduct'll be open in plenty of time, just like we said.'

'Shush,' Deano said. 'Stew's still talking.'

'Really?' Harper was saying to Stewart. 'They didn't include you on the route after you were told they would?'

'Yes. It's going to upset a lot of people – not least Phil's children, Tom and Lana, who pioneered this project in his memory.'

There were disapproving mutterings in the live audience gathered outside the hall.

'We're going to take a break now,' Harper said. 'But before we do, I'd like to make a personal appeal to the Tour organisers to reconsider their decision and give little Egglethwaite the opportunity they fought so hard for. It is still the season of goodwill, after all.' He flashed a winning smile to the camera, and the picture cut away to an Alka-Seltzer ad.

'Bloody hell,' I whispered. I jumped as my phone buzzed on the table.

'Stew?' Tom asked when I examined the screen.

I shook my head. 'Vanessa Christmas.'

I went into the kitchenette to take the call in private.

'Mrs Christmas,' I said when I picked it up. 'Look, I had no idea Stewart was planning to—'

'Save the excuses, Miss Donati. I'm not a fan of blackmail tactics.'

'Well, I'm not a fan of being lied to,' I said, hackles rising. 'Why did you chuck us off the route? If it's going five miles away it could go through Egglethwaite just as well.'

'It was merely felt other communities had a right to consideration,' she said stiffly.

'That's not what you said before though, is it?'

'Well, that was then.'

'I don't see—' I stopped. 'Wait. Is this about that thing on telly with me and Sienna Edge?'

'That was certainly… unfortunate,' she admitted. 'The Départ is a family event. Publicity like that…'

'But you heard what she said to me. What would you have done?'

'That's neither here nor there.'

'Yes it is! It is here or there!' I snapped. 'Come on, Vanessa. If she'd accused you of exploiting your husband's memory that way, what would you have said?'

She hesitated. 'The same as you, perhaps,' she said at last. 'But that doesn't change the fact of it. The organisers saw the footage and they were unanimous.'

'Then it's all my fault. Again.' I blinked back tears. 'Oh God. We worked so hard. The others – the village…'

'Now, now. Don't get upset.' She sighed. 'Blackmail it may be, but it is still Harper Brady on national TV.'

'What're you saying?'

'I just spoke to the organisers and they agree: we can't fight the support your Mr McLean's little stunt is likely to garner. It won't be easy changing at this stage but you've left us with no choice.'

'Oh my God! Then we're back on?'

'That's right. We'll be making the official announcement in the next few weeks. Have a happy New Year, dear.' And she hung up.

When I took my seat back in the living room, the choir were just singing in the second part of the show, Harper and Stewart chatting quietly beside them.

'Well? What did she say?' Deano demanded.

I blinked, feeling dazed. 'She… she's got them to reverse the decision.' I managed a foggy smile. 'Tour's still coming, boys.'

Tom let out a low whistle of relief. 'Thank God. Nothing like a small heart attack to see in a new year, eh?'

I grabbed my phone to text Stew.

You big idiot. It worked. We're back on the route. Love you.

On the TV, I saw the miniature Stew fish out his phone and smile. He whispered something to Harper as the music of the choir faded.

Harper cleared his throat. 'Well, our switchboards have

been going mad here with people ringing in to support tiny Egglethwaite and their Le Tour bid. Nothing the British love more than a plucky underdog, right? But you can calm down now, folks. I've just been informed that the race organisers have found their festive spirit. Egglethwaite and their viaduct shall go to the ball.'

There was a loud cheer from the crowd on the screen, and another from the four of us at home.

'I think you've got one more thing to say before we move on to our next feature, Stew?' Harper said, holding out the mike.

'Yes,' Stew said, flushing. 'There's one person watching I need to say something to, especially as I did the ungentlemanly thing of standing her up for a date so I could come here tonight.' He held something up, and the cameras zoomed in to reveal a small silver star.

'Good idea. Sweeten her up with jewellery,' Harper said with a grin. There was a laugh from the crowd.

'This isn't a present. She has to earn it.'

'What is it?' Cameron asked.

'It's a charm,' Tom said. 'Stew got her a bracelet for Christmas.'

'What does it mean though?' I said.

'Ah, now this I do know about,' Tom said, smiling. 'Wait and see.'

'Are you watching, Lana Donati?' said TV's Stewart McLean. 'The charm goes with something you'll get in the post in a few days. Me and your brother signed you up for BSc Astronomy at the University of Central Lancashire. Part-time distance learning, so you can fit it around work. I know you'll make your dad proud.'

I gasped. 'No. Not really, Tommy?'

'Really,' Tom said. 'I had to steal a few exam certificates from your room; hope you don't mind. Me and Stew paid the first year's course fees between us.'

'Aww. You guys.' I threw myself at him for a hug. 'You're a sneaky git but I love you.'

'Anything else?' Harper said to Stew on TV.

'Er, no, that's me done I think.'

'No it isn't.' His cousin nudged him. 'Go on, tell her. My viewers like a happy ending.'

Stewart blushed. 'Oh, all right. I love you, sweetheart. Save me a drink and I'll be there in time to kiss you at midnight.'

There was loud applause from the crowd as Stewart faded to black.

Epilogue

I shook Tom, snuggled deep into his blankets.

'Oi. Wake up, you.'

'Wur…? Z'it Christmas?'

'Better. It's race day.'

Two hours later, we were dressed – head to foot in eye-watering canary yellow, the pair of us – and ready to inspect the village. Every resident, club and business had been working tirelessly to get the place ready, and there wasn't a window on the main street that didn't have a themed display. Even the undertaker's had a bike-motif headstone.

'Is our display finished?' I asked Deano, who was outside the restaurant with his new girlfriend Shelley, attaching yellow bunting to the front.

'Almost,' he said, stepping back to admire it. 'I think your dad would've approved. It's about his level of daft.'

Stew had been hard at work sourcing old bikes for everyone who wanted to decorate one, and I was quite proud of the medieval effort currently gracing our front window. Deano had even managed to coax Galahad on to it, a lance tucked under his arm ready for a spot of cycle jousting and a yellow jersey stretched over his broad tinman pecs.

'Whose idea were the antlers on the handlebars?' I asked.

'Mine,' Shelley said with a little blush. 'I thought it'd be sort of rock and roll.'

'Shell's dead artistic,' Deano said, giving her backside a proud pat. 'We met at a pottery class.'

She giggled. 'It was like that bit in *Ghost*. He showed me where to put my hands.'

'I just bet he did,' Tom said.

'And you'll be all right in the restaurant this afternoon, will you?' I asked Deano.

We'd wanted to take a few hours off to see the race, so he'd been left in charge of the two waitresses and four temps we'd hired for the day.

'I'll manage. Looking forward to being the boss.'

Tom slapped Deano's shoulder. 'See you later then, guys. We're just going to check out the main street then we're heading up to Pagans' Rock.'

'See you.' Deano plucked Tom's elbow as we turned to leave. 'Oh, er, I sent your picnic ahead with Stew. *Capisci?*'

Tom gave him a significant nod. 'Thanks, mate.'

After we'd inspected the front of Stewart's shop, his bums polished up specially and a now finished Herbert the yarn-bombed bike taking pride of place in the window, we headed to the Temp.

'Nice,' Tom said with an approving nod.

The gardening association had done an impressive flowerbed display: gorgeous petunias planted in red, white and blue strips to form the French Tricolore. At the edges, white rose bushes symbolised the link with Yorkshire. A couple of yellow bikes painted by Egglethwaite Young Cyclists, the group Stewart and I had started up, flanked the bed at each side.

Crowds were already gathering, walking up and down the street examining the windows. Every B&B and campsite in the area had been heaving with cycling enthusiasts for days.

'Let's check the Fox,' I said to Tom.

'*Bonjour*,' Billy said soberly from under his moustache when we'd barged in. He'd gone the full comedy Frenchman: beret, stripy jumper, even a string of onions. In the background, Queen's 'Bicycle Race' blared from the speakers.

'I hope you're not going to offend anyone French in that get-up,' Tom said.

'Nah, it's all good fun. If a French lad comes in, I'll sort him out with a whippet and a flat cap so he can get his own back.'

I winced when I looked behind the bar.

'Do you have to have that up?' I said, nodding to the calendar. 'Those aren't even my real legs.'

'Don't worry, love. No one's looking at your legs,' Billy said with a grin. He nodded at my chest. 'I know those're real.'

'Nice. So are you all set then?'

'Yep. Free brie baguettes for everyone, "La Marseillaise" in the CD player and a range of French wines and lagers behind the bar. Hoping for standing room only by dinnertime.'

I slapped his arm. 'You're a good lad, Billy; I don't care what they say. We'll be in for a drink once it's all over.'

After we left the pub, we walked down the bunting-crossed street to inspect the other windows. Jean had done another topiary bike, Yolanda's caf had a twee little picnic scene with a basketed 1950s-style cycle, and there were a dozen others. Then we popped into the church to make sure the bellringers were ready. Every church on the route had agreed to ring their bells when the peloton passed through, a cacophony of sound from York Minster to Sheffield Cathedral marking the once-in-a-lifetime event.

Finally, we headed to the viaduct, where Sue, Gerry and Yolanda were decorating.

'Bloody hell. Don't go too far over,' I said to Gerry when we got up there. He was leaning over the wall attaching some giant bunting to the outside. 'We don't want our first viaduct fatality today.'

Sue snorted. 'Oh, don't bother, Lana, you can't tell him anything. He's determined his precious bunting'll be visible from space. If he wants to break his neck in the process, good luck to him.'

Gerry finished attaching the bunting and turned to blow his wife a kiss.

'Is this the same Uncle Gerry who thought this was a terrible idea that'd give his sheep a nervous breakdown?' Tom said with a smile.

'Well. Hard to keep that up when I've got the three of you constantly bending my ear about it,' Gerry said with some pretty unconvincing grump.

'Plus he's minting it,' Sue said. 'We made a small fortune letting our fields to campers. The way to a Yorkshireman's heart is through his wallet.'

'Where's Yo-yo?' I asked.

'Over there.' Sue pointed out Yolanda, her hair dyed the vibrant blue of the Yorkshire flag for the occasion, attaching bunting to the other end of the viaduct with a man I didn't recognise.

'Who's the lad?'

'Her latest toy boy. Nephew of someone in her bridge group.' Sue shook her head. 'She'll have to slow down one of these days. Swap the blue hair for a blue rinse.'

'Nah. She'll be going well into her nineties,' Tom said. 'Egglethwaite wouldn't be Egglethwaite without a Yo-yo to sex everyone up.'

'Where are you two going now then? Pagans' Rock?'

I glanced at Tom. 'Yep. It's time for Tommy's important picnic.'

'Ah. The important picnic.' She gave us a kiss on the cheek each. 'Well, good luck.'

Gerry gave us both a hug too. 'And well done on today, kids,' he said. 'Nice to have made history, eh? Next time Rodge writes a book, you'll be in it.'

'S'pose we will. Weird.' I nudged Tom. 'Come on, bruv. Our men await.'

Up at Pagans' Rock, we found Cam, Stew and Flash sunbathing, a blanket spread on the ground with an open basket in the middle.

'Oi. Did you start eating without us?' Tom said.

'Sorry,' Cam said with a guilty smile. 'We got hungry. Just a few olives, that's all.'

'Hmm. Better be.' Tom shot Stewart a searching look, and he nodded ever so slightly.

'How's everything looking?' Stew asked.

I sat down and he shuffled so he could wrap his legs around me from behind. It was our favourite way to sit. He could kiss my neck whenever he felt like it, which was pretty often, and I could snuggle back against his chest. When no one was looking, he could also have a cheeky squeeze of my boobs. That happened pretty often too.

'Great,' I said as Tom sat down by Cameron. 'Very French. Billy's wearing a comedy 'tache.'

'Ha! That I'll have to see,' Stew said. 'How's the viaduct?'

I grinned. 'Yo-yo's dragged some poor lad up there for a decorating date. Fingers crossed they're not at it when the TV cameras arrive.'

'How long now?' Cameron asked.

'An hourish.' I nodded at the viaduct, Gerry's giant bunting fluttering in the breeze. 'The marshals must've opened the gates. Looks like there's already a gang of spectators.'

'So do you two want some picnic?' Stewart asked. 'Deano packed us a couple of bottles of wine, if it's not too early.'

'It most certainly is too early.' I pulled the basket towards me and fumbled out a bottle of something fizzy. 'But since it's a special occasion…'

'Well, cheers,' I said when I'd poured everyone a glassful. 'Here's to all our hard work and general amazingness.'

'Yep. To us,' Tom said, and we clinked glasses.

'Bloody hell,' Cam gasped when he'd taken a sip. 'What Prosecco is this? It's got a bit of kick.'

Stewart shook his head. 'This is the good stuff. Harper donated it from his private stash for us to toast race day.'

'That was nice of him.' I took a sip too and made a face. 'Jesus. He likes it that strong?'

'Yep. Likes his fizz like he likes his women: bubbly, full-bodied and overpriced.'

I nudged him. 'Don't be mean. You know you love him.'

'Yeah. Don't tell him though.'

Tom cleared his throat. 'Hey, Cam,' he said, nodding to a tub on the picnic blanket. 'Try some of this houmous.'

'No thanks. Not a big houmous fan.'

'This is special houmous though. Deano's own recipe. Seriously, mate, give it a try.'

'Honestly, I'm good for houmous. You have some houmous.'

Tom glared at him. 'But this is really, really *nice* houmous.'

I groaned. 'Go on, Cam. Have some houmous or we'll never hear the end of it.'

'Ugh. Anything for a quiet life.' He grabbed the tub.

'There's something in my houmous, Tommy,' he said, peering into it.

'There'd bloody better be, or I'm seriously out of pocket.'

Cameron fished out the ring nestling in the centre of Deano's chickpea goodness, a plain silver band, and held it up in front of him.

'And if you don't like it you can blame Lana. She picked it,' Tom said.

'I do like it,' Cam said quietly. 'I really like it.'

'You going to put it on then?'

'Dunno. It's all houmousy.'

'God, you are such a diva. Lick it off or something.'

Stewart nudged me. 'Am I witnessing the least romantic proposal ever here?'

I grinned. 'Yep.'

'Oi. I am well romantic,' Tom said, glaring at us. 'What's more romantic than houmous?'

Cameron smiled. 'I think you're romantic. Come here, you soft git.' He grabbed Tom's T-shirt for a snog.

'So is it a yes then?' Tom asked softly when they separated, reaching up to sweep Cam's hair back from his face.

'Course it's a yes. It's always been a yes.'

'Cam?'

'Yeah?'

'I love you very much, you know.'

'I know you do. Love you too, Tommy.'

We were lazing in the sun, chatting and feeding Flash scraps of picnic, when the newly engaged Cameron cocked his head to one side.

'Hey! I think they're coming.'

Everyone sat up and peered towards the viaduct. The crowd were cheering wildly, waving Tricolores and Yorkshire flags. Sure enough, a few seconds later the first cyclist, shining in his yellow jersey, zipped by, closely followed by the rest of the peloton. Just a flash of colour and they were gone. It seemed strange, after all those months of work and worry, that history in the making should be such a blur.

'There's your helicopters, Lana,' Tom said, pointing up at them getting aerial footage of the event.

'Nibali,' I heard Stewart mutter. 'Lucky bastard. Wonder if he'll hold it.'

'You OK, love?' I asked him quietly.

'Yeah. Bit weird seeing them go by, that's all. There was a time every dream I had was about wearing that jersey. In my home county too... would've been amazing.'

I shuffled round to look into his face. 'Do you miss it a lot?'

'I did. Never thought I'd find anything that could make

me feel alive the way cycling did.' He twisted a strand of my hair round one finger. 'Then I met this girl.'

'Who was she?'

'No one special. Just a girl. The most incredible, imperfectly perfect girl I ever knew. And when I think about her, I get that same feeling. Like I'm flying and nothing can hold me back. Only, you know, sexier because she turns me on as well.'

'Soppy thing.' I planted a soft kiss on his lips. 'I do love you, Stew.'

'Oh yeah, that reminds me,' he said, rummaging in his jacket pocket. 'You've earned this.'

He handed me the silver star charm he'd shown me seven months ago at New Year.

'Tom told you?' I said, blushing as I attached it to the bracelet I always wore.

'Yep.' He shook his head. 'Firsts in all your assignments. Never knew I was going out with such a swot.'

I laughed.

'So is this it, Lana?' he said as another wave of cyclists were cheered over the viaduct. 'The memorial your dad would've wanted?'

'Yes.' I reached up to stroke his face. 'But it's not the Tour. Not the viaduct either. I know that now.'

'What is it then?'

I nodded at Tom and Cameron, snuggled in a little loved-up world of their own. 'Them. And us.' I traced the shape of Stew's ear tenderly with my fingertips, drinking in those deep grey eyes. 'This is Dad's memorial; what he wrote in his eulogy. He wanted his kids to fall in love and be happy.'

'And are you happy?'

'Happier than I've ever been.'

'And are you in love?'

'You know I am. For the first and last time.'

'And you're mine. Aren't you?'

'Yes, Stew. I'm yours.'

'In that case I'll allow you to kiss me. Since you were good and ate all your lettuce.'

'Mmm. I love it when you talk salad to me.'

The church bells rang out as Stewart's lips met mine, mingling joyously with the cheers and applause of the crowd. And right at that moment, every cheer felt like it was for us.

Acknowledgements

The biggest thanks has to go to my agent, Laura Longrigg at MBA Literary Agents, who first suggested to me the idea of writing a book set during the Grand Départ in Yorkshire and has championed it tirelessly ever since it came to be. Secondly, a big cheer to the team at Welcome to Yorkshire, without whose hard work and enthusiasm Yorkshire would never have hosted such a massive, historic event in the first place so people like me could make up stories about it.

Massive thank you to my editor at Aria, Martina Arzu, and the team there who've worked so hard on this edition. Thanks also go to the team at Mirror Books – Paula Scott, Jo Sollis and Cynthia Hamilton – for their work on this book when it was first published in 2018.

Enormous thanks to everyone who helped whip the story into shape, especially my editors at Aria and Mirror Books, my agent Laura and my beta readers Kate Beeden, Toni Armitage and Mark Anslow, who willingly and without bribes gave up their own time to read and critique my scribblings. All were brilliant and should take full credit for making the story at least ninety per cent better.

I'd also like to shout out to all the fabulous, dedicated book bloggers who give up their time and do such a wonderful job helping authors to promote their books. We do appreciate it, all of us. Thank you.

My ever-supportive family and family-in-common-law have been understanding as always while I once again disappeared from view into the writing cave (aka front bedroom) to write and edit and write and edit and write and edit some more: thank you, Firths, Brahams and Anslows all. Cats, you weren't understanding at all so thanks for nothing, but I love you anyway. And of course, my partner and live-in alpha reader Mark, the inspiration for all my romantic heroes (according to him).

Head-pats and pints to all my friends, especially Kate Beeden, Nigel and Lynette Emsley, Bob Fletcher and Amy Smith, who deserves joint credit along with Billy Connolly for the creation of Stewart's naughty bike racks (thanks, Billy).

Did I miss someone? I always miss someone. Um... Wilsden Band, thanks for the euphonium lessons. Rylstone WI, nude calendar pioneers. Queen (band, not monarch). All the local places that inspired Egglethwaite and surrounds: Hewenden Viaduct, Druids' Altar, Laycock, Heptonstall, Haworth, Harden, Wilsden and many more. And to the people of Yorkshire, who are and always have been our county's greatest asset.

OK, I'm done.

About the Author

MARY JAYNE BAKER grew up in rural West Yorkshire, right in the heart of Brontë country… and she's still there.

After graduating from Durham University with a degree in English Literature, she dallied with living in cities including London, Nottingham and Cambridge, but eventually came back with her own romantic hero in tow to her beloved Dales, where she first started telling stories about heroines with flaws and the men who love them.

Mary Jayne's novel *A Question of Us* was the winner of the Romantic Novelists' Association's Romantic Comedy Novel of the Year Award 2020. She also writes uplifting women's fiction as Lisa Swift, and World War II sagas as Gracie Taylor.